Praise for
Jack Woodville London

"Just as in real life, Jack Woodville London's territory in *Dangerous Latitudes* is a land of spies, rough frontiersmen, Mexican military figures, Indians, and men seeking opportunity, redemption, or both. London has woven a clever spy story with historical events and some of the larger-than-life people who inhabited the Texas-Mexico borderlands to create a colorful novel of the Republic Era."

—Frank de la Teja, Former Texas State Historian

"An expansive historical saga, progressing from Louisiana to Texas and the vast 19th century frontier. A vivid reexamination of a legendary southwestern chronicle, London captures all the fabled boldness and tenacity of the region with skill, assurance and invigorating perspective."

— William Jack Sibley, critically acclaimed screenwriter and playwright, Officer of The Texas Institute of Letters, and Author of *Here We Go Loop de Loop*

Jack Woodville London has tackled a little-touched-upon part of Texas history in *Dangerous Latitudes*, life on its murky frontier after the victory at San Jacinto. Texas in those days was overrun by factions, brigands and intriguers, and London's protagonists seem to encounter all of them. Throughout its pages, the reader is entertainingly reminded of a solid historical truth—Texas in its Republic days was not for the faint of heart.

— Mike Vance, Texas Historian, Documentary and Filmmaker, and Author of *Getting Away with Bloody Murder*

"Espionage meister John LeCarre be aware: There's a new breed of spy on the literary scene. And while protagonist Alexandre LaBranche goes about his role unwillingly and often with minimal success -- George Smiley he's not -- readers will root for him with the turn of every page. Award-winning author London's fast-paced tale, set in the infant days of the Texas Republic, has it all -- the troubled young surveyor who's only desire is to chart Texas' southern border, his horse thieving partners, self-serving politicos, vengeful Mexican soldiers, and, for good measure, a moving love story. Saddle up. *Dangerous Latitudes* is a wild ride."

— Carlton Stowers, two-time Edgar Award winner

"In his historical spy thriller, London cuts a spirited trail through mid-19th century Texas with a rousing blend of espionage and romance. *Dangerous Latitudes* brings to life titanic figures of the state's history like Sam Houston and Jack Coffee Hays, as the battle for the Texas border intensifies in the years before the Mexican-American War. London uses a wealth of historical research and a strong sense of setting to explore themes of race, morality, and manifest destiny in a novel that should find a home with fans of James L. Haley and Doug Swanson."

— James Wade, Spur Award-winning author of *Beasts of the Earth*

Jack Woodville London has tackled a little-touched-upon part of Texas history in *Dangerous Latitudes*, life on its murky frontier after the victory at San Jacinto. Texas in those days was overrun by factions, brigands and intriguers, and London's protagonists seem to encounter all of them. Throughout its pages, the reader is entertainingly reminded of a solid historical truth—Texas in its Republic days was not for the faint of heart.

— Mike Vance, Texas Historian, Documentary and Filmmaker, and Author of *Getting Away with Bloody Murder*

DANGEROUS LATITUDES

ALSO BY JACK WOODVILLE LONDON

French Letters Series:

Virginia's War

Engaged in War

Children of a Good War

Shades of the Deep Blue Sea

A Novel Approach: To Writing Your First Book (or Your Best One)

DANGEROUS LATITUDES

JACK WOODVILLE LONDON

Stoney Creek Publishing

A Member of the Texas Book Consortium

Published by

Stoney Creek Publishing Group

StoneyCreekPublishing.com

ISBN: 979-8-9901289-6-5
ISBN (ebook): 979-8-9901289-7-2
Library of Congress Control Number: 2024919369

Cover design by Ken Ellis.

Opening map by Douglas Brown, Albumartist.com

City map, San Antonio de Bexar 1836, courtesy of The Portal to Texas History, University of North Texas Libraries Government Documents Department.

Printed in USA

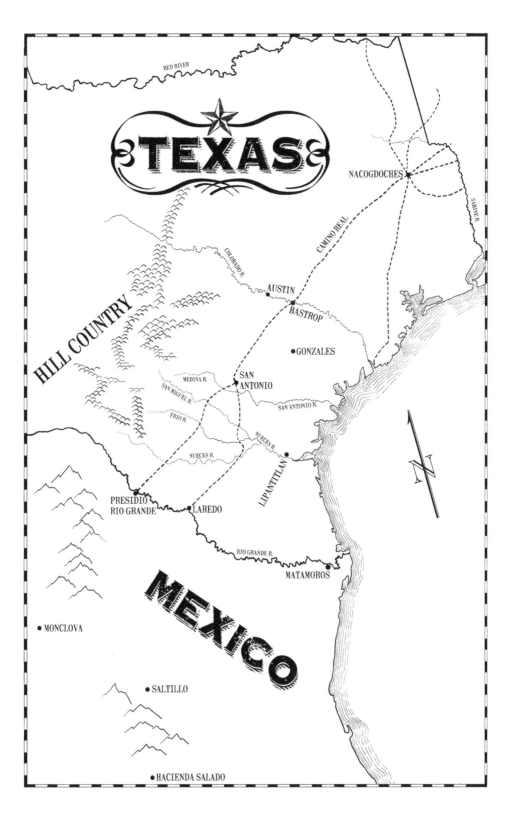

CONTENTS

CHARACTERS

While this is a work of historical fiction, many of the events in the novel did take place during the years that Texas was an independent republic. Characters identified with an * are historical characters. They are listed here in the order in which they appear in the novel.

Alexandre LaBranche: A naïve surveyor from Louisiana

*Alcee LaBranche: Alexandre's uncle, a New Orleans businessman who also became the charge' d'affaires for Texas in New Orleans

*Mirabeau Lamar: Second president of the Republic of Texas, blamed for the failure of the 1841 Santa Fe Expedition in which Mexico captured 300 Texas men

Pennant: A thief and sometimes sailor

Alonzo: A half-Mexican, half-Lipan Apache, Pennant's companion

Noeme: A woman of the Neosho

*Thomas Rusk: Signer of the Texas Declaration of Independence, supreme court judge and, later, United States senator. Law partner of Pinckney Henderson

*Pinkney Henderson: First Texas minister to France and to the

United Kingdom, and first governor of Texas as a state. Law partner of Thomas Rusk

*Sam Houston: Hero of the Texas Revolution, twice president of the Republic of Texas and, later, United States senator and governor of Texas

*Jack C. Hays:Texas scout and ranger, head of the San Antonio Committee of Safety in 1842, US regimental commander in Mexican War 1846-1848

*Samuel Maverick:Signer of Texas Declaration of Independence, captured in Mexican General Woll's invasion of San Antonio in 1842 and imprisoned in Mexico

*Colonel Antonio Canales: Mexican traitor who returned to favor with Santa Anna and who called for the death of all Texas soldiers captured at Mier

*Henry Lawrence Kinney: Merchant with a trading post on the Nueces River near Corpus Christi Bay, suspected of spying for the Mexican army

*Charles Elliott: British consul to Texas in Austin and eventual landowner in Texas

*Colonel Calixto Vargas Bravo: Mexican army officer who commanded garrisons at Laredo and at Presidio Rio Grande

CHAPTER ONE

The wall was stained at about the level of a man's chest.

Alexandre waited in the cramped cell where Colonel Canales had shoved him at sundown and tried to not think about the wall. He shivered in the cold, hunched over, his back pressed against adobe at one end and his feet jammed against the thick wooden door opposite. The only thing he heard during the long night was a harsh laugh outside the wooden door.

"Here, spy," Canales' rough voice hissed from the courtyard. "For you to write to who you loves. Is tradition." There was a rustle near Alexandre's feet as some paper was shoved underneath the door. Then, "Maybe you write your horse thieves," Canales taunted him, and another laugh.

"I am not a spy," Alexandre answered. Canales had walked away. Alexandre picked up the sheet of paper and stared at it.

His first thought was to write a letter as told. He smiled, not happily, but because writing a letter might settle his mind against the image of the bloody wall that waited for him. He found his pencil, held it above the sheet of paper, and had his second thought: there was no one to whom he could write such a letter.

He considered writing to the men he had known in San Antonio,

Sam Maverick and John Twohig and Jack C. Hays. *Indeed*, Alexandre thought, *Hays should carry this last message to those who ought to be held to account for his present circumstances.* But to put their names on paper would relieve Colonel Canales of any doubt that Alexandre was their agent. *If Canales did know, he would shoot me sooner.* As it stood, Canales could not prove whether Alexandre had even known any of them, much less spied for them.

Canales did know Alexandre's horse thieves. They're not my horse thieves, Alexandre thought. Well, perhaps they were his horse thieves, but they'd been Canales's first. More to the point, if he did write a letter to them, he wasn't sure they'd be able to read it. He and the horse thieves hadn't passed their time together reading. Mostly, they had argued.

There was someone else. He could write to her, of course, but he didn't know how to form the words to tell her what he wanted to say. Instead, he thought about the times they had together, not many times, not enough. He remembered each word that she had said to him and he regretted not having told her the things he had wanted to say, his mistakes and imaginings and regrets. But no, he would not write to her or even say her name out loud, for fear Canales was listening. Canales didn't even know she existed.

Alexandre concluded that even to put so much as a single word on paper would risk telling Canales something more than he already knew. He wadded up the page, tossed it at the door, then waited in the dark with his back against the wall, listening for the cock's crow to signal that first light was creeping above the mountains of Saltillo.

There was one person he should write, he realized. He reached for the paper, straightened it, and by the faint moonlight, began.

"Father, this is my last letter. I will be very brief, as my present circumstances require it. I call to your mind our last meeting and remind you of your words to me. I write to relieve your concerns by saying that I have found my purpose in life. I know exactly my prospects. By the time this letter reaches you, you probably will have been told what they are."

Alexandre stopped writing. He wanted his last hour to be spent reliving the past year, not writing a bitter letter. He instead wanted to think about Noeme and Pennant and Alonzo, not his father. He wanted to remember gazing with them across the Texas hills, walking through abandoned missions and riding along hidden trails, swimming in cold streams and sketching the land as no one had ever done before. He loved them and wanted no better memory for the end of his life.

An hour later he heard men outside, soldiers, marching, the sounds of muted commands. They stopped outside his door. A crack of light entered his cell.

"Is time," Canales barked. The cell door opened. "Outside, spy!"

Rough hands pulled Alexandre out by his boots. Another hand took possession of his letter. Someone lifted him to his feet and pushed him toward the wall. There was Colonel Canales, standing in the courtyard, erect, smirking, puffed up with command.

"¡Detener!" Canales barked at the soldiers. They halted. The hands turned Alexandre to face the firing squad.

"¡Attención!" Canales ordered. The soldiers stood at attention.

Alexandre stared at them. The firing squad were miserable soldiers, some barefoot, all shivering, their hands shaking to hold the old muskets they carried. He thought they looked unhappy, like servile men forced to do things they didn't want to do, Mexican versions of his father's Black slaves. Then, in an instant, he realized how he came to be standing against a wall facing a Mexican firing squad, how everything that had happened in the last year could be traced back to one particular evening in Louisiana when he had walked out into his father's sugarcane fields to consider the problem of the slave cabins. Now, as he faced Colonel Canales, and saw how that one thing had led to another and eventually to this, Alexandre LaBranche could not suppress a last smile.

———

Alexandre's ancestors had put their field slaves' cabins alongside a fetid swamp. As a boy, before his mother died, he had not thought much about the swamp or the slaves' village. Later, after he finished his education, he had begun work as a survey engineer on the great canal being built in New Orleans. But no matter how gifted he was in the geographic arts, there had been little work for him because the project was stopped after yellow fever began to kill the Irish diggers. When Alexandre came home to the plantation, he did take notice of the slave cabins and thought the swamp to be not much different than the deadly bogs of the great New Orleans canal. He asked his father for permission to move the slave cabins.

"The yellow fever, sir," he had said. "If we drain the swamp and move the slaves to dry ground, away from the standing water, they won't catch it as much." His father had raised his eyebrows. "They won't get sick as often." His father had snorted at the idea and sipped some rum. "If they aren't sick as often, they'll live longer, sir. If they live longer, they can work longer." His father looked up at this comment. "And you could extend the sugarcane fields onto the new drained ground where their village is now." Alexandre already had brought out the plantation surveys. "If we move the cabins 162 yards in this direction, the land will achieve the purpose." His father looked at the maps.

His father had argued that the slaves liked the cabins where they were, that they liked to take the fish and alligators and raccoons from the swamp, that the ground was good for their little vegetable gardens, and that the slaves knew where each of their places were. But, in the end, his father had agreed.

"But just the field slaves, Alexandre," he had said. "Not the house," by which he meant the slaves who worked inside the plantation home. Their cabins would remain where they were, near the kitchens and blacksmith shops and sheds. "Just the fields."

Alexandre used his pencils and straight edges and geometric compasses to engineer a fine ditch that drained the swamp. When the cane harvest was finished, he had the slaves construct a solid levee along the ditch, then dismantle their cabins and move them.

There had been some lamentation and bold complaining, but before the winter cold arrived the slaves' village had been moved to dry ground. As soon as the season for cold passed, the overseers put the slaves back to work to extend the cane fields onto the newly vacant ground, now irrigated by the drainage from the former swamp.

One evening, Alexandre had walked out into the sugar cane fields to inspect his works. The ditch was draining, the swamp much reduced, and the new crop was nicely cultivated. He was pleased. He walked back to the plantation home, passing by the cabins of the house slaves.

He saw his father leaving one of the cabins. A Black girl stood in its doorway. She was pregnant. Alexandre and his father each looked away. He was quietly proud to see this side of his father, a charitable side, likely delivering some food or clothes or comforts of a slave nature to her cabin. But, three nights later, Alexandre saw the same pregnant slave girl again. This time she was inside the main house, at night, at the door to his father's bedroom. She nodded at Alexandre; he dropped his lamp. The door opened; she disappeared inside.

Once he was back in his own room, he tried to make sense of what he had seen.

Why was she in Father's rooms while the rest of the house was asleep? Alexandre had heard of such cases among the planters and, more often, the overseers, who forced themselves on slave girls.

But, he considered, *was she forced?*

And, he remembered, when his father had been very clear that while Alexandre could move the field slaves, he had been just as clear that the house slaves were to be kept nearby. His suspicion troubled him, and he decided to suppress it.

Father and son avoided each other, but the miasma of the plantation weighed heavily on Alexandre. Two weeks later, his father summoned him to the plantation office.

They sat across from one another, staring, the father dressed in the sturdy clothes that he wore when he went out into the cane fields to watch the slaves at work, the son dressed in fine breeches, a linen shirt and short morning jacket.

"Well," his father said. He glared at his son.

"Sir?" Alexandre suspected why he had been summoned, but not how it would end.

"Well," his father said again. "This cannot continue." His father didn't say whether 'this' referred to Alexandre's habits or to Alexandre's discovery.

Alexandre's habits weren't especially bad ones. He drank little, smoked not at all, did not play at cards or frequent the French Quarter. Indeed, his only real habit was walking around the plantation with a sextant and a timepiece, gazing into the sky and writing down notes of angles and degrees. However, Alexandre's discovery of his father's liaison with the pregnant slave girl had not been so benign.

"You do nothing with yourself because you have nothing to do," his father continued. "You are idle and appear to have no plan."

"That's not so," Alexandre answered. "I work when there is work and I improve my talents when there is no work. That's why your cane fields are larger and the slaves healthier. Perhaps if you took more interest in my...."

"Do you have any more prospects?" his father demanded, knowing that he did not. "Are you in correspondence with anyone about conducting any more surveys? Or to lay out some grand canal? No?" He waited for an argument but was disappointed. "As for your talents, I gave you permission to move the slave cabins, which you did with your transit and chains and bob lines. But the swamp you drained was over a boundary line that had been under water."

Alexandre looked up; it was the first he had heard of it.

"Then, when you moved my field slaves, you put them on the other side of where the swamp used to be, which happens to be on my neighbor's property." He handed Alexandre a letter to prove his misfortune. "I am now obliged to pay rent to my neighbor so that my slaves can enter my land to work my fields. That's your talent, a surveyor who doesn't even know where his own property lines are. So, I ask: Do you have any engagements to survey some other plantation? Lay out a road? Anything? Do you even have any prospects for such engagements?" His father waited; Alexandre had no answer. "Until you have prospects, no, until you succeed in your prospects, you are..."

"My prospects?" Alexandre had heard an alarming note in his father's voice. "What prospects do you mean, Father?"

"You have to have some purpose to your life, Alexandre. I don't mean some little project that I consent for you to do or that one of our neighbors might let you do. Not some other folly that does more bad than good, not again." His father crossed his arms, anger in his eyes, staring over the desk at the aggrieved son.

"This isn't about me, is it, sir?" Alexandre recognized the signs of his father's escalating anger; he had done nothing wrong except catch his father seducing a slave. "This is about you wanting to punish me for seeing what you did."

"No, Alexandre." His father's voice had changed to a growl. "This is only about you. You're doing nothing with your life. You take no interest in running the plantation, nothing more than gazing into the sky and writing notes. You have an education and do not use it. You have talent, but you waste it. Your abilities, if you have any, fail for want of sensible application. I have had your things put in the wagon."

"My things?"

"Your mathematical things, your rulers and chains and what have you. And your clothes. They are in the wagon. You are leaving."

The office became smaller, the walls closer, the humidity suffocating, the hum of mosquitoes cloaking the tension.

"Leaving?" Alexandre asked. "Leaving where?"

"I don't know," his father answered, "but leave you shall. Whether you will be fortunate or unfortunate, find an opportunity or squander your time gazing at the heavens, it's not for me to say and, frankly, no longer my concern. You are a failure. You are leaving here, today, and not welcome back until...."

"That is not fair," Alexandre answered. "That is wrong, to turn me out for what you did."

"What I did? I did nothing. Leave, Alexandre. Go. Goodbye."

Ten minutes later, the disowned son sat on the buckboard of a wooden wagon, reins in hand, worldly goods beside him, cursing his father.

"Damn him. Damn him!"

Alexandre shook the reins. His horse began to walk toward the road that led downriver to New Orleans, and Alexandre told himself that he was not a failure. "I'll show him! I do have a purpose, by God. I'll prove it if it's the last thing I ever do. I'll show him."

———

He tried to find work in New Orleans, but Alexandre soon found that engineering on the New Canal still was suspended, that the new faux bergs of the city already had been surveyed, and that calculating latitudes and longitudes was not much then in demand. He looked into these jobs and more until he ran out of money, then swallowed his pride and sought out his uncle Alcee, a man of business in the counting houses and customs sheds near the river. He went there and asked for his uncle.

"Your uncle, you say?" the clerk asked. Alexandre nodded. "I didn't know that Alcee LaBranche had a nephew. Well, he won't be back today. He's attending a session in admiralty court. Ship called the *Durango*. You might find him there.

"The *Durango*?"

"Yes, the *Durango*. You can see her there in mid-river, riding at anchor." The clerk pointed to the river. The *Durango* and two other sailing ships rocked back and forth on the gentle current of the wide Mississippi. "A Mexican ship. She came into port under escort. Now she's in prize court. That's where Mr. LaBranche will be. I'm not sure what his interest is."

Alexandre walked to the federal court where prize cases were tried, asked for the case of The *Durango*, and waited in the hallway until the session ended.

"Alexandre?" Uncle Alcee asked when he saw his forlorn nephew waiting outside the courtroom. And, within only a few minutes, Uncle Alcee said that indeed he might be able to help.

"I'm sorry to learn that your father has taken such drastic measures, Alexandre, but tell me—do you know anything about Texas?" Alexandre admitted that he knew very little. Alcee then offered to present his mathematical nephew to Mirabeau Lamar.

———

Mirabeau Lamar was a man who did have a purpose, which was to salvage almost any part of the wreckage over which he had presided as the president of the Republic of Texas. His failed attempts to do so, however, had been summed up by Vice President Burnet one week before Lamar came to New Orleans.

"You could have soothed over all your messes, Lamar, the failed schools, the failed Indian wars, even Canales' treachery." Burnet told him, "But no, you wanted to send an expedition off to Santa Fe. 'Don't do it,' Congress said. You did it anyway."

Lamar had believed he could persuade the City of Santa Fe to abandon Mexico and become a trading capital of Texas. He dispatched 300 Texians overland to Santa Fe to do his persuading. The expedition, last heard from in August, had disappeared.

"You lost over 300 men!" Burnet had shouted. "Where are they, Lamar? Every Texian believes they're in a prison somewhere in Mexico, or worse. They blame you," he added, "and Texas is still broke."

And so, as his last act as the president of Texas, Mirabeau Lamar had undertaken a voyage to find money, cash money, bond money, bank loan money, any kind of money, to keep afloat the republic that he had driven into bankruptcy. Mirabeau Lamar was in New Orleans to beg.

While Lamar had a purpose, what he did not have was a plan,

not until Alcee LaBranche whispered in his ear that he just might be able to address all of Lamar's problems.

"We're having a little bit of trouble in the prize court, Mr. President," Alcee had confided to him. "It isn't clear whether the *Durango* was inside Texas waters when she was captured. But, if she was in Texas waters, then Mexico was engaged in an act of war and the United States will not stand for it. The sentiment in this city is such that a public subscription of funds would be forthcoming." Lamar was pleased to hear it. "And Texas would keep the *Durango* and all that is in her under the law of prizes."

Lamar was greatly relieved. Alcee had more.

"But just as importantly, Mr. President, if you find the men," he told Lamar, "the Santa Fe men, the disappeared men of the expedition, Texas will forgive you. The public will forgive you." Lamar was ready to be forgiven. "I believe you can do both, quite easily," Alcee continued. "Permit me to introduce you to my nephew. Here's what I suggest you tell him."

They met in a salon of the Hotel St. Louis on Chartres Street, not two blocks from the slave exchange. The president of Texas took Alexandre's hand, shook it, and saw before him a man of no more than twenty-five years whose fine clothes needed cleaning and scuffed boots needed brushing, a young man whose eyes revealed undisguised admiration when Alcee LaBranche said, "The President of Texas."

"Texas?" Alexandre said, as if he had been asked a question. He had never met a great man, yet here he was in a private meeting with the leader of that heroic nation. He shook Lamar's hand, then glanced toward Alcee, who nodded and quietly took his seat. "I am Alexandre LaBranche, sir, at your service. I am very honored to meet you."

"Mirabeau Lamar, sir." Lamar smiled and indicated that Alexandre should seat himself on one of the fine chairs at the small table. Alexandre almost missed the center of the chair for failing to take his eyes off Lamar, who wondered if the lad would be able to carry on a conversation. "Do you know it?" Lamar asked. "Texas?"

Alexandre's mind raced with imaginings of hardy pioneers in ox-pulled wagons, men who carved rich land out of virgin wilderness, brave men with Tennessee long rifles who faced vast armies of Mexican soldiers on the field of battle.

"I have not had that pleasure, sir," he answered. "But I certainly hope to do so." He imagined that Lamar was himself one of those brave men.

"I hope you will know it, sir, Mr. LaBranche, and soon. Texas is favored by God," Lamar replied. "It's a land of rivers and forests, of fine earth." Lamar described a nation of rich plantations and small cities, farms so fertile that a single family could grow enough to feed twenty. "And a land of free men who do exceptional deeds, Mr. LaBranche."

Alexandre saw before him a sincere man with a kind voice, unexpectedly friendly, dressed in a fine coat and cravat as one would expect a dignitary to dress. At the same time, he tried to imagine Lamar dressed in a buckskin jacket, astride a horse, rifle raised, leading a charge through the cannon and pikes of a Mexican battle line against a cruel dictator whose name he couldn't remember. He asked If President Lamar had himself been one of those exceptional men who fought for freedom.

"I was, sir. It was a hard time. Do you know about the Alamo?" Alexandre had heard of it. "Two hundred of our heroes held off two thousand of the Mexican for thirteen days. And Goliad? Do you know about Goliad? Four hundred of our bravest perished there in defense of freedom. As for me, I had the honor of serving in the cavalry at San Jacinto." Alexandre did not know about San Jacinto. "We were a small army, Mr. LaBranche, a very small army, but we defeated the Mexican, by God. We beat him in just eighteen minutes."

Alexandre was riveted; he had never met a man who won a glorious battle, much less the president of a free nation.

"And we captured Santa Anna! He was sneaking off like a dog, sir. We should have shot him. But we took him, and here we are." Lamar neglected to mention that Mexico had not forgiven Texas for winning at San Jacinto, nor that Texas had not forgiven Mexico for killing every one of the Alamo defenders or for putting the Texians at Goliad against a wall and shooting all four hundred prisoners of war.

Lamar, seeing Alexandre glow with excitement, sensed that it was time to show his fish the bait. He asked Alexandre whether he correctly understood from Alcee LaBranche that the young man had training in the geographic arts.

"Yes indeed, sir. I was honored to study in Virginia, at the school of engineers at the bureau of topography. I am trained in maps and in surveying."

Lamar was pleased to hear it. He asked whether LaBranche could determine latitude and longitude.

"I can sir. In particular, I have mastered the Horrebow method, as refined by Captain Talcott," Alexandre replied. Lamar wanted to know what that meant. "Well, sir, I am able to fix the exact location of any place on the surface of the earth within one minute, and even closer than one minute if I am given the accurate time of day when I take my measurements." Alexandre had begun to relax in the stuffed chair in the fine salon in the presence of an interesting man who was nothing like his own father. "Time is essential for the correct study of a fixed position."

"And are you a mappist? Is that the word?" Lamar asked.

"Do you mean can the boy draw a map?" Uncle Alcee suggested. "What about it, Alexandre? Can you draw a map?" Alcee produced some paper; Alexandre produced his own fine pencils. For a few minutes he bent over the paper and sketched, paused, sketched some more, and quickly drew a detailed map of New Orleans from Chartres Street to the river landing and commercial port. He then sketched onto the map the hotel, the customs house and factors' offices, the tall ships alongside the port, all in three dimensions as an artist might render them, but atop a map grid.

"I am astounded at your skill, Mr. LaBranche." Lamar had never seen such a drawing. "It is as if a man could stand there and see where he was, but on a map. It is remarkable." He smiled, then produced a roll of paper of his own and spread it across the table. "Would you like to see my map, young man?"

Alexandre said that nothing could please him more.

"This is Texas. Do you know the borders of Texas?" Lamar asked. "No? Why, they encompass all the lands from the Sabine River, here" he continued, indicating, "to here. This is the Rio Grande, on the left side of the map. And everything between the Sabine and the Rio Grande is ours, sir, within our boundaries." He let the young man study the map. "It was all settled at San Jacinto, when Santa Anna agreed to withdraw the Mexican army from Texas territory to the other side of the Rio Grande."

Lamar traced the Rio Grande with his finger.

"From the mouth of the Rio Grande at the Gulf of Mexico, then up the principal stream to its source, and then on north to the forty-second degree of north latitude.'" He paused, then looked across the desk. Alexandre followed every word. "That is where Texas meets the United States north of the Rio Grande, at forty-two degrees north latitude. You can find the forty-second degree of north latitude, can you not?" Lamar asked.

"I can, sir." Alexandre answered.

Lamar was pleased to hear it.

"Then I make you this proposition, sir. Texas will pay you the sum of ten thousand dollars, United States dollars, to map the boundaries of the republic."

Alexandre gasped. The offer was staggering, an enormous sum of money. He composed himself, made as if he was studying Lamar's map. It was a good map, drawn with the irregular lines of rivers and the shapes of colonies, and the rough shading that marked ranges of hills and mountains. Degrees of latitude and longitude were printed in the margins. He was not sure he had heard correctly.

"To map the boundaries, sir? Of Texas?"

"Yes, to map them. Half of them, really. We know where the Sabine River is, of course, and the Gulf of Mexico. A priest could find those. And up north, see where it says 'Red River' near the top?

The other side of that is the United States. There is no need to map there. What I offer you is the opportunity to map the rest. This part over here." Lamar pointed to the left margin of the map, the south and the west. "The Rio Grande. Under our treaty with Santa Anna, what's on our side of the Rio Grande is Texas. What's on the other side is Mexico. Our side needs mapping."

The Rio Grande was marked by a winding course from the Gulf of Mexico upriver to Laredo, then onward to Presidio Rio Grande. The rest of the river, and of Texas, everything to the west, was off the edge of the map. The young man wondered what his life would be if he had ten thousand United States dollars.

"Ten thousand dollars?" He was convinced that Lamar had misspoken.

"As you can see, the map is complete up the Rio Grande to Laredo, which is on our side. Your work in earnest would commence at Laredo. From there, you would survey and map as you go." Lamar pointed to a name on the Mexican side. "This is Presidio Rio Grande, upriver from Laredo. We know that the river continues west from there until it gets to a city named Paso del Norte. I don't know how far that is, but it's on the Mexican side. From there it turns north and goes to Santa Fe, where the commercial trail comes in from St. Louis. Santa Fe is on our side." He let Alexandre study the map, then went on with his description.

"But the point is, we don't really have a map of the Rio Grande, not the whole river, not past what you see here, nothing on the river up to Santa Fe and Taos," Lamar continued. "Taos is in Texas too. But no one, not anyone from Spain, not anyone from Mexico, not any human being ever finished the job to find where beyond Santa Fe the Rio Grande comes out of the ground." He paused and smiled. "We offer to engage you to do that very thing, sir, to map all the way to the source of the Rio Grande. Then, from there, sir, north to the US boundary at the forty-second degree of north latitude. That is the job I offer you."

The offer was too good to be true.

"Are there no surveyors in Texas up to the task?" Alexandre asked.

"There are, as you see, a number of colonies in Texas. New cities are laid out every day. The surveyors are fully occupied in marking the leagues and labors, the varas, the boundaries of the plantations and settlements that you see here. But sir, we need a new man, a mapmaking man. And based on your training, sir," here Lamar exaggerated his flattery, "we need you." He folded his hands across his middle section and smiled.

There was a diffuse atmosphere in the salon, as if the afternoon light was filtered through leaded glass windows to render every-thing out of focus, the embroidered settees with soft edges, the brass lamp with a fading wick, two men speaking around the edges of their purposes rather than at the heart of the matter to make each of them look better than he was.

Lamar neglected to mention that if anyone occupied the Rio Grande River, it was Mexican soldiers and Lipan Apaches, both of whom roamed freely almost all the way to San Antonio.

Alexandre left unspoken his surveying error that put his father's slave cabins onto the neighbor's plantation.

Lamar did not think Alexandre needed to know that the only way Alexandre could salvage anything of Lamar's expiring presi-dency would be to find the lost men he had sent to Santa Fe some-where along the Rio Grande River.

Alexandre thought it would be indiscreet to mention that his father had disowned him.

It was enough for each of them that the contract, while not based on a full understanding of the facts on either side, nevertheless was to the benefit of both.

"As I study this map, Mr. President, it would appear the best way to undertake the project would be to sail from New Orleans to your port there on the Rio Grande." Alexandre said it only as a fact, not a challenge. "Otherwise, a man would have to cross all of Texas before arriving at the place of beginning."

"I agree with you, sir. It would appear so from this map.

However, we have no good port on the Gulf of Mexico anywhere near the Rio Grande. It has only been five years since we formed our republic, and a port is on the list of projects to undertake rather than the list of projects completed. I would encourage you to cross the Sabine into Texas, perhaps here," Lamar indicated the Logan ferry on the map, "then proceed to Nacogdoches and continue along the *camino real,* the San Antonio Road, as far as Bexar. Provision there, then set out for the Rio Grande. And you will find good men in San Antonio, men who know the land and can help you in your work. You will find no difficulty in undertaking the project if you first provision at San Antonio de Bexar."

It's too much money, Alexandre thought. *It's more money than my father earns from the plantation in a good year, more than Uncle Alcee takes in commissions from the New Orleans wharves and counting houses.* It was more than he had calculated he might himself earn in ten years or even fifteen years as a successful surveyor of town lots and parishes. He had looked at his hands and covered them, instinctively, as if merely by looking at them Lamar could see what he was thinking. It was too much money.

It was more than the money: it was freedom. From the moment he crossed the river into Texas, he would be free of the plantation. He would be free of his father. He would be his own man in a heroic land.

"I accept, sir," Alexandre answered. "When may I begin?"

Chapter Two

Texas

Alexandre waited patiently while he rode Logan's ferry across the Sabine River to Texas.

Ah, he said to himself, gazing at the riverbank, the thick pine forest, and beyond to the rich black earth. *Here at last.* From the moment he and Uncle Alcee had left President Lamar, Alexandre had expected something to happen, a change in Lamar's mind, problems with the terms of the agreement, a delay in Lamar arranging a letter of credit to await Alexandre in Texas, but nothing had gone wrong. Now, he could barely contain his excitement as the flat raft glided over the shallow water toward the ferry landing. This is a day to remember, he thought, a great day.

The other passengers jostled for position to leave the ferry. He noticed two or three other wagons, several men who led horses by the bridles, and a dozen foot passengers, some Black, mostly White. The bow of the ferry bounced against the dock and the ferry man tied off the docking line. Alexandre waited his turn to steer his wagon onto the landing, then asked directions for the road to Nacogdoches. A workman pointed to a well-worn path through the trees, told him to look out for the fork in the road, and Alexandre rode on, into Texas.

The fork was in a clearing at the edge of the pine forest, less than a half-mile from the Sabine River. Alexandre paused, trying to remember which branch he had been told to take, and chose the road to the left branch. The road left the forest and crossed a broad plain to a low hill and, climbed steadily toward a distant ridge.

As he rode it occurred to him that none of the other ferry passengers seemed to have continued toward Nacogdoches. When he looked back, he saw that most were still at the ferry landing or making their way out of the trees. Some appeared to be making their way to the right-hand fork, but not so many that it proved he had taken a wrong turn. In fact, two horsemen rode on his road, about a hundred yards behind him. He decided to continue up to the ridge for a higher vantage point to study the land and consider whether he might have taken the wrong turn. As the path made its way up the hill the roadbed all but disappeared, becoming no more than a rocky path at its steepest point near the ridge.

The horses of Plantation LaBranche had not been accustomed to pull heavy wagons up steep rocky paths. His horse stumbled partway up the hill, pulling the wagon's right wheels into a deep rut. The panicked horse reared up, twisted the braces, and the wagon rolled over onto its side. Alexandre fell off the buckboard, getting his first taste of Texas. By the time he regained his feet the two horsemen who had followed him at a distance had ridden up. He waved them down; they reined in their horses and stared.

"Would you gentlemen be so kind as to help me right my wagon?" he called out to them, "and then I'll be on my way." One of them may have nodded.

"My name is LaBranche, Alexandre LaBranche." He held out his hand for the horsemen to shake. They did not shake his hand, nor did they give their names. They did, however, dismount and walk to his wagon.

The wagon did need righting. A wheel had buckled, dragging Alexandre's horse down as well. His trunk and a wooden brass-bound box had tumbled to rest a few yards away.

The two horsemen walked around the scene, studying the wagon, the horse, the spilled goods.

"I suggest you," Alexandre said, indicating the scrawnier of the two, "I suggest you take the lead there," pointing to the horse collar and traces, "and try to guide my horse back over to the left. And we, sir," he continued, smiling and encouraging the other man who, behind his brown mustache, was undeniably larger and stronger, "if you and I get underneath the wagon and lift...."

The man with the mustache nodded in agreement. He also nodded to his scrawny partner, who took the horse's reins and began to separate them from the tangled traces. The mustache man and Alexandre bent down to grip the side of the wagon box.

"Not much in your wagon," the mustache man said. "You from around here?"

"I am not. It's my first journey to Texas." For want of an introduction Alexandre decided to himself that he would call the man Mustache. "I'm bound for the Rio Grande!"

"Come over on the ferry, didn't you?" the man continued. He jerked his head back in the direction of the trail, the pine woods, and the Sabine. "Today?"

"I did indeed." Alexandre recognized them as two of the riders who had been on the same raft. "Let's give it a shove. One, two and three!" They lifted, the scrawny man tugged on the horse, and the wagon rose partway before the weight caused it to settle back. "Good, we almost had it. Let's try again."

They failed a second time, but the scrawny man did succeed in freeing the horse from the trace straps and the wagon neck.

"Perhaps if you joined us," Alexandre suggested to him, "we can make it this time. You don't say much, do you?"

"He's not one for talking," Mustache answered for him. "You in a hurry?"

Alexandre nodded and smiled. "Here we go," and he motioned for all three to bend to the task. "One, two, and three," and they strained with all their might. After a shaky rise onto the left wheels, a push, another heave, and a grunt, the wagon passed the tipping point and fell onto all four wheels, bounced once, and came to rest upright. He patted the two men on their backs, then walked over to the trunk.

The trunk's lid had opened, not entirely. The box had not opened at all.

"The Rio Grande?" Mustache asked.

"Yes. I am…" he began to say 'a scientist of the geographic arts,' but doubted such crude men would understand. "… a surveyor. I'm going there to map the river. All of it." The two men may have exchanged a knowing look but otherwise did not seem impressed. "To its source. And, by the way, is this the road to Nacogdoches? Or was it the other fork?" He turned and looked back toward the distant pine forest. A number of people, too far away to be seen clearly, seemed to be milling around the fork in the road near the landing. "And thank you for your help. Now, time's wasting."

Time began to waste at a quicker rate when the boom of a gunshot thundered out of the pine trees. They all turned to look back toward the fork in the road, where the people suddenly seemed to be milling at a much more agitated pace.

"Best be on our way. Make hay while the sun …."

"You got a gun?" Mustache asked. Alexandre shook his head; no, he did not. "What's in the trunk?" he continued. It wasn't much of a question; Mustache already had stepped between Alexandre and the trunk and begun to poke at the lid.

"If you please, sir, those are my…" It wasn't clear how he had done it, but the scrawny partner also had stepped between Alexandre and the trunk. "Let me just close the lid and…" The mustache man stared at him with the same unconcerned gaze the two had held from the moment they had ridden up to his over-turned wagon.

Mustache rummaged around in the trunk, took out the clothes and a leather case, inspected the contents, then replaced them and closed the lid. He nodded to his scrawny companion and the two of them lifted the trunk onto the wagon. The scrawny man then walked over to the brass-bound box and lifted it as well, placing it into the wagon alongside the trunk. He then led his own horse to the wagon and tied the reins to the corner brace.

"We'll be taking these," the mustache man said. Alexandre stood and gaped. "You won't be needing them." He plainly meant to ride away with the wagon and everything that Alexandre owned. "Oh," the robber added, "You got a watch?" He quickly frisked Alexandre, found his watch and a snuffbox, which he took, and a used handkerchief, which he did not. He then mounted his own horse as the scrawny man climbed up to the wagon seat and flicked the reins. "Wouldn't stay around here long. Don't seem too friendly. Good day to you." The robber tipped his hat. They rode away.

Alexandre stood on the grass slope, watching his wagon and horse, the mustache man, the scrawny man, and their horses crest the hill and disappear on the other side. All he could do was stare.

Why'd they steal the wagon? he wondered. It was plain that the wheel had folded. *The axle shafts have to be bent,* he thought. It occurred to him that they'd had to steal his wagon because without it they couldn't have stolen his trunk and survey equipment and, for that matter, everything he owned. He dusted off his hands and knees, then walked briskly toward a stand of wax myrtle shrubs. He looked back toward the Sabine and the pine forest. Still, better my wagon than my life.

He decided to walk back to the ferry landing for help and looked to see what was happening there. He couldn't see very clearly, but what was happening couldn't have been good since several more horsemen burst out of the forest and galloped away on the other fork in the road, as if they were chasing someone, or something. Alexandre decided that walking into a shooting scene was an even worse idea than walking all the way to Nacogdoches. He turned around.

Before long he heard the clop of yet another horse and turned to see if it was someone who could help. Another rider had emerged from the forest and was slowly coming toward him. When the rider was closer Alexandre saw that there was a body draped across the horse behind the saddle. He hid behind some wax myrtle shrubs until the funerary rider passed by and rode out of sight. When that horse, too, was beyond the hill and far away, Alexandre began to jog and walk across the rugged prairie, flitting from the cover of one bush to another and getting as far as he could from the river, the gunshot, the rider and the body.

He soon left the road to avoid being seen, wishing he had taken care to have hidden his compass and also wishing he had taken more care in learning how to use it. He also regretted the theft of his watch and soon lost track of time. He walked across the rough country, crossing fields, pastures, and countless thickets, looking out for a farm, a plantation, a village, anyone who might help him. He approached several farms, each of which was stocked with barking dogs but not with hospitality. As the sun began to set, there was no sign of a town, no smoke rising from a chimney, no broad avenue to a plantation house, and his hunger worsened his anxiety.

Just before dark he saw a farm. There, across a fallow field, was a darkened cabin. No light was showing, no smoke curling from a chimney. No one worked in the field or chopped wood for the picket fences that separated the cabin from a kitchen garden and the livestock pen. He decided to try for the garden.

Images of potatoes and carrots and the vines of red ripe tomatoes crowded his mind and, when he approached the garden, he heard the chaos of loudly squealing pigs and Alexandre entertained the thought of making away with a piglet. But, as he tiptoed toward dinner, he saw why the pigs were making such a racket: a huge wild boar burst through a stand of shrubbery to get to the piglets, wrecking their fence and scattering the terrified hogs. The roaring boar spotted Alexandre and lowered its tusks to charge him as well, then stopped for an instant to choose whether to attack Alexandre or the piglets. The piglets were closer; when the boar turned around to chase them, Alexandre fled back across the field. He ran in the dark, across cotton stubble, stumbling on plowed ground and stumps and onward until he found a dry stream bed.

He had even less experience running in the dark in dry stream beds than he had with catching pig so it did not occur to him that dry streams might have dry waterfalls. Alexandre ran, panting and breathless, until he could no longer see the ground beneath his feet. He paused, bent over to catch his breath, then took one last step and fell headlong into the night, dropping through empty space, flailing, and kicking the air, until something struck his head.

Then he lost consciousness, ending his first day in Texas.

Chapter Three
Nacogdoches, Texas

S everal days later a dispatch rider brought a leather bag into the tidy log building where Thomas Rusk and Pinckney Henderson practiced law. Rusk himself took the bag, told the rider to wait, went into the back room, and read the sealed letter from Texas' *charge d'affairs.*

The New Orleans judges have released the *Durango* and its crew. They will depart for the Gulf any day.

It took Rusk most of an hour to decipher the coded letter. When he had done so, it read:

The passengers were Mexican soldiers dressed as ordinary passengers, sent by Colonel Canales. The *Durango*'s only cargo was five hundred Tercerlo muskets, some small field pieces, and shot and powder. I expect the *Durango* will return to Texas waters and invade toward San Antonio de Bexar.

Three of the passengers, known Mexican agents, did not return to the ship and probably have fled the city. They will not easily be caught out as spies as their behavior is ordinary, their features are not obviously Mexican, and they may not be of that race. I engaged our own confidential agent to follow them. I expect the spies to cross into Texas at the Sabine to gain more information about our strength and to sow mischief.

There was more, but Rusk had the gist of it. He folded the dispatch and returned it to its leather pouch, then rubbed his eyes. He took a quill and began to write his own coded letter:

Dear General: I will be brief. I expect that Mexican agents from the *Durango* will infiltrate Texas, most likely by crossing the Sabine River. They may be here already in that a man, rumored to be a surveyor, has been murdered near the ferry landing. The men of the city have formed a *posse comitatus* and are riding night and day in search of the killer. I will double my vigilance in this area; if the Mexican spies are here, they will be found.

Your servant, Thomas J. Rusk
    Nacogdoches, Texas November 25, 1841

Rusk sealed the letter, put it in the pouch, and called for the dispatch rider. He gave instructions, found a dollar for the man, and sent him on his way.

I need Henderson, Rusk told himself. We must deal with this.

At approximately that same hour Rusk's partner, Pinkney Henderson, entered the storeroom of Palmer's Mercantile Company, which also doubled as the Nacogdoches jail. He squinted in the dim light and saw two men, one larger and with a heavy mustache, the other so gaunt as to be scrawny. Their attempts to stand were defeated for their being chained to a bolt in the wall.

"Gentlemen," he said. "I am Mr. Henderson. I am a lawyer at the bar in this city. I have received an appeal from Mistress Eleanor Goodnough. She asks that I ..." He opened her badly spelled note and read aloud: "'Dear Mr. Henderson. Two honorable and good men are taken to jale in this town and I beseach you to do all in your powr to come to their ade as they are innocent.' I believe you are the men to whom Ms. Goodnough refers. How may I come to your aid?"

The two did not look innocent, not precisely, Henderson thought, but neither did they look like hardened criminals. The mustache man was dressed in dandy clothes that did not fit him, while his scrawny companion was dressed like a starving peasant. *But,* Henderson suspected, *they were not a fancy man and his valet.*

"We are the victims of a misunderstanding, a tragic misunderstanding," the mustached man answered. Henderson noted the exaggerated formality and suspected the man wanted to fool him. He also noted that the misunderstanding appeared to be a physical one as well as a matter of miscommunication; the man and his scrawny companion bore the welts and bruises of a heavy beating. "And because of a failure of listening on the part of one of your fellow citizens, we are as you see us—beaten, chained, and hungry."

"Explain this misunderstanding to me, if you please," Henderson told him.

Mustache did the speaking.

"We were taken by a group of rough men and beaten in the street. Black men. Large Black men."

Henderson wanted to know whether the prisoners knew the large Black men. It was at this point that he sensed the seeds of the misunderstanding, because the answer was not immediately forthcoming. At some length the man with the mustache answered: "I don't make the acquaintance of Blacks, sir"

Henderson found this doubtful; it was not obvious from which race the man's scrawny companion originated, but he was not Anglo. Henderson thought he might be from any race, Mexican, a Black octoroon perhaps, maybe even part Apache.

"Explain to me, then, why they made your acquaintance. Why did these large, rough Black men take you in the street and beat you?" Henderson knew there was more to the misunderstanding than the mustached man was letting on; if slaves beat up a white man, the usual outcome was that the slaves were hanged. Instead, it was the white man and his companion who were chained to the town's makeshift jail. "Took you from what?"

"Our wagon, sir. And that is the source of the misunderstanding." The slaves belonged to Mr. Sullivan, the mustached man explained, and Mr. Sullivan owned the livery stable. "We're accused of stealing our own wagon. We were not stealing it. We were using it for an…" Mustache paused, considered that Mistress Eleanor Goodnough must have explained something to Henderson to get him to come to their aid, and went on with his thin story. "… for an assignation. Of the heart."

Henderson understood assignations of the heart. He had met his own wife when Texas had sent him abroad as a diplomat, and he had married her in London. He also understood Miss Goodnough, who with the other young women at Mrs. Stewart's Female Academy, attended services, sat in a pew, and glanced at every male over the age of eighteen. It might charitably be said that the mustached man could be the height of her aspirations. However, Henderson suspected that she was not the height of his.

"Be plain, sir. If you ask for my help, tell me how you came to be taken in the street, beaten by rough Black men, and brought to this jail. And tell me your names. What is your name?"

"Pennant, sir. I am Stephen Decatur Pennant."

"And your name, sir?" Henderson turned to the scrawny man, who had not spoken a word, nor did so now.

"Alonzo," Pennant answered for him. "Alonzo doesn't say much. And the misunderstanding, to be plain, is that we was testing the repairs to our wagon, sir. It's as simple as that."

Word by word, Pennant's first version of the misunderstanding was that he and Alonzo had gone to Sullivan's Livery to inspect the repairs to the wagon.

"It got bunged up when the wagon turned over." They had hired Sullivan to build new spindles and an axle hub for the wagon. "And we was testing it, that's all, when these two slaves pulled us off and beat the tar out of us. We was going to pay. If the repairs was done proper."

Henderson sensed a dissimulation.

"You are not from here, are you?" he asked. Pennant admitted that they were not. "Where did you stay while your wagon was under repair?"

Pennant answered that he and Alonzo had taken a room in a boarding house that, as it happened, was not far from Mrs. Stewart's Female Academy where, it went without saying, Pennant had made the acquaintance of Mistress Goodnough.

"And, so," Henderson continued, "I understand that you are the victim of a misunderstanding. You were testing your repaired wagon and, perhaps, you were planning to fetch Mistress Good-nough to accompany you in the wagon, when Mr. Sullivan's men saw you riding away from his livery stable and thought you were fleeing your debt for the repairs you had arranged. Is that it?"

"Exactly, sir. You have it."

"And that would explain your clothes. These are the clothes that you thought would make your best impression on the young lady?" Henderson asked.

"Just so."

Henderson rose. Pennant extended his hand and nudged Alonzo to do the same.

"Then you will take our case, sir? Thank you."

"I have not decided," Henderson answered. He saw a cloud cross Pennant's bruised, swarthy face. "First, there is the matter of payment. I am most obliged to have been petitioned by Miss Good-nough to come to your aid. But, just as Robin Hood came to the aid of Maid Marion, Robin Hood nevertheless required some of the king's deer to feed his band of merry men." Pennant didn't under-stand. "To be plain, how, sir, may I expect to be paid?"

It was no small matter. Henderson surmised that if Pennant and Alonzo had money, they would have paid Sullivan for the wagon repairs, and there would have been no misunderstanding. If they had no money to pay Sullivan, they had no money to pay Henderson.

"We expect the arrival of a letter of credit, sir. At the customs house. Drawn on a Louisiana bank." That was a good answer. Henderson himself had solicited the republic to establish the customs house to handle commercial payments for goods coming into the republic. "I believe the letter of credit should arrive any day, sir, if it has not already done so, a fact I cannot establish on my own due to ..." Pennant pointed to the chain on his ankle.

"I see," Henderson continued. "And the second point: I will make a slight investigation for myself into this miscommunication. I know Mr. Sullivan." Henderson, like Thomas Rusk, knew everyone. "Perhaps we can correct the misunderstanding, Mr. Pennant, which I think would be more to your advantage than to answer Sullivan's charge in a court of law. Good day to you." He turned to leave.

Pennant asked him to wait a moment longer and paused before resuming.

"There may be more to the misunderstanding than I have had an opportunity to explain, Mr. Henderson." Henderson paused at the door to the jail. "Mr. Sullivan may have formed the mistaken belief that we were leaving without paying our debt because of the presence of our effects in the wagon." Henderson left the door and returned to face the men. "Our trunk. And our box."

Henderson still was inclined to refuse the case; the two men struck him as too suspicious. But, on the one hand, Henderson needed the money, there having been very little pay in actual cash for his services to the republic. And, Henderson admitted to himself, he felt that he had not been bearing his fair share of his partnership with Thomas Rusk. In the end, he knew there was more to their story; hearing the rest of it might be the only compensation he would receive for a wasted afternoon at the jail. He went to Sullivan's Livery Stable.

Sullivan said there was no misunderstanding and was not inclined to dismiss his charge.

"You will understand, Mr. Henderson, that they owe me fourteen dollars." That struck Henderson as expensive; he asked how the fare could be so high. "It was more than repairing the axle hub and the spindles. They boarded their horses, too."

Sullivan had a counterproposal.

"But I would settle their bill and not press the charge in exchange for one of their horses. And they have to leave town."

Henderson was shocked. A horse of any quality would be worth ten such repairs to the wagon, work which surely had been done by Sullivan's slaves. He suggested Sullivan take a godlier approach.

"And forgive us our debts, Mr. Sullivan, as we also have forgiven our debtors. Book of Matthew."

"Then two robbers were crucified with Him, Mr. Henderson, one on the right and one on the left. Also Book of Matthew. The men will pay, one way or the other."

"But," Henderson answered, "how can they leave town if you keep their horse?"

"They got three," Sullivan answered. "Wagon's just a single rig. One of 'em come into the stable on the wagon, one on a horse, and there was a third horse tied to the back. They can keep the wagon; I want a horse. They can have their portmanteau too. I'll keep the box."

Henderson said that he would relay the proposition to the men but was not at present able to make any binding decisions on their behalf, and might he see the portmanteau. "And the box."

The portmanteau was a clothes trunk. Henderson opened the lid to discover a worn pair of canvas pants, a homespun weather cloak, some underdrawers, four pair of gentlemen's trousers and six fine shirts, together with some cravats, a brim, and a serape. Henderson thought the most likely explanation was that the two men had put some of their own clothes into the portmanteau and that Pennant, at least, had dug into it to dress himself in the ill-fitting dandy clothes that he was wearing when Sullivan's slaves beat the daylights out of him.

He dug further and found the false bottom. Beneath it there were parchment contracts engaging Alexandre LaBranche of the City of New Orleans and such of his assistants and workmen as needed, together with his knowledge, skill, equipment, tools and devices to perform mapping and border surveys for the Republic of

Texas along the length of the Rio Grande River to its source and at such other places as he might be directed by the Republic. LaBranche would draw funds on the contract for the supplies and equipment necessary to accomplish his work, to be effected by a letter of credit which would be delivered to LaBranche at the customs house in Nacogdoches, Texas. There was a map which on the left-hand margin ended partway up the Rio Grande River. He put them back in the false bottom of the portmanteau.

"Do you have the box, Mr. Sullivan?" he continued.

There was on the box's lid a brass plate on which was embossed 'Edward Draper, Philadelphia, 1832.' The contents consisted of a surveyor's transit and sextant, a compass, a collapsing tripod, and a gunter's chain. A leather pouch held sheets of printed columns to write notes and calculations of distances, angles, longitudes, and latitudes.

There also were two canvas bags which, Henderson suspected, had seen life at sea. In one of them he found faded and worn clothes that, by their size, he suspected belonged to Pennant. The same bag was stuffed with dozens of small, colored flags, triangular banners, red, white, blue, some with stripes and diagonals. The other bag contained a pair of cotton pants and a cotton shirt and, to Henderson's surprise, three small cookpots, a ladle, and some kitchen knives.

Henderson thanked Sullivan, then walked over to the customs house.

"Yes sir, Mr. Henderson," the clerk at the customs house told him. "Those two men come here near every day, asking for a letter of credit," the clerk told him. "In a Louisiana name."

"LaBranche?"

"That's it."

"Has it arrived?"

"It has." The clerk opened the safe, sorted the contents, and withdrew a letter of credit, payable on Planter's Bank of New Orleans to the benefit of Alexandre LaBranche, for remit by the Republic of Texas or any bank therein, in such sums as may be presented for demand, not to exceed one hundred United States dollars at any one draw nor to exceed ten thousand United States dollars in total.

Henderson returned to the jail.

"I will take your case," he informed the two men. "But I caution you — it will not be as simple a matter as you might think."

Pennant stood up, as much as he could, and thanked him. Alonzo stared at his feet. Henderson continued.

"I spoke with Mr. Sullivan at the livery stable. He was not amenable to a reasonable arrangement. The misunderstanding, Mr. Pennant, did indeed arise from his observation that you and Alonzo, before the sun rose, had taken from your room at the hotel your trunk of clothes and a bound box and put them in the bed of the wagon at Sullivan's livery stable. You then took your three horses from his stable, hitched your wagon, and were halfway out of Nacogdoches when Mr. Sullivan's stable hands caught up with you and pulled you off the wagon. You do see, don't you, Mr. Pennant, how that could appear to be the act of someone fleeing without paying a debt?"

Pennant agreed that it could be misconstrued.

"And the street where they caught up with you and pulled you off the wagon was near the old Spanish mission. Mrs. Stewart's Female Academy, and presumably Miss Goodnough, were in the opposite direction, on the *camino real*." Pennant had no answer for that. There was more.

Henderson was a diplomat; he knew that bad news was best given slowly.

"I think the miscommunication with Mr. Sullivan may be the least of your worries, sirs. I do have some questions that need further explanation. First, how do you come to be in Nacogdoches?"

The men explained that they followed the ferry road to a fork that brought them to Nacogdoches, where the wagon could go no further without repairs. Henderson's next question was a surprise.

"Can you tell me how a compass works?"

Pennant had no difficulty at all. "It points north. Points on a compass bear off north to set a course." Alonzo whispered something to him. "You fix a bearing with it to get the direction to a fixed object."

They were good answers. It was possible, Henderson thought, that Pennant might be a surveyor or, more likely, someone who picked up navigation at sea.

"What is a league and a labor?" Henderson asked.

Pennant's answer was not quite as good this time. "A league is three miles. Don't rightly know about a labor." Alonzo whispered again. Pennant didn't explain.

"I have seen the survey equipment in the wagon, Mr. Pennant. I would expect a surveyor to know about a league and a labor. And a vara. Do you know what a vara is?"

Alonzo whispered again.

"We come from Louisiana, Mr. Henderson. We don't use the Spanish measures in Louisiana, excepting maybe the league."

"I'm going to leave you now, Mr. Pennant and Mr. Alonzo. I won't be back sooner than tomorrow, so you will have some time to think about whether you've told me everything there is to tell. In particular, I want you to think about two questions. First, how did you know that there would be a letter of credit at the customs house in Nacogdoches?"

Pennant started to answer, but Henderson told him not to say a word until he returned.

"My second question is this: What has become of Mr. Alexandre LaBranche? I doubt that you two gentlemen are surveyors. I think you, Mr. Pennant, may have been a sailor and you, Alonzo, most likely are of the Spanish or Mexican race, perhaps only in part. But you men are not surveyors. Yet you knew that Mr. LaBranche is—or was—a surveyor. You knew that there was a valuable letter of credit in his name, awaiting him at the customs house. And you arrived in Nacogdoches with his wagon, his clothes, and his tools of the trade. So, I fear that your failing to pay Mr. Sullivan may be the least of your troubles. Based on my experience, I suspect that when it is known what has become of Mr. LaBranche, the law may want to take its full course with your necks. Do I make myself clear, sirs?"

Pennant answered straight off.

"LaBranche is alive and well, sir. Or he was when we saw him last. He was standing on a hilltop about a mile or two from Logan's ferry landing. If anything has become of LaBranche from that day to this, it is not for anything that can be blamed on us."

Except for your having robbed him, Henderson thought, *of his wagon, horse, clothes, and tools and left him afoot in a rough country. The two could hang for that the same as if they had killed LaBranche,* which Henderson suspected they had done. Henderson considered whether to tell them that a man, rumored to be a surveyor, had been murdered near the ferry landing. He worried that the rumor might reach Sullivan, who was the one man in Nacogdoches who knew that Pennant and Alonzo had the surveyor's tools, clothes, and wagon. *If Sullivan begins to talk, Heaven help Pennant and Alonzo.*

In either case, they have denied the charge, Henderson thought. It is better if I do not force them to admit the truth, or it could compromise the defense. And, he thought, it might make collection of that letter of credit a bit more difficult.

He bade them good day and, although he would have preferred to go home to his new wife, he decided that he should report his good fortune to his partner.

CHAPTER FOUR

everal days passed before she found him.

When Alexandre regained consciousness, he found himself trapped inside the hard and sharp thorns of a huge greenbrier vine that had ensnared him when he fell headlong in the dark. When the dark became morning, he found that he was suspended midway down a deep ravine. There was a small pool below him; in its reflection he saw that he was hanging above a gully that most likely had been cut by running water during the rainy season.

He struggled against the thorns, but the thick branches were as tough as jail bars and the more he pushed against them the more they ripped into his arms and hands. He took a deep breath and began to see if he could touch or feel anything with his hands to find out how badly he had been hurt in the fall. The vines had him trapped so completely that he spent most of the morning trying to reach around them just to feel the back of his head, where he found a large bump that explained his throbbing pain. When he paused to consider his dilemma, he concluded that he had to tackle two problems.

The first problem was what to do with his future. *I am somewhere between the ferry landing and....* Then he realized that he didn't know the location of a single landmark, not a road, not Nacogdoches, not even the farm where he had fled from the boar ... between the ferry landing and somewhere in Texas. *I rode a half mile to the fork in the road, another half-mile to where I was robbed, and then walked a full day.* He calculated that he was half-way to Nacogdoches, assuming he had taken the correct fork and walked in the right direction. He decided that he would make his way to the first town he found, probably Nacogdoches, make a hue and cry for the two robbers, bring them to justice, then continue to San Antonio to provision for the Rio Grande. He had memorized the cities on the river, Laredo on the Texas side, Matamoros, Mier, and Presidio Rio Grande on the Mexican side. He imagined a river of small towns, happy people who would welcome him as he opened up their world. Then he remembered the second problem. But first, I have to get out of here.

He shouted for help; no one answered. He wondered whether someone would miss him, perhaps someone at the Nacogdoches customs house where he was expected to collect his letter of credit. That led him to wonder whether his two robbers had discovered the contract in his portmanteau and if they would be bold enough to try to impersonate him and collect on the letter of credit for themselves.

The greenbrier vines were as thick as a leg bone, its hard thorns a half inch long, some of which were stuck into his arms and legs and chest, others of which had slashed his face when he fell into the shrub. He watched small birds splash in the pool below his feet, then fly up into the vines. He could not reach his feet, but with some effort he could undo the cuffs of his shirt sleeves. It took him almost an hour to roll them back and wrap them around the vine at his hands. He pulled on the vine; the thorns cut the shirt, and the vine moved. He pulled again, and his hand was free. He pulled a third time, and a dog barked.

Alexandre called the dog.

"Hey, boy, hey. Fetch your master. Hey, boy."

The dog barked again.

"You find him?" a rough voice called from somewhere high on the ridge above him. The dog barked again. "Where, dog?" the voice yelled out.

"Here, boy," Alexandre answered the dog. Then he heard the metallic click of a rifle being cocked. The dog barked again and, in the reflecting pool, Alexandre saw a man step up to the rim of the waterfall and aim a rifle directly at him.

"You got him?" the man yelled. The dog barked twice. "Where, dog? Show me." Alexandre held his breath. The dog barked. The dog attacked. A rabbit squealed as the dog clamped its jaws into the rabbit and shook it. "Leave off the rabbit, dog!" The dog did not leave off the rabbit. "Ain't here for no rabbits, dog! Here! Here!" the rifleman barked. "Here!" The dog held the rabbit in its jaw, looked up the canyon wall, and took off at a run up a steep path. Alexandre heard the rifle bolt being uncocked. "Ain't here to chase rabbits, dog!" the man barked at his animal. Then, in a louder voice, "Nothin'," he called out to someone else up above the ledge. "Thought the dog found him, but it's just a rabbit." Then the sound of boots walking away from the edge, soon followed by the unmistakable sound of a man getting into a saddle and riding away. "Ain't nobody here."

Alexandre began to call out, to say yes, there was someone here, but just before he uttered a word, he decided that yelling for help from a man with a gun in an unwelcome land filled with robbers was unwise. He heard the men ride away.

He waited for silence, then returned to shredding his shirt-sleeves on the thorns. When afternoon came, he was exhausted and napped. When he woke again, it was nighttime.

He resumed his struggle against the woody spikes, wondering whether someone would have reported that Alexandre had arrived on the ferry. He knew that he was becoming incoherent when he began to dream about his father. *Will he repent for disowning me? And for what, a ... liaison with a slave? Or, in Alexandre's worst fears, will he just laugh when he learns that I met my end in a thorn bush? Then, I've got to get down to that water.* The thirst had begun to make his mind wander; he even had a fleeting thought of imitating the dog and catching a rabbit. "I can do this!" he said.

"Shhhh!" a voice said.

"I'll rip my arms and legs out of these damned thorns, and. ..."

At that moment, he felt a small, bony hand clamp over his mouth. A quiet, urgent voice whispered, "Shhh!"

The horses had come back. Alexandre heard them and heard the rustle of branches in the breeze. A dog barked.

"Who...?" he tried to ask, but the hand pushed even tighter against his face and Alexandre could make no sound. He struggled against the branches and thorns, but another bony hand clamped itself to his shoulder to prevent him from moving.

"Shhh," the voice whispered. "Or they'll hear you."

There was the murmur of the deep voices of men on the ridge above them. Alexandre realized that, for reasons he did not understand, someone was trying to find him and someone else was trying to save him. He made himself perfectly still. After another long silence, the horses trotted away, and the voices disappeared.

"Hurry," she whispered. "An' be quiet."

He felt her bony little hands and fingers ripple across his neck and arms, lifting the vines, pulling thorns away from his face. She worked rapidly, tugging and pushing with her rough hands, finding his hands and moving them one way and another. He wondered that she could see what she was doing in the pitch dark. And, unable to make out her features, he realized that she too was pitch dark.

She tugged on the thorns and the birch branches until she freed his head and body. For the first time in days, Alexandre felt the sensation of blood rushing through his body instead of leaking out of it. As she went to work on the vines that bound his ankles, he sought a limb to lower himself to the ground. She helped him limp to the creek bed and to bend down for a drink of the muddy pond water.

"Where am I?" Alexandre asked. He rubbed his cuts, rubbed his face and legs, but was too weak to stand up.

"Men're out lookin' for you," she whispered. "If they catch you, you got trouble."

He could tell from her voice, from the slight dialect and partial words, that she was a slave, maybe a teenage girl, maybe not. But, apart from having fallen into a ravine in the dark, he had no good sense of exactly where he was or even how he got there.

"Who are you?" It did not trouble him that he had been rescued by a slave girl; where he had come from, slave girls were expected to help persons of quality who were in difficulty, even if he could not think of an instance of one actually having done so. It did trouble him that a slave girl had taken charge of him; he decided to take back control as soon as circumstances permitted. "And where am I?"

"Between the river an' Nacodoches."

"Who is trying to catch me?" It occurred to him that very possibly the slave girl might not be there to rescue him. She might just be leading him to be murdered in the dark by the mustache man and the scrawny man. "And why?"

"There's a posse out lookin' for who shot a man down by the river. We got to go." She tugged on his wrist to help him stand, then led him further along the dry stream bed until she found a place where they could climb up out of the gully. There was a field at the top. He stopped.

"Where are you leading me?" he asked.

"Jus' away. Come on."

Alexandre took his bearings. He thought that he saw the outline of a cabin in the distance, probably the farm where the boar had chased him away from the only opportunity he had had to eat since he left Louisiana. In the other direction, there seemed to be some-thing of a road, no more than a cart track, that ran in a roughly straight line, leading in what he judged to be an east and west direc-tion. He turned east.

"Where you goin'?" she asked.

"Back to Louisiana." He began to walk. The robbery had not stopped him, nor the murder, nor even the thorn bushes. *But*, he thought, *if a posse is riding in the dark, looking for me for a murder I didn't commit, I need some civilized help.* The nearest civilization was back in Louisiana, across the Sabine from Logan's ferry. He had only a vague idea of what that help might involve and decided he would make that decision when he got back to civilization.

As he walked, he thought about the message he would send to President Lamar when he was back in Louisiana. He would warn Lamar that two robbers had taken his wagon and tools and his contract for the letter of credit. He would ask Lamar for another horse—and a gun. He would....

She was walking alongside him.

"Where do you think you're going?" he asked.

"I got to get away too. If they catch me, it's worse for me. I'm goin' with you."

"No, you're not. I'm not taking a runaway slave girl with me." What he meant was that men like him didn't rescue slaves. More-over, once he got back to Louisiana, he would have no use for her, nor for that matter would he have much use for himself without his survey equipment and his contract. "You'll slow me down." He wondered if she had anything he could eat hidden in the pockets of her dress but had too much pride to ask.

Instead, he shooed her with his hands, like he was running off a dog. He then set off again, trying to keep a dozen yards off the cart track in case he needed to hide again. She followed him.

"I said go away. I'm not taking you to Louisiana."

"Not goin' with you," she answered. "Jus' runnin' away on my own and happen to be goin' the same direction. Of course, you know your way 'round here. That's how come you fell into the brambles. Maybe I won' follow you." She stepped behind a tree and crossed her arms, waiting for him to walk on, which he did without a backward glance.

The cart track did not run straight for long. It descended to another dry stream bed, turned left and right, entered a stand of pines, turned a few more times, followed the lay of the land up a ridge, and wound its way along a hillside before doubling back on the reverse slope. Every now and then, the road opened onto a clearing or a bit of prairie or a picked-over cotton field. He finally gave out, stopped, crouched down, and rested.

He was hungry and wanted to lie down to sleep. But, getting away from the road had got him lost in the first place, so he walked back toward Louisiana as quietly as he could, stopping when he heard a dog bark or came to a fence or field, hiding from cabins and cattle and horses, unsure how far it was back to Logan's ferry landing.

It was not until the sun began to rise in the distance that he figured out that in the dark he had gotten turned around by the twists and turns in the road. Instead of walking east, he had walked west. Instead of going back to Louisiana, he had walked farther into Texas. He looked for a place to hide. She emerged from the trees behind him.

"I told you to stop following me," he barked. "Get!"

"I'm not followin' you. My momma's momma an' some of her folks is from Louisiana, so I'm jus' goin' there too."

"You're going the wrong way, then," he barked again. "You let me walk the wrong direction. Why didn't you tell me?"

"I don't know which way is Louisiana. You're the white man."

"You're going to get us caught," he hissed at her. "If they catch us, they'll think I'm harboring a runaway."

"You didn't save me! I saved you!" she answered. "You were already gonna bleed or starve to death in the bushes. And I'm not runnin' away with you. I'm just runnin' away. Which way is Louisiana?"

Louisiana was the other way. Nacogdoches was this way, which they learned by seeing smoke rise from chimneys on the other side of a stand of pine trees. Alexandre thought he had found a town to raise the hue and cry against his robbers. At the least, there would be houses and gardens and probably a stream where he could wash. He told her again to go away, then began to walk as quietly as he could toward a creek at the edge of the town.

———

Mary Rusk stood at her front window and watched the Nacogdoches posse ride out of town toward Logan's ferry landing. She then walked to the back porch of her home to oversee the cookhouse but, instead of seeing the cooks, she saw a ragged figure wade out of Banita Creek and toward her kitchen garden. Mary rapped on the porch post to get the attention of one of the mulattoes working in her cook house, who looked up to see the vagabond. She watched the mulatta run after him with a broom, then stop short, broom raised, then broom lowered, then appear to instruct the vagabond to stay where he was.

"He's quality, Misrus Mary," the mulatta reported. "A white man."

"What does he want?" Mrs. Rusk asked. She stared at the white man, who did not look like quality. He instead looked like a scarecrow in torn, filthy clothes. She sent the mulatta back to ask Alexandre what he was doing in her kitchen garden; she returned with the report that he had been robbed and left for dead on the road. She told the slave to bring him to the back porch.

"Stop right there," Mary told him as he approached the steps. "What are you doing in my back garden?"

Alexandre was tempted to ignore the stern woman and go right back to forage in her garden, but he sensed that he was poised between an opportunity to get help and a misstep that could land him in the local jail. He gathered his wits and answered.

"I am lost, ma'am, and I apologize for such an improper arrival. You see, I was robbed some days ago of my horse and wagon and, you can see, my clothes. I have been walking across…"

"Robbed where?" she interrupted.

"Near the ferry landing, ma'am. I set out to walk the rest of the way to…."

"Did they thrash you as well?" she asked.

"No, ma'am, they did not. I am embarrassed to admit that in the dark of night I fell into a ravine and was forced to spend some nights in a thorn bush."

Before she could reply another vagabond walked out of the garden and directly to where Mary was deciding what to do about the white man of quality at her back porch. Mary looked up to see a wisp of a girl, a slender, soft skinned Black girl, dressed in a shift and wearing a shawl on her neck. She was almost as dirty as Alexandre.

"I got him out o' them thorns," the girl's voice chimed in. "An' he decided we'd be better off walkin' back to Louisiana."

"Who are you?"

"I'm Noeme," she answered. She pronounced it 'no' and 'me,' as if she had two names.

"Is she yours?" Mary asked him.

"Yes, ma'am," Noeme answered before Alexandre could deny it.

Mary Rusk was struck by her appearance, dirty and ragged as she was. For a Black girl who had just climbed out of a creek, she had unusual poise; she was not beautiful, but had clear eyes, a fine nose, and a small mouth, especially given how much came out of it.

"We was afraid of robbers, ma'am. That's why we got off the road. Then he fell into them brambles and I had to get him out of that gully and he said he had enough of Texas so we set out to go back to Louisiana. But he got lost."

"Be quiet, girl," Mrs. Rusk ordered. "I meant," Mrs. Rusk continued to the white man of quality, "you. Who are you, sir?"

"I am Alexandre LaBranche."

"Mr. Alexandre LaBranche, you are still lost. This is not Louisiana."

Mary told him to wait on her back porch, that something would be brought to eat. She also sent another slave to give a written note to her husband.

"Come immediately," she had written, "as I have on the porch either the man who killed the surveyor at the ferry landing or the man who Pinkney's clients robbed, or both."

Fifteen minutes later, Alexandre's bite of corn bread was interrupted by the sound of heavy boots on the porch. He looked up to see a solid gentleman with steely eyes pointing a cocked pistol at his head.

"You have one minute to state your business before I march you to the sheriff," Rusk began.

"My business?" Alexandre repeated. "I am a surveyor." He saw a look of surprise in Rusk's eyes. "I came over from Louisiana to Texas to map…"

"My wife tells me that you claim to have been robbed. Where did this this robbery take place?"

"At a ridge this side of a fork in the road near the ferry landing." LaBranche thought the answer clear enough. He was surprised to see Rusk's face become pinched and his eyes focused.

"And when did this supposed robbery happen?"

"It was not a supposed robbery, sir. Two men took everything I owned, even my watch and snuffbox. I do not know what else they would have done, but when we heard a gunshot …."

"A gunshot, sir? You heard it?"

"I did," Alexandre answered. "The robbers heard it too because they finished robbing me and rode off in my broken wagon."

"Sir," Rusk interrupted, "my suspicion is that you are not a surveyor. My suspicion is that you are the man who murdered a real surveyor near the ferry landing. What do you say to that, sir?"

Alexandre was startled by the accusation. It took him a full minute to gather what little dignity he had left to deny it. At the same time, Rusk already doubted that he was looking at a murderer. He saw not only that Alexandre's clothes were in shreds and his face cut and bruised, but also that he had no firearm, no pistol or musket. Even so, Rusk demanded an answer.

"I am no murderer, sir," Alexandre sputtered. "I am a surveyor. I can prove it when the men are found who robbed me and…."

"Prove it yourself," Rusk interrupted. "You don't need your robbers to prove you're a surveyor. Tell me how to do a survey." Rusk realized he had lowered his cocked pistol. He raised it again.

"Of course, sir," Alexandre gulped. "I meant that if the robbers hadn't stolen my survey equipment, I would have used it to show you how to survey. But I can tell you this: I can survey from any fixed point on earth to any other point, measuring the direction, distance, and elevation. If there isn't a fixed point, I can determine one for an exact place of beginning." He saw Rusk's face briefly change expression. "I can measure latitude at high noon with a sextant, compass, and an inclinometer. I can do so at night as well, using a telescope to measure the difference in the meridional distances of known stars. This is the new method, the Horrebow sequence, as improved by Captain Talcott." He expected this to satisfy Rusk. It did not.

"Tell me this, sir," Rusk continued. "Where do you come from? You say you're a surveyor from Louisiana, but you don't sound like you're from Natchitoches, or even Alexandria."

"I am not. I come from St. Charles Parish, upriver from New Orleans."

"You're not helping yourself, sir," Rusk asserted. "I don't pretend to know everything that happens here, but I can't think of any reason for a surveyor from New Orleans to conduct his business in Nacogdoches."

"New Orleans is where I met President Lamar." Alexandre saw the unmistakable look of surprise on Rusk's face. "It is his commission that brings me here."

"What commission is that?" Rusk doubted that Mirabeau Lamar would give anyone a commission to do anything in his last days in office.

"President Lamar engaged me to survey the boundary of Texas, sir, along the Rio Grande River. And to map it."

Rusk was shocked at the idea and said so. Alexandre continued.

"I assure you it's true. I'm hired to map all the way to Santa Fe, then beyond to the very source of the river, and from there due north to the United States."

The idea was unimaginable.

"The entire length of the Rio Grande? You? Alone?"

LaBranche swore that it was true.

"And when did President Lamar give you this commission?" Rusk asked.

"A month ago, sir. We had a very lively discussion about the inadequacy of the existing maps. And he was very interested in my mapping the last part of the river that leads to Santa Fe. But there were details to settle before I could undertake this expedition. And that's what has brought me here. I mean no harm, sir, but as I said to this woman, I was robbed of my wagon near the ferry landing. I have walked…"

"But," Mary Rusk interrupted, "your girl said you got lost just walking back to Louisiana and arriving in Nacogdoches. What kind of surveyor gets lost because he can't tell which way is east and which west?"

Alexandre started to deny that Noeme was his girl. Noeme started to say something about a dark and moonless night. Thomas Rusk cut them both short.

"Lost? It seems the only point on that road that you know anything about is the fork where a man was murdered," Rusk said. "Do you understand why we think you are suspicious?"

Rusk watched the color drain from Alexandre's battered face. He considered asking whether LaBranche was aware that Lamar's term of office had expired and whether he knew that Texas controlled not so much as an inch of the Rio Grande. However, LaBranche seemed so ignorant of the practical aspects of his own profession that Rusk thought it even less likely he would know the practical aspects of the political affairs of Texas. He instead asked a New Orleans question.

"Tell me this, sir. Do you know of a ship named *Durango*?"

LaBranche hesitated, remembering his uncle Alcee's interest in the ship while at the same time wondering what interest a back-water lawyer could have in it. "The *Durango*? Yes, I know a little bit, yes sir." He tried to look innocent of murder while thinking of something that might clear him. "It's a Mexican ship that was taken in waters off Texas and escorted to New Orleans." He tried to remember the other details Uncle Alcee had told him about the *Durango*. "All the passengers seemed to have been Mexican soldiers, and the only cargo was Mexican guns. It was tied up in prize court when I left the city."

Whoever Alexandre LaBranche might turn out to be, Thomas Rusk understood that he would not likely learn the truth if he turned the man over to the Nacogdoches posse. Rusk made a decision.

"Mary," he turned to his wife. "Please find something for him to eat. Tell him where he can bathe and have his girl wash his clothes. I'll send for them shortly." He then turned to Alexandre and Noeme. "And you two: do not even think of leaving this yard. For now, this is the only place where you're safe."

CHAPTER FIVE

Thomas Rusk faced Pinckney Henderson across their only desk, a fine plank table that spilled over with deeds, writs, and dispatches from wherever the capitol of Texas happened to be from one month to the next. They talked in whispered tones so that Alexandre and Noeme, outside their door, could not hear.

"We're in a bind, Pinckney," Rusk proposed. "As partners, you and I, both of us, are responsible for the defense of those two men sitting in jail." He did not add what each of them understood, that Pinckney's interest in them had increased after it appeared that there might be $10,000 to pay for their services. "And at the same time, we have custody of the man they robbed."

"Allegedly robbed, Thomas," Henderson replied, "And so far they've not been accused of having anything to do with robbing LaBranche."

"I assure you, Pinckney, that if the prosecutor learns that Pennant and Alonzo crossed the Sabine River at Logan's Ferry, and that their alibi is that during the murder they were a half mile away robbing a man..." Rusk let the accumulated facts weigh on Henderson's mind. "... he will try to hang your two jailbirds." Rusk took a breath, then continued. "And, unless the posse catches someone else to charge with killing the surveyor at that fork in the road near the ferry, the prosecutor will try to hang that stranger in our back room who claims to be a surveyor but can't tell east from west." Rusk wondered whether he should have sent the man away as he had been inclined to do before Mary pointed out that he couldn't even find Louisiana. "And," Rusk finished, "it requires very little imagination to conclude that the three of them acted together."

Henderson was not quite so sure about that.

"Do you mean, Thomas, they were collaborators? It would be bold for collaborators to act in concert to murder someone near the ferry landing, then leisurely ride a broken-down wagon off into a land that none of them seem to know, overturn it, right it, then rob one another, abandoning one of them to fend for himself? That is too much."

Rusk saw the point. He sipped a cup of bitter coffee and pondered the dilemma again.

"We're still in a bind, Pinckney. There are only two things between them and a hanging jury."

"What are those, Thomas?"

"First, the posse. If it discovers that there's a stranger in our back room who has an unlikely story of what he was doing during the killing, they'll seize him. That's one. The second is Sullivan. If he begins to talk around town about your two sailors having a broken-down wagon full of surveyor tools, we'll be hard pressed to save them."

While the lawyers spoke, Alexandre waited in the back room of their office, doing as they had told him, sitting still and being quiet. Noeme stood beside the door and tried to eavesdrop.

"We're just goin' to sit here?" Noeme hissed. "Why're you agreeing to do whatever Mas'r Rusk tells you? 'Go there, wait here.' We need to be on our way. Louisiana can't be far."

"Then you should leave now," Alexandre answered. "We're not traveling together, so go on. Be gone." He intended to point Noeme toward Louisiana, but he still wasn't sure which direction that would be. "And..." he stopped.

There was something in what he was doing, not just in his words, but in what he intended by them, that he knew was not being true to himself. He realized that the slight and, he admitted, intriguing Black girl had saved him. She not only had gotten him out of the thorns and the gully but also had led him away from armed riders who, he suspected, were the posse. She had followed him when he should have realized he was walking the wrong way and, when Rusk told her to wash his clothes, she had done so. Thanks to her, he was safe, fed, and clean, and he had spoken to her like a dog. Alexandre's mother had taught him better.

"Who are you, Noeme?" he asked, his voice quieter this time. When she didn't answer, he looked directly at her and asked in a different way. "What are you doing here?" She may have smiled, or maybe it seemed to Alexandre that her lips just looked as if they were almost smiling, he wasn't sure. Either way, the way she looked made him pause. "No, don't tell me. If you are a runaway, the more I know about you, the worse it could be for both of us." He put a finger to his own lips to hint that she should not say anything. "I wanted to find Nacogdoches and I found it. I am not going to Louisiana. So, I'll stay here until I get back my..." Alexandre realized he was about to tell her things she didn't need to know. "I'll stay here until I find out what has happened to my wagon. I don't expect you to understand."

What Noeme didn't understand was how Alexandre seemed to know so much about the *Durango*. But, instead of slipping out of the lawyers' back room and running away, she turned away from looking at him and put her ear against the door to listen to Rusk speaking in subdued tones.

"The man claims he was hired by Mirabeau Lamar to come to Texas to survey and map the Rio Grande River, all the way to Santa Fe and beyond. And, if that isn't fantastical enough, he seems completely ignorant that Lamar all but gave away the Rio Grande to that traitor Canales."

"Yet, Thomas," Henderson answered, "I believe that is exactly what Lamar did. There is such a contract in the portmanteau, and I have no doubt that it was signed by Lamar just before the end of his term of office. But why anyone would agree to undertake such a commission is beyond me."

"You've seen such a contract? You amaze me, Pinkney. I thought the man made up the whole story," Rusk answered. "And, yes, it's beyond me as well. But is this that man?"

"Whoever he is, Thomas, and however ignorant he seems to be, we nevertheless must consider whether he's the man who committed the murder near Logan's Ferry." Henderson wiped his forehead and poured coffee for himself. "If we can prove that he is, then we can properly defend Pennant and Alonzo. If they are charged."

Rusk had an answer: "In truth, Pinckney, I don't believe that he is the murderer. The killing was done with a firearm." He told Henderson what he had learned that morning. "We did not find a firearm hidden along our creek or in our kitchen garden. You did not find a firearm in the portmanteau or the box of tools with the wagon in Sullivan's yard, nor do Pennant or Alonzo appear to have possessed one." Rusk paused to consider whether there was another explanation. "It's possible, of course, that he might have had a firearm, and the robbers took it away from him. But that seems implausible: would he have used his gun to kill a man but not to defend himself against robbers?"

They smoked for a few moments, considering what else was possible. Henderson spoke first.

"What about this, Thomas? The *Durango* dispatch warned that there are three Mexican agents bound for Texas."

Rusk took the coded dispatch from his pocket and read from it: "'The men under suspicion are not easily caught out as spies for they are not men who one would immediately recognize from their appearance or features to be of the Mexican race and, perhaps, they are not of that race.'"

"So, Thomas, what if this man who calls himself LaBranche is one of the Mexican agents? You said yourself that when you asked him about the *Durango*, he knew a great deal." Henderson sat back and folded his skinny arms across his skinny chest and waited. Rusk did not answer.

Henderson continued. "A Mexican spy who was in New Orleans would know about the *Durango*, of course, and could claim to be a surveyor with work in Texas. So, perhaps one of the spies discovered surveyor LaBranche's identity and purpose and, once clear of the ferry, he killed LaBranche, took his wagon and goods, and rode away."

"That's a possibility," Rusk replied. "A spy would be clever to take the identity of a surveyor with work that would take him deep into Texas."

Henderson pondered the possibility a few moments more, then rejected it: "But no."

"What's wrong with it, Pinckney? It was your idea."

"It would mean, Thomas," Henderson smiled as he spoke, "that Pennant and Alonzo are those other two spies." Henderson suppressed his amusement at the idea of the two men chained to the wall of a makeshift jail being spies. "I've seen them. No spy would make such a spectacle of himself as those two have done. Imagine, wearing fancy dress to court a young woman from Mrs. Stewart's Female Academy in plain view of the town, then stealing a loaded wagon and horses from a livery stable in broad daylight." It was laughable, the thought of Pennant wearing tight-fitting pants and calling on Miss Goodnough while spying for Mexico.

Rusk smiled as well, but not the smile of a man laughing at Pennant's affair of the heart with Miss Goodnough.

"But," Henderson continued, "if he isn't the Mexican agent, who is he?"

"Well, Pinckney," Rusk answered, "it may be that he's no more than what he says he is, a young, ignorant, rather incompetent surveyor named LaBranche who Lamar tricked into believing that he could wander the length of the Rio Grande River, draw a few maps, and collect ten thousand United States dollars. Maybe it's no more complicated than that."

It was not a very comforting answer. It didn't solve who killed the man at the river, nor whether Mexican agents were involved. It particularly did not solve what to do about Pennant and Alonzo.

"I think our choices are limited," Henderson said. "We can pay Sullivan his $14.00 and give him a horse. That will satisfy the only legal complaint made so far against Pennant and Alonzo, and we can end our representation." Henderson paused to give Rusk time to consider. "Or we can take LaBranche over to the jail to meet our clients and watch what they say. But, if this man is LaBranche, I think that likely will lead to a new legal complaint against them, for robbery if nothing else."

"I fear that—Pinckney!" Rusk stood up and slapped the table. "Why didn't I see it? I know who he is!"

Henderson did not see it, not at first. Rusk brought the dispatch out and showed it a second time.

"Listen to it, Pinckney!" Rusk, swelling with pride, read from the dispatch again. "It says 'I engaged our own confidential agent to follow them.' I think LaBranche is that confidential agent. He's the man hired in New Orleans to follow the Mexican spies!"

Henderson put the tips of his fingers together to form a cathedral and smiled. He quickly saw even more clearly than Rusk how LaBranche's passing himself off as an incompetent surveyor sent to perform an impossible task would be a perfect disguise for a spy.

"Yes, Thomas," he declared. "The facts do fit the case." He paused to consider further. "But, whether we understand completely or we do not, we cannot risk his being taken by the posse. We have to move him onward." He thought for a few moments longer. "The difficulty, Thomas, is that we still have our own clients whose necks we must save. I'm afraid we must act now."

Rusk agreed. They made the decision, then called Alexandre into the office.

"Mr. LaBranche," Rusk said to him, "let me introduce Mr. Henderson. He is not only a lawyer of this city, he also is the recent

Foreign Minister of Texas to France and to England." Henderson bowed.

Alexandre ignored Henderson and answered Rusk.

"Mr. Rusk, I thank you for your hospitality. I am fed and washed and ready to go on with my affairs, which are simple. You said this morning that you don't pretend to know everything that happens in Nacogdoches, but I suspect that you do." He tried to control his nerves, aware that he was standing in his bare shirt with cuts on his arms and hands and subject to the mercy of the two men. "So I ask you: Have two men, dressed rough, one heavyset and with a big mustache and the other quite slender and probably a mixture of some races, come into Nacogdoches in recent days? Those men stole my wagon and things. They might have ridden in on my wagon or, if it broke down again, they might have abandoned it." He tried to be courteous but suspected that Rusk was not being candid with him. "Or do you know where my wagon could be found? I want to go on my way to continue my work."

Rusk smiled politely but not encouragingly.

"Let me begin again, sir. I am introducing you to my partner, Pinckney Henderson. Before he was my partner, he was the foreign minister of our young nation."

Alexandre was skeptical. He doubted that either Rusk or Henderson was a great man, particularly not great men who lived in a village of no more than a few dirt streets and some log and chink houses and buildings, situated in a remote pine forest. Alexandre crossed his thorn-scarred arms and stared at the two men.

"Recent foreign minister, sir," Henderson answered. "Recent. My days of diplomacy in Paris and London are behind me. Nor, sir, am I the more important man among us. Colonel Rusk here is known to every man and woman in the Republic. He was a hero of the great war, then served as the chief justice of our Supreme Court...."

Rusk cut him off. "And now just a humble country lawyer," Rusk inserted, "consulted on a few affairs of state now and then." He paused for the effect his false humility would have on LaBranche. "And it appears that one of those affairs is you. I regret that you've suffered unfairly since coming to Texas, but now is the time to put that behind us. It is time for us to go about your work."

"For us to go about my work?" Alexandre did not see how two self-important lawyers in faded coats and worn boots could have anything to do with mapping the Rio Grande and said so.

"Forgive us, Mr. LaBranche," Rusk said. "but we had to be satisfied that you are who you say you are and that you have the commission you say you have. You have satisfied us. So, let me be plain: my colleague here, Mr. Henderson, knows where your wagon is." Alexandre brightened considerably. "And he has seen your contract of engagement." Rusk smiled at his insider's knowledge of the euphemisms employed to disguise LaBranche's spying. "It appears that you are indeed commissioned to survey and map the Rio Grande border with Mexico."

Alexandre realized that the two lawyers had gone through his things.

"Then, sirs, you must know where my tools are. And where is my wagon? And clothes?" Alexandre was both elated to have found them and furious at the lawyers for dissembling about them.

"Yes, we do know where they are, Mr. LaBranche, and also your servants," Henderson added.

"My servants?" Alexandre asked. "I don't have any servants." They ignored him; it was not important to their plan whether Pennant and Alonzo were Alexandre's servants or his mortal enemies; they had to be got rid of all the same. "I ask again: where is my wagon? And my survey equipment?"

"Here in Nacogdoches, sir, at Sullivan's Livery Stable. And he has repaired your wagon."

Alexandre began to suspect that they might know more about him than they had let on.

"We'll reunite you and you'll be on your way."

"On my way?" Alexandre was hopeful at the proposition; if Rusk was telling the truth, his road to the Rio Grande would begin on the dirt street just outside the lawyers' door. He would gather his things at Mr. Sullivan's livery stable and say goodbye, then find the customs house, take his letter of credit, and start for San Antonio. "Thank you."

"Yes, Mr. LaBranche." There was a new note in Rusk's voice, a sterner note. "If you are LaBranche, you'll be on your way to the Rio Grande. But there is still an unsolved murder, I'm sure you recall, and you are still a stranger in this city. If it turns out that you are not the surveyor LaBranche, you'll instead be on your way to the courthouse where the sheriff, the prosecutor, and a different fate will await you."

Alexandre knew he was trapped. They told him to walk with them down that dirt street, where Alexandre soon learned another fact that made clear that the two lawyers knew more about his future than he knew himself. They stopped at the Nacogdoches customs house. None of them noticed that Noeme followed them.

"Good day, sir," they announced to the customs clerk. Alexandre's mind was not put at ease when the clerk said to Henderson that he was welcome back. "This gentleman is Mr. Alexandre LaBranche. He is here for his letter of credit." They pointed to the visibly startled Alexandre, who had said nothing about his letter of credit, and told him to identify himself.

"I am Alexandre LaBranche," he told the clerk. They told him to say where he was from and how he was occupied. "Of Louisiana. I am a surveyor. At your service."

The customs clerk had served as a foot soldier under Rusk at San Jacinto and believed he owed the man his life. He had been given a job when Pinckney Henderson had persuaded Texas to open customs houses and believed that he owed the man his livelihood. He would have handed the letter of credit to a buffalo robe if Henderson and Rusk had told him to do so. The clerk brought out the document without asking a single question, indicated where Alexandre should sign for it, and handed it over. They thanked him, left the building, and Henderson then politely told Alexandre to give it to him.

"For safekeeping, sir."

"I don't understand," Alexandre replied, which was true. "Safe-keeping from whom?"

"Those who would take it from you, Mr. LaBranche. Robbers. Indians, whose lands you have to cross to reach the Rio Grande. Mr. Sullivan at the livery stable. There is a small debt for repairs he made to your wagon and for stabling your horses. Mr. Sullivan is very particular about being paid."

Horses, plural, LaBranche thought. He began to suspect not only that his time in Nacogdoches would be limited but that his use of his letter of credit also might be limited.

"Unless you have the fourteen dollars to pay, Mr. Sullivan. Cash, not scrip."

"Shouldn't we just go to the bank and draw on my letter of credit?" LaBranche asked. "That is what it's for."

"No," Rusk said. "No. That is not what it is for." They arrived at the livery stable.

Although Sullivan was not surprised to see Henderson again, he was surprised to see Thomas Rusk. "Good morning, Colonel," he said. "How do you fare?"

"Fine, sir," Rusk answered, "thank you. But this gentleman is not fine, Mr. Sullivan. Mr. LaBranche here has lost his wagon and goods. I believe you have them. Mr. Henderson here says you made some repairs, a matter of a broken axle, I understand."

Sullivan said that Rusk must refer to the thieves' wagon.

"I do not know that they are thieves, sir," Henderson intervened. "But Mr. LaBranche here has urgent need of his goods. He is obliged to undertake work on behalf of the republic, and he is greatly handicapped without them. Tell him, LaBranche, what you are to do."

"Surveys," Alexandre sputtered, his face flushed with anxiety. "Mapping. Along the border."

"The border with Mexico," Henderson finished. He gave a benevolent smile to match Sullivan's scowl. "He has come from Louisiana, Mr. Sullivan, and his work is pressing. Please fetch his wagon and horses and we'll have him on his way."

Horses, again, LaBranche thought, plural. And on his way.

Alexandre no longer had any doubts that Rusk and Henderson knew more about where he was going than he knew himself.

"And I understand there's a bill?" Rusk added.

Sullivan sensed that Rusk was in no mood to haggle over the thieves' bill of repairs.

"There is. Fourteen dollars, cash money, not scrip. I should ask sixteen as I've stabled the horses another two nights since Mr. Henderson and I talked it over, but I told him fourteen and I'll be glad of that."

"And Mr. LaBranche's goods?" Henderson added. "His box of surveying equipment? And his trunk?" Henderson wanted to caution Sullivan against greed, but he, too, realized that Rusk and his steely manner had taken over the negotiations. "Mr. LaBranche cannot perform his work without them."

Sullivan sent the two slaves who had beaten Pennant and Alonzo to fetch the wagon and lead the horses out into the street. Noeme looked away from them, then looked away again when a third slave returned with Alexandre's portmanteau and bound box. The slave placed them in the bed of the wagon, then stood aside.

Henderson opened the trunk, rustled through the clothes and papers, closed it, then opened the bound box. He looked carefully through its contents, nodded at Rusk, who nodded back, then told LaBranche that everything was accounted for. When the fetching, opening, and reading had been accomplished, Henderson took out his own leather pouch, counted out fourteen dollars, and handed the money over to Sullivan.

"I redeem your debt, sir. And, if you please, you will walk with us over to the jail." He indicated that the slaves were to tie the horses to the wagon. "You will tell the jailor that you make no further claim against your debtors." He looked in Sullivan's eyes to see whether the haggling was finished; Sullivan looked hard at the horses and the box and decided that this was not a disagreement he should prolong. They walked to the jail.

The jailor wasn't in the least curious when Henderson and Sullivan told him they had come for his jail birds in that Sullivan would press his charges no further. The jailor gladly let them go to be free of having to feed them.

Pennant and Alonzo appeared no worse for having slept on hard floors, eaten cornbread and crackling for three days, and answered nature in a wooden bucket. They were slightly worse when, upon being led into the street, they saw not only the wagon, their horses, Sullivan, his slaves, and a slight Black girl, but also the man they had robbed of everything he owned. They stopped in their boots and gaped.

Alexandre did the same.

"Sirs," he protested, "This is too much. Those are the men who robbed me! They stole this wagon and that horse from me. I demand you arrest them!"

"And you've got it all back," Rusk answered. "Your wagons and your horse and your whatever else you had." Rusk exhibited a smile that Alexandre found disconcerting. "So, take them. Or do you want to press charges and wait in Nacogdoches until there's a trial, Mr. LaBranche? When is the next session, Pinckney, if you please?"

"Two months, Thomas," Pinckney answered.

"Trial?" Pennant chimed in, sputtering through his mustache. "We didn't ...."

"Be quiet, Mr. Pennant." Henderson was universally respected because he was smarter than all the men in Nacogdoches combined. He was universally admired because he had the ability to make all those men listen without raising his voice. Pennant listened. "One more word and you will walk right back into that jail. Do I make myself clear?" He had made himself clear.

"Get in the wagon," Rusk commanded them.

"Stop!" Alexandre sputtered. "I don't want them anywhere..."

"You've got nothing to fear from those two, Mr. LaBranche," Rusk said. He led Alexandre several yards away and continued in hushed tones. "You are under our protection. Those two have been thrashed and jailed and they know that their very lives depend on doing what Henderson and I tell them to do." He waited for more argument, but Alexandre was listening to him. "But Sullivan here is a suspicious man. If Sullivan doesn't believe these two are your servants and that all three of you are leaving together to go off and map the Rio Grande, there is a very real chance he'll turn the three of you over to the posse." Rusk gave Alexandre a knowing smile. "So, my young friend, if you want to map the Rio Grande, then we have to go. Now. Do you understand?"

Alexandre understood. He could refuse Rusk and be handed over to the Nacogdoches posse, or keep quiet, get in the wagon, and set out to prove that he could do something with his life, something important. He looked at the wagon, the robbers, at Rusk and Henderson, and made a decision.

I crossed the river into Texas to prove myself. I might not have expected it to look like this, but it doesn't matter. I am here, I am free, and I am going to map the Rio Grande.

He climbed onto the wagon's buckboard seat and took the reins. When he glanced down, Noeme was staring at him. Her smile was gone.

Why is she staring at me? he thought. *What does it matter to her that I'm leaving? She doesn't belong to me.*

Pennant climbed up beside him. Alonzo made a space for himself between the trunk and the bound box.

"Where are we going, Mr. Rusk?"

"We'll start with the general."

"The general?" Alexandre asked.

"Mr. Lamar is no longer president, Mr. LaBranche. Your business with him is over. The general is the next president. Your business will be with him. Let's get started."

Alexandre flicked the reins. They set out, with Rusk and Henderson riding alongside, leading them away from the jail, across the town square, and past Mrs. Stewart's Female Academy.

Noeme followed behind the wagon until none were watching. Then she climbed onto the back and made a space for herself. The procession turned onto the *camino real*, the old Spanish royal road that crossed Texas from the Sabine to the Rio Grande.

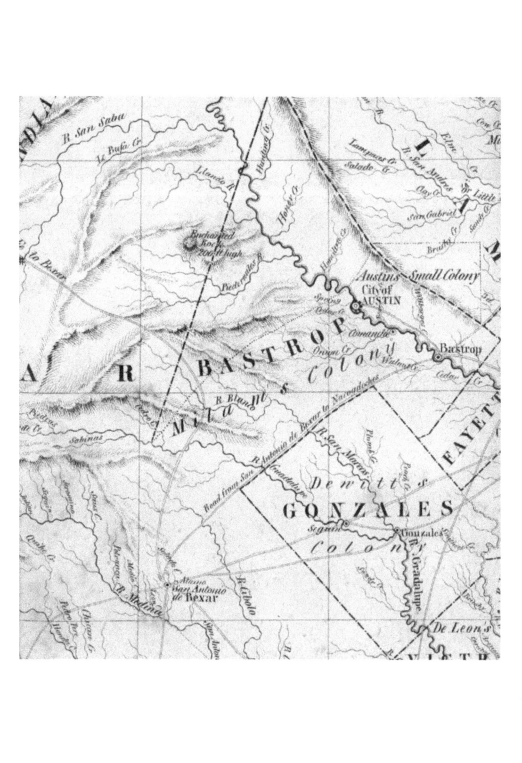

CHAPTER SIX
WINTER 1841-1842, AUSTIN

"**D**o you truly believe him to be an agent hired to follow Mexican spies into Texas?" The general was not a laughing man, but even he couldn't look at the three men without a smile crossing his face. "And those other two robbed him?"

He looked at the three men loitering outside his door, one of them in a tattered shirt, one bowing and smiling like a trained bear, and the third staring vacantly out the window. "Well, thank you, Thomas. Pinckney, thank you for bringing them. Two more thieves and a spy'll be right at home in this godforsaken town full of mud huts and brush fires. But not today. Take some rooms. I'll send for you." Rusk and Henderson were disappointed.

The general was Sam Houston who, after Alexandre left New Orleans for Texas and after President Lamar became former President Lamar, had succeeded to the presidency of the most ill-defended and beleaguered republic in North America. The general also had little time for unexpected visits, even from Thomas Rusk and Pinckney Henderson. But he did have time for spies. He waited until all the unwelcome guests were gone, then consulted his own.

Several days later, Houston sent for them. Two men walked

from the capitol down to Mrs. Eberly's boarding house, found Rusk and Henderson, and told them the general wanted them. The men pointed the way back up to the wooden house where the affairs of Texas were decided.

When Rusk and Henderson found Houston, he was reading the *Durango* dispatch. Houston looked up, nodded at them to find a chair, and resumed. When he finished, he placed the dispatch on the desk, then looked out his window.

A block away, LaBranche, Pennant, and Alonzo sat beneath an oak tree in the front yard of Mrs. Eberly's boarding house. Pennant seemed to be studying Mrs. Eberly while the other two gazed down toward the Colorado River landing a half mile away. The two men Houston had sent to get Rusk and Henderson stayed behind to keep watch on the three from a short distance. Houston smiled, turned away from the window, and faced Rusk and Henderson. He smelled as if he already had drunk a jug of whiskey.

"So, Thomas, Pinckney, you bring me spies and robbers." He laughed, not a deep laugh nor even an amused one, but one they knew well. Houston always listened to his men, but not always happily.

Rusk and Henderson laid out their case with great confidence.

"Sir," Henderson began, "we have brought you Mr. Alexandre LaBranche. He is Texas' secret agent." Henderson referred to the *Durango* dispatch. "We are satisfied that LaBranche was detailed by our *chargé d'affaires* in New Orleans to follow three of Mexico's spies from the *Durango*. Let me explain." Henderson paused to see if Houston rejected the idea out of hand; he did not. "Mexican spies would avoid people. Instead of entering Texas at Gaines's ferry, the better port of entry, spies would instead go to a more remote place, like Logan's ferry, and cross there, which they did. They then would make for Nacogdoches as Pennant and Alonzo did, to watch the *camino real* to San Antonio, or to follow it." He was persuasive; Houston was attentive. "Thus, if our agent was following Mexico's agents, he would follow them wherever they went, including the less conspicuous crossing at Logan's ferry."

Rusk explained the balance of their reasoning.

"Next, this man disguised his true vocation," Rusk said. "like a spy would do. He wouldn't go about telling a ferry man that he was a spy. He would say that he was occupied in some inconspicuous trade, such as a surveyor. LaBranche claims to be a surveyor. He can describe what surveyors do, but as for doing it himself, he would be the most incompetent surveyor I've ever met. He crossed the Sabine, then got himself lost. Then he says that he entertained the notion to return to Louisiana but instead walked west, not east. That's according to his slave." Rusk was satisfied that he had proved his point. He waited for Houston to agree.

Instead, Houston laughed, deep from his belly, almost choking on the end of a chewed cigar that he had bitten off when Henderson told him that LaBranche was a secret agent. He coughed, apologized, coughed again, and then brought out a new dispatch concerning the *Durango*.

"The *Durango*'s already been seen off Galveston and headed to Corpus Christi Bay," Houston read to them. He replaced his dour humor with dour sarcasm. "Those bastards are going straight back into our waters, probably there now, and we could use a spy following the Mexicans for damned certain. But, let me tell you about Alexandre LaBranche." He pointed to the window.

Houston was not drunk, not yet. He was instead in that phase of his ingestion best characterized by rising anger. He continued.

"I think your man LaBranche is the barking dog that caught the wagon. He somehow persuaded Lamar at some hotel in New Orleans to hire him as a surveyor to go up the Rio Grande to see what there is to see. But he's just a plantation dandy who had gone back east to learn something about measuring the earth from the sun and the stars but neglected to learn how to use a compass." He glared at Rusk and Henderson for having even considered that LaBranche was a spy.

"And as for the other two," Houston added, "I think they'd like to be grand thieves, but aren't. I believe that about Pennant, anyway, who was a sailor and probably a pirate. As for his friend, I think

Alonzo may be nothing more than a pitiful creature who Pennant took in. But they are of no importance." He flicked his hand as if he had swatted a fly.

Henderson and Rusk were disappointed, not only that Houston rejected their conclusion, but also that he seemed to know more about the three men than they had learned for themselves.

"We considered all the possibilities, Sam," Rusk answered. "We especially considered whether it was just possible that LaBranche or all three of them were involved in killing that man down by Logan's ferry landing. We do not believe that to be the case, but it is possible." Rusk waited for an answer, did not get one, and continued.

"There is one more fact," Rust said. "LaBranche traveled with a slave."

Houston lifted his eyebrows.

"And not a slave that would be likely to help a man map the Rio Grande, Sam. The slave was a girl, a young, skinny woman."

"And what became of this young skinny woman slave, Thomas?" Houston asked.

"She ran off in the night."

Houston shrugged. The men fidgeted, something that no man other than Sam Houston could make them do.

"Why do you men think the great president Mirabeau B. Lamar offered this man LaBranche ten thousand United States dollars that Texas doesn't have to go map a river that Texas doesn't control?" Houston mused. "Lamar himself abandoned the whole Rio Grande River when he backed the traitor Canales. Do you think your secret agent knows that? Hah!"

That was an inconvenient fact. When a Mexican colonel named Canales started his own revolt against Mexico to set up the Republic of the Rio Grande, Lamar had secretly agreed to support him. Lamar gave the rebels a few companies of Texian volunteers and some weapons and quietly agreed for Canales' fledgling republic to move the Texas boundary a hundred miles north, to the Nueces River. Then, unfortunately, Canales switched sides again and handed the Republic of the Rio Grande back to Mexico and rejoined its army, which now ranged freely all-over south Texas. It also was an inconvenient fact there were no Texians anywhere near the Rio Grande.

"Why did Lamar offer him that contract? I'll tell you why," Houston continued. "Because he needed somebody to go find all those men he sent to Santa Fe on that damned expedition. He thought that if he could get a man to wind his way up the Rio Grande to Santa Fe, if LaBranche found them and if the expedition was a success, Lamar would be the people's hero. The profits of trade would pay off his contract with LaBranche. But, if LaBranche disappeared along the way no one would know a thing about it because the Mexicans would have caught him spying and put him up against a wall and shot him. LaBranche wouldn't be around to blame Lamar for anything, much less ask Texas to pay him ten thousand United States dollars."

Henderson voiced their disagreement.

"Sam, we think it more likely the Santa Fe expedition never reached Santa Fe. Lamar sent them off in the dead heat of a dry summer, overland through Comanche territory. If they had reached Santa Fe, whether they were captured by Mexico or treated as a trade mission, some commercial traveler would have reported it in the United States. But there has been no word they ever reached Santa Fe, not in the American press nor from Mexico." He paused, then added in a solemn voice: "We fear it most likely they suffered the depredations of the Comanche."

"That is our reasoning, sir," Rusk added, "and we believe Lamar must have reached the same conclusion. Indeed, if Mexico had considered the expedition to be military rather than commercial, there would have been retaliation."

"What the hell do you two think the *Durango* was doing if it wasn't retaliation?" Houston thundered. "A ship filled with soldiers and arms preparing to invade Texas? And as for the lost men, well, they aren't lost anymore. That bastard Armijo shot three of them up against a wall in Santa Fe without a trial and marched the rest of them to Mexico. They shoot Texians in

Mexico and then invade Texas? Is that retaliation enough for you?"

That deduction was grave and evident, but it didn't answer the real question. Houston asked it out loud:

"Why'd you two men bring those three to me? I don't need any more incompetent surveyors and failed horse thieves. I'm already surrounded by idiots who've lost their way; we call them senators and representatives."

"Yes, but even so, General," Henderson quietly replied, "you do need spies." He let Houston consider the idea. "Yes, we did conclude that LaBranche was our spy. But, even if he is not, you nevertheless need someone to journey up and down the Rio Grande to see what the Mexican army is doing. Santa Anna sends spies here. You should send spies there."

There were uncertainties.

"Answer this," Houston barked at them. "What if these men do turn out to be the three spies off the *Durango?*"

Rusk had thought about this for a long time.

"Here is one other thing I know," Rusk answered. "There's a slave girl who says she's LaBranche's, but I suspect she's a runaway. One night when the Nacogdoches posse rode out to find the killer, she rescued LaBranche out of a gully." Houston began to twiddle his thumbs and look at his empty glass. "Her story is that LaBranche wanted to go back to Louisiana, but he got turned around two or three times, didn't know which way was which, and walked west into Nacogdoches instead of east back toward the Sabine. In sum, sir, there is little about LaBranche to make anyone suspect him to be a Mexican spy except the story that he is a surveyor. It would be a very good cover story, but whether it's true seems implausible, given his troubles with east and west. I do not believe he tricked us."

Henderson had an even more candid assessment:

"As for the other two being spies, well, no one would suspect them. They robbed a man on a public highway and took his horse and broken-down wagon. They were caught only because Pennant did everything he could to draw attention to himself. He publicly courted a girl in Nacogdoches, then tried to cheat the blacksmith out of his repair bill. In short, sir, if we could not imagine these men to be spies, neither would anyone in Texas suspect them. They simply appear to be too incompetent."

"I can tell you what else they did," Houston barked. "They went to the customs house every day to ask for a letter of credit sent by the president of Texas. That drew my attention to them, you can be sure of that!" Both Rusk and Henderson were unsettled to realize that Houston already knew that fact, one he had not learned from them. "But I want to talk about LaBranche! First you told me he was our spy. Now you tell me that nobody would mistake him for a spy. I think it's more subtle than that. It's not just a question of why Lamar offered him such a contract; it also is a question of why LaBranche would agree to it." He let that idea worry Rusk and Henderson for a few moments, then continued. "Consider, what if he isn't working for Lamar at all? What if he's working for England? That could explain everything."

Henderson, once minister to England, knew something of England's interests. Rusk knew very little. Houston continued.

"Mexico owes more than thirty-three million English pounds sterling to English banks who loaned it to pay for Mexico's war for independence from Spain. Mexico secured the loan with land between San Antonio and the Rio Grande. The English banks would have the right to send a man out to the Rio Grande, look around, and report on the chances of the banks in England ever getting their money back." Houston paused to let the facts sink in. "Mexico wouldn't dare capture the man who could call in their national debt. And, if such a man got wind that Lamar was looking for someone to go to the very same part of Texas to make a map of those same lands, it wouldn't be that hard for such a man to pull the wool over Lamar's eyes by telling him all about modern methods of stars and the moon and an eagerness to go survey the whole region. It would be a spy's dream come true."

Henderson agreed that England might send a spy and that such a man might easily fool Lamar. He did not agree that LaBranche was such a man. More to the point, he was certain that neither Pennant nor Alonzo was in league with a British spy, nor with LaBranche, whoever he might be.

"They robbed the man, General. They left him out there on the road to die. When they walked out of the Nacogdoches jail and saw LaBranche waiting for them, they panicked. Or, I should say, Pennant panicked. They are not allies."

"Well," Houston said, "they will be when I'm through with them. Let's invite Mr. LaBranche back up to the capitol."

———

Alexandre sat beneath the oak tree on the lawn of Mrs. Eberly's boarding house, uncomfortable in his thoughts and chilled despite the late December sun. He tried to concentrate on what he would say to President Houston, on the supplies he would need, on whether to mention Rusk's and Henderson's deceptions and rudeness. His mind instead drifted to something else: Noeme had disappeared.

She had been surprisingly quiet on the journey from Nacogdoches. When they halted for rest or for the night, she had gone about gathering wood for fires and bringing water from creeks. If Rusk or Henderson told her to help graze the horses or to spread their blankets to air before dark, she did so without comment. She cooked what game they killed and served what there was to serve. She might have been slightly more attentive to Alexandre than to the others, doing for him first before doing for them, but no more so than a slave might be expected to do for its owner. At night she made a place for herself to sleep that was apart from the men, but still closer to Alexandre's bedroll than to the others.

A few times, not many, Alexandre might have noticed her looking at him when there was no apparent reason, smiling when there was no occasion to smile. But so quickly had she turned her eyes that she may not have been looking at him, and her small mouth might not have been smiling at all. He had avoided speaking to her.

Then, one night as they camped near Bastrop, Rusk and Henderson had exchanged fireside tales of Sam Houston as a mythic hero in Andrew Jackson's army of 1812, of Houston as a Tennessee politician, of Houston living with an Indian woman near the Neosho. As he listened to them, Alexandre realized that Noeme had sat down quietly behind him. When all rose to turn in for the night, he felt her touch on his shoulder, her thin hand and fingers resting lightly on him, only for a moment. She might have done so to steady herself when she stood. It also was possible, he thought, that she hadn't done so at all, that he had imagined it.

He woke once that night; Noeme stood over him, shivering in the cold air, her shift and shawl not enough to keep her warm. Before he could ask what she wanted, she said, "Good nigh', sir," and moved back toward the embers of the dying fire.

When he rose in the morning, he discovered that she was gone. Now, sitting under the oak tree at Mrs. Eberly's boarding house, he asked, *Why did she leave?*

That was not the first question Alexandre had asked himself. He had wondered how Noeme happened to have found him in a remote gully and why she had tried to save him from the men on horses. He then had wondered at himself for even thinking about an annoying, disagreeable, and lying girl who also happened to be a runaway slave.

But he also wondered, not for the first time, *Why did she tell Mary Rusk that she belonged to me?*

He was unsettled by the memory of seeing Noeme, dirty and ragged as she was, walk out of Mary Rusk's kitchen garden. It was as if he was seeing her for the first time. He had not thought that Noeme was beautiful, but he understood that she was the kind of girl men noticed, slender but coming into her own, longish hair that was straighter than some, high cheekbones, and her face a pleasing oval of light dark skin and clear eyes.

And, he asked, where is she now?

Alonzo was gazing toward the Colorado river.

Pennant was helping Mrs. Eberly to understand the fine points of firing a cannon.

"You got your basic cannon ball, like this here one." He picked up a four-pound cannon ball and held it for her to inspect. "You got hollow balls if you just want to shoot, say, through a door and blow up what's on the other side. And maybe you got no balls at all, you just pack the barrel full of nails and chains and the like, and it'll cut down anything in front of you. Men. Sails. Donkeys. Wagons. Mostly men and sails."

Mrs. Eberly could tell from the way Pennant smiled when he said nails and chains that he preferred them to cannon balls.

"How do you come to know so much about cannons, Mr. Pennant?" she asked, dusting the hem of her skirts with her free hands and smiling at him from underneath well-traveled eyelashes.

They had been told to expect to wait in Austin some days in that General Houston was busy attending to things that Mirabeau Lamar had left unfinished. LaBranche had waited. Alonzo had waited.

Pennant had not waited. He had gazed about the jumped-up village that had become the capital of Texas, looked down the hill toward the river, studied Mrs. Eberly's features and attributes, and considered that she would be a satisfactory replacement for Miss Goodnough. To his delight, she seemed to have some interest in a four pounder that was mounted on a gun carriage not twenty yards from her boarding house. Pennant had sat all one day with Alonzo and LaBranche on her porch, noticing that she glanced at the cannon whenever she walked back and forth into the town or up the hill to the scrubby cedar huts of the capital, and as she went about her chores, shelling beans, gathering eggs, plucking a chicken, rendering fat, and cleaning the front room.

"Have you ever fired it?" Pennant had casually asked her. She told him to stop being plain with her, then denied knowing what he was talking about, then denied having any interest in the cannon. After three days, however, she admitted she had always wanted to see someone fire it. "I'll show you," Pennant offered, and with a local man close by, Pennant had charmed her off the porch and over to the cannon.

"You start with the powder. Amazing, powder is." Pennant waxed briefly about the wonders of gunpowder, then of fuses. He finally came to aiming and, in the end, of what to do when the cannon was fused, powdered, and aimed.

"That gets you to the balls, if you get my meaning."

"The balls," she answered. A brass monkey's rack of cannon balls was stacked behind the cannon.

He explained the fine points of solid balls, hollow balls, and grape.

"That's what you call it when you pack the barrel with nails and such. Grape."

"You know a lot about cannons, Mr. Pennant. Were you in the artillery?"

"At sea, Mrs. Eberly. At sea. From the Floridas to the Mississippi. Guarding the coast. Odd voyage now and then into the Gulf, once or twice around Cuba to the windward passage."

They talked a little about the life of a sailor, without him precisely mentioning the life of a pirate. She asked him about his song.

"What do you do with a drunken sailor, Mr. Pennant?"

"Why, you put him in the bed with the captain's daughter," he leered. He hummed several bars of Drunken Sailor.

She told him a little about the life of an innkeeper.

"Married my first husband, we ran a house for gentlemen down at Indianola and then moved it up to Victoria. Fever took him, but the Lord provided. Mr. Eberly asked me and I said yes. After Captain Hays ran the Indians out of Plum Creek, we figured the new capital was safe. We came up here." She paused and gazed up and down the mud avenue to the rickety stores and wagon yards that lined the dirt road all the way to the river. "Lot of ten-year men here, Mr. Pennant. They were cheats and failures back in the Carolinas or somewhere, then come to Texas. Here they got free land and lied about their slaves and started over. After San Jacinto, they all figured they were brilliant soldiers too, never mind they lost all the other battles, so why not be a congressman or a senator or such? Scalawags, all of them." It was plain even to Pennant that Mrs. Eberly had a low opinion of Texas politicians. "Sam Houston's just another ten-year man," she scoffed. "But they do make us a living. The capitol here is good business, Mr. Pennant. I don't want to move no more. I like it here just fine."

A man walked down the hill into Mrs. Eberly's yard and up to the two men who were keeping an eye on the spies. They pointed at Alexandre, who still sat under the tree, thinking about Noeme. A few moments later, the man told Alexandre he was wanted and led him back up the hill to the capitol. Pennant continued to admire Mrs. Eberly, but Alonzo quietly watched them until they disappeared into the capitol of the Republic of Texas.

The capitol consisted of only two rooms, one marked 'Senate' and one marked 'House,' both distinguished by having wood floors and mortar chinks between the logs of the walls. The two men led Alexandre into the Senate room, where he saw that Rusk, Henderson, and Sam Houston were arrayed around a rough pine desk.

"Mr. LaBranche?" Houston asked. "Or is it Monsieur LaBranche?" He smiled, affable, and motioned for LaBranche to take a seat. "Thank you for coming back to talk with me. General Rusk says you are a surveyor by trade."

LaBranche was charmed by the great man. He acknowledged that he was trained in the geographic arts.

"And," Houston continued, "that President Lamar awarded you a contract to map the Rio Grande River and on up to the United States. Is that about right?" LaBranche said that it was the broad description of what he had contracted to do. "Why don't you tell me, Mr. LaBranche, how you plan to do it? Just set it out for me." Houston smiled again and waited.

"Well, sir, I plan to provision in San Antonio de Bexar. President Lamar proposed that I make my way by land from San Antonio to Laredo, rather than sail to the mouth of the Rio Grande, as Texas has no port there." He waited to see if Houston had any comments. "From there, I would survey upriver toward Presidio Rio Grande, where the Texas maps end. The existing maps do contain latitude and longitude calls, both from Washington and from London, but seem very meagre about geographic features, such as mountains, streams, and settlements. I intend to supplement those with accurate details. Once I survey beyond Presidio Rio Grande, I will continue mapping every physical feature along the river, noting the coordinated details of latitude and longitude, all the way to Santa Fe and beyond."

Houston silently agreed that Rusk was right, that LaBranche knew the words of the surveyor's art. But, he wondered, was he a surveyor?

"How far do you reckon that is, Mr. LaBranche? From, say, Laredo to Santa Fe? And from there on up to the end of the Rio Grande?"

Alexandre had asked himself that question as well. He removed a piece of paper from his pocket, took a quill from Houston's desk, and began to work arithmetic problems, muttering as he calculated.

"The map ends at 101 degrees west. Santa Fe is approximately 105 west, that is four degrees off the map west at approximately seventy miles equals approximately 280 miles west," he mumbled, scribbling as he went. "Then north say by ...." He estimated how far north Santa Fe would be, then began to construct a rough triangle from Laredo to Santa Fe to a point west. "If we take a hypotenuse directly from Laredo and assume the river turns north at the extreme west..." he muttered. Finally, he answered aloud.

"I think from Laredo to Santa Fe by the river would be approximately 750 miles, sir. If there are any big bends in the river, perhaps more."

He was a surveyor. Indeed, Houston thought, he was more than an ordinary surveyor, apart from his problem of not knowing which way was east or west.

"Very impressive, Mr. LaBranche," Houston replied. "How did you know where Santa Fe is? Geographically speaking?"

"The Santa Fe trail from Missouri is well mapped. The chronicles of Major Bennett establish its location very clearly."

"And how long did you tell President Lamar you expected that it would take to do your mapping, sir?" Houston began to twist a piece of string between his fingers, making knots and loops, undoing them, making more.

Alexandre had not come to a conclusion on this point and said so.

"We don't know how far the river extends beyond Santa Fe to its source. It appears no one has located it, no one at all. General Zebulon Pike was in the region thirty years ago, sir, but he was taken prisoner by the Spaniards about 150 miles north of Santa Fe. Where the source of the Rio Grande is from that point, I cannot say. And, from the source of the river north to the United States, beyond the fact it is mountainous, no one knows."

"Did Lamar tell you," Houston barked, "that he was sending you up the Rio Grande to look for about three hundred men he lost somewhere between here and Santa Fe?"

This was puzzling; Alexandre thought he was supposed to find Santa Fe itself.

"No, sir." Something about Houston's manner, about the question, struck Alexandre as odd. "I don't understand what you're asking me. Did President Lamar take some men to Santa Fe? And how did he lose them?"

"He didn't take them. He sent them. About a year ago, your friend Mirabeau B. Lamar sent them off to find Santa Fe. They went out overland, not along the Rio Grande. Supposed to go straight to Santa Fe. Last summer they just disappeared. I thought maybe Lamar had suggested that as long as you're doing this boundary job on the way up the river to Santa Fe, you might see if you could find.... Well, no matter, Mr. LaBranche. Tell me this: did Lamar give you a date to finish this boundary surveying project?"

Alexandre sensed that something was off, something not quite clear about Santa Fe. He wondered if he had missed something, perhaps a part of his duty to search unknown portions of the river as it neared Santa Fe. He answered.

"He did not discuss it, sir. I was given to understand that I might take my time to do a thorough job of the mapping."

"I have another question for you, Mr. LaBranche. Where is your passport?" Houston adopted a mildly malignant smile.

"My passport?" Alexandre had no passport. He had no need of a passport. There had been no suggestion that he would need a passport to work for a country that needed him to define its exact borders.

"Yes, your passport. Surely you have one? Perhaps an English passport?" Houston enjoyed watching LaBranche twitch and shake his head. "Did Lamar not explain that Texas is a foreign country? We are civilized people of a civilized nation, Mr. LaBranche, like the United States. And, like all civilized nations, one must show a passport to enter. Or a visa. That is how we know who people are. So, where is your passport?'"

Henderson looked away. Rusk sensed a cruelty akin to pulling legs from spiders. Houston smiled.

"And your colleagues, Mr. LaBranche? What are their names again?" Rusk said their names. "Have you seen their passports?"

LaBranche had recovered enough of his senses to make an answer for the general.

"They are not my colleagues. I have no business with them." Alexandre sensed that something had changed, that he was being pulled toward a turning point but not told which way to turn, that something to do with his purpose in life was about to change. All he wanted was to look through transits, to shoot the sun and the stars, to measure distances and draw maps of fabled and unknown places.

"I do not have a passport, sir, American or English. I was hired to come to Texas by the president of Texas. Surely that is passport enough. And I know nothing of Pennant or Alonzo, nor wish to." He attempted to puff out his chest, to show Houston that he had his dignity and his purpose, that he was not bound up in the problems of others.

Houston pondered his next point, then made it.

"Tell me this, Mr. LaBranche. Did your two friends out there, Pennant and Alonzo, did they murder that man down at Logan's ferry landing over by the Sabine River? Mr. Rusk has fully reported to me about the murder. It seems to me that your two friends fit the bill for being the murderers. They were on horses. They crossed the river on the ferry. They were seen on this side of the river where the road forks to go over to Nacogdoches. Did they kill the real surveyor, Mr. LaBranche?"

Alexandre's amygdala failed him. He felt dizzy, as if the room itself had moved. His eyes lost focus, and he took a very deep breath to steady himself. He had been prepared to talk about degrees of latitude and longitude, of the details of measuring geographic features along the river and pinpointing their locations, of his technique of drawing maps in a third dimension. He had not expected to be asked about the two men who had robbed him, and said so,.

"I can tell you with great confidence about my plans to determine the latitude and longitude of any point on the boundary of your republic and of my ability to produce a very accurate map of its entirety. I cannot tell you with any confidence about what happened down at the river landing, except for one thing."

"What is that one thing, LaBranche?"

"I do not believe that Pennant and Alonzo were the murderers. At the time of the murder, they were engaged in robbing me of my horse, my wagon, my clothes, my tools, and my papers. When shots rang out from the woods near the river, they took my wagon, hitched my horse to it, and left."

He was mistaken to believe that his answer put an end to it. By this time Houston was on his feet, hands on desk, leaning forward almost face to face with Alexandre. For his part, Alexandre realized that he was snared; the two men who had escorted him from Mrs. Eberly's boarding house had come to his elbows and were prepared to arrest him, or worse.

"So you admit, sir, that the three of you were together at the time of the murder." It was not a question. "A faked robbery would make an excellent alibi for a murder, Mr. LaBranche. An excellent alibi."

"An alibi? Sir, I take great offense at your accusation. I am no murd...."

"A murderer? You deny that you're a murderer?" Houston smiled. He arched his eyebrows. "I say that you may well be a murderer and that your two friends are thieves."

Alexandre was startled at the accusation and, equally, by yet another change of tone in Houston's voice.

"But that's not why I brought you here," Houston continued. "I brought you here because you're a spy. I think you're here to roam up and down our republic in league with those other two scoundrels who came with you, spying and making notes of where fortifications are strong and where they're not strong, of how many men and horses and cannons we have and where they're located, and to make a report of it. And you figured out how to collect ten thousand dollars in the bargain! Do you know the fate of spies, LaBranche?"

Alexandre gulped, shook, and looked around the log cabin capitol for escape. There was none.

"Let me tell you why you're a spy, LaBranche," Houston continued. "You're from Louisiana, which was part of New Spain until 1803. Your family's been there for many generations. But, sir, your family does not care for you. Your mother died. Your father sent you East, to school. You learned arithmetic, as you have proved, but not how to be a Southern gentleman. You learned geography, the famed Talcott geography, at Fort Monroe, but you didn't learn which way the wind blows." Houston took out a cigar, chomped off the end, and resumed. "After you were trained in the geographic arts, you returned to Louisiana where you were engaged in a total of six surveys over a period of five years. They consisted of several homes in uptown New Orleans, which were mistakenly built upon their neighbors' properties. You were let go from the Basin Street Canal when the Irish got sick. You went back home to the plantation. Your father gave you one last chance, to supervise the relocation of his slave cabins, which you moved onto a neighboring plantation. Your father told you to leave home and not come back. When your uncle introduced you to Mirabeau B. Lamar you met a man much like yourself—out of work, money, and opportunities. You, sir, are indeed a spy."

Alexandre could not make sense of Houston's words.

"Oh, forgive me, LaBranche. Sometimes, in my eagerness, I am not clear in my speech. Let me be clear. You are a spy. If you were ever engaged by Mexico, or by Lord Palmerston's English banks, or, God help him, by my friend Andrew Jackson, that engagement is at an end. You now are a spy for me. You are a spy for Texas. Do you understand?"

Houston produced Alexandre's contract from some hidden place behind the desk.

"See this?" he asked. Alexandre nodded that he did. "I'm amending your contract."

Houston tore it into pieces, then told the guards to burn them to ashes. He then uncorked a stone jug, poured foul-smelling whiskey into a tin cup, and began to sip on it.

"You are indeed going to the Rio Grande River to make maps. You're going to begin at Presidio Rio Grande and spy all the way south to Matamoros. You can draw all the rocks and hills and cactus you want, Monsieur LaBranche, but you are going to find and make a map of every Mexican army presidio, encampment, soldier, cook, laundry house, wagon, armory, cartridge press, cannon ball, flag, horse, and tortilla between the Gulf of Mexico and Presidio Rio Grande and send the maps back to me." He took another sip. "Or, you will be hanged for murdering that man down by Logan's ferry landing as surely as you sit there, now shaking in your boots. Do you understand?"

Alexandre gulped.

"I'm not asking you, sir. I am telling you. It is a choice you can make – spy for me or hang for murder. I prefer you spy for me." Houston paused to take another sip of corn whiskey. "But what I am asking you, LaBranche, is whether I should hang those other two idiots who left New Orleans the same day that you did, who stole the horses they rode on, and who stumbled onto the same ferry to Texas that you stumbled onto. Look at them."

Rusk and Henderson stood quietly, marveling at the wealth of information that Houston already had collected about LaBranche and his robbers, none of it from them. Houston knew that the *Durango* had sailed back toward Texas, that Pennant and Alonzo had gone to the Nacogdoches customs house, and details about Alexandre's pitiful career as a surveyor. It was clear to them that Alexandre would not be Houston's only spy, or even his first one.

Houston motioned for Alexandre to be brought to the window. They looked down toward the ramshackle log huts and livery stables, a sawmill and two general stores. They looked at the front lawn of Mrs. Eberly's boarding house where Pennant was edging ever closer to Mrs. Eberly with his talk of hollow balls and his leer of indecent intentions. They looked at Alonzo, silent, gazing toward nowhere. The mustache man and the scrawny man, inepts who had robbed LaBranche of all he owned and failed in the process.

"I understand you hold a grudge against them, LaBranche. I understand a grudge as well as the next man." Houston twisted the piece of string into another knot, then tugged on one end to form a noose. "Should I have them hanged? If you want them hanged, you say the word and they'll pay for robbing you before the sun goes down this very night."

LaBranche began to understand that Houston was not threatening to have Pennant and Alonzo tried in a court of law; he was simply proposing to have them murdered.

"No, sir. I do not wish for them to be hanged," Alexandre managed to answer.

"Good, because you'll need them. I don't believe a man can take a survey wagon up and down the Rio Grande to Presidio Rio Grande and on up to Santa Fe, not all by himself. You'll have them to help you with your hypotenuses, LaBranche, your transits, and your chains. They'll be right there to cook for you and tend the horses.

And they will look after your things when you bring your maps back to me."

"Sir, that is an improper proposal," Alexandre answered. "First, I do not wish to spy for you. I wish to perform the contract I entered into with President Lamar..."

"Ex-President Lamar," Houston corrected him. He quietly gloated to see that his new spy struggled with the fact that Lamar was no longer his employer.

"... as I am a man of my word. But I do not wish to have them accompany me for so much as the first one hundred yards. They would undoubtedly rob me again and leave me to die somewhere out in the great unknown lands of your great unmapped Texas."

"Then I fear that you will not earn your ten thousand dollars, Mr. LaBranche. You see, as much as I believe ex-President Lamar is a fool and an idiot, he entered into a contract with you and Texas is good for its word, signed contract or no. I just think if you happen to be captured by Mexican soldiers, you don't want to be carrying around a document that says Texas is paying you to draw maps on the Rio Grande. But, if you complete the work, you will receive your ten thousand dollars, I promise you, and not before. As for Pennant and Alonzo, I do not believe any man alive can drive a wagon the length of the Rio Grande by himself, surveying and drawing and spying. You need help. They are your help. And if, but only if, Pennant and Alonzo keep you safe and do what you tell them to do, and if you bring your maps and reports safely back to me, that letter of credit will become gold United States dollars. Pennant and Alonzo will receive as many of them as you settle on them. You shall have the rest."

"And if they don't keep me safe or work as I tell them to do?" Alexandre had great difficulty in speaking, both out of panic and because of the sheer idiocy of Houston's task. "Or if I don't return?"

"We will tell your crew, Mr. Pennant and Mr. Alonzo, that their narrow escape from the gallows depends entirely on them keeping you safe," Rusk said in a plain and clear voice. "If you don't return, they don't get paid, nor, Mr. LaBranche, will you likely be in any condition to spend money yourself." He paused to let Alexandre take it in. "Mexico shoots spies."

Alexandre was not very good at surveying landscapes, but he was good at surveying his future. He looked out the window to study the two men on whose threads his life would hang. He saw Pennant talking with a married woman about cannon balls and Alonzo gazing vacantly into space. For an instant his mind returned to his old imaginings of a jolly ride along the banks of the Rio Grande, of happy villagers and expansive vistas, ending in the fabled streets of Santa Fe and the mythical mountains out of which, somewhere, the Rio Grande sprang, of wealth and fame for his discoveries and explorations. But it was only for an instant because, LaBranche knew with certainty, the ending would be different.

He turned to face his captors and wanted to ask them when was the very soonest he could quit this god-forsaken capital and leave them behind, leave their lies and disingenuous threats and crude choices and go home. Instead, he said the only civilized thing that he could safely utter:

"It seems, sir, that you have arranged my death."

Houston laughed.

"No, sir, I have arranged your future, unless you fail in your purpose." He looked LaBranche squarely in the eyes and continued. "Go. I have work to do. Rusk and Henderson here will work out what you need, which will include passports and a little cash advance for supplies. As soon as you have them, you leave for San Antonio de Bexar."

The same two men escorted LaBranche out of the capitol. Houston watched him stumble down the hill toward Mrs. Eberly's boarding house in the same faltering manner that men stumble toward a hanging tree.

"How can you be so sure, Sam?" Rusk wondered at the shabby sight. "How do you know he is not the Mexican agent?"

"Because the Mexican agent is dead, Thomas. I had him murdered at Logan's ferry landing. I thought you had figured that out."

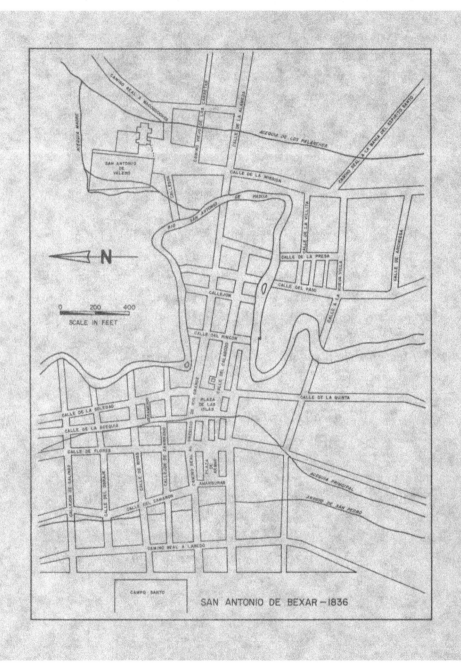

SAN ANTONIO DE BEXAR—1836

CHAPTER SEVEN

1842, SAN ANTONIO DE BEXAR

He agreed to spy.

They loitered about Mrs. Eberly's boarding house, waiting for orders to leave, for instructions, for documents, for winter coats and horseshoes. Then, at first light one morning in February, a man named Hays appeared at Alexandre's room.

"Come with me," he said.

"Come where?" Alexandre asked.

Hays nodded in the direction of Mrs. Eberly's stable. Alexandre found that his wagon had been loaded, the horse harnessed, and Pennant and Alonzo were strapping their sea bags onto their saddles. As for Hays himself, he made no answer, merely sat on his horse while Alexandre put on a heavy coat and climbed onto the wagon. There was on the buckboard a stout leather bag, one Alexandre had not seen before, secured and buckled with two leather straps.

Hays led them out of Austin. They rode south for a very long day, crossing broad rolling prairies and several streams to camp on the bank of the Guadalupe River. Late in the evening of the second day, Hays guided them past the ruins of the Alamo and, about a mile further on, into the main plaza of San Antonio de Bexar. He dismounted, saying only "We're here." Other men appeared, one of whom took Alexandre's horse by the bit and led them down a cobbled street to an old adobe house with a stable yard.

"I'm Samuel Maverick," one of the men announced in a voice that was more congenial than the silent Mr. Hays.' "I've been told to expect you," he added. A slave appeared and began to remove the reins and rigging from Alexandre's horse and wagon. "We'll get your animals situated. We've got some cornbread and beans for you on the table." Maverick pointed to a doorway; a faint light could be seen around the edges. "There's a fire and a bed. Your men can sleep in the back room," he added.

"Thank you, sir," Alexandre replied. "Who told you to expect us? And what do you know about why I'm here?"

"Jack Hays. He told us," Maverick explained. "We've known for a week that three men were coming from Austin who would need a place to stay while they got ready. Mr. Hays doesn't say more than he knows and not always that much," Maverick added. "But you can trust him. Jack C. Hays is a good man." The slave carried Alexandre's portmanteau and survey box into the room, then returned with the leather bag.

After they ate the beans and cornbread, Alexandre dispatched Pennant and Alonzo to the back room, then opened the leather bag to study its contents by the light of a guttering candle. There was a note of only three sentences:

"Use this letter of credit to provision for the journey. Send dispatches by Hays or his men. Burn this communication."

He unfolded the other papers in the bag; they included a one-hundred-dollar letter of credit issued by a bank in Austin for the use of Alexandre LaBranche and a list of supplies one might need for a wagon trip. There was a legal document of doubtful authenticity that described in formal language the geographic boundaries of an enormous area between the Nueces and Rio Grande rivers "to be inspected in connection with the obligations of Mexico in those agreements of deferred bonds issued by the banking houses of Goldsmith and Barclay of London, United Kingdom, dated April 1837 and July 1839...." There were passports.

When Alexandre woke the following morning, he found that Pennant and Alonzo had already left the adobe by a back door. He dressed and went in search of breakfast, which he found at the Maverick home a block away near the plaza. Mrs. Maverick and her slave were waiting and motioned for him to come into the house. Samuel Maverick and Jack Hays were waiting for him at a fine dining table. The slave gave him a proper cup of coffee and some toasted bread. Alexandre did not have to wait long.

"Mr. LaBranche?" Hays said, "I've delivered you. Good day to you." And with no more than a nod, Jack C. Hays left.

"Good morning, Mr. LaBranche," Maverick said in the same kindly tone that he had used the evening before. "Welcome to San Antonio de Bexar. Welcome to my home." Alexandre thanked him and waited. "Breakfast first, then talk," Maverick added.

Mrs. Maverick and her slave were better cooks than Mrs. Eberly. They brought out corn biscuits, coffee, an egg, and something that looked like tomatoes, but wasn't, that burned his mouth. Alexandre studied them, unable to resist the feeling that he was behaving like a trapped dog and equally aware that they were watching him, politely, but without much conversation. When he could do so he put down his fork and sat back in his chair.

"Now, Mr. LaBranche, talk." Maverick smiled and indicated by no more than a look that his wife and her cook should leave them alone. "You asked last night what I know about why you are here. In a word, it isn't Houston's way to explain." Alexandre heard a note in Maverick's voice that might have been evasion but might equally have been resignation. "Something to do with English banks, perhaps. Some land in which they have an interest. I know little more."

Alexandre sensed that Maverick was hesitating to see if

Alexandre would correct him or wait. He waited. Maverick continued.

"I know you're to stay while you get ready. I and others are to help you without prying into your affairs. And I know from those things that whatever you're doing will take you into the frontier."

"What do you mean, into the frontier?" For Alexandre, the frontier was the Rio Grande, and that was almost one hundred and fifty miles away. "Into?

Maverick gave Alexandre a puzzled look.

"The frontier is everything on the other side of San Antonio, Mr. LaBranch," Maverick said. He pointed out his window and across the plaza to a large and surprisingly fine church that dominated the city. "Do you see the cathedral? The frontier begins behind it."

"And Mr. Hays? Is he one of the others who's to help me? He didn't say six words to me from Austin to here."

"Hays doesn't say much. He watches."

"What is Mr. Hays watching, Mr. Maverick? Me?"

"Call me Sam," he answered. Sam Maverick was polite, nothing like the bullying Sam Houston, who would have laughed at Alexandre and swigged from a jug of corn. "Just Sam. Hays and his men are a committee of safety for San Antonio. They're looking for the Mexican army. Comanches. Horse and cattle thieves. Spies."

"On the other side of the cathedral?" Alexandre had a mental image of soldiers hiding in the trees or some version of Pennant and Alonzo stealing someone's wagon in a pine forest. "Are they on the other side of the cathedral? The Mexican army? Or Indians?"

"Sometimes, Mr. LaBranche, yes. And somewhere, always." Maverick drank more of his coffee, waited a few moments, then continued. "That's what Jack C. Hays watches out for." He saw Alexandre's look of doubt at his explanation.

"Sam," Alexandre answered, "if I may be so bold, Sam, I don't understand. If you and others are to help me do something that you believe will take me into the frontier and Mr. Hays is watching for the Mexican army and bandits and Indians in the frontier, I don't see any reason for me to be here at all."

Maverick told him that he might understand better if he saw the frontier. They left the Maverick home and walked to the plaza, where Alexandre noticed that much, maybe all, of San Antonio's affairs were conducted. There were a few shops and offices. A lot of trade was conducted by men selling directly from their wagons. They walked to the cathedral, then around it, and another two hundred yards beyond.

The frontier of Texas was a muddy ditch named the San Pedro River. Beyond the ditch there was a seemingly endless prairie that stretched to the west and south. The *camino real* left the city across a one-horse wooden bridge and disappeared into the horizon. There was a cemetery with a low fence to keep out a few goats and some meagre milk cows grazing nearby. Several men dressed in white cotton pants and shirts and who wore enormous straw hats were hoeing in several fields. Otherwise, there was not to be seen a building, home, ranch, anything of civilization beyond the livestock and the men with their hoes.

Alexandre realized that what Sam Houston had ordered him to do was take Pennant and Alonzo across that vast, empty land to the Rio Grande and look for the Mexican army. He asked again if Sam understood why Houston had sent him.

"Houston keeps his plans to himself. But as for what you're doing here, when Hays and his men ride the frontier, they stop at the Nueces River. That's far enough from San Antonio that if they see the Mexican army, or Comanches, Hays can ride back here in time to warn us." He pointed to the horizon; Alexandre could see the haze of rising hills in the distance. Maverick left unspoken the obvious: Alexandre was expected to go where Hays and his men did not.

They walked back to the plaza, where Maverick shook his hand in such a public way that Alexandre suspected it was for others to take notice and excused himself to attend to a session of court.

Alexandre discovered that, apart from the frontier, San Antonio was a graceful city of stone and tile homes built in the Spanish style under the shade of oak and sycamore trees that grew along the banks of a small flowing river, also the San Antonio, and several irrigation aqueducts. Many of the homes and all the shops and offices had wooden benches by the front doors where people could visit in the shade of overhanging porches. As he walked along, he heard the chatter of Mexican women and the play of children. The smell of unfamiliar foods came through open windows and from behind high garden walls. It reminded him of New Orleans. He continued north along the San Antonio River, crossed several roads that seemed to lead out of the city, and arrived at a small dam. Pennant and Alonzo were perched on the riverbank.

What am I doing here? he asked himself. He looked at the gently flowing stream and the whitewashed homes, listened to the clatter of men setting new tiles on an old roof and to women beating laundry, and realized that the lovely city was his trap. *I'm no spy. If I set out for the Rio Grande, why wouldn't Pennant and Alonzo just rob me again?* He had no good answer for that. *And as for spying, Sam Houston expects dispatches; if I don't dispatch something, he'll send someone to hang all three of us.* He thought of giving up. He could flee, he pondered, but he didn't have anywhere to go, certainly not home. He thought of his father: 'You have no purpose, Alexandre, you have no plan.'

He turned around and walked back without talking to his robbers. He found the adobe house on Salado and opened the shutters to allow light to flow onto the table, then took out his maps.

There wasn't a village, town, or settlement of any kind between San Antonio and the Rio Grande. The map indicated that the *camino real* ended at a Mexican fort on the river, Presidio Rio Grande. He traced down the river and located Laredo, Mier, and finally Matamoros on the Gulf of Mexico. He tried to remember what he had been told about Matamoros, could not, and studied the map again. The only landmark in the vast frontier was the Nueces River, winding its way out of the hills and continuing all the way to Corpus Christi Bay.

He looked at San Antonio's location on the map. The little river where he had seen Pennant and Alonzo lounging on the bank flowed all the way to Goliad and on to Paso Caballo on the Gulf of Mexico. There were towns all along that route, Goliad, Refugio, Victoria. He wondered how long he could wait in San Antonio before he had to choose: flee, spy, or ride to the Rio Grande and keep going.

The next morning, he went back to the Maverick home and asked Mrs. Maverick whether she might tell her husband that he would appreciate the opportunity to talk with him. She said that he would, and Maverick soon joined him.

"Sir," he began, "I don't know what you know about me." Maverick began to protest, but Alexandre asked to be heard. "I'm just a surveyor, Sam, nothing more. President Lamar hired me to map the Rio Grande River." He saw a clear look of concern on Sam's face but continued. "To Santa Fe, and beyond. But when I got to Texas, I was robbed and left to die." He paused, not because he was unsure of what to say but because he had come to realize that the only reason he had not died was that Noeme had rescued him and, he suspected, then led him onward to Nacogdoches. "When I was brought to President Houston, he tore up Lamar's contract, my contract, then ordered me to go to the Rio Grande anyway. But I wasn't going there to survey and map the river; Houston ordered me to go to the Rio Grande to spy on the Mexican army. So, here I am, Mr. Maverick, not a half mile from the frontier, and I don't have any idea what I'm doing."

Maverick took his time answering.

"Again, please call me Sam. Like I said, Sam Houston does not tell people his plans. As for what I do know, I'm supposed to give you a place to stay until you leave. I'm to work with Johan Voss and John Twohig to get you provisioned and on your way." He paused. "And Houston's orders seem clear: you're to spy on the Mexican army. But you don't seem clear about yourself; are you an experienced spy?"

"No," Alexandre answered. "I don't know anything about spying. As for my experience, it's not very impressive. I was taught surveying at the army school of geography in Virginia. But, when I got back to Louisiana, I had few jobs and did not distinguish myself on them. I can use the Horrebow method to find latitude and longitude as well as any man on earth, Sam, but when I try to survey them on the ground, well, sometimes I site things where they aren't supposed to be. Houston somehow found out about it."

"Then I don't know why Houston thought you could be a spy." It didn't make much sense to Maverick.

"Maps," was all Alexandre answered. "Houston wants maps. As he put it, he wants me to draw maps of every Mexican soldier, horse, cannon, and tortilla press on the Rio Grande."

"Can you draw maps, then? Is that it?" Alexandre nodded. "Better than you can survey lines?" Alexandre nodded again.

He accepted a graphite pencil and a sheet of paper, looked away for a moment to concentrate, then bent over Maverick's kitchen table. Five minutes later, he presented Sam Maverick with a drawing of San Antonio. It didn't look like a map.

Maverick was almost speechless. "How did you do this?"

'This' was a graph drawing of San Antonio. There were the Alamo, the San Antonio River, the plaza, the council house on the plaza, the Maverick home, and the cathedral, each in their proper locations and proportions. What was different from a map, however, was that instead of drawing a street grid, Alexandre had sketched everything on the streets and the river in profile, as an artist would have drawn them. He had drawn the buildings themselves, views of the fronts of the homes, shops and the cathedral, their very doors and windows and even their porch benches. He even had drawn the bank, the mercantile, and trade wagons on the plaza, a horse walking across the bridge over the San Pedro, and a few goats grazing beyond the cemetery, all in profile. Maverick ran his fingers over the drawing, shaking his head.

"You have shown me more about San Antonio de Bexar in five minutes than any spy could report in a hundred dispatches." He laughed a grim, knowing laugh. "Mr. LaBranche, you are indeed a spy."

"I might be, if I live long enough, Sam. Those two men who came to San Antonio with me, Pennant and Alonzo? They're the two men who robbed me and left me for dead at the Sabine." Sam Maverick began to understand why Alexandre LaBranche was agitated. "And Sam Houston knew it. He ordered me to take them on as my helpers." Alexandre sighed with the voice of resignation. "If they don't kill me, Houston will. Houston ordered me to send dispatches to him. If I don't, Hays and his men will add me to the list of what they're watching. So, Sam, I can go to the Rio Grande to spy on the Mexican army. Or I can wait to be robbed by my two helpers. Either way, I'm a dead man."

Maverick tried to sound reassuring.

"Well, Alexandre LaBranche, you have some deciding to do. You don't have to leave tomorrow. Hays won't be looking for you to start this soon. And you've got provisioning to do, getting your horse shod and wagon ready for travel. So, while you do, I'm going to think on it."

———

Two days later, Maverick called Alexandre back to his home.

"These two men," Maverick began, "are my friends. John Twohig and Johan Voss." Two weather-beaten and prosperous-looking men stood to shake Alexandre's hand. "You can trust them as much as you can trust me. Here's what I think. If you continue to the Rio Grande, you will find that Mr. Twohig's mercantile will provision you and Mr. Voss's bank will accept a letter of credit to pay for your provisions."

"If I continue," Alexandre answered.

"We can see what you're thinking," Voss said. His accent sounded like "ve" and "tinking." "With Comanches and bandits and der frontier vast, maybe you're thinking you don't go. But you can go if dot's what you want."

"Yes," Twohig added. "We're not going to be surprised if you go on to the Rio Grande. But we're not going to be surprised either if you go back to Louisiana, or simply disappear in some other direction."

"Not our business, Mr. LaBranche," Voss finished. "But if you go, we'll help you."

Alexandre liked them both immediately. They weren't threatening; they weren't persuading, and he believed them. Among the problems, though, maybe his biggest problem, was the vastness of the frontier.

"The Rio Grande is a long way," Maverick resumed, "but not as far as the road from Nacogdoches to Austin. It can be done. There are wagon trains on the *camino real*, trade caravans. Cattle to market. Traders for leather, saddles. The mayor of San Antonio is a trader, a Mexican named Juan Seguin, a good man. He just got back from Saltillo with a herd of sheep. Some of the caravans are big, some just a couple of carts, but, war or no war, there's been trade over that road for hundreds of years and still is. So, a man and a wagon could join a caravan to Presidio Rio Grande or Laredo and get there, especially a man with American papers."

Alexandre wondered what Maverick knew about his American papers, and remembered that the first morning they spoke, Maverick had said he only knew his work was 'something to do with English banks.'

"But the weak link is your two robbers," Maverick continued. "A man couldn't take a wagon to the Rio Grande by himself. So, if your helpers fail you, whether they rob you or not, you'll fail too." Maverick meant 'you will die.' "So, the problem is clear: you have to have helpers you can trust, and you have to satisfy Houston that you're going to spy. Let's look at Pennant and Alonzo. We think Houston will have scared them into thinking that if you fail, he'll hang them. Next, we suspect Houston probably offered them something, made them think that if you succeed, they'll come in for some big reward, a lot of money. Either way, from their side of it, they have two good reasons to keep you alive and bring you back."

Alexandre had not considered their side of it.

"But they also have a good reason to run away," Maverick continued.

Alexandre had only considered himself running away. It made sense that Pennant and Alonso might flee, too. After all, they were robbers.

"What about Hays?" Alexandre asked.

"Hays left yesterday to ride to the Nueces. He'll be gone for weeks. He won't be telling Houston what you're doing, not for the time being. But, as for your robbers: before you do anything, you've got to test them." He waited for Alexandre to grasp his meaning. "We have some ideas."

"And," Alexandre said, "to satisfy Houston that I'm spying?"

"We have some ideas about that, too."

———

The next morning, Alexandre went in search of Pennant and Alonzo. When he crossed the plaza, he found a trader named Kinney who sold merchandize out of his wagon, Mexican merchandise. Alexandre saw the fine boots, saddles, lariats, vaquero pants, and leather.

"Looks expensive," Alexandre said.

"The best," Kinney answered. "Made by Salvador Garza's saddle maker at Rancho Viejo. Matamoros."

"Matamoros? Do you trade down that way?" Alexandre asked.

'I do," Kinney told him. "Leather, tools, dry goods. Some cattle. I trade in cotton and cloth going the other way."

"Don't you have trouble with the Mexican army? Or the Texian army, either?"

"If the army wants something I have, I sell it to them. Either side."

"How would you get to Matamoros from here? Go to Presidio and down the river?"

Kinney's look suggested that he thought Alexandre was impaired.

"My trading post is down on the Nueces, near Corpus Christi Bay. I go from there across the desert to Matamoros."

"I had no idea, Mr. Kinney," Alexandre finished. "I'll visit with you again, if that's alright."

He found Pennant and Alonzo walking out of La Villita, where the Mexicans who had stayed in San Antonio still lived.

"Good morning, young sir," Pennant called out to him. "Been wonderin' if you was okay. Thought you might of run off."

"I have not run off, Pennant. I have made plans. My plan is that I'm going to send word to Houston that I fired you." He had intended to tell them an elaborate lie, but he wasn't a good liar. "I don't trust you, and I don't believe I can depend on you. That's as plain as I can be."

Pennant was speechless. Even Alonzo turned to listen. Pennant answered first.

"You can't fire us! It was Houston hired us to spy for him. He promised us ten thousand United States dollars. You're just mad about that little... uh, misunderstanding." Pennant had risen to arguing height and indignantly waved his arms around.

"You robbed me and left me for dead, Pennant. That's not a misunderstanding. I can't imagine why you think I'd trust you to ride as far as the San Pedro to help me survey a ditch, much less go with me to the Rio Grande to spy on the Mexican army."

"A man shouldn't talk like that about his particular friends, young sir." Pennant was genuinely insulted.

"You are not my particular friends." Alexandre was not a good liar. "And you're not spies; you're robbers. Besides, none of us know anything about spying. We don't know anything about Mexico." He let that idea settle in the air. Pennant scoffed and kicked his boot at the bank of the river. Alonzo gazed downstream. "If the Mexican army caught us spying, they would shoot us. So, no thank you. You and Alonzo are free to go your own way."

Pennant resisted.

"As for spyin'," Pennant retorted, "nothing to it. You just take a look around and remember what you see. And as for the Mexican army, well, most of 'em are barefoot. Sam Houston whipped 'em in eighteen minutes. So, spying on them can't be that hard. All we got to do is just roll along, seeing what we see, you make a few maps, and we bring 'em back to Houston. We collect ten thousand dollars US. Then you go your way, and we go ours." He gave a triumphant smile.

"Can you read, Mr. Pennant?" Alexandre didn't wait for an answer. "Well, Houston can read. He ordered me to send dispatches to him. Send them by Jack Hays."

"Alrighty, that don't sound like a problem." Pennant was eager. "That's what I was sayin', young sir. He tells you what to do and we do it, no questions. And you tell Alonzo and me what you want done and we do it, just like you say."

Alexandre tried to act as if he was struggling with the decision he had already made.

"I'm not putting my life in your hands just because you say you'll be good this time."

"We promise, don't we Alonzo?" Pennant inclined his head toward Alonzo. "No tricks. Just tell us what you want us to do, and we'll do it. Hand o' God." He put his hand over his chest and rolled his eyes toward Heaven.

"Get me a Bible," Alexandre answered.

"I'll swear on a Bible if that's what you want. Alonzo too." Alonzo nodded in agreement.

"It's not to swear on. It's to write dispatches. I need a Catholic Bible, in Latin." Alexandre waited to see if Pennant had more to say. "And, it would be best if you get one without stealing it." Alexandre was confident that it would be impossible for Pennant or Alonzo to get a Bible of any kind without stealing it. If they were caught, he'd be through with them. If not, he would have his codebook. "When I get the Bible, I'll take a few more days to decide. Or you can just quit now." He walked away without looking back.

The next day Alexandre found a Latin bible on his table.

He opened it and began to labor over his long-forgotten Latin, spending an hour in the book of Matthew. When he found the passage he sought, he copied it onto a sheet of paper: '*Opinions bellorum ne turbemini sed,*' which translated as 'rumors of war.' He then added a message in English about the conditions of Goliad, a town he had never been to that was near the Gulf of Mexico, a hundred miles away. When he had finished, he had written:

"*Opinions bellorum ne turbemini sed.* Rumors of war in Goliad. Militia being raised against rumored invasion, but no evidence that a Mexican army approaches. No word about the whereabouts of Colonel Canales. Will report from Refugio."

He added a concluding Latin scripture from the Psalms: "*Facies tua luceat super servum tuum,*" which meant "Let your face shine on the work of your faithful servant."

Alexandre LaBranche had written his first coded dispatch as a spy.

The following day he went back to find Pennant and Alonzo. "I met a man named Kinney. He goes back and forth to Mexico to trade goods out of his wagon, saddles, and tools and cloth and such. Mr. Kinney has mentioned to me something of the activity of the Mexican army. We should report it."

Pennant perked up.

"I understand that if you take the Goliad road along this river you'll come to some old Spanish missions." Alexandre handed them the Goliad dispatch. "Take this dispatch. Ride out to Mission Concepcion, spend a few nights, then one of you bring the dispatch back as fast as you can gallop. Hand it to one of Jack C. Hays' men on the plaza. Tell him 'Dispatch for President Houston. Guard it with your life.' Then ride back to Concepcion."

Pennant shuffled his feet, looked at Alonzo, and finally asked, "What is this?'"

"It's a dispatch. Do not open it. Do not read it."

An hour later, Pennant and Alonzo rode out of San Antonio.

Thus, with certain exceptions, they began to spy.

The spy work enabled Alexandre to enjoy the most agreeable part of San Antonio. He learned to enjoy coffee with Samuel Maverick and a game of cards with Voss and Twhohig. They told him tales of Texas and he told them stories of New Orleans. They told him about fighting in the war; Maverick had been sent out of the Alamo before it fell. Voss and Twohig both fought at Goliad and escaped. Alexandre wondered why they were helping him.

The disagreeable part of spying was the collection of intelligence for the dispatches he sent to Sam Houston. When Alexandre needed to compose another dispatch, he sought out the trader Kinney for rumors of the frontier. One morning he asked Kinney about conditions at Refugio.

"People are always fired up in Refugio and Goliad," Kinney said to him. "They're the first watering holes after San Patricios. They think the Mexican army's always just about to invade."

Alexandre saddled his horse and rode out along the San Antonio River until he found the mission. Concepcion was old and somewhat small, no more than a church and monastery and a few outbuildings. Most of it looked as if it had suffered from a battle. He found Pennant and Alonzo bathing in the San Antonio River.

"This is your next dispatch," he told them. "Tomorrow, ride it into San Antonio and hand it off to one of Hays' men for delivery to Houston. ' They worked out instructions on delivering the next dispatch and the one after that.

The dispatch from Refugio was almost identical to the dispatch from Goliad: rumors of the approach of a Mexican army, but no Mexican soldiers had been seen by anyone, nor did anyone have any information about the traitor Canales. The report from San Patricio, dated several days afterward, confirmed that the Mexican army was nowhere in sight. It ended by saying that a further report would come after Alexandre crossed the vast plain to Matamoros. "For President Houston," they told the riders in hushed and, for Alonzo, heavily accented tones. "Information he waits for."

And, every day, Alexandre considered what to do. His robbers were doing what he told them to do; Hays was out of San Antonio, watching in the great frontier. And, for Alexandre, mapping the Rio Grande continued to hold an allure that fleeing did not offer; even without the promise of ten thousand United States dollars,

accurate maps, maps in three dimensions, would be valuable to the
United States. When he did think of fleeing, he saw his father's
face with the slave girl at his door. Then he thought of Noeme,
and wondered at himself, even considering such a thing. He
wondered how she had found him. He wondered why she had
saved him. He composed the next coded dispatch, supposedly from
Matamoros:

> February 25, 1842. *"Considerate terram qualis sit, utrum fortis sit an
> infirmus habitatores eius"* it began, which translated as "See what the
> land is like, and whether the people who live in it are strong or
> weak," taken from the book of Numbers. Alexandre thought it a
> perfect phrase for a first letter from a foreign land.
>
> Sir, there is at the city of Matamoros a fortification under the
> command of General Vasquez. I judge it to be a miserable force, no
> more than a few hundred men, many of them untrained and bare-
> foot. The cavalry could not exceed twenty men and they on horses
> that appear on the verge of death from the general drought and
> famine of these parts. As for cannon, I believe there to be more of
> them in Goliad and Refugio, and certainly in San Antonio de Bexar,
> than in all of General Vasquez' army. He parades his undisciplined
> soldiers each day toward a bridge over the Rio Grande, drills them
> in ragged formations, and returns to the fortification.
>
> He concluded the spy portion of his Matamoros dispatch by
> declaring:
>
> There is no word of the whereabouts of the traitor Canales, nor
> whether he is in command of any unit in these parts. We leave after
> dark for Mier and on to Laredo, where I will send my next
> dispatches when I find trustworthy riders who can bring them
> to you.

He concluded with a Latin sentence from Thessalonians: "So
then let us not sleep, as others do, but let us keep awake and be
sober. For those who sleep, sleep at night, and those who get drunk,
are drunk at night." He hoped that Houston could find someone to

translate the Latin; half of Texas referred to the president as the Big Drunk.

On a separate sheet of foolscap, he had sketched an entirely imaginary map of Matamoros. There was a cantonment, a bridge over the Rio Grande, a few huts, some map symbols for cavalry and infantry. It was very persuasive.

That night he rode to Concepcion to hand the letter himself to his robbers.

"Wait here for seven days, no less, and then one of you bring it back to San Antonio. Give it to one of Hays' men." He waited for Alonzo to show that he understood. Pennant did not.

"Why'd you say wait seven days, young sir? Why don't you just tell us what day to go take it to San Antonio like you always done?"

"This is a letter that concerns matters that are a week farther away than the others. Are you going to do what I assign you or....?"

"You're running away, ain't you?" Pennant exploded. "You been stashin' us out until you gets clear of us for a week so you can run away. Well, young sir, that's just wrong! You agreed to spy! We got ten thousand ...."

Alexandre cut him off.

"Run where, Pennant? To Mexico? If I'm going to Mexico, I might as well go there to map the Rio Grande. Or do you think I can run to the hill country and face the Comanches? Or I could continue straight down this river all the way to the Gulf of Mexico? There's a Mexican ship, the *Durango*, that was headed for an invasion right there on the Gulf when it was captured and hauled to New Orleans. Word is, it's free again and sailing right back there. So, flee there?"

Alexandre saw an alarmed reaction from both his robbers. Pennant answered:

"No sir, we don't have no business getting tangled up with the *Durango*, young sir. But we ain't doing nothing for Sam Houston neither, not just hanging around this mission." Pennant was chastened, but still demanding. "And we don't particularly care for them priests, neither."

"Then you've got seven days, Pennant. On the seventh day, ride into the plaza and deliver this dispatch. Then I'll decide what we're doing next."

Seven days later, Pennant arrived at the plaza. To Alexandre's dismay, Alonzo rode with him. They handed the Matamoros dispatch to one of Hays' men, then rode their horses to the stables behind the adobe on Soledad.

"What are you both doing here?" Alexandre demanded. "One of you is supposed to be waiting at the mission."

"Too many priests," Pennant answered. "They ain't as hospitable as a man would want. A man'd starve on what they feed and then they want we should pay them. So, yesterday we went down to the creek for a bathe and come back to find two of 'em goin' through our bags. They was lookin' for money." He waited to see if Alexandre was going to argue about it. "Anyways, we done everything you said, and it was time for both of us to leave them priests and their smoke and crosses. What's next?"

Pennant and Alonzo had done what he told them to do. They had not run away. They had stayed at the mission. They had delivered the dispatches. They had acted like spies and had done no harm. They had passed his tests, so far, so he told them what was next:

"We've got one more dispatch to deliver; then we go to the Rio Grande."

————

"I see your robbers have come back," Maverick told him. "Did they pass your test?"

"They did as I told them, Sam. I don't know if that means I can trust them to not rob me on the *camino real*." Alexandre sipped his coffee and took some toast.

Maverick closed his eyes and rubbed his temples. "A word, please?" He waited to gather the word, found it, and spoke again: "You need to leave, Alexandre."

"Leave?" Alexandre was puzzled. Maverick had told him that he could stay for a day or for a month, stay as long as he needed until he was ready to go. He wasn't sure what Maverick expected him to do, either as Houston's spy or as a man who fled. "I haven't finished everything I have to do to prepare for...."

"Yes. Twohig told me you're only partly provisioned. You can't put that off any longer. It's time for you to go. And," Maverick told him in a grave tone of voice, "you're being watched."

"Watched? By Mr. Hays?" Alexandre was both shaken and amused. He assumed Hays was still out on the frontier looking for Comanches and cattle thieves. "If he is watching me, all he'll see is me and Mr. Twohig doing my last provisioning."

"Not Hays," Sam answered. Alexandre would have been the least of Hays' concerns. "He has other worries, Alexandre. You're being watched by priests. They've been following you for days. Twohig noticed them as well, when you looked in on him yesterday."

Maverick smoothed his hands on his breeches, studied his young friend's face. "The priests are still Mexicans, Alexandre. This was a Mexican city long before it was our city. They look to have it back." He paused to let the notion sink in that Alexandre was being careless. "Finish loading your wagon, Alexandre, and get a rifle," Maverick told him. "Some balls and powder. And leave San Antonio. I say no more."

He was satisfied that Alexandre knew what was happening. Maverick had one more thing to say. He put his hands on Alexandre's shoulders and looked in his eyes:

"You can do this, Alexandre. Whatever you choose, you can do this."

Alexandre went the next day to Twohig's mercantile. He bought some water barrels, shovels and a pick, a medicine chest, a fifty weight of dried beef and hardtack, and a canvas tarp to protect him from the elements. He bought a Kentucky fowling musket.

He cashed his letter of credit at Mr. Voss's bank, then walked back to tell Samuel Maverick that he was ready to leave. There was

no one there. When Alexandre returned to the adobe house on
Soledad, he sensed that something was amiss.

The door seemed to be very slightly ajar. The portmanteau on
his bed might have been moved a few inches. He might have heard a
sound in the back room, but no one was in it and its door was
latched. He turned to the leather bag.

The unburned note, the letter of credit, and the legal documents
and passports were as he had left them. What was not as he had left
things was the presence of a sealed envelope. It contained a receipt
dated December 1841, issued to Plantation LaBranche by a New
Orleans sugar merchant. On the back of the receipt was a letter in
his father's handwriting:

Alcee says you are hired to survey a river boundary in Texas.
Good. Succeed and you will find your home open to you, but fail
and you will not. Louisiana has no need of more failures returned
from Texas with their tails between their legs.

His father had written the letter on a receipt, not to save the
expense of good paper or even as an expedient to haste, but to make
clear by the number of hogsheads of sugar delivered and the thousands of dollars received that LaBranche Senior had collected a
successful harvest without him. Alexandre looked for a signature, a
second page, a single word of encouragement, and found none.
Alexandre was needed even less than he was wanted. There was no
reason, or place, to flee.

He found a single hair on the envelope, a long black hair, but
nothing else.

He composed his final dispatch:

There is in Laredo a company, perhaps a small battalion, of
Mexican soldiers. It poses no risk whatever to San Antonio, having
at most two three-pound cannons and a small phalanx of lancers on
horseback. It does not have sufficient food, water, or ammunition to
support an invasion into Texas.

At twilight, he sealed the letter inside a foolscap envelope, put it
in a leather shot pouch, and found Alonzo.

"Ride out to Mission Concepcion, stay two days, then bring this dispatch back and hand it off to one of Hays's riders. Ride hard." It would appear to anyone on the plaza, and particularly to Hays' anxious horsemen, that Alonzo had been riding day and night all the way from Laredo. "Bring it back on Friday." February had passed; Friday would be the 4th of March. "Pennant and I will keep low until you're back."

Alonzo nodded, took the spy dispatch, and rode out of San Antonio along the river path. Alexandre watched him ride out of view, then walked back to the plaza, along Calaboza street and into the only saloon with a light in the window. He saw the trader Kinney.

"Good evening, sir," he said. "How are your affairs? Well, I hope."

Kinney jumped at the sound of Alexandre's greeting.

"Affairs, LaBranche? My affairs are fine if you don't allow for the fact that everybody's packing up and riding out of San Antonio." Kinney was drinking a cup of corn whiskey; Alexandre took one for himself and wondered why Kinney appeared to be agitated. "Hardly a god damned soul left in town. Hard on trade."

Alexandre, quietly grateful for Kinney's gossip about Goliad and Refugio and Matamoros, had planned to offer him a glass of corn. Kinney instead offered Alexandre a fact: the civilians of San Antonio were leaving the city.

"Packing? Leaving?" Alexandre asked. "Leaving San Antonio?"

"Of course, they're leaving. Are you blind, man? The only people still here are Mexicans, a few slaves, and some of Hays' men trying to roll their cannons out of town before the army gets here."

"The army?" Alexandre had an uneasy feeling. It began to occur to him that he had indeed seen fewer and fewer people about the plaza, by which he meant the Mavericks, the Vosses, the families of Texians, and a few of Hays' men. "What army?"

"General Vasquez's Mexican army. They're already this side of the Nueces and headed this way."

Alexandre almost fainted.

"The Nueces?" he sputtered. "What's a Mexican army doing on

this side of the Nueces?" He tried to stifle the note of panic in his squeaking voice.

"Who's to stop them?" Kinney retorted.

"Why ...." Alexandre suddenly understood what Maverick had meant, that Hays' rangers went no further than the Nueces. "The border is the Rio Grande," he finished. He knew that he sounded desperate.

"The Rio Grande?" Kinney laughed. "No one told Mexico it's the border."

"But President Lamar said...." Alexandre realized that he was on the verge of failing in another of Samuel Maverick's warnings, to tell no one his business. It didn't matter because Kinney didn't let him finish his sentence.

"Lamar? He's the one that gave the Rio Grande back to Mexico. Well, he gave it to Colonel Canales, who at the time was a Mexican officer stirring up a revolt against Mexico. Lamar told Canales he could have the land between the Rio Grande and the Nueces for his new country. Canales took it, then rebelled against his own rebellion. Mexico welcomed him back and kept the land." Kinney didn't notice the look of panic on Alexandre's face until he had told him the most dangerous fact. "So, General Vasquez's army is on this side of the Nueces and headed this way." Kinney finished his glass of corn and called for another.

"This way? To San Antonio? When?" He tried to stifle the sound of panic in his voice. If what Kinney was saying was true, the Rio Grande border with Mexico was a myth. Lamar had said it was safe to go to the Rio Grande; Houston had ordered him to spy on the Rio Grande without telling him it was deep inside Mexico. *Both of the bastards lied to me.*

Alexandre now understood why Houston wanted dispatches about Canales. *He was a traitor to Mexico, then a traitor to his own rebellion.* That's what Samuel Maverick had meant, Alexandre realized, when Sam had told him to leave and that Hays had other things to worry about. He had to flee immediately. "When will it arrive? General Vasquez' army?"

"Depends on the so-called Committee of Safety. If Hays defends the city, it'll take a few days. If Hays abandons the city, Vasquez'll be here tomorrow, maybe Saturday. And what with Hays rolling the cannons out of town and emptying the armory, I'd say he plans to abandon San Antonio to the Mexican army."

As Kinney's story of the impending invasion unfolded, Alexandre began to realize that everything he had reported in his dispatches was quite false. Vasquez' miserable force of a few hundred shoeless Mexicans in a small battalion in Laredo appeared to be seven thousand well-armed Mexican soldiers armed with cannons and cavalry deep inside Texas.

"Where are they?" he asked Kinney. "Exactly."

"I don't know. Hays sent a couple of scouts out toward the Nueces to look for them, but General Vasquez captured the scouts. That's why everybody's leaving town."

Alexandre's mind raced. It would only be a matter of time before Sam Houston figured out that his dispatches were complete fakes. The Matamoros dispatch was so obviously false that the minute Houston read it he would send someone to murder him. Alexandre estimated that it would take a day for a rider to take the Matamoros spy letter to the city of Austin and a day to get back.

He could leave on a moment's notice, with or without the wagon and horses.

"So, Mr. Kinney, take me with you." He had not told Kinney about Pennant and Alonzo. "I can have my wagon ready in ten minutes."

Kinney looked at Alexandre with a mild degree of amusement.

"Take you with me? Well, first, where do you propose I take you, my friend?" His voice had the certain sneer that suggested that Kinney considered Alexandre anything but a friend.

Alexandre said to Kinney's trading post, of course, near Corpus Christi Bay.

"Well, then, second, that's not such a good idea. There's almost as many Mexicans about to attack down there as there are up here. The navy's got a ship, the *Durango*, ready to invade at Paso Caballo, and Colonel Valera's got another army riding there direct from Matamoros, might already be in Goliad for all I know. This isn't the best time to go driving a wagon toward those parts."

Kinney gave him an uneasy feeling, as if he were being laughed at. He began to wonder if Kinney had smoked him out as a pretend spy.

"And the third reason, my friend," Kinney continued, "is that I'm not leaving San Antonio de Bexar. I'm a neutral and General Vasquez knows it."

"A neutral?"

"I'm no Texian," Kinney went on. "My ranch is not in Texas, my trading post is not in Texas, I don't claim to be a Texian. Everything I do is west of the Nueces. They say it's in Mexico, I don't argue with them. As far as I'm concerned, and as far as Mexico is concerned, I'm not an enemy. That's why they let me trade back and forth." Kinney laughed, snorted another mouthful of corn, and resumed. "And why would you run? You're no Texian either. For that matter, my friend, exactly what are you doing here?" Kinney emptied his cup and waved for the *señorita* to bring another. "You don't seem to have much business other than asking me about conditions here and conditions there. What do you actually do?"

Houston had worked out what Alexandre was to tell anyone who asked that very question. He reflected that it would work as well for a friend as a stranger. And, like most good lies, it had an element of truth.

"I am engaged on behalf of her majesty's government, sir, her majesty Queen Victoria." Alexandre paused and gathered his wits. "England, sir, which I tell you in compete confidence. May I count on your silence?" Kinney nodded that he was to be trusted; Alexandre continued. "In a word, the government of Mexico borrowed thirty-three million British pounds sterling to keep Mexico solvent after her separation from Spain." Kinney's eyes opened wide. "Her generosity was business-like. The loans were secured by land in what was then called Coahuila y Tejas." Kinney waited for the remainder of Alexandre's story. "My commission is to inspect and report to her banks the condition of those lands."

"Because the little queen wants either the money or the land, right?" Kinney answered. "Victoria. The little queen."

"Precisely. I'm to inspect the lands, survey them as best I can, and report my findings to her majesty's consulate."

It was a good story. If Alexandre was quizzed by the Mexicans, he had papers from the banking houses of Goldsmith and Barclay that described the loans and the land secured by them. If he was hard pressed by any Texians, he was to answer only that he had business on behalf of President Houston.

"Then why," Kinney asked again, "why do you want me to take you to my trading post? When the Mexican army comes, just show them your papers. They won't touch a hair on your head. The last thing Mexico wants is for England to come calling to settle its accounts. *Salud!*" Kinney raised his cup of corn, clinked it against Alexandre's own cup, and drank it off.

"*Salud!*" He tried to not choke on the corn whiskey or on the facts.

Fifteen minutes later, Alexandre was back in the adobe house on Soledad.

"Pennant," he called out. "Things are changing."

Pennant didn't answer, not immediately, and Alexandre feared that he might already have fled. Instead, a few moments later, Pennant walked in from a visit to the necessary out behind the house.

"Changing how? Thought we was headed to the Rio Grande."

Almost a month after he had made his devil's bargain, Alexandre found himself standing on the dirt floor of the adobe house, explaining to Pennant that the dispatch scheme had got out of hand.

"Things are changing, and we knew we couldn't stay in San Antonio forever. Well, forever is now. We've got to stop Alonzo before he turns the last dispatch over to a rider to deliver to Sam Houston."

"Why?" Pennant asked. He could tell from Alexandre's agitation that something worrisome was afoot.

"Because the letter tells Sam Houston that General Vasquez only has a few soldiers in Matamoros and Laredo and isn't equipped to invade Texas."

Pennant shook his head and blinked.

"That's the information you got from your, what do you call that man, your confidential agent? That's the information you got?"

"My confidential agent neglected to tell me until tonight that General Vasquez has seven thousand armed and trained soldiers with cannon and lancers already on this side of the Nueces River. When Hays sent his spies out to find General Vasquez, they were captured. Now Hays has told the women and children to flee the city and ordered the men to clear out the armory and retreat. In short, San Antonio is today in the hands of the Texians. Tomorrow it will be in the hands of the army of Mexico."

Pennant let this information sink in.

"If the dispatch that Alonzo has in his saddle bag reaches Houston, he'll know before he finishes reading it that we've been sending fake dispatches. You know what that means." Alexandre paused. "It means we're alive only as long as it takes Houston to find us."

"I know where he is," Pennant answered. "Alonzo. I know where he is."

"He's riding out to Mission Concepcion," Alexandre answered.

"Well, he's, let me say it this way: Alonzo's probably not riding along the river trail to Mission Concepcion, not exactly."

"I watched him cross the river," Alexandre answered. "Get your horse saddled. We've got to catch him."

"I think it'll be quicker just to walk," Pennant said.

"Walk?"

"If you'd watched Alonzo a little longer, you'd have probably seen him clear the cottonwood trees on the other side of the acequia dam, then double back to La Villita."

"I don't understand," Alexandre said, although he was beginning to. "Why double back to La Villita?"

La Villita was only a few hundred yards beyond the bar on Calaboza, near where Alexandre had found Alonzo and Pennant sitting on the riverbank. It also was where the Mexican population of San Antonio de Bexar lived.

"We might have some, uh, friends there, shall I say?" Pennant slowly drawled out his admission. "In La Villita. If you get my meaning."

San Antonio de Bexar was almost dark. The Maverick home in front of the adobe house was dark. The Gautier and Elliott homes on the other side of the plaza were dark. The cantina now was closed. It was at most a ten-minute walk to La Villita, which was not dark. The Mexican families who lived there seemed undisturbed by the impending arrival of General Vasquez. Pennant led Alexandre to a cluster of adobe huts on *Calle de la Presa*, where they found Alonzo's horse. Alonzo was standing in front of the Casillas adobe home, indifferent to having been caught by Alexandre.

"I thought it was better here," Alonzo explained. It was the longest sentence Alexandre had heard him speak.

An older man and woman came out of the adobe, followed by a younger and rather pretty woman dressed in a white cotton dress and scarf. They looked at Alexandre and Pennant standing in the rough street in front of their home. "This is my uncle, my aunt," Alonzo added. He did not introduce Maria Elena, who avoided looking directly at Pennant. "And my cousin. They took me in." He did not explain when it was that they had taken him in.

They all stood on *Calle de la Presa* and, by the evening's fading light, stared back across the San Antonio River, watching the last Texians of the San Antonio Committee of Safety ride past the crumbling walls of the Alamo, leaving San Antonio to its fate. Alonzo's aunt said something to Alexandre.

"She's asking if you'd like to have supper with us," Alonzo said. "It's pretty good. I helped cook it."

It occurred to Alexandre that he knew almost nothing about Alonzo or, for that matter, about Pennant. It also occurred to him that he was trapped.

"Yes," he said. "Yes, I would."

Dinner was simple, some rice, tortillas, chiles, black beans. Alexandre perched on a wobbly stool at the table with *Señor* and *Señora* Casillas, who smiled and gestured while they ate. Alonzo and Maria Elena ate standing, she fending off Pennant's over-friendly foot and his leers.

Alexandre thanked them, then found his way in the dark back to the adobe on Soledad Street, where he used a candle to burn the dispatch from Laredo and the three-sentence letter of his instructions as a spy. He kept the black hair.

Six hours later, General Vasquez halted his Mexican army at the banks of the San Pedro, where he waited until dawn to take possession of the city.

CHAPTER EIGHT

Alexandre was awakened by the pounding of a musket stock on the wooden door of the adobe house on Soledad Street. When a second pounding threatened to cave the door in he opened his eyes to a vague gray morning light cast through the wooden shutters, the cold air of a March morning that chilled him through his rough wool bedcover. He jumped off the cot and pulled on his pants as the door burst open, two Mexican foot soldiers barging in through the doorway.

"Todo el mundo fuera. ¡A la plaza, ahora!" They waved their guns in his direction and glanced around the room. Pennant and Alonzo were not there. *"¡Fuera de!"*

It was not difficult to sort out that the soldiers wanted him to go to the plaza. When he arrived, he found a hundred or more Mexicans and a few hurriedly dressed Anglos milling around the open space that separated the council house from San Fernando Cathedral. A few Mexican foot soldiers, most barefooted, milled around the edges of the crowd, waving their muskets and calling for the crowd to hurry. Alexandre wandered into the throng and waited. After a few minutes, the soldiers on the east side of the plaza began to nudge the crowd westward, around the cathedral, and toward the ditch of San Pedro creek. There, in the dim and chill morning light, mounted on a tired-looking horse, was the conqueror of San Antonio.

General Vasquez raised his sword in a salute, barked a command, and his army commenced a slow march into the city. He smiled, waved, nodded with favor at two or three officers who rode alongside, and the army waded across the San Pedro behind him. With the help of a dozen sergeants and the foot soldiers who had forced the citizens of San Antonio out to meet him in the first place, General Vasquez led the Mexican army to the plaza. A flag detail marched to the pole in the center of the plaza, attached a Mexican flag to the lanyard, and hoisted it up to fly over the conquered city. Vasquez lifted his sword to salute the flag, the officers alongside him saluted the flag and, with the encouragement of their lieutenants and sergeants, the miserable army of only seven hundred, not seven thousand, tired Mexican soldiers called out a feeble cheer in the dank morning air. The crowd, prodded to do the same, uttered a few unenthusiastic hurrahs and waited patiently to see what was required of them.

For the next hour, General Vasquez issued *pronunciamentos.*

"I hereby proclaim in the name of the Republic of Mexico and by its authority, vested in me, that the laws of the Republic of Mexico are the laws of this place. No law of the rebel army or its leaders shall be given any effect whatever."

"Hurrah."

"I further proclaim that it is the duty of each of you to reaffirm your allegiance to the Republic of Mexico."

"Hurrah."

"Which you will do by signing a pledge. You will be instructed when the pledges are ready for you to sign."

The hurrah was a little less enthusiastic.

"And to take up arms against the rebel army and its leaders when called on to do so."

It wasn't clear from that *pronunciamento* whether a hurrah was required. A feeble voice called out "*si*" here and there, but mostly the crowd was silent to the idea of shooting the Texians.

Vasquez also called on everyone to listen to him read a letter from Mayor Seguin, who had quit the city a week earlier, in which Seguin supposedly announced that he had switched his loyalty to Santa Anna. Vasquez finally announced that the members of the treasonous expedition that Lamar and the Texian rebels had sent against Santa Fe the year before were now guests of the Republic of Mexico.

"It is my duty and, as a soldier, a military honor to inform you, the inhabitants of San Antonio de Bexar, that these rebels who went to Santa Fe are being treated with every courtesy," Vasquez announced. "If there are among you any of their families, take comfort that these men are safe and in good health."

Alexandre tried to not look conspicuous while studying the motley collection of tattered Mexican army uniforms and scrawny horses, surprised at how few soldiers of such a sad military quality were all that had been needed to run the Texians out of the most holy city of the Lone Star republic. He looked around for Pennant and Alonzo in the crowd. He instead saw Kinney, who walked up alongside him and nudged him on the arm.

"What is Vasquez saying?" he asked Kinney.

"He says the San Antonio soldiers who went on the Santa Fe expedition are now guests of Santa Anna. Go get dressed," Kinney said.

"The San Antonio soldiers who went to Santa Fe?" Alexandre interrupted. He struggled with his memory, something that Sam Houston had said about President Lamar sending men to Santa Fe, but he couldn't remember what. It had not seemed important at the time. "Who are they?"

Kinney looked at him with surprise.

"You really were in England for a long time. They were about three or four hundred men that Mirabeau Lamar sent the long way around to Santa Fe to talk the city into joining Texas. They all disappeared last summer. Looks like Santa Anna found them, probably marched them down the Rio Grande to jail in Mexico City. Go back to your house and put on your best clothes. Hurry."

"Why?"

"You're going to meet the general. Wash your face. Put on your boots. Go." Kinney led Alexandre to the Soledad Street side of the plaza, nodded at one of the hungry foot soldiers who allowed him to pass through the crowd. "Hurry."

Pennant was waiting inside the adobe.

"We've got to get out of here," was all that Pennant said. "Soon as it's dark, we got to go."

"Go?" Alexandre answered. "For as long as you were out at the missions, all you wanted was to be in San Antonio. Now you insisted we go. Why? We're in no danger."

"Let's just say maybe it's time to take up spying somewheres else. Maybe even go back to New Orleans, or Galveston. Some say the Indian territory's nice. Why're you putting on your finery?"

"Where's Alonzo?" Alexandre asked, rifling through the portmanteau in search of a linen shirt and his best breeches. "And what are you doing to your face?"

Alonzo was back in La Villita, where he had gone as fast as he could to escape the plaza during Vasquez's interminable *pronunciamentos*. As for Pennant, he was scraping off his mustache and rubbing red San Antonio river mud into his hair.

"What are you doing? What's going on?" Alexandre demanded.

Pennant ignored him, shaving and making himself dirty at the same time.

"Stop!" Alexandre took Pennant by the shoulders, turned him around, and looked his doubtful subordinate in the face. Pennant's eyes darted rapidly around the room, looking at the door, at the window shutter, into the back room. "Why are you disguising yourself?"

"Maybe," Pennant croaked out, "they's some men out there we might not want looking too careful at us. Like I said, it's time to go."

"What men?" Alexandre asked. "Who?"

"Tell you later. Meet you at La Villita. Don't tell anyone you know us."

And with that, Pennant bolted out the door, then slinked away. Alexandre gave up any hope of understanding either Pennant or Alonzo, or of predicting what they were likely to do next. He finished dressing, then found in the leather bag his fake passport and letters of commission and introduction. Ten minutes later, he was back in the plaza, where General Vasquez was being served breakfast beneath a tent awning.

"General Vasquez? Permit me to have the pleasure to introduce you to Mr. Alexandre LaBranche. He is not a Texian." Kinney made a very modest bow to the general; the general nodded back at him. "Mr. LaBranche, I introduce to you General Rafael Vasquez, commander of the Presidio of the Rio Grande and of all forces of the armies of Mexico for the departments of Coahuila y Tejas.

Alexandre followed Kinney's lead with a very slight bow. Vasquez smiled broadly and nodded at the other Mexican officer seated beside him under the awning. Kinney continued.

"General? Permit me also to say that *Señor* LaBranche is more than not a Texian. He is here on behalf of her majesty Queen Victoria of England and…. Who are the banks, LaBranche?"

"My direct employers, sir, are the banking houses of Goldsmith and Barclay. Of London."

"Those two banks," Kinney continued, "of London. England." Kinney saw a mild look of confusion or, perhaps, indifference pass over Vasquez's face. One of the officers seated next to Vasquez whispered in the general's ear; Vasquez's face brightened considerably, then changed again to a look of uncertainty. "Perhaps if Mr. LaBranche explained the details of his commission, General…," Kinney trailed off. Vasquez told him to do so.

"I am commissioned to look over various lands in *Coahuila y Tejas*," Alexandre began. He was not a great liar, but as his story flowed, the lie came more easily. "Goldsmith and Barclay, bankers to the queen, have an interest in certain of those lands." Kinney began to translate the lie into Spanish. Vasquez continued to look uncertain. The officer next to him began to show a look of interest. Alexandre continued. "I am not a banker, sir, so I do not know the technicalities of the transactions, but my understanding is that the government of her majesty the queen is a great friend of yourself and of the Republic of Mexico." Vasquez looked puzzled; his fellow officer turned away with a smile at the unexpected diplomatic exaggeration. "And, as such a great friend, provided some thirty-three millions of English pounds sterling, of English money, in aid of the Republic of Mexico. During her struggles with the King of Spain."

"And during her struggles with the rebel Texians," Kinney added.

Vasquez again looked to his officer for an explanation. He got one.

"Loans."

"Ah, loans. Well," Vasquez said, holding his hands upward and out as if Alexandre had come to collect from the wrong person. "And you are here why, *señor*?"

"My commission," Alexandre continued, "is to report to her majesty, and to Goldsmith and Barclay, on the condition of the security of the loans." He waited. Kinney translated. Vasquez did not understand. His fellow officer also did not understand, not precisely. "I am informed that your honorable Republic borrowed the money and, for security, pledged some thousands of hectares of lands." Kinney translated. Vasquez's companion began to understand.

"What lands?"

Alexandre was prepared. He withdrew the forged copy of the description of lands that Rusk and Henderson had provided in anticipation of an occasion such as this.

"The documents I am provided describe lands west of ninety-seven degrees west and south of thirty degrees north, sir."

"Where are those, *señor*?"

"Ninety-seven degrees west of London is the area bounded by Corpus Christi Bay and the Gulf of Mexico, in the province of Tejas. Thirty degrees north of the equator is at the confluence of the

Guadalupe and Sabinal Rivers. I put that to be some thirty leagues northwest of this very plaza."

Vasquez consulted his officer, then answered.

"I see. Of course, a friend of the Queen of England is a friend of Mexico. We welcome you." He asked his officer another question. "And what do you propose to do, this inspection of lands?"

Alexandre was somewhat less comfortable with this question. He had no experience in banking, loans, or the terms of any agreement whatsoever between the queen of England and Mexico. General Vasquez seemed reasonably compliant; Vasquez's aide seemed suspicious.

"I am instructed to look at the land for myself and report on its condition, in light of the recent difficulties. The rebellion." Vasquez nodded. Alexandre continued. "Is the land occupied, and who occupies it? Is it rich land or poor land? Ranches? Towns? Villages? Farms? Does it produce anything? And, of course, where exactly those things are located."

Vasquez grew tired of Kinney's friend.

"Welcome to Mexico, *señor*. Tell me again your name?"

"LaBranche, General. Alexandre LaBranche."

"We will talk more, I am sure, but there are many things I must do. Good day."

"Good day, sir."

Alexandre stiffened and nodded in a civilian salute, then began to back away.

"A word, *señor*?" Alexandre turned back to see that the officer seated next to General Vasquez was speaking to him. "Colonel Valera has taken Goliad and Refugio." He smiled knowingly at Alexandre. "I thought that you might be pleased to learn that. *Bien hecho, señor*. Well done."

Alexandre gasped. The officer mistook it for an expression of pleasure and continued.

"Tell me, *señor*. Are you working alone in your inspections? For the queen?" Another knowing smile.

"I have my assistants, sir."

"Do you? Well, you must have help, of course. We speak again soon." And with that, the officer waved him away.

————

For all that day and the following, Alexandre did his best to be invisible. Pennant stayed in hiding, but Alonzo came to the adobe house twice, draped in a serape and sombrero and quite dirty. He reported that he had thought it best to burn the Laredo dispatch instead of delivering it.

"And the army is *saquendo* the Texian houses in San Antonio," he said. "Just what is inside. The food and furniture. That is all."

Alexandre already knew that General Vasquez was sacking the city; two soldiers had barged into the adobe earlier in the day but left when they recognized Alexandre as the gentleman they had seen talking with the general. He had ventured over to the Maverick house and found Mexican soldiers loading the family's table and cabinets onto a wagon. The beds, mantelpiece, and linens were already gone. The pantry was bare, and the smokehouse was empty. He found more wagons loaded with the same general plunder from all the houses owned by Texians, from the mercantile stores on the plaza, and from the remains of the armory.

"And where is Pennant? "Alexandre asked. "He said to meet him in La Villita?"

"He's there," Alonzo added. "The soldiers *no estan saquendo* La Villita. Just the Texian houses."

Toward the end of that day, he ventured to La Villita himself. The Casillas family was not at home, but Pennant was hiding inside, sitting on the floor away from the window. When Alexandre found him, Pennant retreated into the more cowardly version of himself, hunched over, face down, knees drawn up. Alexandre asked why he was hiding.

"Why are you two hiding?" Alexandre demanded. "And who is it you might not want looking too close at you? One of the Mexican soldiers?"

Pennant's swagger was gone; the only thing that remained was the look on his face that Alexandre had come to recognize as a prelude to lying. Pennant pulled a sombrero down over his face and turned away.

"I think it best you tell me what you're hiding. Kinney, my confidential source, as you call him, has seen you and Alonzo with me enough to know you're working for me. What are you hiding?"

Pennant thought carefully before answering, another sign that what he was about to say would have a reduced element of truth to it.

"It was like this. I might have been on a Mexican barky, the *Durango*. I wasn't pressed, you know? Ordinary crew, signed on for two or three voyages. I wasn't bound to the manifest, you know?"

Pennant had claimed status as an American seaman and listed Alonzo as his helper.

"I might have signed Alonzo on as my mate. So they wouldn't take him for a Mexican in case we got caught up in something. He's just an Indian, you know, Lipan, something like that."

The *Durango* did get caught up in something. After two voyages between Louisiana and Veracruz, it had anchored off Laguna Madre, at the mouth of the Rio Grande, where it boarded several hundred Mexican soldiers, Tercerlo muskets, gunpowder, some light field pieces, and horses.

"That's when they pressed us, Alonzo and me. We wasn't soldiers, we was crew, just get the ship here to there, you know? But when the *Durango* called in at the Laguna Madre to take on an army of Mexican soldiers, we was shifted to soldiering, Alonzo and me. Then it wasn't long after them soldiers was aboard we heard they was going to start up a little war, starting at Paso Caballo. Would've done it, too, but some Texian ship intercepted the *Durango*. Then a US of A barky come along and broke it up. We was all escorted to New Orleans."

"And someone from the *Durango* is here in San Antonio?" Alexandre asked.

"Maybe. Can't be sure. No need to get up close and personal, you know?" Pennant whispered.

"Because you jumped ship in New Orleans, is that it? You're a deserter. You're both deserters." Alexandre was not surprised, although he was alarmed by the possibility that he was harboring two gallows-birds.

"No, we wasn't deserters." Pennant paused; Alexandre waited. "What happened in New Orleans was like this. The *Durango* was put up in prize court and the crew and soldiers was locked up. Well, after a while, the prize judges let us all out on parole, give us the liberty of the city, close on to two hundred of us. Alonzo and I didn't want no part of that war business, so we accepted what the prize judge said, that we had the liberty of the city, proper like. We figured that liberty meant we didn't have to stay in the jail or go back to the *Durango* either one. I mean, the jailers said we was let go. We was abiding the law of the country that let us go."

"So, you didn't go back to the *Durango*. Now here, in San Antonio, you're afraid that someone off the *Durango* will recognize you?" Alexandre asked.

"Well, it's more like this. There might have been three others of 'em off the *Durango* that didn't go back to the ship neither. They give the slip to the Americans and set out for Texas, you know?" Pennant could see that Alexandre did not know; he was tempted to not tell everything. On the other hand, Pennant also could see that the Mexican army allowed Alexandre to come and go freely, so this was no time to get crossways with the man who could turn him in. "In a word, we might of borrowed their horses. Two of them. And come to Texas."

Alexandre took a few minutes to consider what he had heard: Pennant was a semi-literate, sea-going crook while Alonzo likely was part Indian, part Mexican, hiding behind an aversion to talking. They had fled New Orleans on stolen horses. That would explain how they arrived at Logan's Ferry on horseback and why they robbed him.

"Then, who did you see here in San Antonio, Pennant? Who could recognize you?"

"It could be," Pennant replied, "that maybe that officer you was talking to, he might know who we was."

"General Vasquez? He was on the *Durango*?" Alexandre was doubtful; no general would recognize his lowliest, commonest-looking soldiers in a crowd. That seemed farfetched, even for Pennant.

"Never saw the general before. It was that other one you was talking to," Pennant trembled. "The one you and Houston calls a traitor." He paused and caught his breath. "Colonel Canales."

Alexandre gulped without knowing why. He had met the traitor Canales, without knowing so. He had spoken with him, told him a little of his business and, while Canales was not especially friendly, he had not been sinister in the way Alexandre had expected a notorious traitor to be. On the other hand, Pennant was clearly frightened. Alexandre took a deep breath and plowed onward.

"Are you telling me that Colonel Canales would recognize you because he was on the *Durango* in New Orleans?"

Pennant hunched over until his face touched his knees.

"Nope. It's because he was the one what pressed Alonzo and me into the army down at Laguna Madre. Told the skipper to line up his crew and pick some men, said he needed more soldiers. The skipper give us up to Canales, right then and there on the mole where we was rowin' the soldiers out to the ship. Canales looked me and Alonzo right in the eye and said we was soldiers now." Pennant shuddered. "He's a man with a fierce eye, you know?"

Alexandre understood the anxiety, but he also doubted that a colonel would be any more likely to recognize common soldiers than would General Vasquez.

"Look, there were several hundred of you on the ship. There are seven hundred foot soldiers here in San Antonio. There is no reason to think he would remember either of you at all, much less recognize you."

Pennant was not relieved by the logic of it.

"Maybe they's a bit more to the story," he admitted. He paused for a very long time, until Alexandre kicked his foot, then continued. "It might be the three of 'em off the *Durango* that rode off on the horses we borrowed was not exactly soldiers. It might be they was more like agents, you could say."

"Agents?" For a fleeting moment Alexandre thought of his uncle Alcee, the custom agent, of the cotton and sugar factoring companies on the New Orleans wharfs. Agents.

"Spies," Pennant explained. "Agents. And when everyone else was sent back to the ship, the agents set out for Texas. To spy for Canales, you know?"

Spies? Alexandre's mind reeled with images of men in shadows, hidden pistols, poisons, invisible letters written in code. It then occurred to him that this was too imaginative; two of the agents, the spies, were so inept as to be robbed of their horses by Pennant and Alonzo. He then remembered that he was himself so inept as to be robbed by Pennant and Alonzo.

"You stole the horses from the spies that Colonel Canales had sent to Texas to spy for Mexico?" Alexandre felt his stomach turn over.

"Well, we relieved two of 'em of their horses so they just set out back to the ship. And I won't say those two were the main spies. It was the third one who seemed to be the main spy. Dressed fancy, real American looking fellow, rode a fine horse. He was long gone by the time we got clear of New Orleans. Then we thought he was you when we saw you get on the ferry. You're a dead ringer for the main spy."

"Me?" Alexandre asked. "Why would he...." He then remembered Canales giving him a knowing look when he said that Goliad and Refugio had fallen, and he understood: Canales had mistaken Alexandre to be his main spy. Alexandre looked around the Casillas' kitchen for a club, a hammer, a pistol, anything, to kill Pennant and put himself out of misery as well. He didn't find anything.

"What happened to the third agent?" Alexandre asked, his stomach rolling over again.

"Well, he might of got himself killed."

Alexandre looked incredulous; Pennant continued.

"You see, down there by the ferry landing, right after we crossed over into Texas, there was someone hiding there in the trees. This other fellow, the real spy, well, he come along on his horse, and we figured someone was about to get robbed, so Alonzo and I lit out, got clean away. That's when we found you riding along on your wagon." Pennant stopped and composed himself. "Remember hearing those shots back toward the river? Ain't no doubt those shots was him getting himself killed, the main spy. It was like I said, if a man didn't know better, he could mistake you for him. You're a dead ringer."

Alexandre suddenly understood why Houston was ready to hang him, to hang all three of them.

"Houston believes I'm the third spy, a Mexican spy. And you and Alonzo are the other two! He was going to hang you, and I saved your lives."

"Well, he was going to hang you, too. Don't be all high and mighty about it. You're the one agreed to be a spy for him."

"That's what you've done to me!" Alexandre shouted. "I am not a spy. I am a surveyor. All I wanted was to conduct my survey and map the Rio Grande and earn my reward. That is my purpose in life, to explore and survey and map." Alexandre almost was hysterical by this point. "I don't want to be a spy, not for Sam Houston, not for Mexico. And not for—who?"

"Colonel Canales. And what do you think going up and down the Rio Grande making maps is if it ain't spying? Anyways, maybe it's best Colonel Canales doesn't figure out who we are, Alonzo and me. If he catches us, well, he'll probably figure out sooner or later that you ain't his third spy either. You probably shouldn't tell him yourself neither."

Pennant refused to say any more. He pulled his serape further down over his shoulders and hid under the enormous sombrero.

Alexandre left La Villita, crossed over the river at the dam and skirted the Alamo, crossed the river again, and crept from yard to yard on the west side of the plaza. It made no difference; when he got back to the adobe on Soledad, a Mexican soldier was waiting for him.

"Pachanga. En la plaza." The soldier indicated the direction of the main plaza and repeated himself. *"Pachanga. Ahorita."* Not until he bent his elbow and mimicked drinking, then dancing, did Alexandre understand he was being summoned to a fiesta.

The *pachanga* was in the council house, facing the cathedral. Buglers and drummers had been conscripted from among the foot soldiers to play brassy notes that pierced the dark San Antonio evening, the sound bouncing off the stone walls of the council house. General Vasquez and several other officers had commandeered most of San Antonio's *señoritas,* who were being pushed around the room by young lieutenants whose dancing skills appeared to have been learned on the march. Alexandre recognized several of the other girls as well, and some of their mothers. Kinney appeared with a cup of pulque.

"Colonel Canales has been asking for you," Kinney shouted over the music. A guitar had materialized in one corner, adding to the din.

"Do you know why?" Alexandre darted glances around the room. Smoke filled the air, lanterns swung on their hooks, red and green skirts flashed by. He could barely hear Kinney's shouted comments.

"He wants you because he wants you. A word of advice, my friend. If General Vasquez wants you, he probably wants you to tell him that the Queen of England is his friend. If Colonel Canales wants you, he probably wants you to tell him everything you know. I suggest you tell him."

"Why would he want me to tell him what I know?"

"Don't be stupid. You've been in Nacogdoches. You've been in Bastrop. You've been in Austin. If Canales knows that, he will want to know what you saw there." Kinney saw that Alexandre was about to reply and stopped him. "And he thinks you've been to Goliad. And Refugio."

"Why would he think that?"

Kinney did not have a chance to answer; Canales himself swung and twirled a teenaged Mexican girl around the floor and to a halt directly in front of Alexandre. A nod of his head was all that was needed for the girl to bow and back away; a second nod of his head was all that was needed for Kinney and Alexandre to understand that Canales had more than dancing on his mind.

"*Señor* LaBranche, a question," Canales said.

"Yes, sir." Alexandre did not want to answer any questions.

"This work you do, looking at Mexican lands. You have described a very great deal of land to be inspected. For the Queen of England."

"Yes, sir," Alexandre replied. The pulque tasted sour in his mouth and he began to breathe heavily. Sweat soaked his linen shirt. It was clear that Kinney had said something to Canales about Alexandre's questions concerning Goliad and Refugio and, he feared, about Matamoros and Laredo as well. He began to feel dizzy.

"It is very loud in here, *señor*. Let us go outside." Canales turned and walked out of the pachanga and across the plaza. Alexandre followed. It was quieter there, and dark. People walked around the plaza, not a paseo, just soldiers and local Mexicans going to the *pachanga*, no Texians. Canales ignored them. When he reached the steps of the cathedral, he turned to face Alexandre and resumed.

"I am very interested in this work you are doing, *señor*. Studying our land."

Canales' voice had developed a tone that reminded Alexandre of his meeting with Sam Houston, when Houston told him that he was indeed going to map the Rio Grande, but as a spy. Canales continued.

"How did you find the lands between Goliad and Refugio? Did you find, what did you say to General Vasquez, the condition of the land there, some interesting condition of the land? Yes? Is the land rich or is it poor? What will you report to the queen?"

Alexandre mumbled some complicated words about pasture

lands, ranchos, farms, phrases a man might use to tell a bank what
its security might be.

Canales looked Alexandre directly in the eye and continued. "Ah,
my friend, you said you were sent here to do your inspecting in
light of, how do you call it, 'recent difficulties?' 'The rebellion?' So,
you tell the queen if the land is occupied and who occupies it, no?"

Alexandre was breathing heavily and wanted to throw up. He
had not known when to stop talking; now he did not know how to
start talking.

"Armies? Rebels?" Canales asked.

"I saw no armies." Alexandre was learning that lying was easier
when it involved an element of truth. "I will write that it is farmers,
colonel, some small ranch holdings."

"Well," Canales continued, "from the Bay of Corpus Christi to
the Sabinal is a very great deal of land to inspect. Where do you
inspect first? For your friend the queen?"

Alexandre suddenly had the sense that someone was watching
him, staring at him in the dark, someone other than Canales. He
took a breath of the cool evening air, looked toward the corners of
the cathedral, at the shops that lined the plaza, the flagpole. There
were only Mexican soldiers milling around in the night air. He
found no one looking at him.

"I have provisioned, Colonel, to go to the Nueces." Alexandre
didn't know why he said it or even if it was safe to have said it. *Why
would I choose to inspect the Nueces?* he wondered. Canales and every
man in Vasquez' army would know the Nueces from having crossed
it so many times in the wars with Texas, better than even Jack C.
Hays and his rangers. He believed that Canales was looking into his
soul and finding him to be a liar.

"It is a very long river," Canales replied. "You will have the
opportunity to consider the condition of very much land. It goes
into many of the lands between the Bay of Corpus Christi and the
Sabinal."

Alexandre bowed for want of anything to say.

"With just two men." Canales turned his fierce eye to look

directly into Alexandre's clouding eyes. "Tell me, are your helpers very skilled? Do they help your inspecting?"

Alexandre paused. It was a sensible question; it was a great deal of territory to inspect.

"Just laboring men, sir. They help me with the ordinary tasks."

Canales said that he was satisfied with the answer; Alexandre felt in his bones that Canales was not satisfied.

"I am a military man, Señor LaBranche. I can look at a map and see the land. When I imagine such a map of the land you inspect, I imagine a line from the Gulf of Mexico to San Antonio de Bexar and beyond to the Sabinal. But I do not see a boundary. Do you understand? So I ask, where is the boundary of these lands that interest you? From the Bay of Corpus Christi, do the lands go south beyond the Nueces? How far? And from the Sabinal River, do the lands go west to the Guadalupe Mountains? Or north, or where? I should like to know so that I can see it in my own head, as on a map."

Alexandre tried to collect his thoughts. Sam Houston's fake documents described the land in longitudes and latitudes. The maps that Mirabeau Lamar had given him for his survey of the boundaries of Texas followed the Rio Grande. The fake dispatches he had sent to Sam Houston had named Mexican cities, Matamoros, Laredo, Reinosa. What was the southern boundary of his falsified authority?

"Two leagues to the south of the Rio Grande, sir. It is a very large area of land. Perhaps you know the territory." Alexandre tried to remember the other thing about Canales that Kinney had told him, why Canales was a traitor. The pulque throbbed in his head. His eyes were dry and becoming painful to hold open. "Perhaps, Colonel, you have some advice for me to consider about the land I am to inspect."

"I do know those lands, but at this moment I cannot tell you all that you would require for your report to our good friend, the Queen of England. You must learn very much about the land of the Nueces River to the Rio Bravo, the Rio Grande. What is its condition, is that what you said to General Vasquez? Is it rich or poor? Farm or village? Who exactly occupies this land?" His eyes bored into Alexandre. "*Señor* LaBranche, I should like to know those same things myself that the Queen of England would like to know. As long as you are learning them anyway."

Canales had made his point. He led Alexandre back into the Council House. It was filled with cigar smoke. The guitar thrummed. The bugle joined in, punctuating a *corrido* with piercing notes in the small, crowded room. The walls began to swirl around Alexandre's head. Canales signaled to a private to bring more pulque. Alexandre tried to smile and to nod agreeably, but without agreeing. Canales took this as a sign.

"Do you know why we celebrate the *pachanga* today, *Señor* LaBranche? It is March 6. Do you know it?"

"I do not know it, sir," Alexandre answered. For once, he was telling the truth.

"A very great day, *Señor* LaBranche. Six years ago this day, our army defeated the rebel Texians not one mile from this plaza. At the mission across the river, el Alamo. San Antonio de Bexar is not a city of Texian rebels. It is a city of Mexico. El Alamo is not a place of honor for the rebels, *Señor* LaBranche; it is a place of honor for us. It once was a mission, but in our valiant struggle against Spain, it was a fortress named after my countrymen, mis compadres, soldiers from the town of *Alamo del Parral de Coahuila*. The Texian rebels in the Alamo was an insult to us, to Mexico, *Señor* LaBranche. To me, personally, for the rebels to claim the Alamo is an insult. It is not a shrine to the Texians, it is a place of their shame and our pride. So, we exterminated them, like rats. This day, six years ago today. And in some weeks more, we celebrate the defeat of the rebels in Goliad. They were cowards, at Goliad. They stood up to be shot like cowards. That is why the pachanga. Are you alright *Señor* LaBranche?"

Alexandre was not alright. He had no experience with pulque and, if Canales' probing of his intentions was not enough to make him sick, the pulque was. The floor moved, the walls moved, the smoke and bugle and banging of drums behind the swirl of colored skirts and blue and red army uniforms, all moved. Canales took Alexandre by the arms and helped Kinney get him to a chair.

"The drink, sir," Alexandre muttered. "The ...."

"You are a man, *Señor* Alexandre," Canales laughed. "I never met an Anglo who could take pulque. You are the first! Bravo."

Kenny stood by as Canales saluted Alexandre, then backed away. The last thing that Alexandre heard was Canales' farewell:

"Good evening, *Señor* LaBranche," he said. "I look forward to your next report. Considerate *terram qualis sit.*"

Then there was an explosion.

CHAPTER NINE

The pounding in his head emerged during a nightmare in which Alexandre's father glared at him across the table in the plantation office.

"You are nothing," his father repeated. His father's voice seemed far away, like the sound of his childhood priest reciting the paternoster in a tired and toneless voice. "You have no purpose. You are a failure." Alexandre tried to shout that he had a plan, but he could not remember what his plan was. He tried to pry his eyes apart to see if he had left his plan on the rickety wooden table where Mrs. Maverick's slave set out his bread and coffee in the mornings. He thought he saw her, but it was very dark in the room, much too early for coffee, so it could not be Mrs. Maverick's slave. It was instead Noeme, going through his papers, and he wanted badly to stop the dream and tell Noeme to flee. The pounding on his pulque-dulled temples was louder, more insistent, and his father's shouting came through as *"Despierta se, hora de levantarse."* The command needed no translation; he did pull his eyes open.

Instead of Noeme, there were two Mexican soldiers prodding at him to get off the bed. He had a blurred memory of passing out at the *pachanga,* of an explosion, and wondered how he had got to his bed at all. A candle was lit. The soldiers rummaged through Alexandre's things, stuffing his clothes and boots into the portmanteau, wadding his papers into stacks and jamming them into his bound box. From time to time, one of them motioned with his musket to hurry. They soon carried everything he owned out of the adobe house. Within minutes of his last visions of his father and of Noeme, Alexandre found himself shivering in the cold March air in the stable yard behind the Maverick home, his leather bag slung over his shoulder.

Pennant and Alonzo also were shivering in the stable yard, but with their arms bound by ropes, which, in turn, were held by other Mexican soldiers. The barest light of a March dawn peeked through the iron-grey sky, revealing that during the night Alexandre's wagon, their three horses, saddles, and rigging had been brought out of the stables.

"What is happening?" he hissed to Pennant.

"They took us," Pennant wailed. "They come and took us. I think they're gonna shoot us." Pennant sputtered that he and Alonzo had been captured in their sleep and dragged across town in the dark. He had lost his sombrero but still was draped in a worn serape. His beard was as ragged and his face as dirty as the day before, but he was even more frightened than when Alexandre had left him at La Villita. "You got to help us."

The noise from the plaza was enough for Alexandre to sense that they were not the only ones being knocked out of bed by General Vasquez's troops. The soldiers put the single tree and traces together to hitch the wagon for travel, then saddled Pennant and Alonzo's horses. They loaded the provisions that Alexandre had bought from Mr. Twohig and added Alexandre's bound box, then the portmanteau. Alexandre hoisted up his transit and chains, his siting flags, and, still holding his leather bag, climbed onto the wagon's buckboard seat.

A lieutenant came forward on horseback, looked Alexandre and his men over, and saluted.

"*Sigame, señor,*" he said. He indicated that Alexandre was to fall in line. He led them away from the adobe on Salado and into the crowded plaza.

The entire city of San Antonio appeared to be in motion. General Vasquez's troops were in the process of taking all the wagons and horses in San Antonio and staging them in the plaza. They had little difficulty in doing so since most of the wagons and horses had disappeared when the Texians had fled before Vasquez entered the city. There were few Anglos left in town and, from the best Alexandre could see, none of them had been brought to the plaza.

He saw Kinney's wagon. It had been pulled to the front of John Twohig's store and was piled high with merchandise that Alexandre had seen inside the store only a few days before. Two soldiers were picking their way out of the store and hoisting crates of tools and fabrics onto the wagon bed. While Alexandre watched, Kinney came out of the store, climbed onto the wagon, and urged his horses to lead the wagon around and back toward the river road. Kinney disappeared from view.

Alexandre followed the lieutenant. He steered the wagon toward the cathedral, then around it to the San Pedro, where he turned to see what had become of Pennant and Alonzo. Still bound by ropes, they were being led away in the custody of a troop of Mexican foot soldiers. They rode into the frontier.

It was clear that all of Vasquez's troops were on the move. Horses, undoubtedly ridden by General Vasquez himself and, of course, by Colonel Canales and the other field officers, led the way into the early morning light. The Mexican flag was paraded far in front while ragged columns of scrawny foot soldiers followed across the San Pedro and on to the *camino real* and the prairie beyond the city's edge. The lieutenant rode slowly alongside Alexandre's wagon, directing him to stay in front of him and to join the column that was abandoning San Antonio after only two days of military occupation.

Alexandre tried to make himself understood; he asked with his

arms, with words, with slow, loud speech, where they were going.
The lieutenant turned to answer and said one word only:

"Mexico."

The pulque in Alexandre's system worked its way up his gullet in
search of breakfast, found none, and punished him for having
starved it. As the wagon pounded along, Alexandre's head pounded,
and his tongue began to thicken. His eyes swelled in their sockets.
His nose inhaled a revolting aroma of mule. Alone, not even able to
speak with the lieutenant who guarded him, he began to think.

How did Colonel Canales know that I've been in Refugio and Goliad?
he wondered. He suspected Kinney had told Canales as much, but
Kinney himself knew that the extent of Alexandre's familiarity with
Texas frontier towns was the content of the rumors that he, Kinney,
had himself given to Alexandre. The only others who might have
told Canales were Alonzo and Pennant; Pennant, at least, seemed far
too frightened of Canales to have spoken with the traitor and, again,
both he and Alonzo knew that Alexandre had never been within a
hundred miles of those towns. *And what does he think I was doing
there?* A troubling thought began to form in Alexandre's dulled
mind, that Canales believed him to be spying for Mexico.

The procession followed the *camino real* to the Medina River. It
was a pitiful parade. At its head were the officers on horseback, then
the cavalry and outriding scouts, then the junior officers goading
the foot soldiers to keep moving. There were a dozen Mexican
families who had decided to leave San Antonio rather than face the
revenge that the town's Anglos would wreak on them when they
returned and found General Vasquez gone. A hundred mules,
packed with the city's spoils, followed behind them.

Every soldier had draped himself with something looted from
San Antonio, his portion of the lace, the table linens, blankets, all
the goods that could be stolen from thirty households. The soldiers
walked, hardly marched, alongside the wagons and mules, keeping
them in line and, Alexandre realized, keeping him, Alonzo, and
Pennant cocooned inside the caravan. There would be no quick
dash to freedom, no furtive driving away in the middle of a night.

The lieutenant aimed his sword toward the distant hills that rose west of the *camino real*. There, at least a half mile away, almost invisible on the crest of a ridge, were two dozen half-naked men gazing back at them. It was impossible to make out whether they carried weapons or, as Alexandre assumed, hatchets and spears. They didn't move, neither toward the Mexican army nor back into the hills.

"Indios," the lieutenant said. *"Comanche."* He motioned with his hands and arms as if an Indian was removing his scalp and laughed.

Alexandre considered the half-naked men on the ridge and remembered Rusk's conjecture that such warriors had captured and murdered three hundred men of Lamar's Santa Fe expedition. *Sam Houston should have asked General Vasquez what happened to them. Vasquez was bold indeed with his pronunciamentos to the people of San Antonio that the Santa Fe men were guests of Santa Anna.*

He smiled with remorse that he, too, had become a guest of Santa Anna. He looked back at the Comanche scouts gazing down at them.

Vasquez's army is just a big band of thieves, he thought. How far is Mexico?

He dug into his bound box, found the map that Lamar had given him so long ago, and studied it. The map rather optimistically suggested that they were passing through a land of rivers and bounty. Indeed, the hill country to the west and north did appear to be relatively fertile by comparison to the arid prairies through which they marched.

Perhaps I should write the queen, he mused. *What is the condition of the land? It is miserable. Who occupies it? No one, some Indians, certainly not Texians.* He wondered again how he had lost his way: instead of mapping the Rio Grande and proving to his father that he was a man with a purpose, Alexandre LaBranche had become a prisoner of Colonel Canales. *It's inconceivable that Canales believes me to be an agent of the queen's banks. I'm a dead man.*

The day had arrived that he had told Sam Houston to expect. "You have arranged my death," he had said to the president. Now he was being led to a fate by the Mexican army that, at its worst, would inflict his death, and, at its best, would prevent him from ever returning to San Antonio. Even if Colonel Canales didn't kill him Houston would order his murder once Jack C. Hays reported that Houston's missing spy had fallen in with the Mexican army. He thought of Pennant and Alonzo, bound by ropes and guarded by soldiers. *We're dead men either way,* he thought. He wondered that he was not himself bound by ropes and tied to his saddle.

———

They traveled for six days. Each day, as the Mexican army retreated from San Antonio, he wondered if it was to be his last. He tried to spot Pennant and Alonzo in the slow procession and failed. He wondered if the occasion of his father's visits to the slave cabin had passed and wondered how Noeme had come to search for him in a thorn-filled ravine. He wondered if a man to be shot had no purpose in life and he wondered why in San Antonio he had put off his plan. Late on the sixth day of travel, Alexandre saw a large break of mesquite trees on the horizon, marking a streambud that cut across the desert.

A minor flurry of activity appeared ahead in the column. The mules were led off the path, the foot soldiers began to make camp, sergeants roamed up and down the line, two cavalry officers led several horse soldiers back as outriders to scout behind them. The lieutenant rode up to Alexandre and motioned that he was to accompany them forward.

He followed them for a quarter mile to a mesquite grove that marked the river's edge, where the lieutenant saluted General Vasquez, then wheeled his horse and rode away. A small squadron of privates and corporals were arranging Vasquez's tent and cot, setting up a camp table and a fire pit. Two rather stiff sergeants materialized at Alexandre's side and pinned his arms. He prepared to be sentenced.

"*Cascabels, señor,*" one of them growled. "*Cuidado con el pincel.*"

The other sergeant kicked at some dead shrubbery at Alexandre's feet. *"Serpientes! Cuidase!"*

"Serpents, *Señor* LaBranche," a chilling voice spoke. Colonel Canales had come up behind him. "Have care of the serpents." Canales carried a riding crop and struck the shrubbery himself, for good measure. There were no rattlesnakes in the brush. "They sleep on the rocks but hide in the wood. Take your care." Canales laughed with the casual arrogance of a man who had superior knowledge and superior force. "*Señor* LaBranche, this is as far as you go."

"Is this the Rio Grande? Are we in Mexico?" Alexandre asked.

"We are in Mexico, *señor*. Everywhere is Mexico. San Antonio is in Mexico. This river is not the Rio Grande. It is the Nueces. And tomorrow, we go to the Rio Grande, but you do not. Tomorrow, *señor*, you cease to be among us." Canales sneered at him.

Alexandre clamped his frightened bowels to prevent the final humiliation of his condition.

"Tell me *Señor* LaBranche—you have seen many things on the *camino real*. Have you write some notes to the queen?"

At length, he answered.

"I made mental notes, Colonel. Here there is desert, there are to be found verdant hills and rivers, this land is not rich for farming, that land must be studied more carefully."

"And who occupies it? Is that what you will write? Comanches. They watch us from your verdant hills and rivers. Did you see them follow us? No matter. That is not where you go to inspect the queen's land, *Señor* LaBranche. Not to the hills." Canales waved his hand back in the general direction of the streams that flowed out of the hill country toward the *camino real*. "I believe you say the queen desires you inspect the Nueces. That is what you will do. Tomorrow you leave us. You inspect lands along the Nueces all the way to the bay of Corpus Christi. Do you understand me, *Señor* LaBranche?"

"I understand. And my men?"

"Your two horse thieves? I am shooting them."

Alexandre felt the air go out of his lungs. He sagged toward the dirt at his feet, then recovered.

"They desert my army," Canales continued. He adopted a tone of scorn. "They steal the horses of my agents in New Orleans. They are nothing. I shoot them. They are coming here now." Canales pointed toward a squad of foot soldiers, led by two officers, dragging Pennant and Alonzo along.

The officers led them to a mesquite tree, then tied them to its trunk. A firing squad materialized.

"No!" Alexandre said it with a voice that surprised even him. "You are not going to shoot them. I forbid it! They are my men. I need them!"

"You need horse thieves, *Señor* LaBranche? Does the queen need horse thieves?"

"I need these horse thieves!" he insisted with more vigor than he felt. "One of them assists me with my compass and transits, sir, to keep my bearings. The other cooks. They both do my labor."

"You do not understand, *señor*. They are worth nothing. I give you two men of my soldiers. They help you, not those two *ladrones*."

"No," Alexandre said again. He tried to assume a stern posture. "I am under the protection of Her Majesty the Queen. Those men are under my protection and, therefore, under her protection." He walked directly to the mesquite tree and stood in front of the two shaking men, then turned to face the firing squad and Canales himself. "You can shoot us, Colonel, but if I do not return with a complete and favorable report for Her Majesty the Queen and the banking houses of Goldsmith and Barclay of London, she will demand payment of her loan." He waited for a sign from Canales. "If I do not return myself, sir, England will declare that Mexico is not an honorable country, that Mexico cannot be trusted to pay its agreements. Then England will come for its money and its land." Alexandre drew himself to his full height, then removed his hat and opened his shirt, baring his chest to the firing squad. He waited for the order to the soldiers to raise their muskets. Pennant and Alonzo turned sideways to face him, their disbelief at his courage momentarily causing them to lose sight of their own plights.

Canales shrugged and told the firing squad to stand down.

"Take your horse thieves, then." The firing squad and the officers picked Pennant and Alonzo up by their armpits and marched
them away from the camp. "This is what you do for our friend,
the queen. You inspect the lands and peoples of the Nueces, from
here to the Golfo de Mexico, then south to the Rio Grande at
Matamoros. Can you find exact locations on the earth?" Canales
asked.

Alexandre hesitated.

"Sir, we see the tools in your wagon and in your box. They are
tools to make, how you say, *encuestas? Longitud? Latitud?* No?"

Alexandre almost said that he could locate the exact latitude and
longitude of any place on earth, to mention his knowledge of the
Horrebow sequence as refined by Captain Talcott. He caught
himself, and said nothing, merely bowed his head.

Canales spent fifteen minutes describing what he wanted
inspected. "Our friend, Queen Victoria, she wants to know, are
there Texians on her lands? Do they have an army? Have they made
any ranchos or farms? Is there grass for horses to eat and cows to
eat? The queen would like to know those things, *Señor* LaBranche.
She particular wants to know where there is water for horses. I
expect for you to tell her." He paused for Alexandre to acknowledge
what the queen must have wanted. "When you are finish for the
queen, you leave the Nueces and come to find me at the Rio Grande.
There you will give her report to me as I would like to read it
myself. Surely the man who owes the money may see what the bank
wants, eh? No?"

Alexandre did not answer.

"I have this for you." Canales produced a carefully rolled letter
bound by a green ribbon.

"This, *Señor* LaBranche, you must keep. It is the safe-conduct
pass for you and for the two horse thieves you have chosen to help
you. Do you read Spanish? No? It says that anyone before you give
these presents must give you safe pass and such aides and helps as
you may require from them to do your work. It is signed by General
Rafael Vasquez, *Jefe de Defensores del Departamento del Presidio Rio*

Bravo y Grande. You are safe to go anywhere, *Señor* LaBranche, with this pass. Have it always."

Alexandre had stopped shaking, but he had not entirely grasped what he was set to do and said so.

"You, *Señor* LaBranche, will depart our army tomorrow in the morning. Take your wagon and your equipment and your horse thieves from here all the way to the bay of Corpus Christi. You are to find all water. Yes? Then come to my garrison along the Rio Grande. I will have my dragoons and lancers at Mier or at Camargo on that river. You will bring to me your notes and make your report to the banks. I will send it for you to the embassy in Mexico City."

"The embassy?" Alexandre had not planned for the eventuality that he would actually write a report, much less write one that anyone might send to the British embassy. *I can add England to the list of nations that will consider me a foe,* he thought.

"Yes, *Señor* LaBranche, the embassy of Great Britain in Mexico. I am sure the embassy waits for your report." Canales gave Alexandre another penetrating glare, one that could mean either that he had no more time for England's bank representative or, Alexandre suspected, that Canales doubted that Alexandre had told him the truth. *"Adios, Señor* LaBranche. It is a long way to the bay of Corpus Christi, and you have much to do. Take care of serpents. It would be a sad thing if you did not survive because of a serpent."

Alexandre found his way back to the wagon. His horse thieves were there, unbound, standing by their horses. The Mexican officers were gone. No one appeared to be guarding or even paying attention to Pennant or Alonzo, who stood idly as if there had been no firing squad in a grove of mesquite trees in a desolate prairie on the Nueces River.

"You were right, Pennant. Canales knows that you two stole his spies' horses."

Pennant looked around to see if their guards had returned, if they were loading muskets, gathering ropes.

"They don't plan to shoot us, not today, but they may kill us," Alexandre said. "Canales has ordered us to ride across this Godforsaken desert to the bay of Corpus Christi." He described what Canales had ordered him to do. "So, now we are spies. Our dilemma, though, isn't whether we spy on the Mexican army for Sam Houston or spy on the Texians for Canales."

"Either way sounds bad enough there, young sir," Pennant snorted. He still believed that they were going to be shot, that Canales was just toying with them. Alonzo was indifferent. "What could be worse than having both of those two wanting to kill us?"

"Starving to death," Alexandre said, weary, resigned. "San Antonio is six days behind us. Laredo is at least four days south of here. We don't have three days' worth of supplies remaining. There isn't much water. We will starve."

Alonzo looked up, then whispered something to Pennant.

"Alonzo says don't you worry, young sir, not about that." He was grinning and, for the first time, Alexandre saw that Alonzo too could smile. "Alonzo says we'll eat just fine."

CHAPTER TEN

Sam Houston sat; Noeme stood. Each studied the other. It was Houston who broke the silence.

"I think your mind is clouded," he said. "I think you're seeing what you want to see and hearing what you want to hear. That's a dangerous thing in a spy."

"It is exactly what I heard them say," Noeme answered him. She was accustomed to the president challenging her; it was to be expected. "Canales asked LaBranche about the lands between Goliad and Refugio. Alexandre told him there were farms, small ranch holdings, no armies."

"And what did you hear in that?" Houston pressed her. Alexandre? he thought. That was more familiar than he wanted his spies to be.

"He lied to Canales, that's what I heard in that. Alexandre LaBranche has never been within fifty miles of Goliad or Refugio. He invented a story of farmers and green pastures that do not exist anywhere near those towns and definitely not in February." She wondered in her own mind why she was passionate to defend the surveyor; the most he had ever said to her was that she was not traveling with him. "I ask you to consider this, sir. He told the traitor Canales that he was gathering facts for his report 'to the queen.' Canales asked him if he was going to tell the queen who occupies the land, if it is armies, and LaBranche answered him that he would write that he saw no armies."

"Well, girl, he didn't see any armies in Goliad or Refugio. He's never been there." Houston was getting exasperated.

"Exactly. He has not been there. And he is not an inspector of lands for the banks of England. He's a naïve surveyor caught up in a whirlwind. But he told Canales that he'd been to Goliad and, most importantly, that he was, in their words, working for the queen. Those are the words I heard him say."

Noeme had heard them very clearly indeed, so clearly that Alexandre nearly discovered her hiding in the shadows of the San Antonio cathedral while she spied on his conversation with Canales.

"And what I heard in his words is that he's willing to lie to Colonel Canales and General Vasquez. He tells them exactly what you told him to say."

"So," Houston pressed her, "why would he write those idiotic letters to me from San Antonio, telling me all those tales about horse soldiers riding out of Matamoros and rumors of Mexican armies in Goliad? I think he's just a liar. He lies to me and he lies to Canales. What's the difference? He just tells anybody the last thing he heard, true or not. That's why he told Canales he was working for the banks."

"Forgive me for being bold with you, Mr. President, but that seems unfair. Lying is what spies do, and you told him to spy for you." Noeme had thought about this a very great deal. She had considered the simple answer, that LaBranche was just lying to stay alive. She also considered the more subtle answer, that LaBranche had become comfortable in San Antonio without appreciating that the whole city was in danger of attack. "You said yourself that you never thought he would spy at all, that he would take his wagon and get as far away from you as he could get. Yet he practiced at being a spy in San Antonio. He gathered information by asking about the Mexicans who were threatening Refugio. He learned the organization of Mexican armies, although I admit that he made up what the Mexican armies were doing. He worked out a code in Latin that Mr. Hays' dispatch riders couldn't break. And the lies he told Canales are the lies you told him to tell, right down to the false passports you gave him and his own coded words 'to see the condition of the land, who occupies it.' And he stayed in San Antonio after your rangers and Jack C. Hays and his committee of safety fled."

"Then why'd he ride off into Mexico with Canales?" Houston wanted to know. "I think LaBranche joined the bastards, forgive my language. In fact, Noeme, answer me this: why did Canales seek him out in the first place?"

"I don't believe that Canales did seek him out, sir. It was the trader Kinney who fed the stories to LaBranche about Goliad and Refugio." She liked using the word "trader" to describe Kinney, because it sounded the same as "traitor." She believed he was a traitor and wanted to plant that idea in Houston's mind. "Kinney also stayed in San Antonio when Captain Hays here abandoned the city. I saw Kinney in the plaza when General Vasquez ordered everyone to assemble to listen to his speeches, and I saw him take LaBranche forward to meet General Vasquez and Colonel Canales. I cannot prove it, but I suspect that Mr. Kinney is not trustworthy. Did LaBranche join the bastards, as you say? I don't think so."

What Noeme was not prepared to say was why Canales was eager to adopt LaBranche for himself. He knew nothing of particular use to Canales. San Antonio was full of surveyors. There was nothing about the lands that LaBranche was supposed to inspect that Canales didn't already know: during his time of treason against Mexico he had led his own troops freely to the Nueces, apparently with Lamar's acquiescence. Noeme had her suspicion, but not her facts, so said nothing.

"Kinney's just a crook," Houston answered. "He tells both sides what he tells them so that he can carry on trade with both sides and the Indians too. Hays here tells me that he saw Kinney leave San Antonio."

Jack C. Hays finally spoke.

"I did," he said. "Kinney loaded his wagon and rode out of San Antonio while Vasquez led the army out."

Hays was a man who said little. His men had kept an eye on LaBranche when Pennant and Alonzo began to bring more and more dispatches for delivery to Houston. Hays had not known, however, that Houston had sent Noeme to hide among the slaves in San Antonio to watch LaBranche. Hays wondered whether Noeme had been told to spy on him as well. He continued:

"Kinney was picking over the bones of John Twohig's store within minutes after Twohig blew it up. He took what he wanted, put it in his own wagon and left town."

Hays had come to admire Twohig, even though he too had carried on some trade with merchants from Mexico. Then, when General Vasquez occupied San Antonio, Twohig had gone out to find Hays at the Cibolo to ask permission to try to kill the Mexican officers by blowing up several kegs of black powder at his store on the plaza. Hays had approved. The explosion during the pachanga had come close to succeeding. None of Vasquez's officers was killed, but the attempt added to Vasquez's belief that a huge Texian force was forming outside the city, hastening his departure after only two days. All that Twohig had to show for his sacrifice was a wrecked mercantile store whose surviving goods were stolen, not by the Mexicans who had looted the city, but by Kinney.

"How far did you follow Vasquez?" Houston asked.

"All the way to the Nueces," Hays answered.

"Then what?" Houston continued.

"I watched them from about a half mile away. Vasquez forded the river the morning of the sixteenth and continued toward Presidio Rio Grande. The entire army and all the civilians forded the river and went with him, except for LaBranche and his two men. They turned east along the Nueces and went off on their own."

That was troubling. Houston thought over the implications of his spy heading back into the Texas frontier. Had LaBranche truly gone over to the Mexicans to spy out conditions on the Nueces? Did that mean the Mexicans wanted to use the *Durango* to attempt another attack toward Refugio or Goliad or to make sure no Texian militia was coming to attack Mexico? Or both? Either way, it meant that LaBranche had agreed to spy for the Mexicans. The only consolation was that LaBranche was so incompetent that he would get his spying for Vasquez just as wrong as he had got his spying for Houston.

"I should have just hanged them here in Austin when I had them," Houston grumbled. He wondered whether to send Hays, or even Noeme, to track them down in the vast desert between the Rio Grande and the Nueces. "Should I have hanged them, Noeme?" Houston said it just to peck on her, to remind her that she worked for him. He couldn't imagine why Noeme was taking up for someone as incompetent as LaBranche, especially when he had shown no gratitude for her rescuing him before he bled to death in a gully. "Yes?"

No! Noeme thought. *No! My orders were to make sure that Mexico's agents didn't reach you and that Lamar's mappist did.*

"No, I don't think so."

Houston looked up: it was not Noeme who spoke, but Hays. Hays never said anything about Houston's policies; he only did what he was supposed to do.

"I don't think they set off to spy for Vasquez or Canales," Hays continued. "We kept an eye on them for a whole day after Vasquez crossed the river. LaBranche and his wagon rode a couple of miles east down the Nueces, then his Indian boy, Mexican, whatever he is, crossed the river on foot and shadowed the Mexican army for four or five hours. Once it was clear that General Vasquez was going on to Presidio Rio Grande, LaBranche's boy doubled back to LaBranche and his sorry pirate. LaBranche turned his wagon around and rode off in the opposite direction, upriver. By nightfall they had crossed the *camino real* and made another eight miles. They were headed north, not east."

Both Houston and Noeme sat up to take notice.

"Then, where were they going, Hays?" Houston remembered LaBranche's naïve belief that he could just ride around the Rio

Grande and take surveys and make maps without hindrance. "You know the man can't even use a compass. Maybe he just got turned around again."

"Maybe," Hays said, "but he didn't seem to need a compass. A man can see the hill country from there. Wherever they were going, it sure wasn't back east along the Nueces toward the bay of Corpus Christi or Refugio or anywhere else. I would say they were making for the hill country."

Houston considered this idea for a while, considered whether to send some of Hays's men to look for them. Neither Noeme nor Hays thought it was possible that LaBranche could tell anything to the Mexicans that they didn't already know, nor would LaBranche likely know anything about the Mexicans that Hays didn't already know. He wondered what Rusk would do, or Henderson, and decided that it didn't matter.

"That's enough," he declared. "Leave them go. There's enough Comanches in the hills to keep them busy. They'll show up somewhere, or they won't. One more thing: next time either of you come to Austin, I won't be here. I'm moving the government. Vasquez got too close this time, so we're packing the capitol up and taking everything back to Washington-on-the Brazos." He paused to let that sink in.

Hays doubted that another Mexican army raid into Texas had any chance whatever of reaching Austin but said nothing. Noeme had privileges, as a spy, but she knew that she was Black enough and female enough that Houston would not let her have an opinion about whether to move the capitol. And Houston knew better than any man alive that Noeme and Hays could find anyone; if they needed to find Houston in the future, they would find him.

"Noeme, you disappear until I need you. Jack? Don't let the bastards get that close to San Antonio again, you hear? That's all. Get."

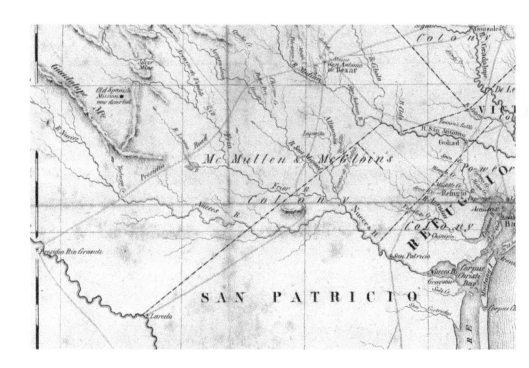

CHAPTER ELEVEN
INTO THE HILL COUNTRY

T he Mexican army made no sign of turning around.

"Look," Alonzo said. He pointed back toward the northeast. The sun glared on the rocks and sand, shielding everything on the horizon. Neither Pennant nor Alexandre could see anything. "Men watching us," he added. "I think Hays, from San Antonio." He explained to Pennant, who relayed it to Alexandre, that he first had spotted them as he spied on General Vasquez's motley departure.

If they are Jack Hays's men, Alexandre thought, *or Hays himself, they'll know from John Twohig that I have limited provisions.* He thought of what else Jack Hays would conclude and was quiet for so long that Pennant thought he had gone to sleep on the buckboard. *If I were to continue east along the Nueces toward the bay of Corpus Christi, Hays will think that I'm spying for Canales. But if I turn back to San Antonio Hays will demand that I report things about the Mexican army that I don't know. That would only lead me back to Sam Houston.*

He chose neither, then looked north toward the faint line of hills in the distance and flicked the reins to start the horse and wagon on their way.

"Where you goin' there, Alexandre?" Pennant asked.

"Neither that way," he answered, pointing toward Mexico, "nor that way," pointing back toward San Antonio. "Both lead to no good. So, I'm going that way," and he pointed due north, "into the hills. You may can come with me or go your own way."

Pennant said nothing, not about fleeing from Colonel Canales nor about his share of ten thousand United States dollars. Alonzo merely sat on his horse.

Alexandre rode alone for a half hour, never looking across the prairie toward Mexico or looking toward the rangers. Pennant eventually rode up along the right side of the wagon, Alonzo on the left. It crossed Alexandre's mind that perhaps they were going to rob him again, take his wagon, and leave him on the desolate prairie. They did not.

They traveled for hours, stopping at meager creeks to water the horses and to ford rocky banks but otherwise traveling in silence until the sun began to set. Small hills began to rise near their path. When darkness made it unsafe for the horse to pull the wagon, they camped alongside a stream.

Alonzo disappeared while Pennant helped unhitch the wagon and water the horses. Alexandre ate a piece of hardtack, sipped some creek water, and reflected that this was the first time since he had crossed the Sabine River that he was not trapped by someone. He knew from the beginning that he had been Rusk's and Henderson's and Houston's pawn. He now realized that by concocting fake spy letters to delay his reckoning and take his leisure in San Antonio, he was the victim of his own false hope. But this was the first time since his father ordered him to leave that Alexandre LaBranche did not have to make a decision. He found a spot of grass and went to sleep.

When he woke, he found that a saddle blanket had been draped over him in the night. The morning sun crested the more mountainous hills that bordered the little valley of the Uvalde.

"Rabbit?" Pennant asked him. "Alonzo went off to have a look around while you was sawin' logs down by the stream. He's good like that. Nothin' better than a bite of rabbit for breakfast."

Pennant waved a chunk of scorched flesh on a stick under Alexandre's nose.

It was enough to draw Alexandre out of the deepest sleep he had had in recent memory. A light frost coated the grass that had been his bed. He shivered and stood.

"We got a little fire goin' over there by the wagon," Pennant added. "It'll get you warmed up."

The stream where they had camped was, Alexandre estimated, more likely to be a tributary of the Nueces than the Frio. The mesquite and chaparral that marked the Nueces off to their left had never disappeared from view as they rode into the hills, but neither had the Frio appeared on their right.

Alonzo was napping behind the wagon. Alexandre had wondered if the man ever slept; he had been little more than a silent presence. He couldn't imagine why Alonzo, with a family in LaVillita, had joined Pennant in a life of piracy, which got them pressed into Mexico's bumbling army on the *Durango*. Now his life was that of a man who stole horses and carried fake messages, a man who faced Canales' firing squad. He gazed around the valley where they had camped for the night.

Considerate terram qualis sit, Alexandre reflected. Those were the first words of the code he used in his fake dispatch from Matamoros. *Considerate terram qualis sit, utrum fortis sit an infirmus habitatores eius*, he had written."See what the land is like, and whether the people who live in it are strong or weak," taken from the Book of Numbers.

Those also were the last words Colonel Canales said to him in San Antonio, at the pachanga, just before the explosion.

How did Canales know what I had written in a dispatch to Sam Houston?

As for *considerate terram*, there was little in the land before him before him to consider. There were no fields or cattle, no structures of any kind, however primitive. There were neither prints nor marks to indicate that anyone had ever been there on horse or on foot. *Are the people living in it strong or weak? That's what Canales repeated back to me at the pachanga.* There were no people living in the hills, none strong or weak, no Texians or Mexicans, soldiers or traders. Alonzo woke. Pennant began to ready the horses and wagon.

Alexandre opened the map that he had carried with him from his first meeting with Lamar. He traced the *camino real* from San Antonio to the Nueces, where the Mexican army had left them, then north to the hill country. Nothing on the ground was as drawn on the map. The course of the Nueces, instead of flowing out of mountains, was a shallow stream in a narrow vale between a range of modest ridges on the west and a seemingly endless series of larger and more verdant hills miles to the east. As for the hills themselves, none were drawn in any correct direction or proportion. He suspected that whoever had drawn the map had not actually surveyed the Nueces or the Frio and certainly had not surveyed the hill country. They were in unknown lands.

"What's your plan, young sir?" Pennant walked up, more eager to please than he had been since long before he had faced the firing squad. "Which way we goin'?"

"We're going into the hills."

By eight in the morning, they had left the stream and valley behind them and set out east through a gap in the landscape. After several hours, they came to a clear, cold river that Alexandre believed to be the Frio. He turned upriver and rode along the Frio for several hours. By late afternoon, they entered a grove of live oak and seemingly lost maple trees that grew along the banks of a gentle bend of the river. A deer gazed at them.

"I'm stopping here," Alexandre announced. Pennant stared nervously across the stream and dismounted. Alonzo quietly slipped off his horse and disappeared into the trees. "These lands remind me of the Shenandoah," Alexandre said to no one in particular, "long green ridges, streams in the bottoms. Hollows. Trees. Grass. I'm stopping here."

"For the night?" Pennant asked.

"It may be the night. It may be days. I'm staying here until I'm no longer staying here. I don't have to decide." He looked toward the grove; Alonzo, almost invisible, had crept to within a few feet of the deer. He looked at the cool, clean, flowing river. He estimated that they were twenty or twenty-five leagues west of where the Comanches had watched General Vasquez's army retreat across the Medina River. "I like it here. I'm comfortable here. I'm stopping."

Pennant also thought of the Comanches.

"We might be comfortable, young sir," Pennant answered. "Can't rightly say we'll be safe. The Comanch can ride them twenty-five leagues in a matter of hours, perhaps minutes. And they's invisible until they aren't, and then it's too late. Maybe not get too comfortable here, that's all I'm saying."

"Did you feel safer standing in front of Colonel Canales' firing squad?" Alexandre answered. "He said you were my horse thieves. Imagine that, my horse thieves. He'll know pretty soon that my horse thieves and I have quit the Nueces. Or did you feel safer with Sam Houston? He was going to hang all of us just on general principles. I expect Houston knows already that our spying for him was all lies." He looked up and saw the deer leap, then spring into the trees and scramble toward a bluff. Alonzo had gotten too close. "Tell me, Pennant, where did Alonzo come from?"

Pennant didn't answer, not immediately. Alonzo was, in his view, something between his mate and his property. *What business is it of LaBranche, he wondered, to know anything about Alonzo?*

"Don't rightly know everything. Not my story to tell. I was loading some cannons onto an old barky down off Galveston, you know? I was gun crew for the barky. Some men brought some labor in, started ordering people around. The labor gang was kind of like their slave prisoners, you know? That's where I met Alonzo, in that labor gang. I snuck him aboard the barky and we sailed off. Been together ever since. Why d'ya want to know?"

Alexandre was satisfied and, when Alonzo walked back to the camp, he changed the subject.

"This place is fine," Alexandre commented. "No Texians. No Mexican armies. No Indians. Food. Water. I'll stay."

Alonzo whispered something. Pennant relayed it.

"They's a mission way over there to the west, Alonzo says." He pointed to a hilltop a league or more away. "Old one, he says. On the upper Nueces. Abandoned for years."

A mission? Alexandre wondered.

"Did Alonzo see it? Where, exactly? What kind of mission? A presidio? Soldiers?" Alexandre wasn't sure why Alonzo was telling him about the mission. Was it safer there, he wondered, than here, where they were protected by a natural cavern and shielded by the trees? "For that matter, how does Alonzo know it's there? Did he see it?"

Alonzo shook his head, then whispered to Pennant again.

"Just a church. Says his grandfather was a priest there," Pennant answered. "Seems like he took up with his grandmother. Had to leave."

This was indeed news! Alexandre envisioned a beaten path of cloaked Franciscans trudging into the hill country to convert the savages, much as they had done at the missions outside San Antonio, then seducing the more agreeable looking ones, also as they had done at San Antonio. He also envisioned that the Indians eventually scalped the Franciscans, hence an abandoned mission.

"Alonzo says they weren't Comanches at the mission. Lipan."

"Is that a comfort?" Alexandre asked.

"His grandmother was a Lipan, he says, part of old Castro's tribe."

Alexandre had never known anyone like Alonzo, of two races, both Mexican and Indian. He had known a lot of creoles, some octaroons, but the Mexicans he had met in New Orleans were the important ones, men of business or shipping. They were loud and impatient, like Colonel Canales, and expected to have their way. As for Indians, Alexandre had never known one before and was not sure how Indians acted.

On their second day in the camp, Alonzo killed a deer. No one asked how he killed it or what he planned to do with it. He unpacked his knives and pots and built a fire. They feasted on roasted venison and foraged lambs quarter salad. They took turns climbing the bluff and fording the stream to look for signs that anyone was watching them.

Each day, Alexandre thought about his choices. Until he had read his father's letter, he had kept the idea of fleeing from San Antonio because Houston's demand that he spy for Texas would get him killed. He had fled into the hills because Canales expected him to spy for Mexico, which, he expected, also would get him killed. He considered the traitor Canales to be the more dangerous.

Does Canales truly believe I'm a Mexican spy? He knows that I sent false information to Sam Houston, the kind of disinformation a Mexican spy might plant to mislead the Texians. But he could know my disinformation only because someone passed the contents of my dispatches on to him. Someone was spying on me.

His first thought was that Kinney must have spoken directly to Canales. But, on reflection, he considered it just as likely to have been the priests at the missions where Pennant and Alonzo carried the dispatches. The priests could have read the dispatches and passed the contents onward until they reached Canales. Samuel Maverick had tried to warn him that he was being watched by priests. And, he thought, who but priests would know the Latin words?

Canales also may believe that I'm the queen's inspector of lands or, worse, believe I'm a spy for Houston posing as the queen's inspector. He knew that both possibilities, that he was believed to be spying for Houston or for Mexico, were dangerous. *Yet, when I stood in front of his firing squad and dared him to shoot me because then our friend the queen would call in the entire debt of Mexico, Canales had just enough doubt to not murder me or my horse thieves, but also enough suspicion to send a dispatch to Mexico City asking about my bona fides.*

Another possibility occurred to Alexandre, that Canales had sent him to cross the desert toward the bay of Corpus Christi to kill two birds with a single stone. *If I were to die in the desert, his problem of getting rid of me would be solved. But if, by a miracle, I did find water and did succeed in crossing that desert to report to him in Mexico, his problem of water would be solved. Canales would win either way.*

It hurt his head to think of what others thought of him. He was happier when he thought about Lamar's error-riddled map of Texas. Alexandre LaBranche was happiest when finding errors in maps and correcting them.

After several days of thought, he concluded that the path to his future was the path to Santa Fe. There was no map from Texas to Santa Fe, whether along the Rio Grande or straight across the unknown western desert. That three hundred men sent by Lamar had gotten lost looking for Santa Fe was proof enough of the need for such a map.

For several more days he considered possible plans. He could leave the hill country and go southwest to reach the Rio Grande above Presidio Rio Grande, then survey and map the river all the way to Santa Fe. Or he could leave the hill country and strike out across the great western desert, mapping a much shorter route to Santa Fe, but without the certainty of finding food and water. In either case, once he reached Santa Fe he could return directly to the United States in the company of Santa Fe Trail merchants or, instead, continue to map the Rio Grande to its source and on north to the forty-second parallel, the very thing that Lamar had hired him to do. And in both cases, his maps would be of immense value in the United States.

I don't need Texas' ten thousand United States dollars, he thought. The United States itself will give them to me.

Over the sixth and seventh days in utopia, Alexandre began to calculate their exact location. He worked for several hours, sighting through his sextant, measuring from his plumb lines, checking his quadrant. He sketched remarkably clear drawings of the route they had ridden from the Nueces to the valley of the Uvalde and from there to the campsite.

In the process, he discovered that one of his lies had come true:

they were camped at the very spot that he had told Colonel Canales was the boundary of his duties for the Barclay and Goldsmith banks. *And here I am, considering the land, and who is in it!*

It was when he hurried to tell Pennant and Alonzo that he knew exactly where they were that four Comanches rode into their camp.

Pennant ran for their old musket; Alonzo stopped him. Alexandre, the sun behind him, thought he had not been seen. The Comanches rode up to Alonzo and glared at him, then said something unintelligible. Alonzo shook his head. They pointed at Pennant; Alonzo again shook his head. They pushed the two aside and began to pilfer through the goods on the wagon.

Alexandre trembled in his hiding place, marveling but fearful, until he realized that the Comanches looked starved and feeble. One of them had a stone hatchet; all of them were half-dressed in skins and were barefoot. Even their horses were decrepit. It wasn't clear whether Alonzo understood them; whenever they spoke, he either nodded or shook his head but did not answer.

The Comanches rummaged through their provisions for a half hour, lifting the water barrel up to drink from the bunghole, tasting the hardtack and jerky before throwing it on the ground. They found the little box of medicines that Twohig had said were essential, tasted some and spat it out, then threw the bottles to the ground. They didn't bother the shovel or pick or, to Alexandre's relief, the horses. In the end, one of them yelled something at Pennant, who wet his pants. The Indians shook one last empty barrel, threw it toward the river, and rode away. Alexandre rejoined his horse thieves.

"Well, Alexandre," Pennant started, "so much for not having any Indians. They knows we're here now. Time to leave."

Alexandre ignored him and asked Alonzo what the Indians wanted.

"Drink," he answered.

"He means whiskey," Pennant answered. "Fire water. That's another thing we can thank your friend General Vasquez for. He rousted us out of San Antonio so early we didn't even get to bring our corn."

Alexandre pointed out that Pennant seemed to have forgotten having been annoyed with General Vasquez for rousting them out so early because he was going to shoot them. An absence of corn whiskey seemed a small price to pay and probably saved them from rougher treatment by the Comanches.

"They come back," Alonzo said. "You see."

The Comanches did come back, forty of them, half mounted, half walking. They surrounded the camp.

A tall, rugged, young warrior dismounted from a strong, better fed horse, walked directly up to Alexandre, and began shouting at him with much flailing of arms and clinching of fists. Alexandre was frightened and waited for the first blow to fell him. Instead, another Comanche, a taller and somewhat older warrior, walked into the circle. He carried in his arms a child, a boy of indeterminate age, somewhere between six and fifteen years. The child was twisted with pain, his eyes closed. His stomach bulged abnormally to one side. The Comanche handed him to Alexandre and stepped back.

"Aguas malas,' the chief said to the three of them. *"Cúralo!"*

He nodded menacingly, then turned and mounted his horse. He made another savage nod, then rode away. The other Comanches shook their spears and arms, then turned to follow. They crossed the Frio, turned as one, gave the men a stern collective glare, then disappeared into the live oaks and the folds of the hills across from the camp.

Alexandre handed the child to Pennant, who almost dropped him. Alonzo caught the boy before he hit the ground and laid him out on the wagon bed. The child's head flopped down; his eyes rolled back in their sockets. Pennant announced that he was dead.

"He's not dead," Alexandre whispered. "but I have no doubt he soon will be. Why did they bring him to us?"

Pennant had never seen a sick boy, at least not on land. Alonzo had never seen Comanches bring a sick Indian, man, woman, or child to anyone, much less hand one over to strangers. Alonzo whispered something to Pennant, who shook his head, then whispered some more. At some length, Pennant emerged from the conference to announce that Alonzo believed that it was a test.

"Alonzo seems to think maybe the Comanch just wants to see if white medicine would fix the little savage. He thinks those four Comanches told 'em maybe we had some white medicine. They figured the blighter's done for, but if he dies, well, Alonzo says this might not be as safe as you wanted."

To flee seemed unlikely. It was obvious that the Comanches had been watching them from the day they arrived and could destroy the three intruders with impunity. Curing the sick boy also seemed unlikely, but trying to keep him alive would be no worse than trying to disappear and at least would gain some time.

"Probably the son of that chief who carried him in," Pennant added. "Alonzo thinks that first warrior wasn't the chief, probably the boy's older brother." Alonzo whispered something else. "No mother. No medicine man."

The child's breath was foul. His stomach was hard as a rock and bulged upward below his chest. He was beginning to turn blue. Alexandre held the boy's head level and washed his face with stream water. He tried to get the child to drink but couldn't get him to open his lips. Pennant suggested they bleed him.

"Got a case of the humours," he announced. "Seen it before at sea. A swabbie'd come down with humours of the blood, turn blue just like this little savage. You bleed 'em, get the bad blood out and the humours they go away." He did not propose that he personally supervise the bleeding, instead handing a knife to Alexandre. "Just make a slit right there inside his forearm," Pennant added helpfully. "Where your veins is, just open one of them and it'll bleed right out in no time."

Bleeding certainly was an option, Alexandre thought. He had seen it many times on the plantation. What he could not remember was whether he had seen any of the sick slaves who suffered from bad humours survive a bleeding. Alexandre realized that the danger was not merely whether the child survived but whether

Pennant might talk him into doing something that would kill the boy.

"Best you be seen to do something there, Alexandre. At least rub some of that calomel on him," Pennant advised. There were no rashes on the child, no open sores, nothing a lotion would soothe. "Won't do nothing for him, but at least the tribe over there'll see you trying something."

Alonzo whispered something else to Pennant. "Alonzo says they handed him to you because the four that picked all over our tools and provisions figured what with all your telescopes and measures that you was the man of science. White medicine."

"Mix some quinine," Alexandre proposed. "I'm going to get some down his throat." Pennant fetched the quinine from the medicine chest and poured a measure into his own drinking cup. "Help me get his teeth apart." Quinine wouldn't hurt the boy and, if he did have the foul humours, might actually help. "Get him by the jaw." Alexandre poured the medicine down the boy's gullet, then watched him gurgle it back out the side of his slack mouth. It did not look good.

For the next few hours, they took turns cradling the boy's head on their laps, not so much from tenderness as the awareness that sitting in that position in the wagon gave them the best view across the Frio to the watching Comanches hid. At mid-day Alexandre took his bound box out of the wagon bed and carried it over to the fire pit, then began to set up his surveying equipment.

He quietly assembled a long gauging rod and attached a quadrant to the upper end. He told Alonzo to walk to the clearing between the live oaks and the water's edge, a position Alexandre judged to be in line with the sun and motioned with his hands to move to one side or another. He unwrapped his transit and assembled it to the wooden tripod, then aimed it directly at Alonzo and, not coincidentally, at the sun. He measured the angle of the sun, then told Alonzo to carry the gauging rod and quadrant to the boy and act as if they were measuring the child with the rod at his side, adjusting the quadrant as if in some way it passed a wave or magic spell over the boy's head.

"We watch over him until dark," Alexandre said in a very loud voice. "Wash his head and check his pulses every fifteen minutes," he added. He assumed, indeed hoped, that the Comanches had watched him and were listening. Neither Alonzo nor Pennant had a better plan.

Alexandre worked for several hours, frequently lifting his arms to the sun and waving his tools around in a manner that he hoped would appear to a Comanche as a worshipful incantation of white medicine. At one point he stopped, climbed up the overhanging rock shelf, took out his transit and gazed to the west, then back across the hills to the east. He climbed back down, then studied the map and made more calculations. The afternoon passed.

The child didn't improve, but he also didn't die. At exactly the last minute of direct light, Alexandre took the others aside and told them his plan.

"I believe that if we're still here when the child dies, they will kill us. We should slip away in the dark, now, go for Santa Fe, and then on to the United States." He paused to see if they had any comment. "It is, by my calculations, just at five hundred miles from here, at approximately 310 degrees northwest. That is my plan."

Pennant and Alonzo shook their heads. Neither thought that the Comanches were likely to escort them out of the hill country and point them on their way across the desert.

"No," Alonzo said. "They see in the dark. If we go now, they kill us."

Alexandre was startled at Alonzo speaking in such lengthy sentences, but he needed an answer.

"What is your plan then?"

"Heal." With that, Alonzo walked back into the circle of light cast by the fire. He rubbed sage and potion of prickly pear on the child's face and lips. He rubbed the boy's forehead, turned his face, and heard a groan, the first sign the child had made. Alonzo turned, faced the moon, lifted his open hands over his head, and bowed. When he finished, he went back to Alexandre and Pennant.

"Boy, make a sound. Air goes in him. Give the foul medicine." The foul medicine was emetic of tartar, a potion so vile that when the first four Comanches had smelled it they tried to throw the bottle away.

Alexandre knew Alonzo was right: they had to be seen trying to heal the boy or the Comanches would kill them all. He pulled the stopper from the emetic and almost dropped the bottle; the aroma had the smell of rotted cream, skunk spray, and human waste. He paused and considered making a dash for the hills, knew that he would be caught and tortured, and lifted the child's chin. With a single flourish, he jammed the vial between the boy's teeth and poured it in. He was certain that he heard a rustling from across the river, expected arrows or hatchets or a murderous assault at any second, but he held the vial inside the boy's mouth until it was empty.

The boy groaned.

Alexandre laid his limp body back on the wagon bed, then washed the child's face and forehead. He barely got out of the way.

With a violent heave, the boy sat bolt upright and groaned from the bottom of his being, choked, coughed, and spewed a huge stream of green, yellow, and thick vomit straight over the back gate of the wagon, then collapsed. Alexandre jumped out of the way, but Alonzo rushed in, washed the boy's face with water, and held him upright. In less than a minute, the child vomited again, chunks of something viscous and leathery that shot across the wagon and landed on the edge of the firepit, with a fair splatter on his legs, his stomach, and on Pennant, who had gotten too close.

"There's more guts than boy there," Pennant yelled. "He's alive." Alonzo and Alexandre, closer to the danger zone, nodded and stepped back. "Watch out."

The child doubled over, reared backward, convulsed, then expelled what appeared to be the entirety of his internal organs, stomach, circulatory system, and intestines, a stream that was more vile than the emetic of tartar that had brought the child to life in the first place. Then, to their astonishment, the boy lifted his head, wiped his mouth with his hand, jumped off the wagon bed, and ran into the river. He splashed face down in the water, scrambled to his knees, then swam and waded until he was on the other side and disappeared into the trees.

"Healed," Alonzo said.

"We go," Alexandre added. "Now!"

Going wasn't as easy as he hoped. None of the horses would go near the wagon, even when harnessed and pulled by their reins. It was impossible to clean the mess out of the wagon bed in the dark. In the end, they rescued a barrel of water and their saddle blankets, then walked a quarter mile upwind along the river. They stood watch in one-hour shifts and prayed that by dawn the vile smell had blown away enough to let them tow the wagon away and pack up. It had.

It was not hard to see why the child had been near death.

"He ate a baby alligator!" Pennant was shocked to see. A half-digested alligator gar lay in the center of the vomit pond. "And ..." Alonzo whispered something. "Alonzo says that's a turkey foot." There was the webbed talon of a wild turkey near the alligator gar, as well as an intact blue gill fish. They began to laugh.

"Probably bet some other little savages he'd do it." Pennant declared. He reflected on his own youth, spent with the other sons of felons breaking into warehouses on the docks, trying to steal cannon balls and sugar cones and anything they could take, all on a dare.

What's this? Pennant asked himself.

"This" was three crude silver disks that had been hammered into ornaments, each no more than an inch across, placed very carefully on the wagon's buckboard. Pennant quietly picked them up and stuffed them into a pocket. Alexandre didn't notice; Alonzo said nothing.

"It's time to go," Alexandre declared. They saddled the horses, hitched the wagon, and rode away from the vale of the lost maples.

They set out to backtrack to their first camp in the hills but had gone no more than a hundred yards before several Comanches appeared on their left. Pennant suggested they prepare the musket for use and told Alexandre to reach for the ball and powder. Alexandre said to do nothing. A dozen more Comanches rode up behind them.

"It's the chief," Pennant hissed, pointing at the older Comanche who had brought the child into their camp. "And the other chief," meaning the younger, angrier sounding Comanche who had led the band into their camp in advance of the medical train. "And all the others. We're in for it. Gimme the…"

Alexandre calmly took Pennant's hand and removed it from the side of the wagon.

The Comanches led them downriver until they arrived at a hard bend that was bounded on either side by steep hills and bluffs. The chief directed them into a declivity between two folds in the hill, then up an incline until the horse could pull the wagon no further. He then motioned for Alexandre to get down from the wagon, took the reins from Pennant and Alonzo, then indicated that they all were to follow on foot.

The declivity made another sharp bend at the summit and there, not fifty feet in front of them, a mine shaft opened right out of the side of the mountain. Old oak timbers supported the lintel and frames of an entrance that was about eight feet wide and six feet high.

"*Almagre*," Alonzo said, pointing at the red dirt that lined the entrance. "*Almagre*."

"What is *almagre?*" Alexandre asked. Pennant didn't know. The Comanches led them into the mine. Someone produced a torch.

The mine hadn't been worked intensively in a very long time. Ruts showed where wagons had cut into the floor. Old iron spokes, a few rusted chains, the remnants of hoist blocks littered the area. The walls, however, were heavily pocked from the chipping away of red ocher and limestone, clear layers of the one compressed into the other. Slag was scattered about.

The chief led them deeper into the mine to a sharp corner, where a second opening appeared. They walked out to find a hidden face of the mountain, completely invisible to the valley of the Frio and to anyone passing through the hill country. A limestone oven had been built to smelt the ore. The chief showed all of this to them with a sweep of his hand, then led them back inside.

He grunted at two of the hardier looking Comanches, who took iron bars from behind a mound of slag. They began to chip and poke at the ore face between the ocher and the copper layers, then to pull out chunks of rock. The chief watched until he was satisfied with one of the rocks. He picked it up, took Alexandre by the arm, and led him back to the opening near the furnace. He then handed the rock to Alexandre, grunted, and tugged at his own braided hair.

Alexandre saw for the first time what the chief wanted him to see: his braid was held in place by a silver clasp. The chief pulled it out of his hair and held it out for all to see. He then pointed at the clasp, at the rock in his hand, and at the oven.

Silver. It was a silver mine.

The chief nodded at Alexandre and Alonzo, jerked his head dismissively toward Pennant, and led them back out of the mine and down to the wagon and their horses. When all the Comanches had mounted their horses, the chief gripped Alexandre and Alonzo on their shoulders, ignored Pennant, and bowed his head. The Comanches turned without another look and rode away.

CHAPTER TWELVE

The Comanches did not return, not in the first few days.

Alexandre was not satisfied that it was their purpose to give them a silver mine; it could as easily have been a kind of jail or, he supposed, a hospital for them to tend to the next Comanche that the chief wanted them to cure. They picked over the last bits of the second rabbit of breakfast. He decided that he was leaving.

"I'm setting out for Santa Fe," he began. Pennant looked up; Alonzo did not. "I can start here and map the route to Santa Fe. From there, I could either join one of the trade convoys on the Santa Fe Trail back to Missouri or I could continue and map the upper Rio Grande north all the way to the United States. I haven't decided which." He waited for Pennant and Alonzo to react; they did not. "I worked out the directions both ways, by following the Rio Grande or by setting out from here to cross the west directly to Santa Fe." He waited; no one answered. "In either case, I want to leave now. The weather is agreeable, there is water, the plants ripen, and game is fertile. If we make twenty miles a day, we will reach Santa Fe before the worst heat settles in, even if we go the longer way."

Pennant chewed his rabbit and sulked. Alonzo said nothing.

"There is no debt," Alexandre continued, unsure whether the men whose lives he had saved would feel obliged to stay with him whatever course he set and equally unsure whether he wanted them to do so. The sun had risen above the hills in the east. Oaks and persimmons showed their early buds. Birds chirped in the mountain laurels above the limestone oven. "You can come or stay," he finished.

"So, you think someone'll pay you more for hikin' across the prairie to Santa Fe than you can make off spying for Sam Houston, eh?" Pennant finally answered.

"I think Sam Houston would pay us with a rope or a firing squad, not with United States dollars," Alexandre answered. "And besides, we haven't spied anything to report beyond watching General Vasquez ride away to Mexico. And Houston knows by now as much as we do because Hays' men watched them leave us at the Nueces."

"That's my point, young sir," Pennant added. "If Houston had told Hays to bring us in, they could have caught us easy out there by the Nueces. Instead, they just watched us ride off up here into the hills. He thinks we's still his spies. And they's another thing, too."

"What's that?" Alexandre hated to ask; Pennant's schemes never bode well.

"You got yourself a safe-conduct letter from Canales, young sir. Ain't nobody going to bother you if you go on down to the Rio Grande and poke around." Pennant said this with the confidence of a man who believed that, despite all evidence to the contrary, Colonel Canales was a man to be trusted and that spying on his country was a simple matter of riding over to the river and looking across. "And anyways, it may be a detour, but it's on the way to Santa Fe. I say we stay here and mine a bit of silver 'til we's ready." He did not say what it meant to be ready.

These arguments were persuasive but not conclusive. Alexandre was not convinced.

"I'm leaving tomorrow, with you or not, as you wish. If I don't start soon," Alexandre argued, "crossing the prairie in the heat will get even harder." He had the notion that beyond the miserable Nueces there would be virgin prairie, more mountains perhaps, and eventually the northern bend of the Rio Grande. No one knew. "I'm losing time." He nodded his head to put an end to it.

"Alonzo says that don't mean anything to the savages," Pennant said. "Time don't. It's light or dark, that's all. If one of 'em said meet me in two hours they wouldn't know what you was talking about." Alonzo whispered something to Pennant, who continued. "Moons do. Mean something. Time of the riding moon, the hunting deer moon. Kill the buffalo moon. That's all. Time to make some deer jerky moon."

Alexandre listened.

"Time to mine some silver moon. If time's just passing," Pennant continued, "I say we fire out some of that ore. Done a bit of that in my time," he claimed. "We did a little silver work ourselves, over at the mines of Penasquito. That was in a break we was takin' from the sea. We wasn't slaves," he said, "not exactly. More like supervisors. Silver mining's hot work, but if them savages can smelt the silver out of these rocks, we can do it."

Alexandre assumed that Pennant was lying about working in a silver mine, but even he knew the rudiments of extracting metal from ore, silver from rock. Dig for ore. Break the ore into rocks. Fire the rocks in the hottest possible oven. Chip out the slag. Collect the molten silver.

"Alonzo here could rustle up some deer, smoke it, something to eat on the road, you know? Easier here than out on the prairie." Alonzo nodded in agreement. "And lessen I'm mistook, we don't have much in the way of cash money for when we do get to Santa Fe. What say we try our hand here a while, maybe see if we can make up a little silver. Who's to say?"

Pennant could see that Alexandre was considering his argument. To make his point, he took one of the steel bars from the mine and poked at the walls. A bit of rock collapsed.

"What could be easier?"

I could do that, Alexandre thought. Produce a small amount of silver, just enough to tide me over in Santa Fe, something to pay for supplies and get me back to the United States.

"And in the meantime, maybe you could show me a thing or two about them survey tools," Pennant continued. "Gonna need to know how to use 'em anyway. If we're gonna map our way out to Santa Fe."

Solutions are easy when there is no problem to solve. Alexandre relented.

"I'll wait one week," he announced, feeling generous in letting his horse thieves play at silver mining. "Then, I'm leaving."

They turned to digging ore from the walls of the mine, hauling rocks to the limestone kiln and smelting the ore, then poring through the ashes for molten silver. They stopped at noon each day so that Alexandre could use his tools to survey their hidden redoubt. He walked to the highest peak above the mine, to the ridges of nearby hills, to the wide plain between the Frio and the Sabinal and took sun readings. Pennant watched over his shoulder.

"It's the Horrebow method," Alexandre mentioned, "as refined by Captain Talcott." Alonzo was fascinated by Alexandre's ability to draw to scale the mine, the cleft in the mountain that hid them, the peaks opposite and the river below. Never had he or Pennant seen such detailed and accurate art. "Fix the latitude and longitude first, then use the disappearing line of perspective to translate the scene exactly onto the map." He decided to spend an hour a day showing them the rudiments of mapping.

Each day passed but, after a week, the silver they produced amounted to no more value than a few Mexican reales or a bit of jewelry of poor quality. Alexandre declared the waiting time was over.

Pennant argued, and Alonzo seemed even less interested than usual, but Alexandre packed his tools. The next morning, they rigged up the wagon and watered their horses. As the first light rose above the nearest hilltop, they rode away from the silver mine.

———

The course of the Frio was serpentine, curving and twisting around the mountainous hills, each of which looked like the last. Each bend seemed familiar, each grove of trees and limestone cliff looked like the campsite where they had cured the Comanche child but was not. When they came to a westward passage, they gave up searching for landmarks and followed it. The passage continued for a few miles, turned sharply around a last hill and abruptly opened onto a wide valley with a broad river that flowed between the mountainous hills of the east and the low ridges of the west.

The landscape expanded onto wide, fertile ground on either side of the river. Small patches of wild corn and barley grew amidst tall grasses. At a curve in the river, there were cypresses that formed a large canopy. Ahead, on the left, they saw another break in the low ridge of western hills.

Alonzo whispered something to Pennant, who relayed it.

"Alonzo think's that old mission's up there somewhere behind that hill up yonder," Pennant announced. Alonzo pointed beyond the cypress grove toward another break in the hills. They rode to look for it.

The mission was hidden behind a fold in the hills at the entrance to a canyon that opened toward the west. There were no prints or tracks on the overgrown ground, neither human nor horse nor mule.

It was forlorn, its church no more than a crumbling rectangular room with a missing door and a broken wooden cross above. It was adjoined to a larger room and a low adobe wall, also crumbling, along whose footings were remnants of other small buildings. The walls enclosed an open plaza that probably had been flanked by sleeping quarters, a kitchen, and farm buildings.

Sparrows and jays nested in the juniper logs of the collapsed chapel roof and weeds choked the rotted window frames and doorways. On one corner of the grounds, a few crumbling crosses marked a cemetery. On the opposite corner, there remained the rubble of a cluster of rooms that had burned to the ground. All seemed equally desolate.

"Why was it abandoned?" Alexandre asked.

"Alonzo heard about it from family tales," Pennant answered. Alonzo shrugged. "His uncle says the priests all left, some with wives to San Antonio, some without wives back to Mexico. He don't talk too much about it."

They built a small fire on the bank of the river near the cypress trees, as much for warmth as to heat their jerky. The wind in the trees, the call of an owl, an animal rustling in the bushes all conspired to put Alexandre's nerves on alert, but there was nothing at the river or the abandoned mission to threaten them. Even so, he took only his blanket from the wagon and left the traces and rigging, ready to hitch up and flee at a moment's notice.

That mission, Alexandre thought, *was large enough for about forty or fifty people.* He conceded that it was overgrown but, even so, there was little evidence of enough farming or livestock pens to feed so many. *And why was it abandoned? Soon the fire was gone as well. He curled under his blanket. Was it abandoned? Or attacked? Burned by Indians?* As if in answer, a flash of lightning lit up the stream and a clap of thunder rolled across the valley. A heavy rain began to fall, and he buried himself as deep as he could inside his blanket. *Why did they build it here?* There had to have been a road, he knew, a road directly to Mexico. His last conscious thought was, *There has to be a road.* He fell asleep.

The next morning, Alonzo led them back to the mission, then through the gap between the western hills that they had seen the day before. After only a few hundred yards, the break became a narrow canyon with a bourn still flowing from the storm. The hills on either side became lower and lower until it was clear that they must be very near the west end of the passage. Their progress stopped when a spur across the path from the canyon walls blocked the way forward.

Alonzo rode ahead, leading his horse up the lower reaches of the spur until he disappeared around to the back side. He returned a few minutes later and called for them to come forward.

The spur did block the passage, at least as far as the wagon was concerned. But when they rounded the spur on foot and climbed higher up the ridge, they saw the entire west open up before them. There were the plains, a distant desert, endless mesquite and cactus, small mesas and rock-filled streambeds. They stood atop the passage that Alexandre had been looking for since he had decided to set out for Santa Fe. He contemplated how much digging would be necessary to clear a path across the base of the spur for the wagon to pass. Alonzo yelled a single word:

"Tracks!"

"Tracks?" Alexandre asked. "What tracks?" *Footprints? Horses? A road?* he wondered. "What tracks? Where?"

They followed on foot, climbing higher up the spur, then over rocky outcrops, thickets of cactus and bear grass. Snakes slithered away. The sun beat down. They reached the summit.

"Tracks," Alonzo pointed.

The spur was not a spur. It was a landslide, an enormous collapse of the canyon wall that covered what probably had been the missing road between the mission and the open west. On one side there was the desert, on the other side, the canyon, visible almost all the way back to the mission. At the base of the landslide, near the canyon wall, there were tracks.

The tracks were ruts in hardened mud, deep outlines of parallel grooves made by the passage of wagon wheels. The tracks ended abruptly under the landslide, probably covered by the same storm that had caused the canyon wall to collapse in the first place. From where they stood, it was clear that the tracks would have continued westward in the direction of Mexico. And, near the tracks, where the sand and rocks and limestone had washed away in the heavy rain of the night before, there was the outline of the bed and wheel rims of a long-abandoned ore wagon. Alexandre went back for the shovel.

They worked for hours to clear away dirt and rock, exposing a wheel here, some of the wagon bed there. The wagon had decomposed so badly that it had caved in not only from the dirt landslide but from the weight of the ore that filled it. The ore itself, however, when they began to uncover it, looked much as it must have done when the priests who ran the mission had forced their newly converted Indian flock to mine it. The wagon had been filled with a rich mixture of ore, rocks streaked heavily with copper, limestone, ochre and, more than anything, with silver, very pure and thick silver.

Each discovery led to more digging. By the late afternoon, they had removed enough of the spur to reveal the contours and outlines of thirteen buried ore wagons. Pennant gazed at the prize and spoke for all of them:

"We're rich."

CHAPTER THIRTEEN
LIPANTITLAN, NEAR THE BAY OF CORPUS CHRISTI

Noeme prodded the goat forward, poking it with a stick, enabling her to watch, unnoticed, the last of the Mexican army as it trudged beyond the waterless arroyo of Agua Dulce. As she studied the miserable foot soldiers retreating into the barren desert, she began to compose in her head a lengthy dispatch to Sam Houston. She included everything she had observed from the moment she arrived up to the moment that Colonel Canales abandoned battle and retreated.

"Sir," she began. "I arrived at Copano Bay to discover that your militia under General Davis had moved to the Nueces River but had left behind its cannon and much of its ammunition. I then learned that more than one-half of General Davis' force had deserted with Lieutenant O'Connor, whose men mutinied over a demand for liquor. I proceeded across country directly to Mr. Kinney's trading post on the Nueces, arriving in time to secure a place of hiding in his goat pens. Later that day, I watched General Davis and Colonel Cameron march past, upriver from the bay of Corpus Christi. I counted two hundred fifty-three men. Two Mexican spies soon entered the trading post and left with Mr. Kinney. I borrowed a goat to enable me to follow them to a place on the prairie near a dry creek opposite Lipantitlan. I observed Mr. Kinney meet with Colonel Canales and heard him describe the size of General Davis's militia and the direction it marched. Canales ordered his Mexican army of five hundred cavalry and two hundred foot militia to move forward under cover of darkness. I abandoned Kinney's goat to the prairie and went to warn General Davis of the Mexican army's forward position. I advised him to retreat from his exposed camp and move his men into the trees alongside the Nueces to protect it from the Mexican cavalry. General Davis ordered my arrest. It being dark, I disappeared into the trees and was not found. I heard Colonel Cameron also urge General Davis to leave the camp immediately and move the men into cover in the trees, which General Davis did. At sunrise, I watched the Mexican cavalry attack the abandoned camp, to no effect. Canales then ordered his militia forward to attack into the trees but, having gotten lost, the Mexican soldiers went too far on the flank and were unprotected, thus bearing the full effect of direct fire from General Davis's concealed men. The exchange of fire was brief, and the Mexican troops withdrew to a safe distance. I then borrowed a goat from the McGloin farm and followed the withdrawing Mexican army. Both men and horses were emaciated from obvious thirst and apparent hunger. Colonel Canales soon issued an order of complete retreat. I followed his entire army across the next two dry creek crossings on its march back toward the Rio Grande River; the soldiers suffered very badly in the heat. I believe many of his men and horses will die from thirst on the retreat to the Rio Grande. I then returned to the Nueces and searched as far north and west as the three rivers for any sign of other Mexican forces. There were none."

Noeme struggled whether to mention Alexandre LaBranche. Even though she hadn't found him on the Nueces, she had satisfied herself that he had not become a spy for Colonel Canales.

No spy, she thought, *not even Alexandre, would have told that traitor Canales that he would find so much as a drop of water or a single field of corn for his army to survive a march of more than forty leagues from Mexico across the south Texas desert.*

Houston had entrusted to her a letter written to Alexandre from Louisiana, which she was to deliver in the event that she found him, and then only if she concluded he was not spying for Colonel Canales. She had said nothing to Houston but privately hoped to find Alexandre somewhere along the Nueces, hoped that he would be grateful to her for delivering the letter, hoped that he would read it aloud to her, hoped that she would learn about his affairs. That had not happened. She did not find him.

Her report, even without mentioning Alexandre, was too long. She set about mentally eliminating what was not needed. She eliminated what Houston would learn in due course from General Davis's own report of the battle. She eliminated that she had warned General Davis of Canales' position the night before battle and that she had advised him to retreat from his hilltop camp into the trees along the Nueces. General Davis had been insulted that a black girl herding a goat had gotten inside his camp without being noticed and, more particularly, that a black girl had attempted to give him military advice. Davis did move his camp, at Captain Cameron's urging. It had been the correct decision, and that was all that mattered. Houston wouldn't care that Davis had distrusted her.

Noeme knew that being treated dismissively by men like General Davis was what enabled her to go unnoticed wherever Houston needed her to go. False appearances, such as herding goats on farms to which she did not belong and entering slave cabins on plantations where no one knew her, caused white men to take no notice of her. That's what gave Noeme the freedom to spy.

She coded onto paper only what Houston needed to know from her immediately.

"Sir: General Davis and Captain Cameron have defended their position at Lipantitlan. Colonel Canales' army did not carry adequate food or find sufficient water to attack across the distance between the Rio Grande and the Nueces at Lipantitlan. Canales withdrew from battle after twenty minutes. I observed his army march back toward Mexico in a starved and emaciated condition. They suffer greatly in the heat and drought; I believe more will die of thirst than from battle. I found no other sign of Mexican forces along the Nueces between the bay of Corpus Christi, Kinney's trading post, San Patricio, and the three rivers."

She chose to not mention Alexandre in her report. She also chose to not mention Kinney's perfidy; that information was best not put in writing and would be better received in person.

She waited until General Davis's own dispatch rider left his horse for a call of nature. Noeme, unseen, then slipped her coded report into his saddlebag, where Houston would find it with General Davis's exaggerated report of his defeat of Colonel Canales' superior army at Lipantitlan.

After Davis's dispatch rider mounted up and galloped away, she silently made her own way back to the McGloin farm and returned the borrowed goat, then began the long walk back to Sam Houston. She knew that it would be a difficult journey, but she needed the time to consider several worrisome questions:

Why, she worried, had Colonel Canales invaded a place of no consequence that could be reached only by crossing a desert where there was no water to be found? Why, she pondered, did Sam Houston entrust the defense of the frontier to men like General Davis who were expected to lead unruly adventurers who were more likely to desert than to fight?

And the most troubling question of all: why had she crept into the adobe house on Salado Street to watch over Alexandre in his sleep the night before the Mexican army had led him away?

No one had seen Noeme arrive. No one saw her when she left.

CHAPTER FOURTEEN
THE HILL COUNTRY

"I agree that it's a remarkable discovery," Alexandre said. "But I'm not going to share in it. I'm still going to Santa Fe."

Pennant was certain that he was making a joke.

"Young sir," he began, "this is a sign from God. Not every day you come across thirteen wagons full of silver what just needs a bit of work. If any of it is half as good as the first shovel full, well, you don't need no ten thousand United States dollars from Sam Houston. You can buy Sam Houston. You can buy Texas, not rightly so as a man might want it. Let's start getting it up to the mine so's we can smelt it." Alonzo nodded in agreement.

"No," Alexandre answered. He sat on a rock to rest and wipe his face. He looked back toward the hills and the mission, then out west beyond the blocked passage. "No. I'm not a miner. I'm not a spy or even a bank inspector for queen Victoria. I'm just a mapmaker. I'm going to Santa Fe."

Neither Pennant nor Alonzo believed him.

"Sir, there's here at our feet enough silver to make us rich. Rich like more'n any pirate ship haul, leastways any pirate ship I know anything about. Rich like'n if you want to go off and explore you can buy more horses and soldiers to go with you than Columbus paid for the Niña, the Pinta and the Santa Maria. All we got to do is just haul it back to that oven up there by the mine and finish smelting it. Then off you go to Santa Fe." As he spoke, Pennant began to look over Alexandre's wagon, to consider just how much ore it would hold, and to imagine how many trips it would take to move the ore back to the limestone kiln to smelt it into wealth.

"I see your covetous eye, Pennant. Are you going to steal my wagon again?" Alexandre stood to face him, much as he had stood to face Canales' firing squad: whatever came next was more than he could control. "Are you still a horse thief?"

Pennant backed down.

"No, no, none of that stealin' talk, young sir. We's particular mates here, all of us. A man don't steal from his mates. We just needs to get this ore back to the mine so's we can go to work on it. And we can't do that just ridin' two horses. We needs the wagon."

A deal was struck. Alexandre would help for as long as it took to get the ore back to the mine. In exchange, Pennant and Alonzo then would supply him with jerky and give him all but one of the water barrels so that Alexandre could set out for Santa Fe.

The distance back to the mine was not great; the men could go from the ore wagons back to the mine twice a day, but the horses couldn't. Alexandre's wagon was adequate to haul his tools and supplies, but neither his horse nor the wagon was sturdy enough to make the journey more than once a day and sometimes just in one direction. They spent more than a week in hauling the ore of just one of the silver wagons back to the mine.

And, after a week, Alexandre regretted his bargain; at this rate it would take months to haul the ore to the mine before he could set out for Santa Fe. But, he reflected, he was a man of his word, regardless of who the thieves were to whom he had given it. He was thinking of that very flaw in his character when they discovered the fresh tracks.

They had ridden early to the valley, then upriver toward the mission and the ore wagons, with Pennant explaining his plan for wealth. "Gonna buy me a barky. Alonzo and I need to get back to the sea."

"And how do you think you're going to cash in your silver to buy that boat?" Alexandre asked.

The question didn't trouble Pennant: "Don't know, bank in Galveston, maybe New Orleans, don't much make a difference."

"So, you're going to ride all the way across Texas to Galveston," Alexandre retorted, "with your saddle bags full of silver? Ride clean through the heart of Sam Houston's militia in San Antonio and Bastrop?" Alexandre laughed, then stopped. "What?"

Alonzo jerked his reins, sat bolt upright in his saddle, and pointed.

"Horses," he said. There were indeed fresh hoof prints along the riverbank. "Five horses. Not Comanches." He followed the tracks on foot to a ford in the Nueces, then stared hard into the hills east of the river. "Today."

The tracks weren't hard to follow. They came from somewhere north of the mission, continued right past the canyon where the ore wagons were exposed, along the Nueces directly toward them, then crossed the river and continued south along the opposite bank. Pennant and Alexandre led the horses into a secluded bend of the river while Alonzo followed the horseshoe tracks, running from mesquite to mesquite, hill to hill, bluff to bluff. Alonzo returned an hour later.

"Mexican soldiers. Riding toward the Frio, no hurry." The Mexican soldiers had followed the river farther south, to the very campsite from which the three men had spent their first night in the hill country before riding into the mountains. They rode in a column with outriders to each side as scouts.

"Convoy style," Pennant said. "Outriders is lookouts. Could be watchin' for the Comanch."

"Could be watching for us," Alexandre answered. "We've got to get out of here."

No one argued about that. The five Mexicans might stop at any moment and double back. They might be watching the three men from a crest of the hills. There could be more soldiers following the vanguard. There was no safety in the open valley.

Alonzo led them straight up the side of a long hill that separated the Nueces and the Frio. From the west slope, they looked back toward the mission; there were no clouds of dust, no evidence of more riders or foot soldiers heading down the Nueces. From the eastern crest, they could see the outline of the Frio north of their own hidden camp. There was little chance of the five Mexican soldiers finding their silver mine; it was so well concealed that it couldn't be seen from the Frio. The bigger risk, obvious when seen from the hill, was that the soldiers would see the tree stumps where first the Comanches and then the three men had cut trees for wood to fire the smelter oven. If the Mexican vanguard turned south at the bend of the Frio they would see evidence of their mining efforts.

They watched for a half hour as the soldiers moved slowly, scanning the horizon, always looking. When they arrived at the bend of the Frio, they stopped. For two agonizing hours, the soldiers rested in the shade of the oaks, ate from their saddlebags, and took a siesta. No one bothered them, not the three men who watched, nor the Comanches, nor anyone else. The riders finally mounted, sent two men ahead on the flanks, and turned north. They did not see the tree stumps.

"Who are they? And where are they going?" Alexandre whispered. The dead heat, the sunlight glaring off the limestone and rock outcrops, the cicadas whirring in the trees combined to make the men hold their breath until the soldiers were out of sight and riding toward the Medina. "We aren't safe until we find out."

Pennant was in favor of hiding. Alexandre was in favor of scouting. In the end, they agreed that Alonzo would follow the Mexican riders. Pennant would return to camp to clear away all signs of life. Alexandre would hide in the hills above the mission to watch for more soldiers. Alonzo was the first to report, three days later.

"They crossed the Medina," he said. "Toward San Antonio." He reported that when the five soldiers neared the city, they had spread out and moved with greater caution. Alonzo had kept within a few hundred yards of them until they reached the arroyo de Leon, no more than a few miles from the San Pedro. One of them minded their horses, the others changed their uniforms for peasant garb and set out on foot.

For two days Alexandre hid on the crest of a hill above the abandoned mission where he could see anyone who followed the Mexican soldiers. Back at the mine, Pennant had picked up the debris of their hauling ore and their smelting, then used sage brush to sweep away their own horseshoe prints and wagon tracks. There were no more soldiers or anyone else. The three tried to figure out what they had seen.

"They didn't gallop. They didn't ride like deserters," Alexandre concluded. "They didn't hide in the folds of the hills. If they were looking out for anything, it was Indians, not us. They went for a reason."

"Comanches watched too," Alonzo added. "I saw them." If the Comanches had watched the Mexicans, the Comanches also had watched Alonzo.

They waited for a week, not lighting a fire, not swinging a pick or digging for ore. Alonzo scouted while Pennant and Alexandre fed and watered the horses. Then, eight days later, Alonzo alerted them that the riders were coming back. The three men led their horses into the mine, hid the wagon, and took their rusty musket up to the crest of their mountain perch to watch. The same five Mexican soldiers returned as they had come, riding back from the Medina to the Frio. They wore their uniforms and, while they still did not gallop, they also did not stop for a siesta or use outriders to scout their flanks. They were going back to Mexico.

"Spies," Alexandre said to no one in particular. "But what are they spying?"

They spied on the spies. The Mexican soldiers crossed the Nueces, turned toward the mission, passed it, and finally left the hill country through a larger canyon far beyond the mission. From there, they continued across the prairie toward Mexico.

For days Alonzo stood watch near the Mexican passage while

Alexandre kept a lookout above the abandoned ore wagons and the mission. Pennant rode back to the Frio in case other riders entered the hill country from that direction. Nothing happened. There were no more riders, no Mexican army, no explanation for the five spies.

A week went by without another sign of anyone else coming from Mexico. They cautiously resumed hauling ore from the wagons to their silver mine. Then, a week later, Alexander's horse threw a shoe. Hauling ore came to a halt.

CHAPTER FIFTEEN
LAREDO

They tried to nail the horseshoe back onto the hoof but made a poor job of it at best. Indeed, all the horses' hooves showed the signs of shoes worn down to the live sole.

"We don't get some new shoes on 'em soon all they hoofs is going to crumble," Pennant declared, with reason. "They can't abide this rock much more." They all had seen their horses stumble more every day with the worn and heat-loosened horseshoes that had been nailed on months earlier. "I know a little something about horses," he added, with a thief's superior knowledge of other people's property. "They all get balky. So, long as we're there anyways, we could use some other goods too."

"As long as we're where?" Alexandre was on alert for one of Pennant's schemes. "And what other goods?"

"Nothin' against Alonzo's cookin' but maybe some real food, you know? A bit of flour. A bisket sounds pretty good." Alonzo whispered something. "Right, even a tortilla sounds good. You could use some biskets and tortillas out there on the desert eh, Alexandre." He paused, trying to appear solicitous. "And long's we's gettin' horseshoes and some food, we might as well get something to work the silver. Best thing is a mold. Can't rightly make silver coins proper without we got a mold."

Improvement of their finished product was of no interest to Alexandre, but essential to Pennant and Alonzo. In their first efforts to smelt silver, they had poured steady drips of molten rocks into their spoons, all manners of hollowed river stones, hardened knot holes from dead cedars, even remnants of rusted iron lamps found inside the mine. No two silver bits came out the same, much less as identical coins or bars or anything else. "This new ore," Pennant continued, "best thing is we make it up into bars an' coins, so we need a mold. And some tongs. Be easier to handle if we had some tongs."

"I said 'what do you mean as long as we're there?'" Alexandre demanded. "Where is there? It isn't San Antonio. If we showed up in San Antonio, Hays would demand a spy report on the Mexican army. At the least he would expect us to have made some maps of the Rio Grande." Alexandre briefly remembered long ago, when he happily set out to map the border. "We don't have either one."

It went without saying that Jack C. Hays would take them to Sam Houston for hanging or, perhaps, save time and shoot the three men himself.

"Well, by there, I didn't rightly mean to go back to San Antone. I had more in mind Laredo."

Alexandre thought Pennant was crazy.

"If I wanted to be killed by Mexicans it would be hard to find a better place than Mexico." Alexandre had long since ceased to think of Laredo or anywhere else on the Rio Grande as part of Texas. "Laredo is twice as far from here as San Antonio, maybe more. And why would anyone in Laredo give us horseshoes, nails, and food?"

"And coffee, and a mold. We could use a shot mold, that'd be fine, just make up silver coins shaped like musket balls or such, long as they's all the same. Bit of salt wouldn't go down bad either."

"I am not going to Laredo," Alexandre barked. He rose to his full height. His eyes flared.

"'Course we are," Pennant answered. "You've got that safe

conduct from Colonel Canales. You can go anywhere you want in Mexico with that. And you won't have to pay cash money for no tongs or food or horseshoes! The Mexicans will give 'em to you. Isn't that what your letter says? They have to give you safe pass and such helps and things as what you need to do your work. You won't need any money."

"We'll have no need of money after Colonel Canales shoots us."

"Canales said you was to go looking for him at Camargo or Reinosa, not Laredo." Alonzo whispered something to Pennant. "And they ain't much of a fort at Laredo either, maybe just provisions. Lot safer'n goin' to their big army fort at Presidio Rio Grande. Thought you knew that."

A few days later, they rode through across the most desolate landscape Alexandre had ever seen.

"It's all thickets and cactus," he moaned. "This dirt won't even grow enough weeds to keep a goat alive," a fact already disproved by Pennant's having stolen one from a Mexican shepherd they had passed one evening. "Why would anyone go to war over a desert?" *And,* to himself, *will there even be a blacksmith in Laredo?*

As they approached, Laredo opened up slowly, small outlying farms, then a few earthen huts with stick roofs, children chasing chickens, dogs, all slowly giving way to a more cosmopolitan village of adobe and plaster similar to San Antonio, except much smaller and more barren. A few people stared at them, then went back to their own affairs as the men rode slowly toward the bell tower of St. Agustin. The three passed by a few doorways with cookpots, the smell of posole and chiles, a stable, and a small shop with a wooden floor where gourds and pots were for sale. The plaza was flanked by the church, the alcalde, a building of shops shared by a *portales* arcade roof. Men in sombreros bustled to get out of the heat; women sold tortillas from blankets. On the far side of the plaza, an open space between the buildings revealed a convent and, beyond, the Rio Grande. The river was almost dry.

That's the fabled Rio Grande? Alexandre thought. The water flowed in a broad shallow stream between banks that were seventy-five yards apart. It's hardly the Mississippi, or even the Sabine. *I could walk across it. I could survey it, map it, and record its coordinates, all in a single day.*

There was a small military fort on the opposite bank. They rode across the river to the few desultory soldiers who guarded the courtyard of the garrison. An officer walked out, straightened his tunic, and addressed them.

"Who are you?" he asked. Alonzo answered that they needed help with shoeing their horses. "Go away," the officer followed up. "This is a garrison, not a livery stable." Alonzo asked if there was a blacksmith. "No, they've gone to Presidio Rio Grande. There's nothing here for you. Where did you come from?" The officer signaled his soldiers, who walked smartly to the three ragged men and reached for the reins of their horses.

Alexandre unfolded the letter of safe conduct and handed it to the officer.

"From Colonel Canales," he added.

The officer took the safe conduct, read it and reacted as if Alexandre had handed him a bucket of lightning bolts. The officer stood smartly to attention and saluted.

"Calixto Vargas Bravo, coronel, jefe y commandante de guarnición de Laredo en el departemento del Rio Bravo en Coahuila y Tejas, señor, a sus órdenes, señor." A torrent of Spanish flowed over the parade ground as Calixto Vargas Bravo welcomed them to Laredo and to all that he could offer to assist them.

Within minutes, he had begged Alexandre to surrender their horses and handed them over to the care of a corporal, who led them and Pennant away. A second corporal escorted Alonzo to the quartermaster's stores. Colonel Bravo himself took Alexandre into the officers' quarters and asked in jovial and not-understood Spanish about Colonel Canales and the queen of England.

They were in Laredo for less than six hours, and Pennant had been correct: the Mexicans gave them what they asked for. By the end of *siesta,* they were reunited on the garrison parade ground. Their horses had been shod and their saddlebags burdened with horseshoes, nails, and a fine ball hammer. A large canvas bag of cornmeal, salt, beans, chiles, and coffee and an iron cooking grill had been roped to Alonzo's saddle. Alonzo stood quietly by while Alexandre chatted affably and unintelligibly with Colonel Bravo. The only thing missing was Pennant who, after a brief search, was discovered trying to seduce a rather jolly spinster beneath a shade tree behind the garrison's stable.

"Alonzo, tell Colonel Bravo that we're grateful for his hospitality." Alonzo did so. "And that we haven't enjoyed such generosity anywhere since leaving Louisiana." That much was true; while the farrier shod their horses and the quartermaster rounded up food, Colonel Bravo had invited them to dine at his officer's table. "And tell him that if we could ask for anything it would be only to stay longer in Laredo," which was false, except for Pennant, given the shy flirtations of the spinster. "But, because our equipment and tools are unguarded, we must return to camp this very evening."

They might have lingered even longer if Alexandre's inadequate Spanish had succeeded in falsely clarifying for Colonel Bravo the work that he had undertaken on behalf of the Goldsmith and Barclay banks.

"Be so good as to inform Colonel Canales," Bravo answered, "that I have given my complete and generous assistance to his good colleague, *Señor* LaBranche, and his two aides." Alexandre and Alonzo assured him that they would do so. "And if you do not find Colonel Canales, do you have anything for him that I may deliver on your behalf? From the Queen of England?"

We have to get out of here, Alexandre thought. *The more el coronelo wants to talk about Canales and Queen Victoria, the closer we get to the wall where they line us up to shoot us.*

"Please tell him, Alonzo, that we shall do so." Alonzo did so. "And that we regret missing Colonel Canales at Camargo and Reinosa," which Alonzo also conveyed to Colonel Bravo. "But my report of inspection is not complete. You may say that we found the condition of the land to be very barren. We found that no people occupy it."

"But Colonel Canales is not at Camargo or Reinosa," Colonel Bravo replied. "He is at Ramireno, less than ten leagues from here. His vanguard arrived yesterday." Alonzo translated; Alexandre changed color. "I beg you to stay the night, my friends," the colonel continued. "You can speak with him yourselves, when he leads his regiment past Laredo tomorrow or, at the latest, on Thursday. He marches to join General Woll at Presidio Rio Grande."

While Alonzo translated that Colonel Canales was one day away, Alexandre and Pennant struggled to not fall off their horses.

"Thank you for your generosity, sir. We must go." Bravo seemed not to understand. "We must return to our camp." Bravo still did not understand. "Our tools and equipment aren't protected; we must go," Alexandre tried again, displaying by pantomime the act of riding away. "There." Alexandre pointed in the most opposite direction of where he understood Colonel Canales to be. Bravo reacted immediately.

"¡No vayan en esa dirección! No es seguro," Bravo answered in a grave tone of voice. "Guerra." Bravo improvised his own pantomime: soldiers marching, rifles firing, cannons booming. "Guerra." He pointed across the river toward the great trackless desert from whence Alexandre and his silver miners had just come. "Guerra."

War? Alexandre understood the word as well as anyone. War, where? War, with whom? War, when? His mind raced with visions of soldiers marching into plazas, images of fusiliers kneeling to fire, lancers and dragoons attacking. He saw the befuddled General Vasquez on horseback and the menacing Canales at the head of real troops. He knew the answer before Bravo could say it.

"El general Woll avanzará en San Antonio," Bravo answered. "Desde el presidio del Rio Bravo." He pointed to the north.

Alexandre understood. From the first time he had looked at the map of Texas when he sat with President Lamar in the drawing room of a New Orleans hotel, he had seen that Presidio Rio Grande was the far edge at the west end of the map, connected to San Antonio by the camino real, the same road General Vasquez had used in retreat.

"Por eso mi guarnición está vacía; los soldados están con el general Woll."

"I regret," Alexandre answered, "that I will not be able to witness Colonel Canales leading his troops past Laredo. Our duties are many leagues north of the river." He assured Bravo that the warning of war would cause them to return to camp by a different route, a more southerly route. "The queen would be quite distressed if her inspector of lands got caught up in a war, Colonel," Alexandre added as he settled his boots into his stirrups and saluted. "It is not our fight, sir. Adios, Colonel, and gracias."

"No es adios, mi amigo. Es hasta la vista." Bravo saluted. His men stiffened to attention. Alexandre saluted in return.

None of them breathed until they were an hour north of Laredo. Then they laughed and inhaled the fresh air of freedom. They bragged of the bounty Colonel Bravo had settled on them.

"Rice," Pennant said to no one in particular, as he counted out the bags of food. "Frijoles. Dried beef. Look at this!" This was salt. "Even a bit of coffee. Lord, I ain't had coffee in months. Alonzo, you must a cleared out their store."

Alexandre had not seen this Pennant before, a Pennant who was more like a happy housewife than a pirate or a thief. The thief soon reappeared.

"Got a little surprise of me own," he said. With a flourish, he dug into his own saddlebag and withdrew a parcel wrapped inside a stolen serape. "Look at this!"

He held up a shot mold, a slab of steel with cavities on its face that were the shape of musket balls, rifle balls, and, at the larger scale, a cannon ball.

"Four pounder," Pennant announced. "Fill it with lead, four-pound cannon ball. Mold's not the best of shape, but it'll make silver for us just fine. Thought we'd borry it for a while."

The smallest mold would form a ball of silver large enough to make Guanajuato reales; a man could sell a dozen pieces of that size and live for a year. If they could fill the cannonball mold a dozen times with silver smelted from the pure ore of the buried wagons, they would never have to work another day in their lives.

"Yes sir, I admit, the farrier wasn't payin' no mind while I was watchin' him shoe the horses. Good fellow, won't say nothing against him as he did his work right and proper, except that he didn't notice my interest in the cannon balls. Would of took a cannon too if I could of found one."

We are, Alexandre thought, *no longer an imposter and two horse thieves. We are men of action.*

The horseshoes worked. They arrived at the mine in half the time it had taken them to ride to Laredo, then led the horses to the sweet banks of the Frio to graze and rest. But, when they climbed into the mine, they found evidence of visitors. There were piled up some rough blankets made from buffalo hide, several stone cook pots, and some bags of dried pine nuts, berries, and corn.

"The Comanch is taking care of us, young sir," Pennant bragged. "This ain't no jail. We're set!"

They were not set.

One week later, the four old Comanche warriors who had first invaded their camp walked straight into their breakfast of salt meat and beans. The warriors shouted, grunted, and waved their arms furiously; the men had no idea what they wanted. The warriors were burned from the sun, their faces haggard. But their eyes were painted, and their arms were wrapped with war thongs. All carried lances; one had an old musket. They demanded the three men follow them.

They left the mine, crossed the Frio, then rode west across the hills until they arrived to overlook the Nueces. The Comanches pointed down from the perch toward the river below. There, along both banks of the river, were more than two thousand Mexican troops. The vanguard already had passed the old Spanish mission while its baggage train stretched well back, far beyond the entrance to the canyon where the remaining ore wagons were still concealed by the landslide. Between the vanguard and the baggage trains there were regiments of dragoons, squads of cavalry and, behind them, the regimental flags of a general officer and his staff. They led yet more regiments of grenadiers and foot soldiers armed with Tercerlo muskets and Baker rifles. The caissons of a dozen cannon rolled along behind the foot soldiers. The army moved slowly through the hill country at two or three miles to the hour.

"Them five Mexican spies," Pennant said. "They was scouting the way for that army down there."

"That army down there is the army our friend Colonel Bravo said was preparing for war," Alexandre concluded.

"That army down there, young friend, is marching to San Antone," Pennant answered.

There was little doubt of it; Bravo had told them as much in Laredo. The army followed precisely the route that the five spies had scouted a few weeks before. It would lead the army down the Nueces to the gap in the hills, then east to the Frio, then back through the hills to the Medina River and right into San Antonio. No one would ever see them coming.

"We forgot," Alexandre added. "that Colonel Bravo told us there would be a war. We rode right across the *camino real* where Canales left us at the Nueces but, because we didn't see any signs of an army, we forgot about it." It went unsaid that they didn't see such an army because General Woll had led his army far above the Nueces crossing to sneak through the hills and surprise San Antonio from the north. "But," he finished, "it's not our fight."

"Will it be our fight if they find our silver mine?" Pennant asked. "It's not like we grew them trees back. It'll be a lot harder to hide the stumps and what not from a couple of thousand men on foot than it was from five spies galloping the other way on their horses."

One of the Comanche warriors took Alonzo; they disappeared amid the rocks and mesquite trees. Two hours later, Alonzo reappeared.

"We got within ten yards and watched up close." Alonzo had seen the army deploy outriders to scout ahead of the dragoons. "They're fed and watered," Alonzo said. "Horses. Men." The implication was clear; General Woll did not intend for his troops to linger on the march. He continued.

"There," Alonzo pointed. Neither Alexandre nor Pennant could see anything. "There," he said again. Then, in the vast distance, they watched the outriders, then the flags of the dragoons and their horses heading steadily toward the passage to the Frio. For a half hour the men watched the progress of the vanguard, then the entire cavalry, and, finally, the first companies of foot soldiers. "There."

At last Pennant and Alexandre saw what Alonzo had seen: forty Comanches on horseback broke from cover and rode directly toward the advancing Mexican army.

When the two forces were a hundred yards apart, the Mexican cavalry rolled out on its flanks to encircle the Comanches. The Comanches continued to ride directly toward the army. When they were fifteen or twenty yards from the soldiers, three warriors advanced. The other Comanches halted.

"Look," Alexandre whispered, as if the sound of their voices would carry down the mountainside to the river and into the din of the colliding forces. "It's the chief who handed us the boy." The two companions who rode forward with him were the angry warrior and the child himself.

"It's our lad," Pennant whispered. "The boy." Their sickly child sat as tall as he could in his saddle, healthier but no larger than when they last had seen him swimming away. "No!"

The cavalry had merely gotten out of the way of the infantry. A dozen foot soldiers charged their *Tercerlos*, kneeled, and fired a volley directly into the three Comanches who had come to meet them. The child was killed instantly. The chief fell from his horse with musket balls in his chest and head. The warrior charged, raising his ancient musket. He was shot from his horse, then shot a dozen more times on the `ground. The cavalry then attacked the rest of the Comanches from the flanks. Not more than a dozen escaped. The battle at the Nueces lasted no longer than five minutes.

The men sagged against the rocks and trees that hid them,

watching the Mexican army. It resumed its march through the hill country, no more deterred by the Comanches than if they'd swatted flies. The army rode directly over the field of dead warriors, ignored the Comanches' surviving horses, sent no outriders to pursue the few who had gotten away. Alexandre, Pennant, and Alonzo could do no more than hold their collective breaths.

"Those savages never done nothing," Pennant said. "They never hurt nobody, least not the Mexicans."

"Those savages gave us your fortune," Alexandre answered. "They gave us food and blankets. They let us live in their lands, and their land is being invaded."

"They kilt our boy," Pennant replied.

"Yes," Alexandre said, "And now it is our fight."

CHAPTER SIXTEEN

"That goddamned Canales feinted an attack on General Davis down at the Nueces while those other bastards were sneaking through the hill country," Houston shouted. San Antonio had fallen, again, this time to a Mexican army led by General Woll. "Don't say a goddamn word!" Houston growled.

Noeme had no intention of saying a word. Houston had the facts; it was not her place to analyze them or to advise what to do about them. Her place was to do what Houston told her to do once he decided what to do.

"How the hell did those sons of bitches get all the way to San Antonio and not one person saw them?" he continued.

This was not, strictly speaking, a fair question. Bigfoot Wallace had warned that there were some Mexican strangers in San Antonio. Jack C. Hays had arrested two Mexican spies at Mission Concepcion; the spies had not survived the arrest. One local Mexican had warned the mayor and Judge Hutchinson that two thousand Mexican troops were within a few leagues of the city.

"But we didn't believe them, sir," Hays said. "There had been bandits all up and down the Cibolo and the Guadalupe, as many as a hundred of them. We captured some, threatened some, but we didn't find any Mexican armies."

"What kind of ranger outfit are you running, Hays? How could two thousand Mexican soldiers surround San Antonio before you knew they were there? What the hell are you doing out there?"

It was not in Hays' nature to argue, not with his men, not with Houston. It also was not in his nature to defend himself over a tongue-lashing; his goal was to protect the people Houston sent him to protect, and Hays had failed to protect them. What was in his nature was to say exactly what he knew.

"It was more than that, sir," Hays answered. "We were warned down to the last hour. Look at this." Hays handed Houston a large sheet of foolscap on which there was drawn a map. Houston glanced at the drawing, then pitched it onto his desk.

"Two days before General Woll invested San Antonio, sir, Mr. LaBranche appeared in the city. Judge Hutchinson was holding the fall term of court, and every lawyer in the Bexar district was in the courtroom. Mr. Maverick came walking in with LaBranche and said to stop court, to listen to what he had to say."

"LaBranche?" Houston was surprised. He had heard nothing of LeBranche being back in San Antonio.

Noeme was just as surprised. Her head snapped up to listen, but she said nothing.

"Yes, sir," Hays answered. "It was him. At first, I didn't believe it was Mr. LaBranche; he was worn an pretty ragged. I hadn't seen him since his party separated from Colonel Canales at the Nueces last March and rode off into the wilderness. But LaBranche stepped up and Judge Hutchinson told him to speak and be quick about it. Mr. LaBranche said to us, 'Sirs, there's a Mexican army not more than two days away.' We didn't believe him. Some of us were suspicious because of his being seen with Canales in the past. Then he said 'They are coming to San Antonio. I watched them marching down the Nueces to a vale of the Uvalde.' And to my shame, sir, I said that it wasn't true because we had men down on the *camino real* who reported that the road from Mexico to San Antonio was clear.

Mr. LaBranche said that the army was not on the *camino real*. He said the army was far north of the *camino real,* inside the hill country, and progressing through the mountains toward San Antonio. When he said that, sir, the men in the courtroom laughed at him." Hays collected his thoughts. "Then he drew this map, sir."

This time Houston did look at the map. It was remarkable. Houston knew the geography of Texas as well as any man. He had seen the maps that Stephen F. Austin had sent around the United States to attract settlers. He had seen the Tanner maps that Jim Bowie had followed to the San Saba in search of a lost mine. And he had seen the land office maps, some submitted by Samuel Maverick. They were child's scratches in comparison.

Alexandre's map was so detailed that it might have been a picture. He had drawn the peaks and valleys of the hill country at an oblique rather than an overhead perspective, thereby showing the landscape as a series of mountains as a man might see them from a saddle. On the left there was the vale of the Uvalde with the Nueces flowing down a broad plain, a passage eastward to the Frio, through more hills to the Sabinal, on to the Medina and, finally, the San Pedro. Alexandre had marked by a solid line the route that General Woll used to lead the Mexican army to the very edge of the city. In its own right, the map was remarkable; as a warning, it was the finest piece of spying that Houston had ever seen.

"Except that you didn't believe him, Hays. Is that what you're saying? He drew you the order of battle for an enemy ten times your size and you didn't believe him?"

"Yes, sir. Most of the men said LaBranche was making it up. They thought it would be impossible to lead dragoons, infantry, cannon, and a baggage train through those mountains. Some asked how LaBranche could have known they were following that exact route if he had broken off and ridden to San Antonio."

"Well?"

"He said that General Woll had sent spies over that same route a month ago. And there was more. LaBranche said he'd been living in the mountains, but didn't know that the army was coming until his friends the Comanches warned him. He said it was the Comanches who led him to see the Mexican army marching through the hill country."

Houston laughed.

"That," Hays added, "is what the men in the courtroom in San Antonio did, sir, they laughed, because Comanches don't befriend white men in the hill country. Comanches kill white men and take their horses."

"Go on," Houston ordered.

"I went out there to look for myself. I rode the *camino real* as far as the Medina, then back to the San Pedro. Then I scouted all the other roads that enter San Antonio." Hays made no effort to hide his failure. "When I reported that I found no trace of General Woll's army, the prosecuting attorney had LaBranche arrested."

Houston said nothing. Noeme clamped her hands hard on the edge of her chair to prevent herself from saying anything. Hays waited for Houston to explode. Houston did not. Hays continued.

"That night I went out one more time. I rode to the Salado and then over to the mission trail along the San Antonio River. When I returned, I couldn't get back into the town. General Woll's army had surrounded the city. That is how the sons of bitches got all the way to San Antonio, sir, exactly the way LaBranche told us they would." He paused to let the facts sink in, then concluded. "I failed, sir."

Houston knew, everyone in Texas knew, that General Woll had captured San Antonio, almost without a shot. What Houston had not known, because there had been no one to tell him, was how Woll had managed to surround the city without a single scout discovering his army in advance. Now he knew. That was not why he had sent for Hays.

"When did you learn that General Woll took all those men in San Antonio as prisoners?" Houston asked. "The judge and the lawyers and city council and the businessmen? Woll captured fifty-two men right in the middle of town. What I mean is, when did you learn about that?"

It was a different version of the first question: 'How did the

Mexican army surround San Antonio without you discovering them?' This version was 'How did the Mexican army spirit away fifty-two men, all the men who had been in Judge Hutchinson's courtroom and at Samuel Maverick's house, and remove them from San Antonio without you stopping them?'

Hays was patient and honest in his answer.

"We didn't know he had taken Judge Hutchinson and Mr. Maverick and all those other men until after the fight at the Salado," Hays answered. "It wasn't until then that we got someone into the city who told us what the conditions were under General Woll."

Houston nodded, not in approval but in understanding. He paused to think, then asked:

"Well, Jack, that's what I asked you to come report about in the first place. Get on with it. What happened at the Salado?"

"It was like this, sir. Matthew Caldwell brought up about a hundred and fifty volunteers to the Cibolo, good men, and my ranger company, forty-two of us. Caldwell moved us forward to a ravine on the Salado. That morning he sent us up to the edge of San Antonio, to show ourselves. Eight of us rode almost right up to the Alamo before the Mexicans finally saw us. McCulloch and I kicked about until some Mexican cavalry came out. They chased us back toward the Salado, where we joined back up with Caldwell and the men. Then there was what I would call a skirmish for a couple of hours before the Mexican sent out his big guns." General Woll had sent two cannons and two hundred more cavalry to chase Hays and McCulloch, then added four hundred foot soldiers and a regiment of dragoons. "Colonel Caldwell had the men proper there on our side of the arroyo, sir. When the dragoons rode up, we shot their horses out from under them. When the Mexican infantry marched across the prairie toward our ditch, Colonel Caldwell's men simply killed them. I don't know how many, sir. We lost one man, Mr. Jett."

"And the Mexican, sir?" Houston asked.

"I don't know to the man, Mr. President. I think we killed about sixty, sir, and there were probably two hundred of them wounded trying to make their way back to safety. It was getting on to dark by then and I didn't want my rangers wandering around in the dark counting Mexicans."

Houston didn't smile or frown, say he was satisfied or dissatisfied. Hays continued.

"It was all Colonel Caldwell could do to keep the men in the line after the shootig was done. They wanted to chase the Mexican back into the city and shoot more of Woll's soldiers. But the fight had been successful, sir. And one of the Mexicans we killed was Vicente Córdova. He tried to get to Colonel Caldwell's flank, and the men killed him and all his Indians."

Houston sifted this information. That someone had killed the infamous Córdova was good news, but most of Hays' report was about Colonel Caldwell's battle.

"Did you see what was happening a mile away, sir, with Captain Dawson?" Houston asked.

"No, sir," Hays answered. "I could not see that part of the battle."

"I'm told that Captain Dawson's men never reached Colonel Caldwell," Houston continued.

Hays had not been in a position to see. One of Colonel Caldwell's scouts had discovered that a rear guard of Mexican regiments had surrounded Dawson's volunteers.

"As best we can figure, Jack, there were almost sixty men with Dawson. Only two escaped. So, what happened to Dawson's men? Their women want to know. I want to know. What happened to them?"

Even Jack C. Hays shrank at the memory of the battlefields the following day, with General Woll back inside San Antonio and beyond the range of attack, he and Colonel Caldwell's men had found them.

"We came across Dawson's body, sir, and thirty-five more. We knew they were ours. They were naked."

Houston was furious.

"I hoped for better from General Woll than stripping the bodies of brave volunteers on a battlefield. That son of a bitch's no better than Santa Anna. They're no army, they're just a mob of marauding murderers." Houston vented his temper for a few moments, then continued. "And did we strip the Mexican's bodies, Jack?" Houston asked.

"No sir. Our men took a few things, boots. Bigfoot found a pair of pants."

Houston laughed. Anyone big enough to have pants that would fit Bigfoot Wallace was a big man indeed. He would forgive Bigfoot, but he would not forgive the Mexicans for stripping the clothes off thirty-six Texians and leaving them for the coyotes and the fowls.

Houston was not a man to punish the messenger. Hays' admission that he had failed to discover General Woll's army before it surrounded San Antonio was a confession that Hays felt keenly but that Houston regarded as the same failure of every man in the Bexar district. All were told; none believed. If pressed, Houston could himself confess to having failed at one time or another. He trusted Jack C. Hays with what mattered.

"We've got to know who survived, Jack. Dawson's men. We have to know who the prisoners are. And what happened to them."

"Yes, sir," Hays answered.

"And where they are. Find them, Jack."

"Yes, sir."

"Thank you, Jack. You may go."

Jack C. Hays was not a man to argue or to wait around for others. He did not do so now; he loosened the reins of his horse, swung into the saddle, and rode away.

For the next hour, the great man sat with his arms folded, his eyes fixed on the window as if something might appear that he hadn't seen before. Nothing did. Twice, Noeme stood up, once to leave, once to speak; Houston twice shook his head. She sat back down and did not speak. At the end of an hour, he resumed.

"It's not just the women, Noeme," he said. "The women down in Fayette and Gonzales and Victoria, whose men went off with Dawson and didn't come back." It hurt deeply; he knew some of Dawson's men, almost all of Caldwell's, and many of their widows. They had stood beside him, or commanded under him, or had volunteered for dozens of fights and skirmishes and battles from Buffalo Bayou to Victoria and Lipantitlan, from Refugio and Goliad to Plum Creek, brave men. "And it's all those men that Woll captured inside San Antonio the first day. We don't even know who they are, most of them. All we can guess is that Woll took every Texian in San Antonio and hauled them away. There won't be a judge or reeve or banker left in the place, or any of the lawyers who were there for the fall term. All gone."

He liked not only that Noeme was invisible and willing to go anywhere on a moment's notice, but also that she was smart. He liked that no one would believe a black girl was free or that she could read. He reached into his jacket pocket and took out a folded letter, opened it, read it, then handed it to Noeme.

"To His Excellency the Honorable Samuel Houston, Office of the President, Washington-on-the-Brazos, Republic of Texas, greetings:

On behalf of Her Majesty, Victoria, Queen of The United Kingdom of England, Ireland, Wales, and Scotland, and as the representative of Her Majesty's government by her commission as consul for the Republic of Texas in subordination to the Ambassador to the Republic of Mexico, the Envoy Extraordinary Minister Plenipotentiary, the Right Honorable Sir Richard Pakenham, I bring to your attention the inquiry of that official which states the following question:

Mr. Elliott: Is there known to you a person or persons who represents himself or themselves to be acting on behalf of the banking houses of Barclay and Goldsmith, St. James, Westminster, London, in the matter of inspecting certain lands, said lands themselves being represented to serve as security for bonds, loans, and credits issued by such banking houses on behalf of Her Majesty the Queen to the Republic of Mexico at divers times between the years 1827 and 1841 and being situated in the former administrative districts of Coahuila y Tejas and now including some portions of the Republic of Texas? The foundation of this inquiry is that certain messages have been provided to the embassy of Her Majesty the Queen in the City of Mexico that describe the assistance, cooperation, aid, and protection afforded to such person or persons in the conduct of such inspections and particularly including land that is situated between the Nueces River and the Rio Bravo—Rio Grande Rivers, such assistance etc., including letters of protection and assistance on behalf of the Army of the North in the Department of Coahuila Y Tejas of the Republic of Mexico.

Respectfully,

Richard Pakenham, Embassy of her Majesty the Queen, City of Mexico

President Houston, I am unable to reply to the Ambassador at present, I being only very recently appointed to my post. Accordingly, I would greatly benefit from your knowledge of this delicate question. I share with you this inquiry from Ambassador Pakenham with the express request that, if any such person or persons are known to you, that you please make fully known to me in my capacity as consul etc., as aforesaid, your knowledge of him or them in order that I may make proper investigations and replies to the Ambassador in keeping with the subject. I look forward to your answer to this inquiry.

I send to you the continued wishes of my office and of the office of the Ambassador and of Her Majesty the Queen for your health and well-being.

Yours faithfully,

Charles Elliott, Consul of Her Majesty, Victoria, Queen of The United Kingdom of England, Ireland, Wales, and Scotland, to the Republic of Texas, in Austin, this 31st day of August, 1842.

The flourishing sentences and carefully disguised subjects and verbs were unfamiliar to Noeme, but the subject was not. When she finished, she folded the letter as it had been given to her and returned it to the great man.

"It seems that I came up short," Houston said. "About your friend LaBranche." Noeme had never heard Houston admit error before; this did not seem the time to say so.

"Did you look at this map that Hays brought?" Houston asked. "It's almost like you're standing there on the prairie looking right at the hills and rivers in person." He sighed. "He did exactly what I told him to do. Mind, it took him a while to get around to it, laying about in San Antonio for a month or two, but just look at this. Every horse, cannon, soldier, wagon, and tortilla press, just like I told him. And no one believed him."

Noeme waited for him to say what he wanted her to do, if he wanted her to do anything. In the end, she asked:

"Do I wait for Mr. Hays to find out who the prisoners are?"

Houston thought about that question as well and came to a decision.

"No. I've got to chase Woll back into Mexico. The people will demand it and I demand it. I've ordered General Somervell to organize two regiments in San Antonio, but it'll take him a while to get an army together." He paused to organize his words. "Once Santa Anna learns that I'm sending an army to the Rio Grande, he'll order General Woll to dispose of the Dawson prisoners. If he hasn't shot them already, he may shoot them then, or at least march them to prison deep in Mexico just like he did Lamar's Santa Fe men."

Houston put his fingers together, nodded, gazed, and thought some more.

"But, if this letter from our friend Elliott is correct, someone in Mexico is asking about the bona fides of your friend LaBranche. If he turns up in a prisoner pen, his life isn't worth a horseshoe nail." He then answered the question that Noeme wanted to ask: what to do?

"We have to find him," Houston went on. "If LaBranche is a prisoner, we're too late." He paused to see if she understood the urgency; if unmasked as a Texian spy, Alexandre would be shot. But, if he was unmasked while falsely posing as an English bank agent, Texas' fragile relations with England would be shot. "You must find him before General Somervell and Captain Hays attack Mexico."

Noeme had wanted to find Alexandre from the night almost a year before when she had disappeared from the back of his wagon while Thomas Rusk and Pinkney Henderson herded him and the two horse thieves to Austin to meet Sam Houston. She had wanted to talk with Alexandre, really talk with him, from the moment when she had listened to him evade Colonel Canales' prying questions on the steps of the San Antonio cathedral. What she did not know was what exactly it was she wanted to do when she did talk to him. What could she possibly say?

"I will find him, sir," she answered. "But what then? "When I find him, what am I to do with him?"

CHAPTER SEVENTEEN

It was the finest hour Alexandre had spent since the day he escaped San Antonio. They awoke one morning to a hard frost that covered the ground. The meat that Alonzo had dressed had frozen inside their makeshift smokehouse; a rime of ice topped the water in their cistern. Then, when they woke and walked out to start a fire, they found the four old Comanche warriors who had led them to witness Woll's massacre of their leaders. They were sitting on three heavy buffalo hides.

He bowed to the warriors and put his hand on his heart. Pennant looked to see if they had stolen anything. Alonzo tried with uncertain Spanish and even more uncertain Lipan to offer breakfast. The Comanches nodded their heads and chanted. One of them pointed toward the disappearing moon and made an indecipherable signal with his fingers; Alexandre thought it looked like a galloping horse that suddenly laid down. The Comanches wrapped the men in the buffalo robes, refused Alonzo's offer of jerky, and disappeared.

Despite the loss of horseshoes, despite the Mexican army riding through their passages to the abandoned mission and the hidden wagons of silver ore, they had persisted. As autumn settled on the hill country, Alexandre and Pennant hauled ore from the last few wagons to the smelting kiln at the mine. Alonzo fed them on deer and turkey and with greens and herbs he gathered from the rocky hills and the lush bottom lands near the rivers. And occasionally, while the horses rested, Alonzo fired the oven for Pennant and Alexandre to smelt the ore into silver, very fine silver. While they worked, Pennant lectured Alexandre on his folly.

"Now let that be a lesson to you, young sir." Pennant had taken to calling Alexandre "young sir" as his name. He levered his shovel into the mound of ore, lifted, pulled, and shoveled another pile onto the mound near the oven.

"And what lesson would that be?" Alexandre asked. He helped pick the rocks out of the ore.

"Truth is the worst policy. You lie to people, they give you what you want. You tell people the truth, they put you in jail," Pennant said.

Alexandre laughed.

"We go to Laredo, young sir, and we tells 'em we needs some horseshoes and a bit of cornmeal and maybe some salt and the commander-in-chief of the whole shebang falls all over hisself to meet our every need. Coulda said 'Ali Baba'and he'd a granted all three of your wishes and give you three more. No need to mention his forty thieves."

"It was not Ali Baba," Alexandre answered. "It was Aladdin of the forty thieves who had the three wishes. And there was more to getting what we needed than telling Colonel Bravo we wanted some horseshoes and a bag of cornmeal. There was the matter of the safe conduct letter."

"There you go, always lookin' for the bad," Pennant answered. He swung a pick into the pile of rocks and ore, swung it again, and broke up enough to call for the shovel. "Thieves and wishes ain't so bad, young sir, and they wasn't nothing wrong by you using that safe conduct. That's why your friend Canales gave it to you."

They had not the least idea that Noeme was twenty feet away, hidden in a dark recess of the mine near the entrance to the oven.

Laredo? Noeme wondered. *Canales? What safe conduct letter?*

"He is not my friend, Pennant," she heard Alexandre answer. "Canales left us for dead in the desert."

Noeme had never been certain whether Canales had left them for dead in the desert. Hays' rangers had not been able to say more than that General Vasquez had left the three men at the Nueces and that they had watched Alexandre turn toward the hill country.

"But then you go off to San Antone," Pennant continued. "Then you tell the truth, you tell 'em the Mexicans is coming, the Mexicans is coming. They call you a liar and put you in jail for raising a false alarm." He shoveled another load of ore and stood aside so that Alexandre could sort it. "Seems like a lesson to me. You lie, you get fed and your horses get took care of. You tell the truth, and they put you in jail. Hard to think you can't learn it; you was the one they put in jail."

"I was in jail for an hour. Samuel Maverick stood my surety, and they let me out. He took me back to the adobe house on Soledad, where I slept in my old bed until the alarm bell rang out in the plaza. You could hear the Mexican soldiers shouting to surrender and the Texians firing wildly down the streets, but you couldn't see for the fog," Alexandre added. "Not twenty feet, it was that thick. I made my way over to Mr. Maverick's home. He said he figured that no one would charge me with raising a false alarm now. He told me to get on my horse and get out before the fog lifted. That was the last I saw of him."

Pennant knew the rest of the story; Noeme did not. Alexandre had ridden the back streets of San Antonio to the San Pedro creek, then passed through the Mexican lines without being seen. It took him two days to ride to the Frio river, then back up into the hills to their mine.

Weeks after Alexandre escaped San Antonio, they had heard the distant sound of rifle fire. They rode to the lower reaches of the hills and hid in the shrub, where they watched a small band of Texians harry General Woll's Mexican army in retreat on the *camino real* to Presidio Rio Grande.

"Sorriest battle I ever seen," Pennant had announced. "Proves my point. Best leave 'em all alone, Mexicans, Texians, all of 'em. They all just wants to bluster and such. A man could get killed. Better off here making silver."

They had become very good at making silver. After their successful venture into Laredo, they had begun to cast silver in their purloined shot mold. The ore had produced over one hundred balls of very fine silver, each large enough to slice into coins the size of ocho reales. It was only a matter of time before they could produce silver the size of cannon balls. Every day, it became harder for Alexandre to leave.

Late that afternoon Alonzo made his way up to the mine, through it, and out to the limestone oven and told them to ready the fire to roast some deer.

"Venison again? Bah!" Pennant moaned. "Know what I'd like, Alonzo? A fish. Ain't had a good fish since we was on the *Durango*. Nothin' against your deer meat or all them rabbits, just a little change is all I'm saying. Slap a fish on the grille, that'd be fine. Remember that time we was off Mobile? How much ore we got there, young sir?"

Noeme had watched Alonzo stalk a deer a half mile from the bend in the Frio. From there it had been a simple matter to stay in the shadows and watch him kill the creature, then field dress it, then to follow him back to the mountain, up the declivity, and slip unseen into the mine itself. She had quietly hidden near the opening to listen to them.

"Time for supper, young sir. Enough for today. First dog watch! Eats!"

Noeme decided that it was time to reveal herself. She flitted unseen out of the darkness and made her way to sit on a small boulder near Alonzo's makeshift kitchen to watch them make room for cooking.

"Good evening, gentlemen," she said. "May I join your company? I should like to rest if I may, before we go on." The men almost collapsed where they stood.

"Who the hell are you?" Pennant demanded. He and Alonzo

should have recognized her but did not. "Get the hell out of here. You're trespassin.' You ain't welcome here." Alonzo whispered in his ear. "And how come you to be here anyways? Who are you? Git!"

Noeme smiled but otherwise paid him no attention.

Alexandre, who had told himself to stop thinking about her, recognized Noeme immediately. He dropped his ore at his feet, walked closer, and studied her to be sure that it was indeed her. He asked the same questions, but in a different manner:

"Is it you?" and "How did you find us, I mean?"

Noeme looked exactly as Alexandre had last seen her on the road from Nacogdoches, striking but not beautiful, a woman he had known even then that he would not easily forget. She still was slender but seemed to have filled out more, grown more. He tried to not stare at her long hair and high cheekbones, her small mouth with its faint smile at the corners.

"Or were you even looking for us?" He sat down, unsure of what to ask.

"Good evening Mr. Pennant and Mr. Alonzo," she answered. "Do you not remember me?" She watched the clockwork gears of Pennant's agitated mind spin in a feeble effort to remember. "I certainly remember you. We met when Mr. Rusk and Mr. Henderson were concerned that you gentlemen would be prosecuted for cheating Mr. Thompson of his livery bill for repairs to the wagon you stole from Mr. LaBranche. We sat near one another for several days in Mr. LaBranche's wagon until I had to quit the journey." She turned her gaze toward the wagon. "I do believe that Mr. Thompson earned his bill; Mr. LaBranche's wagon seems to have survived the year better than you have done, sirs," she laughed.

It was true enough. The men had long since given up the pretense of mending their clothes, shaving their beards, or even using a razor to trim their hair. At present they were covered in ore dirt creased by pick-and-shovel sweat and rock breaking fatigue.

"How long have you lived in this cave?" she asked.

"Would you like some water, ma'am?" Alexandre answered, without answering. "And dinner? Alonzo has some deer on the fire.

We have some greens and onions. Will you share it with us?" He affected a falsely confident voice, even, clear, and formal, the voice he had used to tell Colonel Bravo that they were on a mission for the Queen of England, the voice he had affected to tell the San Antonio men that he had seen the Mexican army riding through the hill country.

"I would, sir. And yes, I would share your dinner." She smiled at him, more than she had intended to smile. "We have much to talk about."

The men were uncomfortable. A woman, a Black woman with straight hair. A woman inside a camp so well concealed that only the Comanches who had led them to it knew how to find it. A woman who spoke as Noeme spoke.

"What happened to your voice?" Pennant asked. "You don't sound like a slave. You used to talk like a slave."

"It is a voice I use when I am supposed to be thought a slave." She waited for them to understand what she had said. "It works quite well with men like you. But I think we are past that now. And I am not a slave."

They ate around a campfire, uneasily picking at the deer and barely tasting the onions and lambsquarter leaves. Noeme gave them a peace offering of sugar she had carried from San Antonio to sweeten what she had come to tell them. They boiled some of their Laredo coffee, Pennant grumbling about eating with runaway slaves, Alonzo shaken by her having had no difficulty in finding them in a place that could not be found. Alexandre was quiet, ending the meal with a remark.

"You said we had much to talk about." It was almost the first thing Alexandre had said since he had got up the courage to ask her to share their dinner. "What are these things we have to talk about?"

"What I want to know first, lady, is how you come to find us?" Pennant demanded.

"A child could find you," Noeme answered. "General Woll's army trampled everything in its path with a thousand horses and the boots of two thousand soldiers. All I did was follow his trail of broken trees and crushed earth from the banks of the San Pedro to the Frio." She watched Alonzo squirm at how easily she had tracked them. "How did you come to take up silver mining, I might ask? It is not a thing that was mentioned about you."

"Who?" Alexandre finally asked. "Who mentioned things about us?"

"Right, lady," Pennant added, "that's what I want to know. Why'd you come here? We was peaceable men afore you showed up. Who tole you to come find us?"

"President Houston," she told them.

That silenced them. Pennant and Alonzo still believed that they were in as much danger from President Houston as from the traitor Canales. It didn't matter whether he sent a Black woman or Jack Hays or Satan himself to find them; nothing good would come of it.

Alexandre understood: what better subterfuge for Houston than to deploy a Black woman in the guise of a slave as his unseen agent. He was disappointed that it was Houston who had sent her and, at the same time, embarrassed to discover that he wanted her to have sought him of her own accord.

"Why?" he asked. "What does Houston want with us?"

"He wants you to map the Rio Grande. No, that is not accurate. At this moment, he needs for you to make a map of a very specific place across the Rio Grande." She paused to let them absorb the message. They were not happy to hear it and even more unhappy with what she said next: "Houston needs for you to find the men General Woll took from San Antonio." They all stood up to protest. She continued: "If you're to understand what Houston needs, I have to tell you what has happened."

Noeme told them of the battles that took place after Alexandre fled San Antonio, stories they did not know.

"After General Woll left the city, we learned from Mrs. Elliott and Mrs. Jacques, of San Antonio, that on the very first day, when the Mexican army surrounded the city, all the men went to the Samuel Maverick home to take up arms. When a heavy fog lifted, they could see that their situation was hopeless and surrendered.

The Mexicans took their arms and put them under guard, more than fifty of them, all the Texian leaders of the city. The mayor, the judge, the lawyers, the sheriff, all of them became prisoner. Three days later, a detachment of the Mexican army marched the San Antonio men away."

"Young sir, here come mighty close to bein' took prisoner with 'em, then," Pennant grumbled. "He got out in the fog."

"We know that," Noeme answered.

"You knew I was in San Antonio?" Alexandre asked. "How do you know these things?"

"It is what I do," she answered. "Major Hays reported to Houston what you did to warn the city. What I have to tell you is that among the men who General Woll took as his prisoners are Mr. Maverick, Judge Hutchinson, Mr. Twohig, Mr. Voss..." She began to say their names, particularly the names of men who had been friendly with Alexandre in San Antonio months before. "We believe they're in Presidio Rio Grande. When your name was not listed among the prisoners, I concluded that you had escaped the city."

"Why was Jack C. Hays concerned that I escaped San Antonio?" Alexandre asked. Noeme, he knew, had a purpose in seeking them out, but he didn't know what it was. "He paid no heed to me when I was there."

"And he admitted the failure was his," she answered. "Yours was a noble act poorly repaid. I have seen the map you drew. President Houston has seen it. Never in history did anyone have a warning as accurate and complete as the warning you gave the men of San Antonio. If they had listened to you, the things that followed would have gone differently. As it is, these men are in grave danger."

Alexandre had figured out why she was there.

"And Sam Houston has sent you to find me because he wants us to find them," Alexandre answered. "The prisoners he wants us to find are the same men who laughed at my warning and put me in jail. And why us? Houston threatened us with hanging. I must say, I fail to see the incentive."

She had thought a great deal about this question; it did not have an easy answer.

"Because you're not known to be Texians. Because you have a right to go where you must go, to look at the land that Mexico pledged to English banks." She paused. "And because time is very short. President Houston commissioned General Somervell to form an army to attack Laredo. He was ordered to surprise the Mexican army, but his men made a spectacle of themselves in San Antonio, all drinking and fandangoes. He ordered the detention of Mexican priests and requisitioned beeves from ranches far beyond the missions. His plans couldn't be more obvious and are probably as well known in Mexico as they are in San Antonio."

"And President Houston wants us to find the prisoners before Somervell reaches the Rio Grande," Alexandre replied. It was not a question, but she acknowledged that it was so.

"He fears that the Mexican will do them a mischief if Somervell attacks," she explained.

"A mischief?"

"Take them to prisons in Mexico City, like he did with the Santa Fe men. Or worse."

Alexandre studied her as she spoke. Noeme disturbed his fragile inner peace more than he had feared. The discovery that she was not a slave and that she spoke English with such elegance only clouded his thoughts. Why, he wondered, couldn't he ignore her for her own qualities?

No one spoke for minutes. The sun set below the peak; the campfire died to all but a few glowing coals. They sat in shadow, the men uncomfortable, Noeme's features difficult to make out. They considered what she had said was expected of them and then considered that if they had been so easy for her to find, they also would be easy for others to find. They might not be trapped, but they were no longer free. Houston had put more at stake than just their lives; he was risking their silver. Pennant spoke first.

"I ain't goin'," he said. Alonzo whispered something to him. "Alonzo says he's with me. Tell Houston we said no."

Noeme nodded.

"I have a story for you, Mr. Pennant, about Mrs. Eberly. Do you remember Mrs. Eberly?" she asked in a very kind voice. "President Houston moved the capitol away from Austin to Washington-on-the-Brazos. When he sent men back to Austin to collect all the government records, Mrs. Eberly fired a cannon at them. They dropped the records and ran." Noeme waited for Pennant to react. He hung his head. "When President Houston sent me to find you, he said that you would refuse to help because, in his words, 'Mrs. Eberly's got more courage in her little finger than Alexandre's two horse thieves have got put together.' He thinks you have less bravery than a woman who runs an inn for politicians, Mr. Pennant. He considers you a coward and predicted that you would refuse to go."

The fire died. The night air passed through the camp, rustling the mesquite branches and carrying the calls of the owl and the coyote. Pennant and Alonzo retired. Noeme wrapped herself in a cloth from her bag. Alexandre sat in the cold night air and wondered how Houston could ask that of him.

"Houston said that I would become his spy or he'd have me hanged for killing a man at the Sabine River. Now he wants me to risk my life to rescue the San Antonio men, his men, who put me in jail for trying to warn them. Why should I do that?" he asked.

Noeme had learned that it is better to listen than to argue. She listened. Alexandre continued, recalling his treatment at the hands of Thomas Rusk and Pinkney Henderson and of his being led by the nose in San Antonio by a man named Kinney.

"And I'm known more in Mexico than you may realize. A Mexican officer named Canales has mistaken me for a spy that Mexico sent from New Orleans to inform on the Texian army. Canales left us at the Nueces River, expecting me to go to the bay of Corpus Christi to spy on the Texians in that area. I was to report to him in Reinosa."

"And did you?" she asked. "Spy in the bay of Corpus Christi? And report to Colonel Canales?" She had to be certain of him.

"No. As soon as General Vasquez's army was out of sight, we

turned away from the Nueces and came here. We've been here ever since. I have no wish to see Colonel Canales again."

She told him that Colonel Canales last had been reported at Matamoros.

"President Houston ordered a naval blockade that bottled up the *Durango* at Laguna Madre. Most of the Mexican army of the North has left Presidio Rio Grande to go down to Laguna Madre." She paused, then led him back where she wanted him to be.

"Why are you here? I have told you why I'm here, Alexandre. Why are you here? This isn't what you set out to do. Have you given up?"

"What do you know of giving up?" he answered and immediately was ashamed he said it. It was he, not she, who had attempted to turn around and go back to Louisiana the moment she, not he, wiped the blood from his face after she rescued him from his foolish tumble into a ravine. It was he, not she, who had written entirely fake dispatches to Sam Houston to disguise that he was hiding in San Antonio in order to buy time. "I apologize. I don't know what your life is like. Are you really a free negro?"

"I am a free woman. I was never a slave." She gave Alexandre a moment to consider that, wondering whether it would make a difference to him. "And whether I am negro or not, I cannot say. I do not think of myself in that way. I am from the Neosho," as if that explained her. And then: "Does it matter?"

"No."

He said it didn't matter and hoped that he was being truthful. He only wanted to know more about her. He had populated her with imaginary features and idealized desires and was quietly pleased that she was the Noeme of proper English and hidden skills. He was less pleased that she was the Noeme of Sam Houston and wondered what that entailed.

"I must tell you something else," she said quietly. "because the risk is greater than you understand. Someone has told the English ambassador to Mexico City that someone is posing in Texas as an inspector on behalf of its banks." She waited for him to reply; he did not. "It is possible that questions are being asked about the ruse that you three are working in the name of the Queen of England. Is that how you came to be in Laredo?"

"Is there nothing about me that is a secret from you?" he asked. "This is too much."

"There is much that is a secret, Alexandre." She caught herself using his given name and checked herself. "I didn't know about Laredo until I heard you and Pennant talking of it before I walked into your camp. I apologize for having listened to you, but I listen before I act." He said nothing. "And I didn't know you had a letter of safe conduct." It was not much of an apology for spying on him; she would not have accepted it if their positions were reversed.

"I've brought another letter for you," she continued. She reached inside her clothing and produced the envelope. "I carried it with me to Lipantitlan to give to you."

"What is Lipantitlan?" he asked.

"It is an earthen fort on the Nueces, near the bay of Corpus Christi. Houston sent me there because of rumors of Colonel Canales leading an invasion there. Do you know Mr. Kinney?"

He said that he did.

"Mr. Kinney's trading post is there. I think Mr. Kinney is a traitor. I watched him meet with Colonel Canales and show him where General Davis' camp was. I tried to warn General Davis about Canales' position, but he wouldn't listen to a Black woman. Colonel Cameron understood and persuaded Davis to move the Texians. If he hadn't moved the men to the trees during the night, Canales would have overrun them." Alexandre didn't appear to be interested. "I took your letter in case you were there. I took it many places where you weren't. I haven't read it. I believe no one has. Would you like for me to leave you alone so that you may do so?"

Is that what she is, Houston's messenger?

She made room for him to sit beside her to read by the glow of the fire. He sat. She didn't move and breathed only with care. He expected it to be from Sam Houston, dark instructions on conducting a mission in enemy territory, threats of reprisals if he refused or failed. The letter was not from Houston; it was from Alcee LaBranche.

He read it twice before speaking.

"My father was taken ill in February. I can't be certain that he's still alive." Then, as an afterthought, "It seems that my birthright may be in question." Alexandre suddenly felt weary, weary of carrying silver ore to the mine, of hiding, of his inability to talk to this strange woman. He folded the letter and sat on it for want of a pocket in his clothing.

"What is a birthright?"

"My father owns a plantation. I expected to inherit it, but I might not." He took the letter out to study again. "My uncle is a man of business in New Orleans. He has taken charge of my father's affairs. It was he who introduced me to President Lamar to seek the commission to survey the entire Rio Grande River." He laughed with wistful sarcasm. "What grand plans I had then, to map the boundary of Texas all the way to the United States. A grand expedition, and for money. Now Lamar's gone, I'm here, and my Uncle Alcee is in control of my father and his plantation. I could suggest that Uncle Alcee will rob me of my inheritance, as he has a capacity for sharp practices, but I don't know that. This letter was written seven months ago. I doubt they believe I'm still alive."

She sifted through the ideas of his life, a life of plantations and family, birthrights and inheritances.

"Do you have brothers or sisters? Your mother?" she asked. She knew something of sisters.

"My mother did not survive me. If I have a brother or a sister, my father would not acknowledge him. My uncle most surely will not."

"I don't understand," she said, fearing that probably she did.

"My father would not recognize another child as his because he would own the child. He would send it to work in the fields with the other people he owns."

"Is that why you left?" she asked. He didn't answer. "Should you

go back to your plantation? Your birthright? Is that what you want?"
She was free. She could leave. She held her breath.

"No," he finally answered. "I had no taste for the plantation, no
interest in it. My father and I were not on good terms. He said I was
a failure, that I had no purpose in my life, nor even a plan. I've done
nothing to prove him wrong. I even failed here," he said. "I set out
for Santa Fe, but I'm still here helping Pennant with his dreams of
silver."

She asked him why he wanted to go to Santa Fe.

"To escape them all," he said. "Houston, Canales, the Comanches.
We were alive, and that was enough. I decided that I'd find my way
to Santa Fe, then join up with some merchants on the trail to
Missouri. And, I told myself, along the way I would make maps,
great maps, of the unknown river."

She asked why he didn't continue with that plan.

"I worked out a route to Santa Fe, but one morning we were
suddenly surrounded by Comanches. This is hard to believe but,
instead of scalping us, they gave us the chief's sick son and told us to
cure him. Don't ask how, but we did. And, as soon as he could stand
up, he fled from us as fast as he could. We began the trek out, but I
failed there as well. The tribe surrounded us and led us to this
mine."

He paused to consider how to explain the rest of his story.

"Then we became comfortable. We had food. We were safe. Then
we discovered silver." He told her about the ore wagons near the
mission and his promise to remain for as long as his own wagon
was needed to bring the silver to the limestone oven at the mine.
"Even the Comanches make it harder to leave; instead of scalping
us, they come every now and then to see if we're alive. They bring
us things. Bags of corn and squash. Tools that I am sure they stole
from someone. The buffalo robe you're sitting on. In short, I used
the promise I gave to help Pennant and Alonzo haul ore in my
wagon as an excuse to put off leaving to find Santa Fe. Hardly a
success."

"I disagree," she answered. "You're here, you're industrious.

You're alive. And, Alexandre, I have seen your map. Never has anyone drawn a map like the one you drew for the men in San Antonio. Even Houston was struck by it, 'a work of art that a child could read,' he said." She paused to choose her words. "I don't believe that you have failed. I believe that your success is yet to present itself. It will."

They waited by the flickering light, listening to the rustle of leaves by the camp, the call of a distant owl, the ripple of cold water in the Frio far below. He felt her beside him, heard her breath.

"I have no wish to go back to the plantation. I'll make my own way, or I will not."

"And I will help you," she whispered. "If you wish."

———

Pennant was overjoyed to find that Noeme had left in the night. Alonzo was bewildered that she had disappeared with as much stealth as she had used to appear in the first place. Alexandre dashed their complaints because Noeme had not left them.

"She is at the river," he said. "I think she has gone to bathe." Pennant stood up. "And you may not go and see for yourself." He drank from a mug of camp coffee to start his system. "Sit down. I need to tell you this: I am going to Mexico."

Even Alonzo was alarmed at this announcement.

"I decided last night that I should do so. I will go by myself."

"You're not right in the head, young sir. Well, you've never been all that much up here," Pennant tapped his skull, "but this is worse'n anything you ever done. I say no." Alonzo whispered something to him. "Alonzo says no too. Listen: how you gonna find them prisoners, I ask you that? Mexico's a big place. An' if you find 'em, what're you gonna do with 'em? An' if they catch you, then what're you gonna do?"

Alexandre sipped at his coffee and gazed at the breakfast fire.

"Stay here, mine your silver, and wait for us to return," he answered. "I expect that we'll need a week to reach Presidio Rio

Grande, find them, learn their fate, and then find General Somervell."

"We? You takin' that runaway slave girl to Mexico? You know once she's over the river, she's free. Why do you think she took this job? She tole ol' Houston yessir, I'll find them three and take 'em to Mexico an' we'll get those prisoners for you an' all the time she was thinking 'I'll get me across the river an' I'll be free an' all those fine gentlemen from San Antone can sit in a Mexican jail an' rot for all I care.' You'r gonna get yourself killed, young sir."

He had an answer: "If I get myself killed, you and Alonzo won't have to worry about how you share the silver."

Noeme returned as quietly as she had left. She heard Pennant asking the questions that Alexandre should have been asking. When they saw her, they glared at her, but she sat down to listen. Alexandre explained his plan.

"The Mexican army is hundreds of miles downriver at Mier, below Laredo. I'll go into Presidio Rio Grande with my letter of safe conduct. I'll ask for horseshoes and food just as we did in Laredo, then nose around until I find a place big enough to hold that many prisoners. If I find them, I'll make contact, and when I know their condition and what will become of them, I'll map it for General Somervell. Then we'll come back here."

Noeme listened quietly until Pennant accused her of trying to get Alexandre killed.

"Why'd you want to do that to him?" he demanded. "You go. You're a free woman on the other side of the river; you go over and do the finding and the mapping and leave young sir here alone. What do you need him for anyways?"

Noeme hated the answer. Pennant was right, that she would be able to cross the river and the Mexicans would consider her to be a freedwoman, escaped from the slaveholding Texians. That, however, would not be enough.

"Mr. Pennant," she said, "there isn't the least chance I would have brought Houston's spy mission for Alexandre to risk if I could do it without him. But I cannot carry a written message," she began. "If the message was taken from me, the prisoners would be punished and removed. An alarm would be sent out and the authorities would call up any garrisons in that part of Mexico to answer Somervell's expedition. Now do you understand?"

Pennant did not. Noeme was reluctant to articulate how stupid he was. Alexandre answered for her.

"The prisoners don't know her; if she did find them, they wouldn't trust her word." He waited for Pennant to figure it out. "They'd see her as a black woman in Mexico and think she was a runaway slave. At the best, they wouldn't believe her. At the worst, they would tell her nothing or would lie about their conditions. As for believing me…"

Pennant and Alonzo finally understood: the San Antonio men were prisoners precisely because they had not believed Alexandre the last time they met. They would believe him this time.

"They won't make that mistake again," Noeme said in her soft voice. "Now, it is time for us to go."

She put her meager bag in the wagon and walked over to the small stand of trees where the horses were stabled. She watched as Pennant glared at Alexandre as he would a traitor or a fool.

"I'm going despite Noeme, not because of her," Alexandre said. "You should know that she has offered to return to Houston and say that we could not be found."

"Don't go, young sir. I see nothin' good coming of this." It was a rare touch of concern that Alexandre had not expected from his horse thief.

"I'm going," Alexandre resumed, "because I'm needed. Samuel Maverick and George Voss and John Twohig helped us when we were in San Antonio. When I tried to warn them, Mr. Maverick believed me. He got me out of jail and saved me from his own fate. I'll do the same for them."

Pennant and Alonzo helped to harness the work horse and hitch the wagon, then led them down to the Frio. When the wagon was out of sight, they shook their heads.

"She's going to get him killed," Pennant grumbled. Alonzo whispered something back. "And us too. I know you're right, but I don't have to like it."

They made their bedrolls and filled their saddlebags. They led their horses out of the camp and rode. An hour later they caught up with Alexandre and Noeme at the crossing of the Nueces, where the four of them turned south toward the *camino real* to follow the road into Mexico.

Chapter Eighteen

Sullivan's spindle repairs held, but the axle hubs did not. When the four spies forded the river a league from Presidio Rio Grande, a wheel fell off and Alexandre's wagon turned over again.

"I believe this is how we first met you, young sir," Pennant wheezed. Alonzo dismounted and, as he had done at the Sabine, untangled the reins and braces so that the horse could walk free. Alexandre and Alonzo removed the surveying tools and the boxes, barrels, and tents they had carried to show that they truly were inspecting lands and peoples rather than looking for prisoners of war. "Fact of the matter is your axle is busted. We needs to get the wagon back up on its wheels and pray it'll make it to repairs."

As he had done at the Sabine, Alexandre told everyone what to do. "Put your weight here under the box, that's it, and you," meaning Pennant, "under the buckboard. On my count of three, one, two, three, LIFT!" The wagon budged and fell back. "Once more and one, two, three, LIFT!"

Noeme studied them, half expecting Pennant and Alonzo to rob them again and leave. The operation needed adjusting.

"On LIFT," she said, "I'll place the box under the axle so it doesn't fall all the way back down." Alexandre counted to three, they lifted, and she shoved Alexandre's box of survey equipment under the axle. "Now, this time, on LIFT," she said, "I'll brace the wheel on the axle while you push." Alexandre counted again, they lifted again, and she forced the wheel back over the hub and straightened it. The wheel held.

They put the braces and reins back on the horse and walked the empty wagon up the riverbank to the hard ground above. One by one, they went back to the river's edge to carry up all the weight they had taken off.

"I've got to make a decision," Alexandre announced. "Someone has to stay here with our things, and someone has to go with me into the town." They agreed. "And as Alonzo must translate, he has to come. I think that means that you, Pennant, will guard the wagon and our equipment until we come back for you."

Pennant's brow wrinkled as he considered being left alone on the Mexican side of the Rio Grande. The river did little to distinguish it as a boundary. It was wide, very shallow, and so little water flowed that the land on either side of the Rio Grande was a desert punctuated by sage, mesquite and cactus. No farms sprouted alongside the *camino real,* and the only visible evidence of ranching were some parched goats and a few cattle. There were no signs of life behind them across the river, neither men nor horses, cattle or goats, nothing to suggest that a single living thing existed in the landscape. Pennant would be lonely but, he surmised, safe.

"I'll stay," he decided, "but don't see no need for the girl to go. Just a lot of explaining to do and no good answers from what I see." He had a point; if asked, what was Noeme doing with them? Was she a slave? A runaway? A cook? And if Colonel Bravo had reported that Colonel Canales' three *norteamericano amigos* had been in Laredo, there would have been no mention of a slave or of a woman who looked like a white woman with black skin and straight hair. "Who's she supposed to be?"

"It is not my way to show myself to people," Noeme answered.

"You did not see me in San Antonio. You did not see me inside the mine. They won't see me in Presidio Rio Grande."

They left Pennant, unhappy, with his horse, a broken wagon and their boxes and barrels, and rode the other two horses into Mexico.

Noeme studied the desolate winter landscape. It was even more barren than the prairie at Lipantitlan, the relentless brown of the desert broken only by dormant creosote shrubs and a few leafless trees along the Rio Grande. She thought of her home along the Neosho, the water flowing through gentle hills and fertile prairies, cold in winter, hot in summer, endless stands of cane and reeds that the tribes used to thatch their homes. Everything she loved was on the Neosho: her father, her mother, her sister, her tribe. Yet there was nothing on the Neosho for her.

"What is the Neosho?"

Alexandre's voice broke the grim silence. Noeme was startled to hear him ask about the very thing she was thinking.

"The Neosho is a river, on the Arkansas, in the Indian territory. It is a perfect place, flowing water, rich forests, fertile land. The people of the Neosho are Osage, a gentle people. Good and kind people. Very tall, very brave people. It was my home."

She told him about the bountiful trees, herds of buffalo, wild horses and the gentle hills of endless grass.

"My father is John Rogers. He traded as far as Tennessee. He was often gone for weeks, sometimes months, but he always came back."

Alexandre pondered the facts. John Rogers was not an Indian name, and his freedom to come and go between Arkansas and Tennessee implied that John Rogers was not a slave.

"My mother's father is Cherokee. My mother's mother is not Cherokee. She is dark, like I am dark. My father did not mind her color, or mine. The Osage did not mind our color. Tiana, my sister, my older sister, is not dark."

Noeme, Alexandre concluded, was most likely the daughter of a white man and an Indian woman who was the daughter of an Indian man and a Black woman, or perhaps a Black man and an

Indian woman. Images of wigwams along the Neosho, council fires, tall men with painted faces formed in his mind.

"My father said we had a higher calling. He said if we could read, we could take ourselves anywhere we might choose to go. When he came back from trading, he brought us books and slates and lessons. I read about many places, and I wanted to go. Tiana read also, but she did not have another place she wanted to go. She stayed with the Neosho. I left."

That was enough to tell. A father named John, a trader. Mother. Tiana. Reading. Leaving. She had told him as much of her past as he had told her of his. No, she would tell him one more thing.

"Sam Houston lived in the Neosho. Tiana was his wife. One day, he wanted to go to Texas. Tiana did not want to follow him. I did."

Alexandre wanted to know when she came, and why she followed her sister's husband to then-Mexico, and exactly what did her being Sam Houston's agent involve? But he found himself tongue-tied by her, so when he attempted to ask, "Why did you follow Sam Houston to Texas?" it came out as:

"Houston was going to hang me." She smiled but listened. "When I told him that I had been engaged by President Lamar to survey the Rio Grande, that fabled boundary that we just crossed between evil Mexico and brave Texas, Sam Houston bullied me into becoming his spy. He told me I would agree to be his spy or he would hang me. He offered to hang Pennant and Alonzo, too."

This time she laughed.

"Not really," she answered. "He approved the money to provision you in San Antonio while you faked at being his spy." She had thought it was adventurous.

"I did fake spying, that is true. Then I forgot about spying until I watched General Woll's army shoot my friends." *No*, he thought, *I became a spy in Laredo, when Colonel Bravo told us that General Woll was preparing to invade Texas.* "Why did you follow Sam Houston?"

"Houston was never going to hang you, not unless you were indeed the Mexican agent from the *Durango*," she said. "I told him that you were not. He was waiting for me to report to him what I had witnessed at the Sabine ferry landing. I told him that the Mexican agent was dead and that two horse thieves had tried to rob you. I also told him that the horse thieves were not the Mexican agent's conspirators but more likely just two incompetent sailors who had stumbled into stealing the wrong horses. Houston didn't know what else to do with the three of you, and you were very devoted to mapping the Rio Grande. He said when you took out a map and worked out a problem with lines on the earth and distances you became like a child, so that was just his way of sending you on to do your job." She let him consider what she had told him. Then, in a quieter voice, she added: "I would never have allowed him to hang you, Alexandre."

They rode in silence for another half hour until the first adobe houses emerged above the cactus to denote the town of Guerrero and their entry into Presidio Rio Grande.

"Houston enjoyed your dispatches from San Antonio. When he read *'qui ebrii sunt nocte ebrii sunt'* he called for Anson Jones to come read it with him. 'Anson, listen to this: Those who are drunk are drunk at night.' He laughed out loud and said that writing in Latin to call him Big Drunk was very inventive for a spy dispatch." When she had listened to Houston read it, she realized that there was more to Mirabeau Lamar's surveyor than an inability to know which direction to turn. "How did you come to write them?"

"I made them up. A man named Kinney gave me rumors about Refugio and Matamoros. Pennant stole a Bible for me so that I could copy Latin verses to obscure the reports." He was proud that he could compose clever falsehoods with double meanings.

"Houston knew you had never set foot in any of the towns you wrote about. He has men in all those places: Goliad, Refugio, San Patricio, everywhere, men who served under him at San Jacinto. They report very often what is happening on the frontier."

"Did he know I was still hiding in San Antonio?" he asked, a bit embarrassed at how tame it all seemed in looking back.

"I think that Houston believed you never left the city," Noeme answered. "He sent me to spy on General Vasquez in San Antonio.

When I saw Mr. Kinney lead you to Colonel Canales, I took it on my own initiative to see that he didn't create any mischief."

"You followed me in San Antonio?" he asked.

She did not answer. Instead, as they neared the first adobe houses of the town, she slipped off the back of his horse and vanished into the shade of a mesquite thicket.

"What do I do?" he asked.

"Ask for repairs," she called back. "And some food. I'll find the prisoners." She paused, then: "I'll find you."

At first, he saw little to distinguish Presidio Rio Grande from Laredo, but as he and Alonzo rode further into the village, the difference was obvious: Laredo was asleep; Presidio Rio Grande was very much alive.

They passed an adobe church and burial ground. There were men working nearby, dressed in white pants and serapes, assembling corrals for goats and donkeys. One lot was given over to workers cutting *piñon* logs. On the next was a yard laid out with stacks of mud bricks. There were merchant shops like those in San Antonio, a barber, a tavern, a potter, and women cooking in the front yards of their homes. Chile ristras hung from the roof beams, children chased after each other and the goats, and someone behind closed doors ran the shuttle of a loom. There were butchers for goats, for pigs, a specialist in chickens, and at every shop and stall there were people bargaining, arguing, buying, refusing.

The main road opened onto a plaza where an infantry platoon stood in formation. Beyond the plaza there were the long, low row buildings of a barracks and the military headquarters of the presidio. Soldiers scurried across the plaza, in front of barracks, and on to the quartermaster stores, the stables, and the armory. There were parade grounds in the distance where officers put their horses through maneuvers.

"*Atencion, peloton!*" a sergeant barked. The platoon stiffened.

"*Al hombro, armas!*" The platoon raised their rifles, crossed them to their shoulders, grasped the stocks, and snapped their free hands back to their sides.

"A la derecha..." The platoon faced right. *"Marcha hacia Adelante!"* The platoon set off, marching down the company street toward the parade ground. Alexandre had found the heart of Presidio Rio Grande.

They dismounted and led their horses to the headquarters building, where they tied the reins to a post. Alexandre withdrew his letter of aid and assistance. They walked in.

"Señor LaBranche!" a voice called. A torrent of unintelligible and rapid-fire Spanish flowed from across the reception room. Alexandre was stunned to see Colonel Calixto Bravo rise from behind a desk, smiling with obvious pleasure, and walking with extended hand to meet them. Another torrent of Spanish resulted in a junior officer fetching an *equipale* chair for Alexandre, motioning for him to sit and for Alonzo to stand by his side.

"He asks what brings us to the presidio," Alonzo whispered.

"Tell him that our wagon has broken near the river and could he help us to repair it," Alexandre replied.

"Colonel Bravo says with great pleasure," Alonzo translated.

Coffee was produced, a bit of fried tortilla and beans, enough to tide them over until *siesta.* The junior officer excused himself, only to return in a quarter hour. Bravo smiled and unleashed another torrent of joyful Spanish.

"He asks if you have met with Colonel Canales since we last met in Laredo," Alonzo relayed. Alexandre said that he had not and was surprised at Colonel Bravo's evident look of disappointment at his answer. "Colonel Bravo says that Colonel Canales is presently at Mier but hopes to see you very soon."

Bravo regained his cheerful bearing and gave orders to the young officer.

"I am to lead them back to the wagon," Alonzo translated. "You are to enjoy the comforts of the *alcalde* until we return." "What is the *alcalde?*" "The civil governor. He will show you the village, as Colonel Bravo must attend to some matters of the army."

Another torrent of Spanish. Alonzo translated again.

"And will you permit him the honor for you to stay in an officer's barrack room for as long as is necessary to repair our wagon and get our supplies? He is very pleased to see his old friend again."

"How will I communicate with him? Or the alcalde?"

"It will all be very simple, he says. You are his guest."

Alexandre had the sinking feeling that it was too simple. Bravo led him to the alcalde, unleashed another friendly torrent of Spanish, and left him.

Until siesta, Alexandre walked around the presidio in the company of a man he did not understand. Every few steps along their way, the alcalde would stop at a door, or a tree, or a grassless pen, and praise the sight for its untranslated qualities. Long before naptime Alexandre knew the location and nature of the municipal records, the family names of the more important sarcophagi in the cemetery, the registry of priests at the village church, the art of a man making Mexican saddles and boots, and the operations of a metal forge where spurs, buckets, pump handles, nails, hammers, pliers, and locks were fabricated. He learned that a red flag outside a butchery meant that a pig had been slaughtered that very morning. The alcalde was proud. Alexandre was anxious.

"*San Juan Bautista?*" the alcalde asked. Alexandre smiled and shrugged. "*Vamos.*" They set out to walk beyond the village and the parade ground. About a mile from the presidio, a large stone bastion rose up from the landscape. The monastery consisted of some half-dozen stone buildings enclosed within a high adobe and stone wall with a stout wooden gate. On one corner of the bastion, a bell tower and cupola rose to mark the location of the church. They entered.

"*Esta es la misión de San Juan Bautista,*" the alcalde said. Every few moments, he used the words "mission," "padres," and "Indios" such that Alexandre understood San Juan to be a source of pride and industry. As they walked, Alexandre noted that the plan of San Juan Bautista was not unlike the long-abandoned mission on the Nueces near the silver ore wagons. There were buildings for kitchens, granaries, ovens, gardens, and barns for the livestock. Fields, an orchard, and a pasture were tended outside the walls. Along the west wall there was a long row of rooms whose use could only have been sleeping quarters. Some of the doors were secured with bolts and padlocks.

"Can we see?" Alexandre asked. "See? Look? Visit?"

A bell rang, loudly, one time. The alcalde stopped, put his hand to his ear, and waited. It rang twice more.

"*Siesta!*" the alcalde answered.

The alcalde led Alexandre back to the presidio headquarters. Colonel Bravo was absent but the same young officer now escorted Alexandre to a plain, clean adobe room in the officers' area of the post a hundred yards from the plaza. There was a fine litter with fresh bedding, another equipale chair and table, a candle, a carafe of water, and his portmanteau.

"You things with mans," the officer told him. "Horse for *heradura,*" he added, not helpfully. "*Carretón* for fix."

"My men?" Alexandre asked. To be put away in a room was unsettling. It seemed that Pennant and the wagon had been brought to the presidio, if he understood the word "*carretón,*" but they were nowhere in sight, nor did he have the least idea how to find his horse. He wondered where Noeme was.

"*Siesta.*" The lieutenant bowed and left.

Alexandre couldn't sleep. For the next two hours he went to the door, looked outside, saw neither man nor animal in motion, and retreated. He walked to the plaza and back, then to a grove of trees where he hoped that Noeme would be hidden in the shade and was not. He walked back. At twilight a church bell rang once, paused, then chimed out six bells. Siesta ended. Alonzo appeared at his door.

"They have the wagon and horses," he said. "Ready tomorrow, maybe. Pennant is at the taverna."

Alexandre was nervous about the tavern. Colonel Bravo had neither asked for the letter of safe conduct nor seemed concerned about the cost of hospitality for his visitors. Pennant was unlikely to be a quiet visitor.

"What is Pennant doing?" Alexandre whispered. A few glasses of mescal and the company of a woman, Alonzo replied. "How is he paying for his mescal?"

Alonzo shrugged, then produced two small silver musket balls they had molded at the mine. He handed one to Alexandre, then took the other and pressed it between the metal hinges of Alexandre's door. When he closed the door on the hinges, the silver came out as a very flat, round coin.

""Take me to him," Alexandre insisted. *Pennant is using the silver for drinking and women in the heart of a Mexican fortress. If we're unmasked, we'll be put up against a wall and shot.* "We've got to get him out of there."

The tavern was filled with soldiers, a few women in colorful clothing, a stout bartender pouring clouded drinks into tin cups, but no Pennant. Alonzo asked if the *norteamericano* with the mustache could be found but was met with shrugs and a few winks. Two men offered mescal to Alonzo while the barman poured a cup for Alexandre, who choked on it. They backed out of the tavern as soon as they reasonably could escape. By then, it was dark outside.

By looking into every open doorway along the commercial road, they found the wagon in a livery stable. The wagon was in a corner, propped up on stumps, its wheels leaning against the wall. Two men were energetically using an adze and plane to fashion new hubs for the axle. Alonzo asked about their progress.

"Mañana," they were told. *"Tal vez ...."* Tomorrow. Maybe.

They walked on in search of Mustache Man. Noeme called from the shadows.

"Have you been to the monastery?" she whispered. "Don't stop walking," she said from the dark.

"Yes," he whispered back. "I may have found a gaol. There were padlocks on the sleeping quarters."

"I saw them too," she answered. "There were saddles in the stable, Texian saddles, not Mexican. Some of the prisoners are here or were here."

They walked and talked, he in the street, she in the shadows.

"I don't think there were enough locked rooms at the

monastery," she said, "not to hold sixty prisoners. And no horses, just saddles."

He knew she was right. If the prisoners had been brought to Presidio Rio Grande, he thought, they hadn't stayed there very long. There was no place to hide them. He considered another question: *Why is Colonel Bravo in Presidio?*

"I'm suspicious," he told her. "The officer at the presidio is the same officer who helped us at Laredo," he said. "He is very friendly, but he always has someone escort me. Our wagon has been taken apart and our horses hidden, supposedly being shod. Pennant has been lured away by a woman from the tavern." He let her consider that. "I don't believe there is anything here for us. We need to get away."

Noeme started to reply, but another Mexican officer approached them on the street. Alonzo dropped behind. Noeme receded into the darkness. With smiles and gestures and a flow of Spanish, the officer nudged and pushed Alexandre back toward the plaza. He eventually understood that he was being led to Colonel Bravo's personal quarters for dinner.

For the next two hours Alexandre smiled and shook hands with a half-dozen Mexican officers, all eager to tell him about rifles, horses, the beauties of Monclova and Saltillo, none of which he completely grasped. More than one spoke of a *'feroz batalla en Mier."*

At every opportunity, he used the words "New Orleans" and *"Estados Unidos"* and especially *"los bancos de Barclay and Goldsmith."* In between opportunities, he picked at more food than he had seen at any dinner in his life, most of it so hot that it hurt to chew. He washed it down with rice and beans and a vile drink that made him cough. Over every enchilada, every chicken drenched in mole, every stuffed pepper, Colonel Bravo maintained a running chatter about Queen Victoria and the *desierto* of the Nueces and the Comanches. Alexandre feared a repeat of the *pachanga* of San Antonio, but none was mentioned. A dessert, a tequila, and then one of the officers led him back to his adobe cabin and bid him *buenas noches.*

He waited in the dark until the encampment was quiet. There

was neither the chatter of soldiers nor the clicks of horse hooves on cobblestones, not even the barking of a dog. He eased open his wooden door to see what could be seen and to hear what could be heard. Nothing.

Alexandre waited another half-hour, then left as silently as he could. Twenty minutes later, he was back at San Juan Bautista. He crept around the walls of the monastery, through the bean fields and the corrals, past the kitchens and ovens, but found no way to get inside the walls at night. When he arrived at a place he believed to be near the locked rooms, he held his breath, stood absolutely still, and listened.

"Hssstt..." he hissed at a blank adobe wall. "Hssst." There was no answer, no reply from prisoners, no men rattling tin cups against bars or singing baleful songs of distant homes. The padlocked sleeping quarters were empty.

He made his way back to the presidio and to his room.

Did I leave the door ajar?

He took off his boots and touched the door. It swung freely.

"Hello?" he whispered. There was no answer.

He walked on bare feet across the floor, felt for the litter, sat on the equipale, and undressed. He stared into the dark, reached for the candle, put the candle back, and climbed into bed.

General Woll captured almost sixty men in San Antonio, he reflected. But there were only four sleeping quarters that are padlocked, and no one is in them. He considered the logic of the problem. Guerrero is a small town. The presidio is not well defended. San Juan Bautista could not hold sixty men for very long. Where will General Woll have sent sixty prisoners? He suspected Woll had sent them on to Mexico City and prison. We have to leave. He fell asleep while mentally calculating the different routes to Mexico City.

It was a troubling sleep, and one that Alexandre would not forget. In his dreams, he imagined being with Samuel Maverick, sitting at his table, sharing a glass. Mrs. Maverick was there, holding a baby. Then, it seemed, his own father was there as well, also holding a baby.

He then dreamed that he was back in the adobe on Soledad Street, in his litter. Someone filled his arms and covered his mouth. He dreamed he removed the blanket, yet still his arms were filled, and then his chest was warm to the touch, as if someone lay against it.

Hair gently fell across his forehead and his face. He tried to brush the hair, but again it fell over him. Small, thin, strong arms closed around him and held him. Breath soothed his brow, his face, and then he was kissed, gently, then deeply, and with passion such as he had only imagined. He tried to wake, but the lips parted only to say 'shhh' and then kissed him again, deeply, warmly. He was powerless to stop. He didn't want to stop.

She did not stop. She stroked him, took his hands to caress her and, when he could bear it no longer, she took him to her. She held him and made him hold her body to him, rocking him into her and keeping him until ecstasy overwhelmed him and they collapsed in union, a single body, and slept together.

She was what Alexandre wanted, had always wanted, and he was content. He dreamed that they would wake, and go away, and leave all of this behind them.

When he did wake, the morning sun creased the wooden shutters. His blankets were tucked around him. His clothes were on the chair, just as he had left them. There were no footprints on the floor, no finger marks on the cup or the carafe. There was no stray clothing or wisps of long, dark, straight hair. The door was closed.

Maybe it was only a dream, he thought.

He dressed and went out into the parade ground. Colonel Bravo was waiting for him.

The colonel gestured for him to join him for breakfast at the portale in front of his quarters. Bread and coffee had been set on a low leather table; equipale chairs were positioned around it. Bravo gestured for him to sit down and take a bit of the bread, to have a taste of the coffee. He looked to see if she was in the shadows of the building. She was not. As he began to drink from his coffee, he was taken from behind. Hands gripped Alexandre's arms and pinned him to his chair.

"I am sorry, *Señor* LaBranche," Colonel Bravo's young officer said, walking from behind to face Alexandre. "Colonel Bravo apologizes and says that he is obligated to obey his orders."

Alexandre looked to Colonel Bravo for help, but Bravo shook his head. He tried to stand, to lift his arms, but the strong hands had been well chosen for the task of pinning him in place.

"Colonel Bravo says he ask if you meet with Colonel Canales, *Señor* LaBranche," the officer continued in halting English. "You tell him no, so he is ordered to do this."

A squad of Mexican soldiers appeared, rifles ready, bayonets fixed. The soldiers lifted Alexandre by his arms; the squad formed around him. He looked around wildly for Noeme, for Pennant even, or Alonzo.

"They are taking you, *Señor* LaBranche. And Colonel Bravo says his orders are to say this to you." He took out a sheet of paper and began to read: "'*Considerate terram qualis sit, utrum fortis sit an infirmus habitatores eius.*' I do not know it, *Señor* LaBranche, but Colonel Canales tells him to say it to you." Colonel Bravo gave Alexandre a slow, sad look. "Now, these men will take you. You will see what the land is like. You will see if the people is strong or weak. Colonel Canales says *Señor* LaBranche, you look at them well. They are the last things you ever see. *Adios.*"

CHAPTER NINETEEN

Alexandre's guards led him through Saltillo past the Plaza de Armas to a garrison where a captain of infantry ordered them to take him down from his horse. The captain then took him into the barracks, through several guard rooms, where they entered a large orderly room.

Colonel Canales, flanked by several soldiers, was waiting for him.

"Well, LaBranche, do you see if the land is rich and the people is strong?" Canales sneered. "Did Colonel Bravo tell you at Presidio Rio Grande to look because it is the last thing you see? Did you look?"

"Hello, Colonel. Yes, he did. And as for the land, I looked, but I didn't see anything. There is a difference," he answered.

Alexandre had paid little attention to the Mexican landscape while Colonel Bravo's guards led him more than a hundred miles across the Valle Dorado and over the mountains of Sierra de la Rata. The people who lived along the way, however, had been kind. When they fed Alexandre's guards, they fed the same food to him. When the guards slept, he slept. He had spent much of the journey to Monclova wondering whether Colonel Bravo had told them to guard him loosely so that he might escape in the night. But, at Monclova, the *comandante* changed his guard. The soldiers who led him on to Saltillo stole his greatcoat and his boots and tied his bare ankles to the stirrups. He was given little to eat, less to drink. Now, delivered to Colonel Canales inside a Mexican army garrison, he knew that there would be no escape.

"I order Colonel Bravo to bring you here because you are a spy for the traitor Houston." Canales relished the pronouncement of revenge. "I bring you here to shoot you."

Alexandre was stopped from collapsing only by the soldiers who held him in their grip. His face went pale, and his head began to spin. He had made the mistake of believing his story about the English banks and believing that the army of Mexico believed it as well. He struggled to speak.

"I am not a spy," he managed to say.

"Of course you spy, LaBranche," Canales sneered. "You have write your spy reports to the traitor Houston. That is why I know you are Houston's spy."

Alexandre was perplexed by the comment. He had known since Canales gave him the letter of safe conduct at the Nueces that Canales had read at least some of the fake dispatches, or at the least that he knew of them.

"Colonel, you knew about the letters to Houston when we were with General Vasquez. You could have shot me then." His mind raced to finish his alibi. "Instead, you gave me a letter of safe conduct. I believed then that the letters to Sam Houston proved to you that I was not Houston's spy."

Canales told him to explain. Alexandre continued:

"Did you read those letters, Colonel? Or did you only hear about the letters from someone when you were in San Antonio? Perhaps a priest? My horse thieves had the letters with them at Mission Concepcion."

"*Entonces?*" Canales shrugged. "You admit you wrote the spy letters." He turned to give an order to the soldiers.

"The letters prove, Colonel, that I was not a spy for Houston because the letters hurt Houston's cause. When I wrote to tell him that there were no Mexican armies near Goliad or Refugio, your own troops were invading those same cities. That did not aid Houston's cause."

Canales had not considered that the letters the priests had read to him might have helped the Mexican cause. He paused and listened.

"And my report to Houston about Matamoros, sir, the one with the Latin verses you quoted to me the night of the *pachanga* and again at the Nueces River?" Alexandre had nothing to lose by reminding Canales of the contents of the one letter that Canales seemed to have memorized. "Do you remember saying to me '*Considerate terram qualis sit, utrum fortis sit an infirmus habitatores eiu?'* I wrote quite falsely in that letter to Houston that General Vasquez was at Matamoros with a cavalry of no more than twenty men on starving horses. Houston believed it and did nothing to reinforce San Antonio, even though on that same day you and General Vasquez had already crossed the Nueces. You captured San Antonio the next day. That clearly hurt the Texian cause. I am not Houston's spy."

"Maybe it proves you are just an incompetent spy," Canales answered. "And I don't believe you. I ask you, why did you write any letters of a spy to Sam Houston?"

"Because Houston said he would hang me if I didn't." Because, Alexandre realized, Sam Houston was no different than Antonio Canales. They both were violent men who wanted to know what the armies of the other were doing. "Houston gave me no other choice if I was to go about my commission for England, sir. I was trapped by him then much as I am by you, now."

"It only proves you were a bad spy," Canales said. "It is normal, *Señor* LaBranche, the law of countries, to shoot the spies, even the bad ones." Canales cared little about the fake dispatches; he had not understood what the priests said about them. His anger with Alexandre, his distrust, arose from losing his army at Lipantitlan.

"And then you lied to me, spy." Canales felt obliged to tell the men he intended to shoot his reasons. "I leave you at the Nueces so you will inspect the land all the way to the bay of Corpus Christi. Then I wait for you at Camargo, spy, and also at Mier, for you to bring me the report you are making for the little queen. I wait for you to tell me is there water in the Nueces, is there cattle, so I may decide what my army needs if we go there. But you do not bring me a report. I learn that no one sees you along the Nueces or the Bay of Corpus Christi. So, you lie to me, and you disobey me. I shoot you just for that."

"I did not lie to you, Colonel Canales," Alexandre answered. "Yes, you told me to go to the bay of Corpus Christi but, no, I did not tell you that I would do so. And, yes, you told me to bring you a report to Camargo, but I did not agree to do that either. Then, you left me in the desert."

Canales wasn't in a mood for parsing words.

"I waited for you, LaBranche. You disobey me." He turned again to order the soldiers to take Alexandre.

"You left me on the upper Nueces with almost no provisions," Alexandre answered. "I did not believe you truly intended for me to go hundreds of miles to the bay of Corpus Christi without food and water. And my work for the English banks, for the little queen, was in the other direction, in the hill country. I rode directly into the hills and have been there ever since." He gathered his thoughts and continued. "I am not a spy, Colonel, nor am I a Texian. And I am not a liar. I'm just an inspector for two English banks that loaned money to Mexico so that your nation could fight for its independence. If this is how Mexico repays its loans, I would like to go back to Louisiana."

Canales considered the point: he had left the spy and his two horse thieves in the desert with no food or water. But, as for being in the hill country, Colonel Bravo had been very clear in his report that LaBranche had appeared in Laredo and had refused to wait there to meet Canales.

"First, spy, I ask you this: if you are no spy, why do you take your horse thieves and your tools of making spy maps to Laredo? That is the work of a spy." He waited. "You can no answer that!"

Alexandre did have an answer.

"I'm sure Colonel Bravo also told you that we did not bring any tools to Laredo. We came for horseshoes and some food. When Colonel Bravo asked us to stay longer, I told him that we had left my equipment at our camp. I left all of it in the hills, and I went back to the hills.

"Prove it," Canales said. "Prove you were in the hills."

"Prove it?" Alexandre answered. "What proof would you like?"

"Describe me something you know in the hills, something a man can know only if he is a long time in the hills, something that you would make in your report to the little queen."

Alexandre thought of the silver mine and the wagons of ore and rejected them. He would not enrich a man who was going to murder him.

"There is a mission," he answered. "It is long abandoned. It is north of the vale of the Uvalde, at the upper end of the Nueces River, near a canyon that opens east and west onto a track that goes across the desert, then continues south to Presidio Rio Grande."

Canales was startled. He himself had never heard of the abandoned mission until General Woll's scouts reported it before the attack on San Antonio. But that was not enough to save Alexandre.

"That only proves you saw a mission. You could see a mission in one day. What is it you see for months, spy, with your measures and inspections?"

"I left the Nueces at the vale of the Uvalde and studied the land north and east to the boundary of my commission, which was at a coordinate that was stated to be at the confluence of the Sabinal and Guadalupe Rivers. I may add, sir, there is no such place; those rivers do not join. The existing maps have many such errors. I studied those rivers to their sources and also studied all the other rivers in the hill country. I measured the altitudes of the hills and mountains and the passes between them. And I studied the fertile land that is at the foot of every hill and mountain. The maps I was making would have shown the English banks that the land securing their loans is very good land. Those maps would have told the queen that the land in those hills is rich and that no one occupies it."

Canales began to consider that Alexandre LaBranche was more complicated than he had believed. A man that complicated, he suspected, must be an even more clever spy who disguised his purposes with fakery.

"If you are a great mapmaker of nations, Spy," Canales continued, "show me your rivers and your hills and fertile lands. *Guardia!*"

The guards went away to find what was needed. They returned and spread a large sheet of paper and pencils on a table. Canales ordered Alexandre to draw a map of the hill country.

An hour later, the traitor Canales stared at a drawing unlike anything he had ever seen. Alexandre had drawn a mapped landscape of precise hills, rivers, and lush pastures. The perspective made it appear as if someone was looking westward across mountaintops toward the Nueces and, in the distance, at the ruins of the mission. Alexandre had penciled in unmapped passages between the Frio and the curving banks of the Sabinal and the headwaters of the Medina. In a small inset he drew the mission, its crumbling doorway, collapsing chapel, and the priests' quarters that had been destroyed by lightning. He sketched the low hills on the west bank of the Nueces and the view toward the passage through which General Woll had led his army. He did not draw the entrance to the canyon where they discovered the ore wagons, nor the curve in the Frio that hid the entrance to the mine. Canales had difficulty concealing his surprise.

"You observe, like a spy," Canales said. "But for months? The Comanches would kill you. They steal your horses," Canales insisted.

"We saw very few Indians, sir. Our horses are old, and we had no whiskey; they did not bother us."

Canales had his own surprise:

"The drawing does not save you, spy. I have write to Mexico City about you." Canales looked to see if Alexandre showed alarm; his face revealed fatigue and resignation. "The embassy of England does not hear of your work for the queen. It has no record of you. You lie, Spy, about working for your queen and your banks."

Alexandre realized that nothing he could say would change Canales' decision. But he would not concede merely to ease the conscience of his tormentor. He made his last reply:

"My commission was not issued from the embassy in Mexico City, sir. Barclay and Goldsmith engaged me through their corresponding bank in New Orleans. That is the usual way of business, sir."

"I don't believe you, spy. A man facing a firing squad tells a lie to save his life." He did believe Alexandre, but not enough. "Take him," Canales said to the soldiers.

They marched him out of the orderly room and through a door that opened onto a barren courtyard.

There were on two sides walls with rows of wooden doors so short that a man could enter only on his knees. Each door was held in place by a padlock and bolt. The fourth side of the courtyard was enclosed by a high wall, bloodstained at about the level of a man's chest.

The guards led Alexandre across the yard to one of the low wooden doors, opened it, forced him to his knees, and pushed him inside the stone cubicle. There was no bedding, no cup or plate, no water, not even a bucket for his toilet. The only light entered through a crack in the wood at the edge of his cell door. He expected that his stay would be short.

"I give you one night to pray, LaBranche. Then tomorrow I shoot you. *Pase buenos noches, Spy!*"

The door closed. The bolt was shoved into place and the lock snapped shut.

———

Alexandre spent his last day remembering the events that had brought him to a prison cell in Saltillo. He sat in silence broken only by the occasional barking of orders in Spanish outside in the prison yard, *"A la derecha, Adelante!"* He passed some of his time thinking about the day he met Mirabeau Lamar in New Orleans. "Ten thousand United States dollars," Lamar had promised him, to map the Rio Grande River to its source. "Just this side of the river," Lamar had added. "It's ours. The other side is Mexico's." Alexandre remembered thinking that it was more money than his father might earn in several years on the plantation. *It is too much,* he had said to himself, and it was.

He remembered being robbed by two half-wits singing about a drunken sailor and being rescued from a thorn-choked ravine by an annoying Black woman who told Mary Rusk that she belonged to Alexandre. Since that day he had been threatened, entertained, befriended, and tricked, but in the months and days before Colonel Bravo's soldiers took Alexandre away from Presidio Rio Grande, he also had been rich, been in the company of friends, and had become a man of action. He had spent his last night of freedom in the arms of a woman he loved. What more, he wondered, could a man ask of life?

Sometime during the night, he heard a rustling sound at the wooden door and realized that someone had slid a sheet of paper into his cramped cell. He heard Colonel Canales hiss from outside, "Here. Is for you to write to who you loves. Is tradition." Then, "Maybe to your horse thieves." Alexandre unfolded himself, picked up the sheet of paper, and stared at it.

He had no intention of writing to his horse thieves or to Noeme, but he did try writing a letter to his father in the dark. He knew that Canales would read it, probably would not deliver it, so told his father only that he had found his purpose in life. His real purpose, he realized, had been to gaze over the Texas hills, to draw them as no one had ever done before, to swim in cold streams and wander through abandoned missions and along lost trails. He had helped enrich the men who robbed him and loved a woman, who happened to be Black, in a way he was sure his father had not loved anyone. His father might understand, but Alexandre still was not sure that he understood himself. He instead tried to relive every time that he had seen Noeme, from the moment her bony limbs picked him out of the thornbush to the time her fine arms held firmly to her as she whispered terms of love to him in the dark. He thought of each word that she had said to him and how he had failed to say to her what he felt. He had been so foolish, he thought, to not figure out that Houston had sent Noeme to find him, and more foolish still to have thought that because she was Black, he could not be drawn to her. *And you, Colonel Canales, you don't even know she exists.*

Alexandre did try to pray, the first time since his father dismissed him from the plantation. He asked for Pennant and Alonzo's safety and for forgiveness of his sins, of which he could recall only a small number. He wanted to pray for one more day with Noeme but asking for another day of fornication seemed impious. He decided he would not apologize to God or to his father for having fallen in love with her and found that he was strangely happy. Alexandre LaBranche was prepared to face the firing squad.

When a rooster crowed somewhere outside the walls, he buttoned his shirt and pulled on his boots. He soon he heard the snarl of heavily accented English growl his name through the wooden door.

"Traelo afuera!" were the first words Alexandre heard when morning light peaked through the crack in the wooden door. "Bring him out," Colonel Canales barked. The wooden door creaked open. Rough hands reached inside to pull Alexandre into the prison yard. They lifted him to his feet and gripped his arms and put him up against the bloodstained wall. Colonel Canales stood ten feet away, facing him. Canales spoke first.

"Well, spy. This is the last thing you see," Canales barked. *"Utrum fort?* Now you know is the people strong or is they weak." Canales' grim laugh was frightening.

Alexandre squinted to adjust his eyes to the light inside the prison yard and thought that Canales looked like a rooster, puffed out in his officer's uniform with rows of dubious medals, a rooster and six banties with shouldered muskets.

"*Utrum fortis,* Colonel," Alexandre answered. "*Fortis,* with an 'i' and an 's.' Or did you mean *utrum fort?* That would be Latin for 'the people are maybe.'" He wondered at himself for making a Latin conjugation joke at a time like this.

Canales paused to let the effect of the death sentence sink in. "Are you ready?" Canales hissed at him. "*¡Escaudron, listó!*" The firing squad lifted their muskets.

"Lipantitlan," Alexandre said in as loud a voice as he could muster. "I know why you lost the battle!"

"*¡Apuntanses!*" The firing squad aimed their muskets.

"There was a real spy was at Lipantitlan, a spy who lied to you, so your army was ambushed. You trusted the wrong spy."

"*¡Esperenses!*" The firing squad paused. Canales walked right up to Alexandre's face. "What spy?"

The firing squad lowered the muskets.

The guards marched Alexandre back to the orderly room. The map of the hill country still lay on the table where he had left it the day before. The soldiers gripped his arms, waiting, until Canales walked in and told the guards to stand outside the door.

"You were tricked by a man named Kinney," Alexandre said. Canales shook when he heard Kinney's name. "Kinney is the man who introduced me to you and General Vasquez in San Antonio." That meeting in the plaza after General Vasquez' interminable pronunciamentos seemed to have happened in another lifetime. Alexandre remembered it only because, after the explosion during the *pachanga,* Kinney had stolen everything that was worth stealing from John Twohig's mercantile store and ridden out of San Antonio.

"I don't believe you, spy," Canales shouted at him. "You were not at Lipantitlan. You know nothing about Lipantitlan." But, Canales knew, Alexandre had heard something.

"I left Laredo with new shoes on my old horse and went back to my camp in the hills. You know that Houston sends men to ride the *camino real* from San Antonio to the Nueces. I shared a campfire with them one night, near the mouth of the Sabinal." Alexandre pointed to the location on the map.

"What is that to me?" Canales demanded. "I have no business with Kinney."

"They told me that Kinney was seen coming out of his trading post to meet at Lipantitlan the night before the battle." Alexandre saw in Canales' black eyes that he was right. "You were overheard talking with him near your army. He told you where the Texian camp was so that you could plan your attack. But the camp wasn't there. The next morning, when you attacked where Kinney sent you, the Texian army was gone. Then, when your army pursued them near the river, the Texians ambushed them from the cover of trees until your army retreated. That is what I was told by one of the Texians at the Sabinal."

Canales was shaken by the story, but it did not make Kinney a spy. It only meant that it was known that Canales' army had been ambushed. He tried to show composure.

"This proves nothing, *Señor* LaBranche. It is known that Houston's cowards hid in the trees."

"The Texian army had its own scouts at Lipantitlan. The next time Kinney went to San Antonio, he was accused of treason for aiding you at Lipantitlan. He escaped hanging by swearing that he lied to you at Lipantitlan about the location of the Texian camp the night before battle. He swore that he had shown you the location of a campfire that he knew the Texians already had abandoned and that he knew they hid in the trees at a place where your army would have to pass. Kinney told them that he was a hero of the battle, not a traitor, because he led your army into that ambush. They let him out of jail."

Canales let loose a string of Spanish curses. He threw his shako hat against the wall and grabbed the table by the legs and shoved it over, spilling the map and everything else. The guards rushed in, fearing that Alexandre had attacked him, and stood back at attention while Canales raged about the room.

"And," Alexandre added, "he said that he hid his cattle from you. He knew your men would starve. You listened to a lying spy, sir."

An hour later, the guards took Alexandre from the guardroom, past the orderly office, and out the garrison entrance near the Plaza de Armas. Two soldiers handed him his stolen greatcoat, then shackled his hands. Colonel Canales and a squadron of lancers arrived on horseback. The guards took Alexandre by his arms and, with hands shackled, lifted him onto another horse.

"I do not shoot you today, spy. ¡Adelante!" Canales commanded, and the squadron rode toward the plaza. "Maybe tomorrow."

Alexandre saw the cathedral of Saltillo, an elegant stone church with intricate bell towers that flanked an ornate porch. The governor's palace faced the cathedral from across the plaza, where arcades sheltered church and government offices and the places of business of scribes and lawyers. An open wagon market was bustling in the commerce of tools, clothes, saddles, and food, reminding Alexandre of the market wagons in San Antonio; he craned to see if he recognized any of the vendors. Crowds parted as they rode through. Several blocks beyond the plaza, the squadron passed a high stone wall that, Alexandre realized, was a real military prison. Women crowded the gates and were pushed away by burly soldiers with old muskets and dull bayonets at the ready. He expected to be put in the prison, but the procession rode onward, soon leaving Saltillo.

"Where are we going?"

"I take you to the other rats, spy," Canales answered. "The rats of Mier."

Alexandre listened stoically, unsure what were the rats of Mier. He knew only that Colonel Bravo's young officer had told him in broken English that Colonel Canales was in a great battle at Mier.

"Why were you not with the other Texians at Mier? The coward Cameron was there with three hundred rats. I capture all of them. I take you to meet them."

"I am not a Texian, Colonel. I know nothing about Mier." Alexandre understood what Canales meant by rats; he didn't understand what he meant by the coward Cameron.

"Houston sends General Somervell and a pitiful army to Laredo, but Colonel Bravo already has move his garrison, as you find out, so there is not a battle at Laredo. The coward Somervell retreats but leaves the traitor Cameron to take half of his army to Mier. I capture all of them." Canales took satisfaction in seeing that his report made Alexandre slump in his saddle.

Alexandre slumped because he realized that he had been a complete failure. *I risked going to Presidio Rio Grande to find Samuel Maverick and the civilian men from San Antonio before General Somervell attacked Mexico. I didn't find them. Then Somervell's army, or half of it, was captured by this crowing rooster at Mier. I did nothing.*

It took all the first day for them to ride south from Saltillo. The rough road climbed up switchbacks on rough cart track roads to a mountainous ridge, only to descend, then climb again to more mountainous ridges. The land was bare, the mountains no more than a series of sharp walls of rock. When Canales grew bored with bragging about his victory, Alexandre pondered whether anyone would learn what was to become of him. He wondered if Canales would forward to his father the letter Alexandre had written to from his cell and wondered if his father was alive to read the letter. He wondered if Colonel Bravo had captured Pennant and Alonzo. He wondered if Noeme had escaped.

They reached the last of the folded mountains near the end of the second day. Their path overlooked a vast desert that opened onto the interior of Mexico. Alexandre had a sense of foreboding that, from that point forward, he was entering an alien land on a journey from which there would be no return. The ride across the desert was made worse for want of water. There were no streams, no springs, and the few ranchos he saw were the graveyards of dying goats and cattle.

At the end of the third day, they saw a cloud of dust coming toward them. As they approached, the cloud of dust revealed twenty horses, and soon, twenty dragoons. Its captain rode ahead, recognized Canales, saluted, and ordered his men to halt. Canales dismounted, the captain dismounted, and the two of them walked away from the squadrons. Alexandre soon saw an eruption of furious shouting, waving of arms, and a significant amount of bowing and saluting. The two men walked back to the squadrons, where Canales barked orders at the dragoons.

"Here I leave you, spy," Canales announced. "I see you soon. Do you know *ley fuga?*" Alexandre did not. "It is necessary, *ley fuga*. When a man tries to escape, the law shoots him when he is caught. Do not try to escape or you do not live long enough to see me again. *Ley fuga*."

Canales mounted his horse, tugged at the reins to wheel it away, and took command of the dragoons, then led the dragoons away toward the mountains in the distant east. One of the guards who had led Alexandre from Saltillo to the middle of the Mexican desert ordered him and the remaining guards to continue. The cold air chilled them, cutting through Alexandre's threadbare greatcoat and with the desert sand piercing the soles of his boots. His wrists chafed at the irons and his back sagged from fatigue. They traveled another six hours.

Late on the fourth day, they rode through a land of piñon and sage to a grove of trees and an irrigation acequia. A quarter mile away stood a large hacienda. The procession rode to the gates, entered, and dismounted.

A sergeant arrived, talked with the squad leader, then ordered that Alexandre be taken off his horse. A blacksmith arrived to knock off his irons. Another guard led him by the arm to a high wall where, soon, a large wooden door swung back. Alexandre was pushed inside. The door closed behind, leaving him facing a corral filled with broken-down men.

The Mier prisoners were ragged. Most were dressed in buckskin and homespun; many had battered hats of one kind or another. Few of the Texians had boots. Some wore moccasins and some had no shoes of any kind. Almost all of them were wounded, some openly bleeding, others sickly. Somervell's army looked pitiful indeed.

Alexandre looked to see if any of the men he had been sent to find were among them, Samuel Maverick or Mr. Voss, John Twohig, or Judge Hutchinson. There was no one he recognized.

"Who are you?" one of them asked him.

"LaBranche. Alexandre LaBranche," he answered. "Once of New Orleans and, once, of San Antonio."

Some of the men crowded around him for news.

"Any idea what become of General Somervell's army?" another said, more of a declaration than a question.

"No, I was gone from San Antonio before General Somervell marched for Laredo."

"Any word from Sam Houston?" someone asked. "Canales tricked us into surrendering, the bastard. Houston should be coming for us."

"We surrendered as prisoners of war," another said. "Canales marched us off to Monterrey, then said they was gonna shoot us. They can't shoot us. We're soldiers. We're prisoners of war."

"I don't know what Sam Houston is doing," Alexandre answered them. He doubted that Houston was doing anything, just as Houston had done when Mexico captured San Antonio twice.

"How'd you come to be in a place like this?" someone asked.

"Canales had me seized at a place called Presidio Rio Grande," he answered. "I was looking for Sam Maverick and Judge Hutchinson and the men General Woll took prisoner in San Antonio."

"They're long gone, LaBranche, Alexandre LeBranche. We didn't see any of them. They was marched off to prison before we got here."

Alexandre didn't see three hundred men in the courtyard. He was relieved to see perhaps only a fourth that many and hoped that Canales had exaggerated the number of rats he had caught at Mier.

"How did they capture a hundred of you?" he asked.

"It wasn't a hundred of us," one of them answered. "We was nearer two fifty. About two weeks ago, Captain Cameron told anybody healthy enough to want to try that he was ready. About a hundred and eighty of 'em overpowered the guards and escaped." The man and the others who listened to the tale grinned at the escapade. "We're just the ones who was too sick to run."

Hacienda Salado was quiet for several days. Alexandre settled in with the Mier prisoners. He slept on the ground with them, ate sparsely from vats of rice and watery beans, and slept some more. It was the only peace he had experienced from the day that Noeme appeared in the silver mine on the Frio.

Alexandre did learn that Canales had been right about one thing: General Somervell's army never fired a shot. He pieced the facts together from the survivors. Somervell captured Laredo without any opposition from any Mexican army; there was no Mexican army at the garrison. He then announced that his expedition had succeeded in invading Mexico and ordered his army to turn around and go back to San Antonio. About half of his army thought he was a coward and refused to retreat. Captain Cameron led those men downriver and across the Rio Grande to attack Mier. They enjoyed early success but quickly ran out of shot, powder, and food. Cameron was forced to surrender all of them to Canales the day after Christmas.

The Mexican army forced the Mier prisoners to walk on foot across the sierra to Monterrey, where it was announced that they were not considered to be prisoners of war. Canales declared them to be mercenaries and ordered them all shot. The men were relieved when the military governor of Monterrey forbade the executions. Canales left for Saltillo; the men of Mier were marched onward to Hacienda Salado. All the Mier prisoners wondered what had become of Captain Cameron and the men who escaped with him.

Then, one morning, word went through the prison yard that a squadron of dragoons had captured them in the desert. By that time, all the Mier prisoners had learned what Alexandre had been told: the rule that applied to escaped prisoners was called *ley fuga*.

CHAPTER TWENTY

On the fourth day following the Feast of the Epiphany, the village priest in the remote Mexican village of Progreso entered his small church to discover a nun and two grown acolytes on their knees in front of the altar, their hands folded in silent prayer, faces cast down. As he approached to give them benediction, he looked up at the humble wooden Christ on the Cross that had hung behind the altar for generations and noticed something that had never appeared before: Jesus had shed a tear.

"It's a miracle," he said, and dropped to his knees to pray.

When the priest stood, he found that the strangers had disappeared. He wondered if it had been a vision, turned to see if the tear had disappeared, which it had not, then pushed his way into the congregation that had begun to arrive for mass.

"Have you seen them?" he called out. "The strangers. One is a nun. They were here, praying, and then disappeared."

"They're at the jail," a widow answered. "I saw them at the window."

The nun and her two companions were indeed at the village jail, praying in silence. The priest made his way through the dozen or so

Progresos who had formed a circle around them, approached the nun, and asked if she would let him pray with her. The nun's two companions lifted her by her arms. She stood, and the bars fell off the jail window.

The crowd gasped.

The miracle of the jail was not especially consequential; there was only one prisoner, a goatherd accused of the theft of a bucket. He was set free immediately. The nun and her acolytes finished their prayers and left Progreso, riding on their wagon.

Word of the miracles at Progreso spread from village to village. The miracle workers themselves passed through Sabinas, Escobedo, and other hamlets, always praying in the local church and leaving behind evidence of a miracle, a vial of the blood of St. Peter, a silver calvary no larger than a thumb. By the time of their arrival in Monclova, the story of the itinerant nun caused a small crowd to await them near a local church. A dozen of Monclova's most reverent citizens and the parish priest prayed with them.

After a lengthy silent prayer, the nun lowered her forehead to the floor before the altar, stood, and made the sign of the cross. Her two companions did the same. All three bowed in penitence, then made their way back through the nave, out the door, and across Monclova's plaza. They heard the shouts from inside the church.

"Stigmata!" someone cried out. "Stigmata!" Jesus's handprints from the cross, complete with nail holes and a bit of blood, were visible on the floor where the nun had knelt to pray. "It's a miracle!" another wailed. "Lord have mercy." "Christ have mercy."

———

"Hurry," the nun whispered to her two acolytes.

By the time the crowd caught up with them, the three pilgrims were on their knees, praying in silence in front of the door of Monclova's local jail. The crowd stood back. After a very few minutes, the three stood up. The nun opened her arms, touched the chain that had secured the jail door, and lowered her face. The chain clattered to the ground. The door opened wide. The priest shrieked.

"Please, pilgrims, who are you?"

One of the men answered.

"Itinerants, father, to the church of *San Pedro Encadenado.*" The pilgrim lowered his face. "In the city of Mexico." Saint Peter in Chains was not one of Mexico's better known or most-worshipped saints. "We take a disciple to the pantheon in that parish," the pilgrim continued. "His remains. He was of holy orders."

He withdrew a fine linen paper letter written by the bishop of San Antonio who asked of all to whom his messages were presented that they offer humble food and shelter to the three who escorted the remains of The Very Reverent Pedro Feliciano Martin y Porras, of the Diocese of Linares, to eternal rest in the pantheon of *San Pedro Encadenado* in the City of Mexico. He gave the letter to the priest, who read it, made the sign of the cross, and returned it.

"Free the prisoners!" someone shouted. Someone entered the now unchained jail and returned with two scruffy drunks and a man convicted of fighting in a tavern. "Pray for them," the crowd demanded.

"Is the nun holy?" someone asked. "Has she seen visions?" Someone thought to ask the nun directly: "Have you witnessed miracles?" The nun kept her head lowered inside her wimple and cloak and said nothing. "Not often we see a black nun."

"A Poor Claire," the women were told. "She has taken their vows of silence."

"What about the other one?"

"He only mumbles," the scrawny acolyte explained. "Mute since birth. We must continue. The road is long."

"Is that a coffin?" someone else asked them, crossing himself. The coffin on their wagon bed was bound by chains, but only to keep it from opening when the wagon bounced along the difficult roads.

"It is."

They left Monclova with gifts of tamales, jars of water, and three fine serapes to ward off the cold of the mountains on the road to Saltillo.

The pilgrims found Saltillo, unlike Progreso and Monclova, to be a crossroads of northern Mexico. It was a city, a trade center, the capitol of Coahuila, and a fine plaza. It also was General Vasquez's winter quarters.

Pennant pointed to a Mexican flag flying above a high wall and, following it, they discovered the military prison, a walled courtyard adjacent to an army guardhouse. Soldiers stood guard, muskets at the ready, on either side of a heavily barred wooden gate. Women, wrapped in cloaks, queued in the early morning hours to bring food to prisoners. They halted at the prison gate.

"It's her," one humble woman said to another. "The Nun of Progreso." The women crossed themselves and spoke of the nun's miracles, which seemed to have multiplied between Progreso and Monclova. There were whispers of dry cows suddenly producing milk, a burning building not scarred by flame, cripples throwing down their crutches. "And the jails! She prays for the prisoners." A sergeant nodded. The gates opened.

The prisoners of Saltillo were wet, cold, hungry, disheveled men in dismal condition. Most were starved, some clearly diseased, eyes bulging, hair falling out, with sores and scabs on their exposed ankles and wrists. Many wore the cotton pants and shirts of peasants. Some had serapes, no more than two or three had coats. Several lay on the dirt floor, near death. Straw was littered around the walls. Rats scurried everywhere, fighting for scraps and bugs. One corner was a surface latrine.

The nun walked to the center of the courtyard and bowed her head in silent prayer, nudging her mute acolyte to join her. The other walked among the prisoners, asking how long they had been in prison, whether any had been taken away recently, inquiring as discreetly as he could whether anyone had seen a scrawny *norteam-ericano*. Some ignored him, some crowded around, others held out hands to beg. No one told him anything.

A few minutes later, the gates opened again; the women who had been outside now surged into the prison to bring food and blankets to prisoners. They joined the pilgrims in the center of the courtyard and hoped to witness a miracle. No miracle occurred inside the prison, neither a stigmata nor a tear of Jesus nor steel bars falling from cell windows, at least not a miracle the prisoners or their women recognized. The miracle instead was in the form of a prison guard who marched into the courtyard to the prayer circle and stood directly in front of the nun.

"You have to leave. There is no more time," the guard said to them. The speaking pilgrim nodded. The mute clamped his mouth closed and waited for instructions. The nun kept her face down under her cloak. "And it is dangerous. Hurry! You must go, now!"

The nun did not move.

"She's not allowed to speak, Sergeant. She's in holy orders," her acolyte answered. "What is the danger?"

"The *comandante* has ordered the prison closed. To prevent a mass escape."

A mass escape seemed unlikely. The prisoners were feeble, the walls high, the gates thick and guarded. The nun listened carefully. The guard continued.

"It's because there was an escape of *norteamericanos*, from a hacienda. They went into the mountains."

All three faces looked up from prayer.

"*Norteamericanos?* Prisoners?" the pilgrim asked. He quickly hid his face in his serape to avoid eye contact.

"They were in this very prison until thirty days ago. All Texians, from Mier." The nun struggled to hear, recognizing the words "Texian" and "Mier." "Like devils! I guarded them myself."

"What hacienda?" Alonzo asked, making an effort to seem threatened."

The guard didn't know.

"They were being taken to prison in Mexico City. Hurry, you must leave or…" 'Or' meant that he was himself in danger of being reprimanded by his officers. *"Adios."* He rounded them up, nun, acolytes, ladies of Saltillo, all of them, and the guards led them out the gate.

"Bless you, sister! Bless you, brothers!"

The nun folded her hands and nodded to all who looked at her. Her acolyte spoke.

"We escort the remains of the blessed Father Pedro Feliciano Martin y Porra to eternal rest at the church of his namesake in Mexico," he said. The journey is far, the way difficult," he told them. "By our calling we are obliged to minister to the jailed and imprisoned, the hopeless and the lonely, inside bars and walls everywhere our journey leads us. It's time for us to leave."

The crowd felt obliged to help their mission. The women reported that Mexico's valiant army had led repeated contingents of *norteamericano* prisoners through Saltillo for months. General Ampudia had more recently brought many Texians from Mier, a famous victory on the Rio Grande.

"And Colonel Canales brought another here only a few weeks ago," someone mentioned.

"Just one?" Alonzo asked.

"They will be on the road to San Luis Potosi," someone added. "And that's the way to the city of Mexico." Some faithful came forward to bestow more serapes and shawls, baskets of tamales and rice, sacks of black beans and white beans. "And it will be cold," they were told. "You must cross La Muralla," said another. "God be with you."

"And with you also," Alonzo answered.

As they rode away from Saltillo, they heard the murmur of a dozen poor women who discovered that the simple twine ropes of their rosaries had been turned into tiny silver chains. They turned south to cross the mountains that guarded the road to San Luis Potosi.

"Well, what now, sister?" Pennant grumbled. "It's cold as hell, they ain't no water to speak of, and we don't know where we're goin.' You got a plan for this?"

"We don't change the plan until we find him," Noeme answered.

"A church, a miracle. A jail, a miracle. And if we find him, that will be a miracle."

"The miracle's if we don't get rounded up," Pennant grumbled. "They's Mexican soldiers all over the place looking for them escapers." The wagon creaked as it lumbered its way through the Sierra Hermosa to the desert beyond. "We might be wantin' Alonzo out front scoutin' a bit, in case they's soldiers on the road."

"Escaped prisoners won't be on the road. They'll be hiding in the mountains." They all wondered whether Alexandre was among them. "Nor will they go far; there isn't enough water." There was neither stream nor pond anywhere within sight. "And," Noeme added, "we're safer together. If Alonzo were to be caught alone, they would treat him like a prisoner, and we would have no interpreter."

They stayed together, facing the wall of mountains that blocked their way forward.

During the next two days, they crossed six mountainous ridges and dozens of smaller ones before they found themselves again in a vast desert. Meagre herds of cattle and goats pecked at snatches of starved plants. They saw occasional haciendas, far from the road and far apart, but no towns or villages. Finally, by sunset of the fourth day, they rode toward the lights of a large ranch. At dark, they arrived at a walled hacienda. A Mexican flag fluttered above the gates. A soldier called down to them from the wall.

"Where are we?" Alonzo called back.

"Hacienda Salado," the soldier on the wall told them.

CHAPTER TWENTY-ONE

The three pilgrims waited outside the gate.

"Who are you?" the soldier called down to them.

"Pilgrims. To the city of Mexico," Alonzo told him. "Can we have shelter for the night?"

The gates swung open. They drove the wagon through. An officer walked forward to meet them.

"Welcome to Hacienda Salado, Sister, Brethren. I am Capitán Jose Garcia." He waved his arm to indicate the size of a very large hacienda. There were two large buildings inside the walls, white-washed stone rooms with tiled roofs that surrounded a large, formal courtyard. "We are not prepared for visitors. We can offer food and water for the night," Garcia continued, "but you must sleep outside the walls."

Alonzo trembled as he said his prepared lines.

"Is there a chapel? We are pilgrims, escorting the body of the most holy Father Pedro Feliciano Martin y Porra to his eternal rest in the pantheon of San Pedro Encadenado." They each held their breath as Alonzo pointed to the chained coffin on the wagon bed. "We should like to recite evening prayers."

Garcia looked at the coffin and at their wooden box of posses-sions. He studied the three miserable travelers, a nun and two men draped in serapes to protect them from the cold, then ordered a soldier to remain with the wagon while he led them to the chapel.

One side of the courtyard was formed by kitchens and stores and a smokehouse. As they crossed the courtyard, each of them glanced furtively through a passage to the back of the hacienda enclosure and saw a much larger second courtyard. It had a granary, barns, pens, and coops. On one side of that courtyard there were corrals; on the opposite side, a large solid wall separated the hacienda from the desert. In the center of the corrals and the court-yard, shuffling aimlessly and sitting in twos and threes and fours, were about seventy-five prisoners.

"Who are they?" Alonzo asked.

"Devils," the officer answered. "Rebels. We captured them on the Rio Grande when they attacked Laredo and Mier. They're danger-ous. That is why I cannot let you stay inside the walls."

The chapel was little more than an altar, a crucifix, and a plank floor sheltered by a tiled porch roof built into a corner of the front courtyard. There were stubs of votive candles behind the altar, none lit. Noeme lowered her face to the ground in front of the altar and made herself appear to pray. Pennant and Alonzo knelt beside and slightly behind her.

"*Domine vobiscum did you see them?*" Alonzo prayed. Noeme nodded. "*Ángele Dei, they are Texians.*" She nodded again. "*Et quod angeli et beati qui S. Petri ad vincula we have to see if he is here en liberabo eum.*" Pennant nodded. "*Credo in Spiritum Sanctum, what do you want to do? Remissionem peccatorum, Amen.*

What Noeme wanted to do was walk into the groups of Texians to look for Alexandre for herself, find him, lead him out the gate, and start on the road back to Texas. What was possible, however, was more limited: they were inside a hacienda in the middle of the Mexican desert, masquerading as religious pilgrims, surrounded by soldiers with muskets. She remained prostrate for almost twenty minutes, considering what she had seen and what she might plan, then held out her arms. Alonzo and Pennant lifted her to her feet. She bowed her head and put her hands together, and they backed away from the chapel.

Capitán Garcia led them back toward the gate and away from the view into the back courtyard. A woman from the kitchens met them and handed a folded cloth to Capitán Garcia.

"It's a simple dinner, I'm afraid," he told them when they reached the wagon. "It's what we all eat, tortillas, rice, beans, chilies. This is all I can offer tonight." He handed the food to Pennant, and a soldier lifted a carafe of water onto the wagon seat. "You'll be safe outside the walls. There are trees and an acequia in that direction," he pointed, "where you can stay for the night. And, if you wish, we can bring you more of this," he indicated the pot of beans and tortillas, "for your breakfast."

"Thank you very much, Capitán," Alonzo answered. The gate opened, a foot soldier took the horse's bit and led them out of Hacienda Salado.

They located the acequia and the grove, then steered the wagon around behind them, away from view from inside the hacienda. As desperate as they were, the three pilgrims were where they hoped to be: they had found some of the Texian prisoners, they knew the nature of the prison that kept them, and they had a sense of the men who were in charge.

When night fell they set about what they had planned to do. Pennant unlocked the chains that bound the coffin, unscrewed the corners, and slid the lid back. Noeme and Alonzo lifted the dressed skeleton of Father Pedro Feliciano out of the way. Pennant removed the false bottom of the coffin and, together, they lifted out the silver. They put a small bag of silver into the wooden chest of Noeme's religious vestments and buried the rest, along with Father Pedro Feliciano, in holes that Pennant and Alonzo dug in the midden. Pennant unwrapped a polished signal mirror stolen from the *Durango*. When the moon was at its lowest, the night darkest, the hacienda quietest, Alonzo disappeared. Two hours later, he returned:

"He is here," Alonzo announced.

———

At first full sunlight, while one of the Mexican soldiers was at morning prayer, Hacienda Salado experienced a miracle: several of the dried-out votive candles in the small chapel burst into flame. The man shrieked, ran for his fellow soldiers, dragged two or three back to the chapel, and they, too, witnessed the miracle when the rest of the votives ignited. No one noticed the aroma of spirits on the candle wax.

Even Pennant, who worked the signal mirror that had lit the candles, thought that it was something of a miracle that it succeeded. He climbed down from hiding in a niche in the hacienda wall and scurried around to the gate to meet Noeme.

The miracle worked so well that it took ten minutes of pounding on the hacienda gate before anyone heard them. Capitán Garcia stood in near disbelief near the main door of the *residencia,* gazing at the chapel, at the prisoners, and at his own men while they marveled at the candles, all of which soon sputtered out.

"Good morning, Capitán," Alonzo began. He listened to Garcia's breathless story of the miracle. "It is the holy sister," he continued. "These things happen everywhere she goes. Progreso, Monclova, Saltillo…."

Garcia gazed at the black nun standing alongside Alonzo, head bowed, and forgot all about the wagon and the third pilgrim.

"What things happen?" he asked. "What happened in…"

Alonzo recited some of the miracles of jail doors opening, stigmata, tears on Jesus' lacrimal glands.

"Permit me to show the holy sister what has happened here," Garcia finished. He led Alonzo and Noeme to the chapel, forcing his way through the throng of astonished soldiers and more than a few curious Texians.

"Here," Garcia said, "this very altar—the candles burst into flame this morning, just as one of the soldiers was at prayer." Alonzo nodded and shrugged. "Others saw it, him, and him," he pointed. "They had no flint, no powder, nothing. It was... a miracle." Garcia turned to face the black nun with a very reverent gaze: "Who are you, Sister? Is this your work?"

"She cannot answer you, Capitán," Alonzo explained." A vow of silence. But it is in jails and prisons that she ministers. She prays to San Pedro, the patron saint of prisoners. And," Alonzo and Noeme turned to look at the Texians, "you have prisoners. She would like to pray for them."

Garcia agreed at once.

Noeme walked through the courtyard, stopping to look at each man. Some she knew from Houston's assemblies of militia on the Brazos, others from Fayette County. Some she recognized from General Davis's miserable little army of the Nueces at Lipantitlan. Houston's use of a Black woman to spy for him continued to serve in its own hateful way; not one of the men in the courtyard recognized her until she came to Alexandre. She shook her head at his disbelieving eyes and turned away to avoid giving herself away. By nine in the morning, the miraculous nun had prayed over everyone in the hacienda except Capitán Garcia.

"Would you like her blessing?" Alonzo asked. Garcia nodded that he would. He called a sergeant, gave him orders for the morning's duties and inspections, then led the miraculous nun and her translator back to the chapel.

Noeme and Capitán Garcia knelt. Alonzo whispered something. Garcia nodded, stood, and removed his cartridge belt and case, handed them to Alonzo, and knelt again. Noeme took his left hand, bowed her head almost to the floor, and firmly brought Garcia down to pray alongside her. He began to say the *pater noster*, then a verse to the Virgin of Guadalupe, and finally an ave. He stood. Alonzo returned his cartridge belt to him.

Alonzo spoke to put the plan into motion.

"The holy nun would ask you to give her one of the prisoners."

"A prisoner?" Garcia sputtered. "I can't give you a prisoner."

"She says that you are holding an innocent prisoner who should not be here. He is not a Texian rebel. She will show you the prisoner."

They walked across the courtyard to Alexandre. He was as hungry, dirty, ragged, and unshaved as the rest, and Garcia said so.

"You ask me for that prisoner?" Garcia, doubtful and suspicious, took Noeme by the arm and led them out of the prison yard toward the main gate. "I don't have authority to give…"

Alonzo interrupted him.

"Does your pouch weigh heavily on you, Capitán?" Alonzo asked. "She sees you carrying your belt heavy."

Garcia put his hand under his cartridge pouch, lifted it, paused, and lifted it again. His eyes widened. He opened the cartridge pouch.

"Oh my God," he gasped. "Holy Jesus, son of God; Holy Mary, mother of God." He showed them the open pouch. It was filled with musket balls.

All the musket balls had turned to silver.

Noeme looked at Capitán Garcia, put her hands together, and bowed her head. Garcia couldn't take his eyes from twenty silver musket balls. Alonzo had the presence of mind to stay with the plan.

"She says that the angel struck off the chains that bound San Pedro in his prison, capitán, "Alonzo said. "You should do the same. She asks why you will not set that innocent prisoner free."

Garcia struggled with the question. There was no circumstance in which Colonel Canales had given permission to him or any of the officers to let any of the Texians go free, except by shooting them. But she was the Holy Nun of Progreso and Monclova. And Garcia suddenly had become a wealthy man.

"Why does she want him?" Garcia asked. "Why does she say this prisoner must not be here?"

Alonzo made a show of consulting the holy nun of Progreso who, by nods and shakes of her covered head, made a show of answering him. Alonzo turned to Garcia and asked,

"She says that there are written orders on your desk that say he is to be free, not held."

"I don't have a desk," Garcia answered. A crack appeared in his faith in the holy nun.

"There is a table in the recibidor," Alonzo said. "She asks, is it not your desk? There you will find the orders she mentions."

The letter of safe conduct lay where Pennant had hidden it amidst a scroll of documents on a wooden table in the receiving room of the main house. Neither a sergeant who lied about having been inside the room the entire morning nor any of the soldiers who had come and gone into the room during Garcia's sojourn with the nun had noticed the letter. Garcia refused to believe it was even on the table; when he was persuaded to read it, he began to tremble.

"The holy sister asks if the letter doesn't say that all people who read it must provide such aid and assistance to *Señor* Alexandre LaBranche as he requires to do his work?" Alonzo asked. Garcia agreed that it did. Alonzo continued. "But she doesn't know about military things, Capitán, and asks if a man with the title General Rafael Vasquez, *Jefe de Defensores del Departamento del Presidio Rio Bravo y Grande* is a superior officer to a capitán and if his orders must be obeyed?" Garcia could only look away.

A lesser man would have handed Alexandre over to her immediately. Garcia, trapped between duty, wealth, and fear of holy retribution, was not a lesser man. He gathered his strength and asked the only question he could imagine:

"What is this work that he does, Holy Sister?" Even Garcia could sense that an explanation was called for if a man who was to be given all aid and assistance as he required was instead locked inside a hacienda with Texian rebels on their way to prison in Mexico City. "Why is this man so important?"

"This man is so important, Capitán, because without him his horse thieves could not continue to spy on the Republic," a deep, guttural, and immediately recognizable voice said from the doorway to the *ante-recibidor*. Colonel Canales walked into the room and stared coldly into the eyes of Capitán Garcia, then Alonzo, then

Pennant. "A man important enough for the traitor Sam Houston to send his horse thieves and a nun to perform magic tricks to frighten ignorant people to set him free."

Noeme looked Colonel Canales in his cold eyes and replied in impeccable Spanish:

"A man who is so important, Colonel, that his particular friend, the Queen of England, will send her navy and her army to look for him if he doesn't return with me. And," she paused to let Canales reflect on her threat, "if they do not find him, Colonel, they will come to find you."

Each of them stopped, stopped moving their arms, turning their heads, shifting their feet. The holy nun with a vow of silence had a firm voice with clear commands. She continued.

"These men are not spies, Colonel. They are who they say they are, engaged by the banks in England to see the conditions of the land that Mexico has pledged to secure the loans that financed your war of independence from Spain. They are not Texian spies, and they are not your spies. Would you like to read the report that Mr. LeBranche had prepared for the English banks?"

She withdrew from her flowing robes a sheaf of handwritten pages and handed it to Canales. Each page had a different title: Settlements along the Lower San Antonio, Guadalupe, and Nueces Rivers; Fertility of the Copano Bay-Corpus Christi Estuary; A Corrected Survey of the Geography between the Medina, Sabinal, Frio and Nueces Rivers at twenty-nine degrees north latitude, with observations of Roaming Bands of Indians, Buffalo, and Horses. There were descriptions of drought and salt-barren lands between the Nueces and the Rio Grande, mentions of the Vasquez and Woll invasions of San Antonio, and mentions of the Texian efforts to follow them back to the Rio Grande.

Canales glanced at the titles, then tossed the pages on to the desk.

"Shoot them," he said. "Shoot them all, and shoot LeBranche too." He gave the order to Garcia, then turned to leave the room.

"Or," Noeme continued, "you may wish to read the other report.

It is the report that will be delivered to Mr. Charles Elliott, the English consul to Texas, one week from today, if Mr. LaBranche, Mr. Pennant, Mr. Alonzo, and I do not arrive back in San Antonio. It says that the lands in question are rich, fertile, and excellent for farming, for cattle, and for industry. It says that there are rich mines of the purest silver known only to Mr. LaBranche and his, as you call them, his horse thieves. It says that all of these are in land that is under the control of the Texian armies and, therefore, that Mexico has no possibility of using that land to secure its debt because the army of Mexico in those regions is too weak to sustain an invasion and take the land back from Texas. It failed twice at San Antonio, once at Refugio, and once at Lipantitlan, an invasion that you know well, Colonel, because you're the Mexican officer who failed at Lipantitlan to defeat a force one-tenth your size. This is the report that England will receive if you shoot us. I would recommend that as soon as we are buried you send messengers to Mexico's feeble navy to watch for the British Navy, because it will come to collect the debt." She paused, then finished her declaration. "As I said, Mr. LaBranche and his helpers are particular friends of the Queen. I have heard you say it yourself, Colonel. You know it is true."

"What do you want?" he answered.

"It is true, Colonel," a man said.

They all started at the sound of Capitán Garcia's voice.

"About the silver, it is true. Pure silver, Colonel." Garcia fumbled into his cartridge pouch and removed a fistful of silver musket balls, which he displayed to the room. "I don't know if she finds it or if she makes it with miracles, but she has it. Silver."

Canales wasn't fooled by miracles, but he was taken in by wealth. He weighed his own thoughts: *Where did Garcia get a pouch full of silver musket balls? Are there really hidden silver mines? Or did the nun have some other way to come with enough silver to bribe LaBranche' guards? Or should I shoot them all and be done with it?* He revealed the slightest concession merely by asking Garcia how much silver.

"Twenty pieces, sir. After the miracle of the votives, she caused my lead musket balls to become silver musket balls." He handed them to Canales; they were silver.

"What do you want?" Canales repeated.

"I want to leave Hacienda Salado with Alexandre LaBranche, with Pennant and Alonzo here, and with my wagon and horses and goods. Now."

"For twenty pieces of silver?" Canales snarled.

"Yes, for twenty pieces of silver, and soon enough to stop the report of Mexico's inability to defend its territory that will go to Consul Elliott if we don't return. And I will leave enough silver with you, Colonel, to make you a wealthy man. That is what I want."

"What silver for me?" Canales asked. He wasn't surprised that she had bribed Garcia, who Canales thought would have handed Alexandre over for one silver musket ball. He was, however, impressed that Noeme had planned far enough ahead not only to increase the bribe but to have another bribe for himself. "What silver?"

"I will ask you, Colonel, what I asked Capitán Garcia: must you obey General Rafael Vasquez, whose name is on *Señor* LaBranche's letter of safe conduct? If you wanted to be able to revoke your letter of safe conduct, perhaps you should have issued it in your own name, but you did not. I offer you this, Colonel: give me Alexandre LeBranche, open the gates, and we leave, and you will be rich. Or close them and shoot us, and you will cause a war that Mexico cannot afford."

"How will I be rich?" Canales asked.

She walked to the door of the *recibidor*, gazed at the cannons that flanked the main gate, and told them to follow her. At the base of each cannon was a brass monkey of four-pound cannon balls. She nodded at Pennant, who unstacked one of the brass monkeys. There, in the middle of the bottom row, was a cannon ball of pure silver. Even Canales was astonished at its brilliance. He pondered his choices, then ordered Capitán Garcia to bring the prisoner LeBranche.

"So this is the famous Holy Sister of Progreso?" Canales continued. "They speak of you in Saltillo, bars falling off jails, a stigmata somewhere, and magic candles in Hacienda Salado. Permit me to say that this is your final miracle, holy sister. You are leaving Hacienda Salado." By this time, a contingent of cavalry had joined the guards at the gate, watching the haughty commander and the holy nun. "You have opened the jail doors for this man who says he is a friend of the Queen of England. I say that he is a liar, Sister. He lies to me about Queen Victoria and her banks of England. He lies to me about his inspection. Twenty pieces of silver would have been a fair price for him. A silver cannon ball is better. He is yours. Take your imposter, sister, and go. Leave."

Alexandre, dazed, ragged, and disbelieving, was brought into the courtyard and led to the wagon.

"Go, spy, with your horse thieves and your black witch. If I ever see you again," Canales growled, "I'll shoot you myself. Open the gates."

The witch, the horse thieves, and the spy mounted the wagon. The gates opened. Pennant flicked the reins. The wagon inched forward. Then, as they looked beyond the hacienda, they saw a cloud of dust over the hard sand of the Saltillo road. It was kicked up by the horses of a regiment of cavalry, leading back into captivity almost two hundred men on foot. The escaped Mier prisoners had been caught.

"Hurry," Noeme hissed. "Faster! Pass the gate!" Even Alonzo heard the note of panic in her voice.

It was too late.

The cavalry led the ragged prisoners back into Hacienda Salado, two by two, their hands tied behind them and ropes linking them to one another. The men stumbled, halted, fell, were dragged and pulled, struggling across the bitter desert floor. Guards prevented the wagon from leaving while the cavalry formed a column through which the prisoners were marched. Noeme recognized some from Somervell's roundup of men in San Antonio, others from General Davis' motley force at Lipantitlan.

The pilgrims waited for the better part of a quarter hour while the Mier prisoners filed slowly back into the courtyard. When the last of them passed the wooden gate, Alexandre said his first words since he had been brought from his place on the ground.

"I don't know how you found me, and I don't know how you managed to ransom me," he said. He shook Alonzo's hand, then Pennant's. He embraced Noeme and held it, then said the rest. "I owe my life to you. It is no small thing for you to have it in your hands and a terrible thing for me to take it back. But," he told them. "I can't abandon them." He pointed to the Texians as the gates began to close on them. He moved as if to get off the wagon. Pennant grabbed his arm.

"What do you think you're going to achieve by staying here? And abandon them to what?" Noeme asked. "We went to Presidio Rio Grande to find the San Antonio men that General Vasquez seized, to draw your great maps for General Somervell to rescue them before he invaded Laredo. These are not those men."

"No," Alexandre answered. "They aren't. But I finally understand how to survive Colonel Canales. I believe that me staying among those prisoners is the only thing that will keep him from shooting them. He believes me just enough, believes in my role with the little queen and with your letter to the English consul that I can keep him from taking a chance of shooting us." Alexandre looked at her, looked back at the courtyard filled with the arrived prisoners and his friends of the last weeks, and remembered what she had told him at the silver mine above the bend of the Frio. "You told me that my success in life was yet to present itself. It is presenting itself now."

"Alexandre," she pleaded. "Do not do this. Your success in life will be to save these men, not become one of them. We have to leave now to get back to Texas and make your maps of every Mexican road, jail, village, mountain, and cantonment between the Rio Grande and these prisoners. That is the only way Houston can send an army to save them. Only you can do this. Not me, not Pennant here, or Alonzo. Please," she pleaded. "Come with me, Alexandre. I need you."

Alonzo flicked the reins. Alexandre wavered, then called out:
"The men, Colonel?"

"The men?" Canales called back. "You're free, LaBranche. Go."

"The prisoners. What are you going to do with them?" Alexandre
asked.

"The prisoners? Shoot them. It's the law. They escaped; we
captured them. That is why we brought them back to Hacienda
Salado, to shoot them. Leave yourself, LaBranche, or I take you back
and shoot you with them. Silver only buys so much." He slapped
their horse on the rump, and it jumped forward. "Or the witch will
need more than one coffin on her wagon."

The gates of Hacienda Salado slammed behind them.

———

The desert offered nothing but hard sand and dirt, relentless cactus
and suffering brush, low mountains in the distance and the miserable oasis of the hacienda. They halted on the far side of the acequia
and the grove of trees.

"The coffin," Alexandre said. "Was it for me?"

"No," Noeme answered. "The coffin was to help us find you. We
filled it with miracles. No one looks in a coffin."

They sat in silence, staring at the hacienda walls, at the main gate
and the small doorways where laundrywomen entered and left to
dry clothes on the shrubs. It was a fortress.

"None of the men we set out to find are in there," Alexandre said,
to break the silence. "Mr. Maverick, the judge, Mr. Twohig. The San
Antonio men were all taken away to Perote before I got here. That's
where they were taking us, Perote prison." He paused. "All these
men here are from General Somervell's army. The Mexican army
captured them at Mier on the Rio Grande. Those who were led back
this morning escaped several weeks ago. The men who stayed
behind were too sick and wounded to try to escape. They thought
the others had gotten back to Texas."

"Well, young sir," Pennant said, "they didn't make it to Texas. We heard about them in Saltillo. Heard about you, too. We was thinkin' maybe you was Scot free yourself. We was thinkin' to turn back, but Noeme here said we press on."

Alexandre was all but broken himself. "Canales wanted to shoot me at Saltillo. I was led out to be shot at dawn." He tried to not cry.

"How did you survive?" Noeme asked, putting her arms around him.

"I told him I knew why he had lost the battle at Lipantitlan. Do you remember what you told me about seeing Canales talking with the trader Kinney the night before the battle?" she remembered. "I told Canales that Kinney had lied to him at Lipantitlan and led the Mexican soldiers into an ambush, that he escaped hanging in San Antonio by saying that he had lied to Canales about the location of the Texian army."

For the first time since before they entered Presidio Rio Grande, Noeme laughed out loud.

"I may have misunderstood about his cattle, too. I told Canales that Kinney hid his cattle from Canales' army, so the army starved. I said I learned it all from one of Hays' men near the Sabinal River, then went back to making maps for the little queen. It was enough to make him pause. I think now he intends to shoot Kinney."

Watching Noeme laugh and seeing Pennant and Alonzo grin and punch each other on the arms was better for Alexandre's soul than the idea of fleeing Mexico. But he had more to discuss.

"Why did you come for me? This is too dangerous."

"Truth, young sir," Pennant answered, "Noeme here, she and Alonzo followed along after you right when Colonel Bravo snatched you there at the Presidio. When they couldn't find a way to get you loose, she stole your things out of that room you slept in, then come up with this here plan to fetch you. That was afore we was even back across the Rio Grande."

Alexandre knew Pennant was a liar. This time, he knew Pennant was telling the truth.

"She don't run from nothin,'" Pennant said.

"Noeme? Pennant, Alonzo, this is a debt I can never repay."

Alonzo had already taken the shovel to the midden and was digging deep into the filthy earth when Noeme told Alexandre the rest of her plan.

"We bribed Capitán Garcia with twenty silver musket balls," she said. "And bribed Canales with a silver cannon ball. We were prepared for more." She nodded at Alonzo. Alonzo dug up another silver cannon ball and handed it to Alexandre, who was astonished. "This is how hard your friends worked to save you, Alexandre, smelting their silver for a chance to set you free. And, if twenty silver musket balls and one cannon ball can buy one man's freedom," she continued, "I believe that thirteen wagons of silver should be enough to buy the Mier soldiers' lives."

Before the sun rose the following morning, the miracle nun of Progreso was back inside the hacienda, praying in the chapel. It was not long before the men told Canales that she was there, not much longer before he came to her himself.

"I told you to leave, sister. You have no business here. This is not a place for nuns and peasants."

"I can produce more miracles. See for yourself." She held out a small bag, also filled with silver. Even Canales could see that it was fine silver, purer than anything he had seen, even from the silversmiths of Taxco.

"What do you want, Sister?" He knew it was not a miracle, at least not a theological miracle.

"Their lives." She stared directly into Canales' eyes. "All of them. You would be wrong to shoot them."

"For a bag of silver?" He sneered, but there was a note of uncertainty. "No. It is the *ley fuga*. When a prisoner escapes, the law shoots him. No."

"Not for one bag of silver, Colonel. For enough silver to pay the banks of Barclay and Goldsmith every shilling of the pounds sterling that Mexico owes to England. Enough silver to purchase American warships for Mexico's navy. Pure silver. As pure as this."

"I do not believe you. Where is this silver, holy sister?"

"The men's lives, Colonel."

"I do not believe you."

"Then you will risk a war, Colonel. Not just a war with Texas, but a war with the United States. If you shoot two hundred prisoners of war, the civilized nations of America and Europe will consider Mexico to be a lawless state, not a Christian nation, not a nation of honor. And shooting prisoners will not solve Mexico's dispute with Texas. Shooting them will make the United States invite Texas to become a state. And then there will be a war with the United States. You know it's true."

Canales studied Noeme. He had the sensation of having seen her before but dismissed the idea. He also had the sensation that she was some steps ahead of him in the negotiation.

"Where, I ask again, is this silver?"

"I will not reveal anything to you without a promise," she insisted.

"I will not promise anything to you without proof of this pure silver."

He knew immediately that she had won. By merely suggesting the possibility that he might promise something, he had let slip that he could promise something.

She knew it as well. She gave instructions.

"Please send for Capitán Garcia, he of the silver musket balls. I will take him with me. Whether you find that I can perform miracles will depend on the report that Capitán Garcia will make to you."

Twenty minutes later, Canales stood on the hacienda walls with a telescope, watching like a naval captain studying the sea, as Noeme led his young officer across the barren plain. They soon disappeared from his view behind the banks of the acequia and the grove of trees.

An hour later, he watched Garcia return.

"I don't know how many, Colonel, but they have buried more silver cannon balls in the desert."

"Then I'll go out and take them. Assemble the men," Canales ordered.

"She told me you would say that. I was to tell you that if you attempt to take them, the silver will remain buried in the desert and the rest, she was very particular, the rest will remain in its place."

"The rest? What does that mean, Garcia? Where's the silver she promised?" Canales asked.

"It's in Texas, Colonel. She has given specific instructions sir, she said this exactly: 'When it is published in the American newspapers that all of the Texian prisoners are alive and safe in Mexico City, I will deliver the wagons of silver to the *comandancia* of Presidio Rio Grande in exactly seven days.' She especially mentioned the newspaper of New Orleans, sir."

"Wagons?"

"Her words, sir. Wagons."

"Of silver of this purity?"

"Yes, sir, as she told me." Garcia paused to be certain that he repeated every word that Noeme had dictated to him. "She said that it is enough silver to purchase ships for a Mexican navy. However, she has left in San Antonio a sealed letter; if she does not return to retrieve the letter, the location of the silver will be revealed to President Houston, because it also is enough to purchase a Texian army."

"*Hija de puta!*" Canales shouted. "*Alacran!*"

"But if the men live, Colonel, she'll deliver the wagons to Presidio Rio Grande herself."

"How many wagons, Garcia?"

"Thirteen, sir.

———

Two hours later, Canales rode to the grove of trees. He found the pilgrims waiting for him.

"I agree," he said.

"Then you will have your silver," Noeme answered him. "And we will be on our way."

"And these are my terms," Canales added.

"There are no terms, sir," Alexandre answered for the four of them. "The men will not be shot."

Canales ignored him.

"These are my terms, Holy Sister. I take today all the silver that you buried here. It must be as pure as the cannon ball you gave me." He turned to face Alexandre. "Or I shoot them all. Today."

Canales reached into his waistband and withdrew a flintlock pistol. Noeme thought he was going to shoot Alexandre on the spot; Alexandre thought he would shoot Noeme. Canales instead raised the pistol to point in the air, then fired it. Almost immediately, the hacienda gate swung open. A half-dozen dragoons and a dozen foot soldiers rode out of the hacienda and made their way to the grove. They formed a squadron in front of Colonel Canales and stood smartly to attention.

"Tell them where to dig," Canales said.

Noeme said no, but Alexandre told her yes. Pennant and Alonzo tried to look away; Canales paid them no attention.

"You have the advantage of me, Colonel," Noeme said. Canales ignored her. "You have my silver, and you also have the prisoners. You want the rest of my silver in exchange for doing nothing, for not shooting men in your safekeeping."

"The prisoners are in my safekeeping until I have my thirteen wagons of silver. When I have the national silver," he corrected himself.

"And you will not shoot any of the men," she pressed him.

"If you meet my terms, yes."

She led them one by one into the filthy midden and beyond. The foot soldiers produced shovels and dug where they were told. Within a half-hour, all the silver cannon balls had been unearthed. One of the soldiers walked to the wagon bed, studied the coffin, Noeme's box of vestments and rosaries, and their food. He took their bags of black beans and white beans and handed them to the men who held the silver cannon balls. They put the balls into the sacks, then turned in formation and marched back to the hacienda.

"I have your word, sir," she said a final time.

"I am a man of my word." Canales turned to his capitán of cavalry. "*Adios,* Holy Sister. *Adios,* Spy and horse thieves," Canales sneered. Without further threats or remarks, he turned his horse and cantered his way back to the hacienda.

"What do we do now, lady?" Pennant asked.

The March wind blew across the hard ground. Sand whipped into the air. The distant mountains had a mean, poisonous aspect. The road to Salado was pocked by the drift of blowing dirt.

"We leave," she said.

———

They stopped when the night was too cold to continue. There were few stars, obscured by clouds, and the moon was no more than a sliver of faded crescent. The wind rustled the dying branches of the trees. The horse refused to sleep.

They waited all that night and into the next morning. Then, at first light, they saw Capitán Garcia approach with a dozen cavalrymen to surround their wagon. He rode to Noeme, bowed, and handed her a folded cloth.

"What's that there, lady?" Pennant asked. "Did the dogs bring us something to eat? We's a bit short of food since they took our beans."

"No," Noeme answered. "It isn't food." She unwrapped the cloth. In its center there was a wedge of silver, apparently cut from one of the cannon balls. She held it out for them to see. "No."

She understood immediately the message that Canales was sending. Her face twisted in pain, her shoulders sagged. She felt hot tears roll down her face.

Alexandre held the silver wedge up and squinted at it in the sunlight, then passed it to Pennant.

"What's this?" he gasped. The silver wedge was very good silver, hard, shiny, and without bubbles or pits. But, by looking carefully, he saw what Noeme had seen: two dull red streaks running through the wedge. "The damned dog."

"Almagre," Alonzo said. "Red. Earth."

"Ochre," Noeme said. "An impure streak in the silver." She was shaking at Canales' treachery.

Garcia nodded to the cavalrymen. Four of them dismounted, seized Alexandre by his arms, and tied his hands. They pointed him back the way they had come.

"I am instructed to give you this message from Colonel Canales," Garcia said. "The silver is not pure. You, Holy Sister, are not a person of your word. But Colonel Canales is a man of his word."

The cavalry was much faster, even leading Alexandre on foot, than Noeme and the wagon. By the time that she, Pennant, and Alonzo reached Hacienda Salado, the gate had been closed. The guards on the wall told them to go away as the sun began to set against the wall of the rear courtyard.

The shooting began almost immediately. The first musket cracked an explosive boom that rolled across the desert floor like a grenade. Noeme, Pennant, and Alonzo were so startled that they thought it was thunder, then refused to believe what they knew was gunfire.

As their hands covered their faces and their voices shrieked in grief, a second musket volley cracked across the desert. The boom of black powder was punctuated by shouts from inside the hacienda, shouts of fury, grief, disbelief.

"They're shooting the men," she said. "It's murder."

"Lying dog said they weren't no shooting," Pennant growled.

"Perro satanico," Alonzo added.

BOOM! And then, BOOM!

The shooting continued for what seemed like hours. At one point, it stopped, and the pilgrims prayed that it was done. Instead, after a pause, a crack of musket fire signaled the next round of executions.

Noeme tried to count the volleys but could not. With each boom, she began to cry, then shout. Pennant flinched, turned his face to look to the desert, to the acequia, at the midden, anywhere but Hacienda Salado. Alonzo covered his head with his arms and hated the half of the race into which he had been born.

BOOM!

They waited until the shooting ended, and until dark, but no one opened the gate. No one left the hacienda or entered it that night. At first light, a sentry looked out and saw that they still were sitting on the wagon. Eventually, another officer rode out and chased them away.

CHAPTER TWENTY-TWO
APRIL, 1846

S
am Houston stumbled.

Mrs. Eberly's boarding house was of the German style, built of stone and wood, with two floors and an outside staircase to reach the guest rooms above. When Houston drank more than he should, he tended to stumble. When he was home Margaret checked his swearing and his temper and especially his temperance but, when he was in Austin without her, his work habits led to his irritability and his irritability led to a bottle and the bottle led to stumbling.

It did not help that he was forced to live above a woman who had tried to wreck his plan to rid himself of the city of Austin. When General Vasquez invaded San Antonio, Houston had ordered the capitol to be moved from Austin to Washington-on-the-Brazos. Mrs. Eberly had turned a six pounder on the archive building and fired off a cannon blast at the men who Houston had sent to fetch the government records.

Anson Jones had arranged a truce between Houston and Mrs. Eberly, just as Anson had arranged so many other truces in Houston's affairs, but Anson had not been able to arrange a truce with Houston's bottle. Houston crawled up the stairs, fell against the door, almost set fire to his coat with the lamp that Mrs. Eberly had lit for him, and finally managed to stumble into his dark room over-looking the state capitol of Texas.

It was a dark night. April leaves on budding branches further darkened his room. With relentless inefficiency, he staggered across the floor, fell across the bed, and remembered the lamp. The glass chimney swayed in the dark, yet somehow righted itself and the lamp came to rest in its proper place on the wobbly table near the bed. Houston attacked his clothes. The jacket struggled against his arms, the boots stuck to his wet feet, and his cravat almost strangled him for want of its knot refusing to budge as he tugged at it. He snapped two buttons in undoing his breeches and resolved to leave his shirt until morning, then lay back against the pillows and burned his hand in snuffing out the lamp. The ceiling stopped its circular motion. Houston closed his eyes.

A voice buzzed in his head:

"*Igitur non dormimus sicut et ceteri, sed vigilemus, et sobrii simus.*"

Houston stirred, hated the buzzing voice in his head, and closed his eyes again.

"Thessalonians, Mr. Houston. '*Qui enim dormiunt, nocte dormiunt et qui ebrii sunt nocte ebrii sunt.*'

Houston was drunk, but awake. He turned his head from side to side; he could not see anyone in the dark.

"It means 'So then let us not sleep, as others do, but let us keep awake and be sober. For those who sleep, sleep at night, and those who get drunk, are drunk at night.'" There was a soft laugh, not a kindly laugh. Houston fumbled for the lamp.

"You don't remember me, do you?" the voice said. "The last time we spoke, you said that you'd hang me for murdering a man down by Logan's ferry landing. Have you forgotten?" Alexandre waited.

He was patient. He had sat two years in Mexican prisons with little to do but wait and to watch his fellow prisoners. He had watched them die; he had watched them take care of each other, and eventually he had watched them leave.

"Let me remind you. I'm the man President Lamar hired to come to Texas to map the border along the Rio Grande. Lamar omitted to tell me that neither Texas nor Mexico considered the Rio Grande to be the border. When I got to you, you tore up my contract with Lamar and then offered for me go to the Rio Grande as your spy or else you would hang me. Don't try to stand up. You'll just hurt yourself."

Houston fell back against his pillows, his mind unclear, his memories struggling to match the declarations and accusations.

"What do you want?" was all that Houston could mumble.

"I brought you a map."

Houston was too drunk to grasp that someone was in his room in Mrs. Eberly's boarding house. He had spent the evening making speeches with Thomas Rusk and Pinkney Henderson and thought that he was just having a normal case of the horrors from drinking too much. Then he felt something land on his face, a broad sheet of heavy paper that curled as if it had been rolled. He thought he was being attacked and flailed at it with his hands.

"Take the map, Sam Houston," another voice said from the dark. "Alexandre has gone to a great deal of trouble to make this map for you. It would be one crime too many against him if you threw it away."

"Noeme?" Houston had known her voice far longer than Alexandre's. "Is that you?" He shook off the worst of his drunken state and succeeded in sitting up. "Where are you?"

"I'm right here, Sam Houston, in the shadows. That's what you liked about me, that I could spy for you because no one would notice me in the shadows."

"Where've you been, Noeme? I needed you." Houston managed to be petulant that the Black woman who had done his bidding from Louisiana to Lipantitlan to San Antonio and the hill country had disappeared for three years.

"You sent me to find Alexandre LaBranche. I found him. He brought you a map."

Houston's fog began to lift. He had missed Noeme, missed telling her to go places where he couldn't go to watch things he couldn't watch and report things that his generals wouldn't tell him. He tried to remember telling her to find someone named Alexandre LaBranche and wondered why LaBranche would bring him a map.

"What kind of map, Noeme?"

Alexandre struck a match and lit the lamp. Houston jerked back when he saw them.

Alexandre LaBranche had changed. He was both harder and thinner than when Houston had last seen him. His face was now a man's face, a firm jaw, high cheek bones and a nose that might have been sculpted. He had fine dark eyes that had seen hard things. He was taller than many, but his shoulders were rounded, as if he had been stooped over for a long time.

Noeme moved from slightly behind Alexandre to stand beside him. She, too, had changed. Noeme's hair was no longer tied back in a slave's bun and her heart-shaped face was perfectly poised with its small mouth and wide eyes. She looked neither Black nor White nor Indian, and even though he was drunk, Houston wondered how Noeme managed to be invisible while she had become enchantingly beautiful.

Houston knew that they were not part of his dream, but still might be part of his horrors.

Alexandre picked the map off the covers and handed it to him.

Houston tried to focus on the map. He would not have known what it was if Alexandre hadn't written the word 'Matamoros' in bold letters on one corner.

"The last time I wrote to you about Matamoros," Alexandre said, "I lied to you about what was there. It's hard to imagine. but that probably saved my own life. Do you remember me writing in Latin 'to see what the land is like and are the people weak or strong'? This, Houston, is what Matamoros is like. It is not for me to say if the people there are weak or strong."

Houston looked at the map and felt that he might have been standing in the plaza. The Fuerte Casamata dominated the city, with its hard stone walls, battlements, and cannons facing a bend in the Rio Grande River. Alexandre had numbered the buildings of the military cantonment and inserted a map legend that named them as barracks or parade grounds for infantry, artillery, cavalry, and support troops. He had placed military symbols on them to show the size of each unit and written comments about the actual strength of the Mexican army. He had sketched in the cathedral, about a half mile away, and in one corner there was a small ugly building marked "Jail, where Mr. Kinney was held." Across the river from Matamoros there were land features marked as *"resaca de palmas,"* and *"chapparal at palo alto."*

The old Sam Houston reasserted itself.

"Why the hell'd you two bring me a map of Matamoros?"

"We understand that you've become a senator, you and Mr. Rusk. You should have had a pretty good idea of what the Mexican army was like after your failures at San Antonio and Mier. But you didn't know anything about Matamoros, so we spied on it. We brought you the map so that when you get to Washington and people expect you to know what an American army is facing, you won't be an embarrassment."

"And," Noeme added, "it seems to us that someone should see what is going to happen there."

"What's going to happen there?" Houston asked.

"The president of Mexico and the mayor of Matamoros have issued proclamations for every man in Mexico to come to the defense of the city because Texas is no longer a province in rebellion. Texas is now a state of the United States, and there will be a war. General Arista is leading the Army of Northern Mexico toward Matamoros right now."

"What happened to you, Noeme?" Houston asked. "You sound angry. Where have you been the last three years? Hays told me that you left San Antonio dressed like a nun, riding in a wagon with a coffin chained to the wagon bed." Houston had been angry when Jack C. Hays reported that Noeme had soon disappeared across the Nueces. "I was afraid they got you. What happened?"

"You sent Alexandre to find Mr. Maverick and the San Antonio men. The Mexican army seized him at Presidio Rio Grande. They marched him to Saltillo, where the traitor Canales put him against a wall to shoot him, but, as he said, his Latin from the Matamoros letter saved him.

Along with what I learned from you about Mr. Kinney at Lipantitlan, Alexandre thought.

"As for me, Mr. Pennant and Mr. Alonzo and I performed miracles, Sam Houston. We went to every church and jail in northern Mexico looking for Alexandre, and we found him, in with the Mier prisoners at Hacienda Salado. We just couldn't bring him home because Colonel Canales reneged on the bribe we paid him."

It was not a story Houston had heard.

"We bribed Colonel Canales to let Alexandre go," Noeme said. "We bribed him with silver, a lot of silver. He made a show of setting Alexandre free."

"You gave Canales silver, Noeme? Where did you get any silver?"

"Mr. Pennant and Mr. Alonzo and I mined it and we cast it. We gave Canales and another officer twenty pieces of silver and three silver cannon balls."

Houston gasped.

"And we had more, Sam Houston, a lot more. I agreed with Canales that if he promised to not shoot the Mier prisoners, I would deliver thirteen wagons of silver to Presidio Rio Grande on the day that American newspapers reported that the Mier prisoners were safe in prison. Alexandre left with us that very hour. That night, Canales sent soldiers to recapture him. They took him back to Hacienda Salado."

Alexandre resumed the story.

"Canales put me back in with the Texians in the hacienda courtyard. That afternoon he came to me and said, 'Now, LaBranche, your friend the nun and your horse thieves do not keep their word.' One of the pieces of silver that Noeme had given to Canales was a silver cannon ball." They could hear Houston gasp in the darkness. Alexandre felt tears stream down his face. He found that he had difficulty breathing. His jaw tightened. His mouth became dry. Noeme gripped his hand more tightly.

"'The nun,' Canales said to me, 'she promise me the silver is pure and so I agree to not shoot the prisoners.' He held a slice of the cannon ball with two thin streaks of red ochre running through it. 'But you see? The silver is not pure,' Canales said. 'I judge ten percent impure. She does not keep her word, so now I keep my word.'

"Canales made me fill a jar with seventeen black beans and the rest white beans, one hundred seventy-six in all. Then he made his announcement:

"'Rebels,' he shouted, 'It was the order of his excellency General Santa Anna that all of you be shot as escaped prisoners.' We were stunned. 'You all know it is the *ley fuga*. But,' Canales went on, 'I persuaded Santa Anna in his mercy to let me save most of you.' To me Canales said, 'I shoot ten percent, LaBranche, the same percent not pure as your black witch's silver!' And, to the men, he said 'The spy LaBranche has put beans in this jar. You will draw. If you draw a white bean, you live. If you draw a black bean, we shoot you. You have one hour to write a letter.'

"Canales made me hold the jar while every one of the men was prodded forward, put a hand into the jar, and drew out a bean. None of them looked me in the eye. Some joked about finally winning a lottery or being lucky. Others wept. An hour later, Canales began to shoot them."

Alexandre was weeping. Noeme held his hand, and he continued.

"The Mexicans didn't kill them easily," Alexandre resumed. "Their muskets were old, and the soldiers didn't know how to aim them, so a lot of their shots hit arms or legs or missed altogether. Canales ordered them to load again and fire again. They shot some men five and six times before finally killing them. One man, a boy, really, was shot in the face and fell, then began to crawl. They shot him again. Another cried for being wounded in the stomach. They shot him again. The shooting continued for two hours until all the men who had drawn black beans lay dead in the courtyard of Hacienda Salado."

Houston was unable to speak. He stared at Alexandre and Noeme, then shook his head. He stood, he stumbled around the littered bedroom, went to the door, opened it, looked out by the light of a waning moon at the mud streets and log huts of the capitol of the newest American state.

"What happened after the men were shot, sir?" Houston asked.

"Canales ordered that their bodies be left where they fell. Four days later, a priest took them to Cedral for burial. Then they marched us to prison. We walked on foot to the city of San Luis Potosi, where more of the men died from disease and fatigue. One day, they herded us into another hacienda and a troop of Mexican cavalry arrived.

"That night they told us that Santa Anna had issued another order. Because one hundred eighty prisoners had escaped from Hacienda Salado, but they only recaptured one hundred seventy-six of them, there was a decimal error. Shooting only seventeen was one man short of ten percent. This time there was no lottery. They seized Captain Cameron, put him in chains, and murdered him that same night."

Noeme completed the story.

"Captain Cameron was the man who saved General Davis at Lipantitlan, Sam Houston. He told Davis to move the troops into the trees, away from the attack, where he could ambush the Mexican army. Canales hated him."

They sat in darkness for an hour before anyone spoke again.

"Your name wasn't on any prisoner list, Mr. LaBranche," Houston said in breaking the silence. "Mr. Waddy Thompson and the American merchants in Mexico obtained lists of all the prisoners. They visited the prisoners themselves. You weren't among them."

"Do you understand, Mr. Houston," Noeme asked, "that for more than one year, I didn't know if Alexandre was alive or was dead?"

Alexandre? Houston thought.

"When the shooting stopped, Mr. Pennant, Mr. Alonzo, and I made our way back to Texas," Noeme said. "When we got to San

Antonio, the city had heard that the Mier men had escaped. We had to tell them that the men had been recaptured. We still believed Canales had murdered all of them."

"Yes, Noeme," Houston said. "So believed we all. We didn't know for a long time that only seventeen were shot and one hundred sixty were not shot."

"Shooting even one was infamy!" Alexandre snapped. "The traitor Canales promised Noeme that he wouldn't shoot any of them, but hours later, he picked out ten percent of the Mier prisoners and shot them. Your men, Sam Houston."

The room was so hot the atmosphere felt as if was burning. Alexandre's fury and Noeme's hostility smothered all of them more than they could bear. It was a long time before Alexandre resumed.

"They took me to Santiago Prison in Mexico City. The guards separated the sick prisoners from the wounded and the wounded from the able. The able were sent on to Perote Prison. The sick were left to die. But I was hidden. From the day that the Mier prisoners arrived until two years later, when Mr. Elliott's dispatch was delivered to the British minister in Mexico, I was kept hidden in the disease ward of that prison. I was the only American there."

"Mr. Elliott, sir?" Houston replied. His voice faltered, the timbre of his speech softened.

"Mr. Elliott, sir, yes," Noeme answered, "the British consul to your fine republic. Perhaps you remember sharing with me the letter in which Mr. Elliott officially asked if you knew anything about someone claiming to be a representative of English banks going around inspecting lands along the Rio Grande. I remember it well. That was the day Captain Hays brought you that remarkable map Alexandre had drawn to warn the city of San Antonio that General Woll was about to attack. You replied to Mr. Elliott, falsely, that you knew nothing of such a person. I say falsely since you and Mr. Rusk and Mr. Henderson fabricated the story that Alexandre was so employed, all to make him your spy. It was after you lied to Mr. Elliott that you sent General Somervell to attack Mexico at the Rio Grande."

Noeme gave Houston time to remember, then continued.

"You failed them all, Sam Houston. When Britain and the United States learned of the treatment Mexico rendered to the Mier prisoners, you refused to come to their aid. I learned that you wrote to Mr. Elliott that those men had gone to Mier without your orders, and that you and the Republic of Texas were not responsible for them. Such was the bravery with which you led Texas against Mexico."

By now, Houston was sober. In the dispersal of his alcoholic vapors, he began to realize that Noeme despised him.

"When I couldn't find Alexandre's name in the prisoner lists," she continued, "we went to Mr. Maverick, who had been freed and was back in San Antonio. We told him that Alexandre had been captured while searching for him and the other men. I told him the exact details of my knowledge of Hacienda Salado."

Noeme unleashed her anger and her intelligence on the great man.

"Mr. Maverick knew you wouldn't help, so instead of coming to you he went directly to Consul Elliott. Mr. Maverick shared with Consul Elliott the knowledge that Alexandre, Mr. Pennant, and Mr. Alonzo had been forced by you to pose as agents for the English banks, and that Alexandre had been seized with the Mier prisoners. Mr. Elliott sent a diplomatic dispatch to his superior, Mr. Pakenham, the British ambassador to Mexico. Mr. Pakenham found Alexandre in the disease ward of the prison of Santiago."

"But," Alexandre continued, "as I was neither a Mier prisoner nor a San Antonio prisoner and, as you had expressly denied to Mr. Elliott any knowledge of me, I was not to be freed."

"But freed you were, sir," Houston retorted. "You are here in my bedroom, as free as any man."

"I am free because two years later, after the last of the surviving Mier prisoners were released, Mr. Elliott and Ambassador Pakenham instructed the government of Mexico that, unless I was released from Santiago Prison that same day, the government of

England would find it convenient to call in the loans its banks had made to the government of Mexico."

There was nothing for Houston to say. He could have told them that during those two years he had worked as the president of Texas to avoid war with Mexico, to seek peace with the Indians who raided across Texas, or that he had exterminated the murderous Moorman gang. He could have given them the details of his secret negotiations with President Tyler to annex Texas as a new American state. But he knew that stories he told to defend himself would mean nothing to those he had failed.

"Well, Mr. LaBranche, have you come to kill me?"

———

Manuel Alvarez looked up from his piles of buffalo hides, wool blankets, and silver jewelry to see who had entered the mercantile rooms of the American Fur Trading Company of Santa Fe. Two men, one scrawny and of indeterminate ancestry, the other an Anglo man with a large walrus mustache, had walked into Alvarez' store. It was late in the afternoon, the hours of trading were at an end, and Alvarez was busy. The men ignored the trading tables and walked directly to where Alvarez sat behind his desk of business.

"Mr. Alvarez, sir?" the mustache man asked.

"I am, sir. As you can see, my trading company is at the end of its trading day." He folded his arms to suggest the two men leave, then looked gravely at a stack of hand-written bills of lading and excise documents. "Perhaps you passed by the wagon yard, sirs. The wagons may not depart until I approve these records. If you'll excuse me."

The men did not excuse him.

"Mr. Magoffin told us as you is the American consul and all that you is the man we want. 'He'll see you quick as mercury' was his words. And then he said quiet like 'He don't much care for Armijo, you see. Armijo was to have Mr. Alvarez murdered a couple years back.'"

Manuel Alvarez did not care much for Governor Armijo because four years earlier Alvarez, as the American consul in Santa Fe, had tried to interfere with Governor Armijo in his mistreatment of three hundred men on a trade mission from Texas who he tricked into surrendering to Armijo's army. Armijo had starved, stripped, and seen to the dispatch of the men, then ordered them force marched to Mexico. Alavarez also did not care for Armijo because the governor then had suggested to several of the rough men of Santa Fe that they would not be sorry if the American consul was found dead. Alvarez had been beaten, his stores looted, and his home set on fire. As Mr. Magoffin had told Pennant and Alonzo, if there was any one man in Nuevo Mexico who would be happy to see an American army ride into Santa Fe, that man was Manuel Alvarez.

Alvarez walked to the front of his store, closed and bolted the door, extinguished the lamps, and led the two men out the back door of the trading company. They avoided walking through the plaza in plain sight of the governor's palace, instead making their way toward the peralta and the wagon yards beyond. When they reached the stables and corrals, Alvarez turned on the two men.

"Do you see those teamsters?" He pointed to a dozen burley men who were working on their wagons. "I can have you killed, sirs, as surely as you stand there. They will dispatch you without asking. And those men?" He pointed to a better dressed group of men, men with fine pants, leather jackets, men with rifles. "They will not hesitate to do what I tell them to do. So, what did Magoffin tell you to see me about?"

"This," Pennant said. He reached, carefully, inside the lapel of his fine coat and withdrew a sheet of parchment. "He said that this would interest you."

He handed the parchment to Alvarez, then gestured to Alonzo to step away to show that they posed no threat to the American consul. For his part, the American unrolled the parchment, looked at it a second time, then quickly rolled it back up.

"What is this?" he demanded. "Why does Mr. Magoffin think I would see you about a .... What is this? A drawing?"

"It's a map, sir. This particular map is at *Paso del Norte*, right where the Rio Grande stops flowing south and starts flowing east toward the *Golfo de Mexico*."

Alvarez knew maps. He had lived in Spain, in Cuba, in Washington, and had traveled across all of civilized northern America by the use of maps. But, while the parchment that Pennant had handed to him was a map of the Rio Grande, it was not like any map Alvarez had seen before.

The drawing showed every feature of the approaches to the city of Paso del Norte along both sides of the Rio Grande. It displayed each bend, curve, bank, and ford of the river. There were fine details of the pass between the mountains of Chihuahua and Nuevo Mexico, showing the elevations of peaks and the ridges where the mountains extended toward the road leading into the interior of Mexico. There was, in Alvarez' immediate assessment, more information on this drawing about the military approaches to northern Mexico at Paso del Norte than if a spy had described it from personal observation.

"Where did this come from?" he hissed. "If you're caught with this, they'll shoot you."

"That's why we is givin' it to you, sir. Not sure we spelt it all right, but you can see them notes in the sides. That's the latitudes and longitudes of places. Alexandre taught us how to do it. We used the Horrebow method, as refined by Captain Talcott. Works pretty good."

"What is this?" Alvarez asked, pointing to a line along the lower edge of the map.

"Calls it a scale. Alexandre taught us how to do scales. This here is a mile, a U.S. mile. If you want, you could take a ruler and measure on the map from this place to that place. It would tell you how far it is. This here whole area is only about four miles square."

Alvarez didn't know what to say. Existing maps of the land between Santa Fe and Paso del Norte depicted one crooked line for the Rio Grande River, smaller lines for the few roads, and small boxes to indicate the location of Albuquerque and the other villages along the way, all on one sheet. The map in his hand was at least fifty times more detailed than any map he had ever seen.

And who, Alvarez wondered, are these men? The two looked like mongrels who, to judge from their clothes, had robbed a rich widow. Yet here they stood before him with what could only be described as a drawing that would enable a military commander to attack the Mexican city of Paso del Norte with as much information and preparedness as if he had personally walked every inch of the land and city.

"Who are you?" Alvarez demanded. Without saying so, he had begun to walk toward the sheds by the wagon yards where the teamsters and guards were supervising the wagon train being put ready for departure. "Who are you to walk into my store and give me a map that could get us all shot?"

"Mr. Magoffin said you was the man to get them up to the right people in Missouri," Pennant said. "To General Somebody."

"Why would I be that man?" Alvarez asked.

"'Cause you is the American consul for the United States, 'cause you don't particularly care so much for the governor here, and 'cause they's going to be a war," Pennant said. "An' Mr. Magoffin says what everybody knows anyways; when they's a war, Santa Fe and Paso del Norte is going to be in the middle of it." Alonzo whispered something to Pennant, who resumed. "And you, sir, you is the man who fills out all the forms to let the wagon trains start off on the Santa Fe trail up to Missouri. And that's where General Somebody is. In Missouri."

"How do you know so much about it, sir?"

"Well, 'cause Mr. Magoffin's son is marryin' a girl up in Missouri and she's comin' back here with General Somebody on the next wagon train in. And, as Mr. Magoffin says, they don't send generals to guard a wagon train to Santa Fe."

"General Kearny."

"That's the one," Pennant answered.

"Sir, I asked you who are you? I ask you that again: why should I trust you?"

"Well," Pennant said. "first, Texas hired Alexandre to survey the Rio Grande River from the Golfo of Mexico to where it comes out of the ground." Alonzo whispered again. "We hired on as Alexandre's helpers. He taught us the mappin' business. I did the calculating. My friend Alonzo here is pretty good at walking into places like Paso del Norte and nobody pays him attention."

Alvarez waited for the rest of a doubtful explanation. It came.

"And you should trust us because we hate Santa Anna and Colonel Canales," Pennant said. "Did you hear about the Mexicans shooting prisoners in cold blood, sir? Made 'em draw beans and then shot 'em up against a wall."

By this time, every literate person in North America had heard about the decimation of the Texians at Hacienda Salado.

"We was there. We got nothing against the Mexican people. Good people. Give you the serapes off their backs. But they're ruled by a group of evil men, sir, what we hate. These maps is to help General Somebody…"

"General Kearny."

"Right. Help General Kearny walk his army right down the Rio Grande to Paso del Norte and Chihuahua City and right into the middle of Mexico."

"These maps? There's more?"

"Yes sir. While Santa Anna had Alexandre in prison, Alonzo and me went back to our camp in the hills, to wait, do a bit of work. Then when it was time to do some surveyin', we started at a place called Presidio Rio Grande. We mapped ever inch of that river, ever side creek, arroyo, resaca, Indian camp, place to ford the river, mountain, cactus, and peanut from there to Santa Fe."

Alonzo whispered something else, and Pennant continued.

"Eight hundred thirty miles, sir. As the river flows. They's a big bend in it I don't think no white man ever seen before. Canyons, bears, and then a big sort of desert like until we come up on Paso del Norte. That's where we bought the clothes. Took us a while."

Alvarez admired their ill-fitting clothes. Pennant wore a cutaway black coat and striped trousers. Alonzo had a buttoned velveteen jacket and a silk blouse with a ruffle at his neck. Each had polished leather boots and a beaver hat. Alvarez wondered where they got the money, then decided to not ask.

"Why do you say there will be a war, sir?" Alvarez asked.

"'Cause the United States is making Texas to be a state and when they do there will be a war. And it'll all be about this river." Pennant tapped the map with a finger and winked. "Will you do it?" Pennant asked.

"Do what, sir?"

"Get these maps to General Kearney, up in Missouri."

"I will. Where are the maps?"

"Don't worry yourself on that," Pennant answered. "We got 'em hid okay. You tell me when the next wagons leave for Missouri. We'll meet you in the wagon yard with the maps. You put them on the wagons and our business is done, leastways until Alexandre and Noeme shows up."

"Alexandre?" Alvarez asked. "Is he then released from prison?"

"He is. Dumbest thing Santa Anna ever done," Pennant snickered.

"And Noeme?" Alvarez asked. "Who's Noeme?"

"His woman. She's the one planned this whole thing out."

———

Houston asked if LaBranche had come to kill him because that is what he would have done if their places had been exchanged.

"No," Alexandre said. "I came because, when we leave this room, I want you to close your eyes and see every one of the seventeen men who answered your call being pushed against a stone wall in a miserable hacienda in a desert far from home and hearing the words I heard in Saltillo. *"¡Escaudron, listó!"* *"¡Apuntanses!"* and the word that I waited to hear, that were the last words they heard: *"¡Fuego!"* I want you to see their faces, the fear in their eyes, hear their screams, and watch their ragged bodies drop to the dirt. I want you to see the ghosts of those men every night for the rest of your life."

"And I," Noeme said, "I came because when you go to bed every night and put out your lamp, I want you to wonder if this is the night that we come back in the dark and remind you that for every heroic deed you claim from defeating Santa Anna at San Jacinto, there are bloodstains on your heroism because you sat behind your desk in the capitol and did nothing while your men were being murdered."

"When you go to church with your wife ..." Noeme added.

"And when you give great speeches in Washington...." Alexandre said.

"And when men and women gather to hear you talk about your devotion to Texas, we want you to see the faces of those men who died and all the men who lived whose clothes were in shreds and had no shoes and here put in chains and marched a thousand miles into Mexico to sit in prison because you did nothing. That is what a president looks like when he says he's a hero, but in truth, does nothing."

"That is what we want you to see every minute of your life, Sam Houston. That is why we came."

"Goodbye, Sam Houston," Noeme said. LaBranche said nothing more. They walked out of the bedroom and down the stairs of Mrs. Eberly's boarding house.

The great man struggled to walk to the window where, through the spring-laden branches of an oak tree, he saw LaBranche hold Noeme's hand as she climbed up onto a solid, well-made wagon. He watched her reach for LaBranche, who joined her on the wooden seat and flicked the reins to lead their wagon and horses away from Mrs. Eberly's boarding house.

They rode in silence for a long block before Noeme asked him.

"Should we have told him? About the other maps?"

"No," Alexandre answered. They had discussed it a dozen times, two dozen, and each of them had changed his and her mind another dozen times. In the end they had agreed to not tell Sam Houston that there were more maps.

After they had finished in Matamoros, they rode to General Zachary Taylor's army encampment at Point Isabel to give him twenty-five maps of the Rio Grande River between Presidio Rio Grande and Matamoros. Each map displayed elevations, streams, ravines, farms, and, in the case of cities, the streets, buildings, bridges, and roads. In Mier and Camargo, notations on the map read "detail of Mexican army presidio, encampment, soldier, cook, laundry house, wagon, armory, cartridge press, cannon ball, flag, horse, and tortilla, as commissioned by the Republic of Texas." Neither Taylor nor his commander of engineers nor his artillery officers had ever imagined having such detailed espionage of an enemy's lands. General Taylor pronounced them to be exceptional.

From Point Isabel they made the difficult journey to the Nueces River, then on to San Antonio. They dined with Samuel and Mary Ann Adams and with John Twohig and Johan Voss and waited for the return of Jack C. Hays from a ranging expedition. When he returned, they gathered in the Maverick home and give another set of maps to Hays.

"These are for you," Alexandre had said to Hays. "I hope you will trust me this time."

Hays had studied the maps, seeing on page after page details of the Mexican villages of Nava and Progreso, the cities and military presidios of Monclova and Saltillo. He saw where LaBranch had marked *"Buena Vista—note for battle"* on a large plain between the enfilading ridge lines of two small mountain ranges. There were maps of San Luis Potosi, the city of Mexico, and Perote, home of the infamous prison, and a map of the ports and harbors of Tampico and Vera Cruz.

Chief among them was a drawing of a pathetic hacienda in the deserts of Zacatecas state. Hays saw Hacienda Salado as the men of Mier had seen it—the gates, the chapel, the grove of trees and acequia, and the corral. When he stared at the courtyard wall where

Canales had conducted the murders, even Jack C. Hays had shed tears.

There was a final map. It displayed in minimal detail the village of Cedral, south of Hacienda Salado. On it was written the single notation: 'Burial of the Mier prisoners.'

"I trust you," Hays said. "I will find them."

Alexandre and Noeme left San Antonio to face Sam Houston. Now, as they rode away from Sam Houston, they agreed once more it was better not to have told Houston about the other maps. Noeme changed the subject.

"Do you think they'll miss us?"

"Who?" Alexandre answered.

"Pennant? And Alonzo?"

"Why would they miss us? They have a fortune in silver."

Pennant and Alonzo did have silver. There had not been thirteen wagons of it but there had been thirteen wagons of ore as well as the ore in the mine. For two years, Pennant, Alonzo, and Noeme had worked it until they produced more silver than one wagon could carry. They used some of it to purchase the best of every instrument and tool to be had for determining the location, elevation, distance, and features of anything that could be surveyed. They took their tools and wagon to Galveston, where they waited on the docks until the day that the American ship Creole hove to at anchor. Their hearts nearly burst when the passengers disembarked, and Alexandre was restored to them.

Of the remaining silver, one-half now was in Santa Fe, hidden under false floors in the bed of Alonzo's and Pennant's wagon. The other half was hidden under the bed of the wagon that Alexandre and Noeme rode through the capital of Texas.

"They're bounders, you know," Noeme declared. "Not Pennant and Alonzo; they're just horse thieves. I meant Houston, Rusk, Lamar. All of them. They used you. They used me."

"Yes," Alexandre answered. "That's how great people go about things, promising to do what they can't possibly do, then using people like us to make it appear that they almost succeeded. They take credit if something works and blame others if it doesn't."

"That's the kind of bounders they are." She had gotten her temper up in Houston's bedroom; she would let it come down when she chose.

"Houston would say it was all for the greater good, that someday people will say they were great men." Alexandre flicked the reins. "We know what heroes are. All the Texians lost to Mexican firing squads and prisons, those men are heroes." The horses walked on, pulling them and the wagon further away from the great man. "But, but who's to say who is a great man? In Matamoros and Reinosa, the traitor Canales is a great man. In the city of Mexico, Santa Anna is a great man."

"And none of them know what you know," she laughed. "The bounders. They don't know where Texas ends and Mexico begins. They don't know where the Comanches mined for silver in the hills. They don't know that Alonzo is a very fine cook or that Pennant has silver balls."

"Or where the source of the Rio Grande is," he answered. "But it's somewhere. All it wants is for us to find it."

"And we will. When we do, you'll claim your ten thousand dollars. Houston won't pay it, no one will pay it, but you'll claim it and watch Houston retreat again. There are some wrongs that cannot be righted in a lifetime, Alexandre," she said. "The Neosho believe that your father knows who you have become. I believe that."

His father was dead, the wrong that could not be righted. Uncle Alcee had taken over the plantation. Alexandre could not see a way clear for him and Noeme to free the slaves or sell the fields or redeem himself in his father's closed eyes.

They clip-clopped along for another block.

"Why did you ask if Pennant and Alonzo would miss us?" he asked.

"Because they're waiting for us in Santa Fe," she answered.

"Yes."

"But you're pointed toward Louisiana." She aimed a finger at the morning sun climbing in the sky in front of them, over the heads of the horses, over the trees, above the shingle roof of the log cabin capitol. "One more time, Alexandre: The sun rises in the east. Santa Fe is in the west."

He sighed and began to draw on the reins to get the horses ready to turn.

"Do you remember the first time we met? You were going to walk back to Louisiana, but you walked farther into Texas. Imagine that—a mapmaker who can't tell east from west."

"I remember." He remembered every minute of that day. "I was just turned around. I think it was you who made us walk to Nacogdoches." he said. She laughed. "I believe you did it on purpose."

He decided it was time to ask her the question that had been put off so many times.

"Why did you tell Mrs. Rusk that you belonged to me?" he asked. "That day we walked out of her creek, into her garden, and she asked me 'Is she yours?' Before I could say anything, you said 'Yes Ma'am.' Why?"

Noeme smiled.

The sun was now behind them, the Colorado River in front of them. They forded the river and turned toward the cold springs a mile away. When they reached the cool shade of Mr. Barton's pecan trees, with no eyes to pry on them, Noeme moved closer to Alexandre, turned, put her arms around him, then kissed him with the passion of an eager bride.

"Because I did," she said. "Belong to you. You didn't know it then, but I knew."

They stayed a few minutes longer, composed themselves, and then told the horses to walk on.

"We have places to go, Noeme."

"Yes. The source of the Rio Grande."

"The forty-second parallel."

"We will find them."

"It's a long way," he said. "I propose we start by going to find our horse thieves. It does seem that we need them."

Author's Note

I have tried to bring the Republic of Texas, its heroes and villains and ordinary people to the page in a way that makes them familiar and credible and invites the reader to be a part of their story as well. All the underlying events in *Dangerous Latitudes* are based in fact.

Writing historical fiction challenges the author to create a language and geography that, to borrow from David Mitchell, may be described as "bygonese." While such fiction often is anchored by actual events, its worth is not to teach a history lesson but to render homage to the characters who pass through them, both the real and well-known and the unknown, men and women whose experiences can only be imagined. Thus, while the events that underly this novel did take place in Texas and Mexico between 1841 and 1843, Alexandre, Noeme, Pennant, and Alonzo are fictitious.

I chose to put offstage the most critical event of Texas history of that era, the Santa Fe Expedition of 1841. Like the murder of Hamlet's father, this very real tragedy lurks just out of view. President Mirabeau Lamar, a hero at San Jacinto but a political villain afterward, sent 300 soldiers and merchants from Austin to Santa Fe to 'encourage' that city to secede from Mexico. It is that expedition that in the novel leads Lamar to commission a naive Alexandre

LeBranche to map the Rio Grande while secretly hoping that Alexandre might find the 300 Texans, who seemingly had vanished, and thereby restore Lamar's political fortunes.

The actual Santa Fe expedition was a disastrous failure. The three hundred men became lost before reaching the Red River. Bands of Comanche and Kiowa attacked them, a prairie fire trapped them, and they ran out of food, water, and ammunition. The Texans surrendered in New Mexico without firing a shot and none of them ever saw Santa Fe. Nevertheless, Mexico was enraged and vowed revenge. It began when the Mexican army marched the survivors almost two thousand miles to prisons deep inside Mexico. There was no word of their whereabouts for some nine months. Lamar's party lost the next election and dumped the problem in the lap of his successor, Sam Houston. Houston, and Texas, needed spies, people who could go unnoticed into places of great danger and report on the preparations that an infuriated Mexico was making for revenge.

Like Hamlet's handwringing, Mexico's revenge took place onstage, both in the novel and in the real Texas of 1842. Six years after the fall of the Alamo, Mexican armies crossed the Rio Grande and captured San Antonio (and the Alamo) twice. Houston's real-life spies, particularly his rangers, failed him. I invented Alexandre, a mapmaker with a cover story, and Noeme, a brilliant woman of indeterminate ancestry and great courage to whom no one would pay attention, two people who could go unhindered into places of great danger to report on the movements of the Mexican army. They, with Pennant and Alonzo, are witnesses to the real-life Mexican invasions of San Antonio and the imprisonment and executions of Texan prisoners in Mexico.

Mexico's invasions, together with the cruel imprisonments and executions of Texas prisoners, swayed American sentiment in favor of annexation of Texas. In turn, once Texas became a state, the United States provoked a skirmish at the Rio Grande that erupted into the Mexican American War. Mexico's reaction to Lamar's ill-advised Santa Fe adventure eventually cost Mexico all of Texas, New Mexico, the American West, and California.

Unfortunately, most of the extraordinary events of that period are little known except to scholars of Texas history. They are a hidden trove of war, audacity, bravado and villainy, courage and cruelty, yet bookshelves are especially thin on historical fiction set during the ten years of the Republic of Texas between 1836 and its annexation as a state in 1846. *Dangerous Latitudes* is my attempt to open a window onto it.

I have tried to present Texas, Alexandre, Noeme, Pennant and Alonzo in a way that invites the reader to be a part of their story. To the extent you have enjoyed your time with them, I am deeply grateful. As for any historical errors in *Dangerous Latitudes*, the fault is mine.

Jack Woodville London
Austin, Texas
August, 2024

About the Author

Jack Woodville London is a historian and author who is Director Emeritus of Writing Education for the Military Writers Society of America (MWSA). He first studied creative writing under crime fiction author Peter May in St. Céré, France, and is presently a postgraduate student at Rewley College, Oxford University. He lives in Austin, Texas.

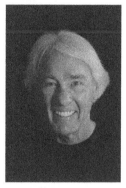

Jack is also a speaker and seasoned writing teacher, who participates in speaking opportunities with state, national and international historical and writing groups, including MWSA, the Writers League of Texas, SouthWest Writers, Historical Novel Society, and Historical Writers of America. Jack and his work have been featured in national, regional and local print, television, radio, podcasts and social media. He was given the President's Award by MWSA in 2022 for his contribution to teaching the craft of creative writing to military veterans.

Jack's previous books include the multi-award-winning French Letters trilogy, about the American generation that came of age in World War II and their children, *Shades of the Deep Blue Sea*, and *A Novel Approach* (the accepted text used by the Military Writers Society of America to introduce veterans to the basics of writing).

jwlbooks.com
jack@jackwlondon.com

Looking for your next book?
We publish the stories you've been waiting to read!

Scan the QR code below to get 20% off your next Stoney Creek title!

For author book signings, speaking engagements, or other events, please contact us at info@stoneycreekpublishing.com

StoneyCreekPublishing.com

www.ingramcontent.com/pod-product-compliance
Lightning Source LLC
Chambersburg PA
CBHW050338230125
20447CB00007BA/13